Louisa Heaton lives on Hayling Island, Hampshire, with her husband, four children and a small zoo. She has worked in various roles in the health industry—most recently four years as a Community First Responder, answering 999 calls. When not writing Louisa enjoys other creative pursuits, including reading, quilting and patchwork—usually instead of the things she *ought* to be doing!

Cursed with a poor sense of direction and a propensity to read, **Annie Claydon** spent much of her childhood lost in books. A degree in English Literature followed by a career in computing didn't lead directly to her perfect job—writing romance for Mills & Boon—but she has no regrets in taking the scenic route. She lives in London: a city where getting lost can be a joy.

TWINS FOR THE NEUROSURGEON

LOUISA HEATON

THE DOCTOR'S REUNION TO REMEMBER

ANNIE CLAYDON

MILLS & BOON

First Published in Great Britain 2021
by Mills & Boon, an imprint of HarperCollins*Publishers* Ltd,
1 London Bridge Street, London, SE1 9GF

www.harpercollins.co.uk

HarperCollins*Publishers*
1st Floor, Watermarque Building,
Ringsend Road, Dublin 4, Ireland

Twins for the Neurosurgeon © 2021 by Louisa Heaton

The Doctor's Reunion to Remember © 2021 by Annie Claydon

ISBN: 978-0-263-29775-1

09/21

MIX
Paper from
responsible sources
FSC® C007454

TWINS FOR THE NEUROSURGEON

LOUISA HEATON

MILLS & BOON

To all the midwives, doctors and obstetricians
who save lives and ensure healthy deliveries,
as much as they can,
every single day.
You are greatly appreciated x

PROLOGUE

Eleven weeks ago

THE SECOND SHE got through the door to her hotel room, Samantha Gordon kicked off her heels with a heavy sigh and let her bag drop to the floor. In the darkness of her room, she padded over to the big window that revealed the Paris skyline at night in all its wonderful glory.

There was the Eiffel Tower, gleaming in gold, the beating heart of this city. And all around it yellow and red veins of light, as drivers drove their cars to various destinations. The tourists, the city's lifeblood, and the residents were all going about their lives as if nothing incredibly significant had just happened in hers.

How did life just carry on?

Sam envied them their ignorance. Wished that she could be out there with them, taking in the delights of the city one last time. Dining on crêpes, or macarons, or crème brûlée. Walking by the river or the palace, or hoping for one last glimpse of beauty at the Louvre. Sucking up the energy, the culture, the passion and hope within this city and somehow bottling it to take it back home with her to Richmond.

She wished that she could pretend that this day hadn't ever happened at all.

Instead she was here. Standing in the dark. In this hotel room, alone. Knowing that her actions today had resulted in a beautiful girl no longer being in this world. A wonderful young girl. Emmeline. An eleven-year-old who had already been through so much, who had been tired, who had *begged* them not to do another surgery.

But it hadn't been Emmeline's call.

That decision had lain with her parents, and Sam knew that they were somewhere out there in this vibrant city of light, broken, in pieces, also questioning their decision today. Mourning. Grieving. Maybe even blaming each other. Who knew? Would today's decision rip them apart? Emmeline's mother had been sure surgery was the right thing. Her father not so much. It was certainly a decision that would be with them for ever.

Sam knew that. Bad memories had a way of clinging on. Of digging into your psyche, clawing into you with painful ripping talons, changing it, changing *you*. Bad memories were studied, provoked. Feasted on. They popped up when you least expected them to ruin your day. A phantom of the past. Haunting you for ever.

'I'm so sorry, Emmeline,' she whispered, pressing her forehead against the ceiling-to-floor windows. And she told herself, there and then, that she would never forget this girl.

Ever.

She deserved to remember her. She deserved to be reminded of her. The ghost of this girl would remind Sam every day that she needed to be sure about every single decision she made.

A gentle knock at her hotel room door brought her

back to the present. She almost didn't answer it. The idea
of facing people...seeing anyone...

Sam wanted to ignore it. Wanted to just lie on her bed
and stare into space for a while, and maybe later order
some food to her room. She'd not eaten very well the last
couple of days, having caught a tummy bug. But now she
could feel her hunger.

Tomorrow she had to be up early for her flight home
at eight-twenty. That meant getting to the airport an hour
or so earlier, which meant getting up at... She groaned at
the thought of such an early wake-up call. Hiding beneath
the quilt seemed like such a wonderful idea right now.
Maybe she could phone the airline? Change her flight to
a later one? There had to be more than one flight to London tomorrow, right?

'One second!'

She padded across the floor in her bare feet and picked
up her bag, hung it off the back of a chair. Then she
picked up her heels and placed them off to one side, before peering through the spyhole in the door. She wasn't
just going to open her door this late at night when she
wasn't expecting anyone.

Yanis?

Yanis Baptiste was one of the neurosurgeons she'd
been working with on this exchange between her hospital in Richmond—St Barnabas's, affectionately known
as Barney's—and his hospital, Hôpital St Albert.

It was a month-long exchange. Sam and a few other
doctors from various hospital departments had come over
to Paris, whilst some of the Parisian doctors had gone
over to London to work. It was something they'd been
doing for a few years, and this year Sam had volunteered
to go, having heard so many wonderful stories from other

doctors who had taken part. They had informed her of just how much knowledge they had gained from the exchange. Plus, it would be a chance to soak up the local culture. See the sights, too.

Sam was always looking to expand her knowledge. Always trying to find new ways of doing things and learning...

But what was *he* doing here? This late at night?

She opened the door. 'Hey... I wasn't expecting a visit.'

She smiled at him. It was hard not to. Yanis Baptiste was a very handsome man. Dark hair, piercing blue eyes. Cheekbones you could cut yourself on and lips that... Well, the first time she'd met him she could remember thinking that she'd happily suck on his bottom lip. Or bite it.

It had been kind of distracting, working with him, but Sam had behaved herself, despite the constant flirting and the knowledge that they were both single consenting adults.

'There is a tradition here at St Albert that when we lose a patient we raise a glass to celebrate their life.' He held up a bottle of red wine.

Well, if it was *tradition*... Plus, Sam was ready for a drink of something stronger than the tea she'd been about to make herself. And there was no way she was going to raid the mini bar and be faced with an extortionate bill when she left.

She stepped back, opening the door wider. 'Come on in.'

Yanis smiled and stepped past, and she was met by his usual scent—something exotic and masculine. Briefly she closed her eyes to enjoy it, breathing him in, letting it soothe her ragged soul, before opening her eyes again and closing the door.

Yanis was looking for glasses, which he found above the mini bar. 'You like Merlot?'

'Sure.'

She wasn't sure where to sit. There were only two places—the chair next to the small table in the corner, or on the bed—so she just stood, watching him, as he popped the cork effortlessly and poured them both a glass.

He handed one to her and raised his own. 'To Emmeline.'

Hearing him say the young girl's name caused a lump in her throat. Reminded her of that sweet girl's smile.

'To Emmeline.' She clinked her glass against his and took a sip. The wine was beautiful and ran over her tongue with a gentle caress of flavour.

She looked at him over the rim of her glass, drinking in the sculpted beauty of his face. He had such expressive eyes. The kind she could lose herself in if she wasn't careful.

'You were upset when you left.'

He stared at her so intently... It wasn't an accusation. More of an observation, inviting her to speak about how she felt.

'Yes, well...losing a patient will do that to you.'

'It is always a difficult thing.'

She needed to sit down, so she sank onto the edge of the foot of her bed. 'It just hit me hard, you know? She didn't want that surgery. She'd had so many already. She was tired. Done. She didn't want it any more—the fight. How many times did you tell me you'd gone in before?'

Yanis sat down next to her. 'Three.' His voice was sad.

'Three times… Three times in her short life that poor girl had gone through brain surgery to scrape out a recurring tumour. No wonder she'd had enough!'

It hadn't been just the trauma of surgery she'd needed to get past each time, but the recovery from surgery, too. Each one taking longer than the last.

'We could not leave it. You know that. Doing so would have resulted in her losing function and dying. It would have been a terrible way to go.'

'But she would have had more time! Time with her family. Time with her poor parents and her little brother. Time we took away from her today.'

The guilt was hitting hard, and Sam took a larger slug of her drink.

'It would not have been quality time—you know that.'

'But she begged us, Yanis! She *begged* us! And yet her parents told us to do the surgery because they trusted the medicine, trusted what we were doing, and look what happened!'

Yanis dipped his head. 'We gave her counselling and prepared her in every way we could, Sam. We could not have known that she would stroke out like that today. Her previous surgeries have all been relatively straightforward.'

'But we knew it was a risk.'

He turned to look at her. 'There is always a risk. We did the right thing, Samantha. You have to believe that. Her tumour was slowly eating its way through areas of her brain that would have caused her to lose all function. Speech. Swallowing. Movement. Imagine her life without those things. She loved to swim. To play on her trampoline. Today we tried to give a young girl another six months of normality.'

'Well, today we failed.'

She got up and went over to the bottle of Merlot and poured herself another glass, before filling his as well.

'I just wish that...'

She fell silent as tears threatened, swallowing hard to gain control of her emotions, thinking of her own experiences, her own childhood spent in doctors' offices and hospitals. The fear she'd felt. It could have been her. At any time in her childhood, this could have been her.

Yanis stood before her and looked deeply into her eyes. 'Wish that what?' he whispered.

'That it could have been different.' A tear slipped from her eye and rolled down her cheek.

Yanis took their glasses and put them down, and then he pulled her forward into his embrace.

She went willingly, her body yearning for the comfort that only another person could provide. Yearning for the warmth and the security and the safety. Yearning for a connection that she had not had for a long time.

Being here in Paris had made her feel so alone—something she'd not expected when she'd first packed her bags for a month in the city of love. She'd imagined meeting some French waiter or barman. Someone who would catch her eye and maybe provide some fun and laughter in amongst the hard work she would do here. A lighter side to her life. A brightness. A connection. Fun.

But she'd been so busy at the hospital, so exhausted when she came back to the hotel each night, she'd not really had time to sightsee or enjoy the city for what it was. But Yanis she knew. They'd known each other only for a month, but they had worked together a lot in that time, and she trusted him as a professional.

So she sank against Yanis's chest, sighing heavily into

the warmth of him, the strength of his arms around her, and closed her eyes in bliss as he stroked away her concerns and her cares, one hand on her back, the other stroking her hair. Her tears dried up and she realised they were swaying gently. He was rocking her, soothing her, and it felt so good and so right that she almost didn't want it to end.

Lifting her head to look at him, to smile and say thank you, she was suddenly caught in the tractor beam of his intense gaze and the words got stuck in her throat.

Yanis looked down at her with a question in his eyes, a want and need of his own, and suddenly she realised just how upset that he must be, too. Yanis had *known* Emmeline. Much better than Sam had. He had worked on her for every surgery, had watched her grow over the last few years, had no doubt hoped for a better outcome than the one they'd experienced today. And yet here he was, comforting *her*.

She could see, sense, *feel* just how much Yanis needed this, too.

'Yanis…'

'Oui?'

'Will you kiss me?'

She'd never in her whole life asked a man to kiss her before, but she had to right now. She knew Yanis wouldn't do so without her giving her consent first. He would never assume that she wanted him to kiss her just because they were comforting each other. But something had changed within her as he'd embraced her. It was as if her whole body had come alive.

She'd felt so weary and tired when she'd made it back to her hotel room—hours operating on someone's brain would do that to a person—but now all that world-weariness had gone and she felt alive for the first time in ages. She just knew that she wanted something to happen between them. It felt right. This was her last night in Paris. That was all she knew and that was all she needed to know. If they were going to celebrate a life, then why not enjoy the one they were living right now? Take a chance...strike whilst the iron was hot.

Who could truly know how much time they had left on this earth?

Yanis was here with her in this hotel room and she deserved to enjoy him as much as he would enjoy her. Why not comfort each other?

He placed a finger beneath her chin, lifting it ever so slightly as he stared deeply into her eyes. She saw his pupils, large and dark with arousal, and in that moment she knew she had never looked into a man's eyes that were so intense. So beautiful. So exotic.

The feel of his lips lightly brushing over her own sent fireworks exploding throughout her body, and a heat began to build within her as her hands began to clutch at his clothes.

Don't let me go.

His lips trailed down one side of her neck, feather-light, gentle, and the occasional quick touch of his hot tongue against her skin made her nerve endings dance in delight.

Her heart began to pound within her chest. She needed this. This oblivion. Being with Yanis like this would take away all the pain of losing Emmeline and would, for a brief while at least, take away her own past, her own regrets, her own grief.

His lips found hers again and he deepened the kiss. She began to loosen the knot of his dark tie, her fingers hungry for the buttons of his shirt, so she could get past those, feel the wonder of his skin. Feel the heat of him. The strength. The flexing of muscles moving beneath flesh.

She shrugged out of her blouse, felt Yanis's hand at the zip of her skirt before it fell to the floor. He lowered her gently onto the bed and she pulled him close, not willing to be apart from him for a second, arching towards him, meeting him, relishing the weight of him above her, his skin against hers.

His body was a delight, and exactly as she'd imagined. From the very first day at St Albert she had noticed Yanis—before they'd even been introduced.

He was tall, at least six feet, and his straight, dark hair was exquisitely styled to look as if he'd just been dragged out of bed. But he was still groomed enough to look professional. Just watching him move, she knew that he looked after himself. Broad shoulders, a trim, neat waist in his slim-fit shirts, trousers that accentuated his backside and thighs.

He was a man who knew how to dress for his shape. Or was that just a French thing? That innate sense of style that all French people seemed to have so effortlessly? It would not have surprised her to see him strolling down a catwalk, or even to find out he modelled in his spare time. She'd seen the way people looked at him. Nurses, patients, other doctors, even one or two men had cast an appreciative eye over the delectable Yanis Baptiste. A double take, a second look just to make sure that their eyes hadn't been deceived.

And he was *single*. How that was possible she didn't know, but right now she was very glad that he was—

especially as his mouth was doing such wonderful things as it trailed over her stomach.

Did he notice her scars? Did he wonder? Did he have questions? She felt shame begin its deep burn and suddenly wanted to hide, to cover herself, but that feeling went away when he simply carried on, without stopping or pausing. Without speaking.

He said nothing as his lips trailed lower, his tongue lapping at her belly button, his teeth nibbling ever so gently over her hip bone, his fingers hooking into her underwear and sliding them down, so she ignored her feelings and pushed them away.

She lifted her hips to make it easier for him and closed her eyes in ecstasy as his mouth trailed up her left inner thigh.

Her fingers caught in his hair…

And then… *Oh, yes!*

She simply lost herself. It was as if all thoughts vanished, all cares were washed away, and all upset and shame disappeared, to be replaced by wonder and heat and delicious excitement as she thrust her body against his mouth, never wanting it to stop, never wanting these sensations to end. He drove her onwards, upwards, higher and higher as his tongue slicked over her flesh, and just as she thought she might explode, his lips came back to her own and she tasted herself upon him.

'Sam…we should protect ourselves.'

She nodded. 'I'm on the pill. Do you have a condom?'

He shook his head. 'I didn't come here expecting to…' He looked down at her body, smiled. 'I haven't been with a woman for a long time.'

'I've not been with a man for a long time.'

She grinned and pulled him towards her. Urging him

on, wrapping her legs around his waist, she gasped with pleasure as he slowly filled her with the long length of him and began to move slowly, watching her every expression.

Sam gazed into his eyes, holding on tight, riding the wave that was coming. She was unable to look away, not wanting to look away, needing to have that connection, to see into his soul, for him to see into hers.

Briefly, she worried about what he might see… worried that he might sense she was broken and could never be fixed and because of that he might stop. So she closed her eyes to him, denying him that kind of access, and buried her face in his neck as her body began its ascent.

She felt the build of it, the surge, the sparks of electricity, the fizzing of nerve endings as the current suddenly exploded and she cried out, clutching him tight, her nails scraping his back as he came, too. She felt him thrust even deeper, stronger, and then, after a few breaths, he slowly stilled and began to kiss and caress her collarbone.

The delicate kisses were a balm for the frenzy of before.

He pulled back to look into her eyes. 'Are you all right, *ma chérie*?'

She nodded, smiling, but unable to open her eyes and look at him. She suddenly felt ashamed. Ashamed and fearful over what they had done.

Had he seen the real her? The Sam Gordon she liked to keep hidden? Had he glimpsed her secret?

Now that it was over—now that she'd had what she needed in that moment so she could forget—she wanted him gone.

Before he could ask too many questions.

CHAPTER ONE

Present day

THERE WAS NOTHING quite like the feeling of stepping into an operating theatre. This was the place where the magic happened. Where the fight for life was not just black or white, but many shades of grey. Here, the inevitable could be fought. Here, the surgeon's skill battled disease, or old age, or trauma, and triumphed.

The operating theatres were probably the most important rooms in the hospital. Not that Sam thought any less of the wards, where patients recovered, or the rehabilitation department, where patients relearned old skills so that they could return to something resembling normal life. It was just that in Theatre was where the battle began, and without her skills, her knowledge and her ability, those patients could not begin down their road to recovery.

Walking into Theatre scrubbed and sterile, ready for her gown and her gloves, her mask and headset, was a ritual, a practice that made her feel as if she had all the power in the world. And *control*.

It was a heady feeling, and one that she had been determined to have her entire life.

Her patient already lay on the table, anaesthetised and connected to a respirator. Beside the anaesthetist, machines beeped and gasped, monitoring oxygen rates, heart rate, blood pressure and temperature.

'Let's run it,' she said, as a nurse fastened her gown at her side.

'Dante Jackson, four months of age, here for a shunt due to hydrocephalus.'

'You've checked the tags?'

'Yep. It's the right patient on the table.'

She nodded, glad that all seemed correct. Over on the wall were Dante's recent scans, lit up from behind, and she examined them one last time. She didn't really need to. She knew exactly what was happening inside this little boy's head. But it was a ritual. She always did it. She checked and double-checked. She made sure. There was no room for mistakes or surprises in her theatre. This was a room in which she was always in control.

'Scalpel.' She held out her hand and her nurse assist placed the blade into her hand.

Time to begin.

As ever, she muttered her little mantra beneath her face mask. 'Above all, do no harm...' Then louder, for the rest of the staff, she said, 'Let's make a difference, everyone.'

She felt the rest of the theatre team relax, even saw a few eyes crinkling at the corners as they smiled. It was a habit, a practice that enveloped them all together as a team. Almost a good luck routine. It was like a footballer always wearing the same pair of socks for a match, or an actor always cracking his neck before going on stage. It made Sam feel better and everyone else, too, because it made them feel she was on her game.

Which she was—even if she did feel a bit off today...

It was the strangest thing, but she felt sure it was nothing, really.

Whenever Sam felt ill, or off in some way, she always told herself that it was nothing. That she was imagining it, or that it was just a psychosomatic echo left over from childhood. Of course, in reality she knew that she *could* get sick. People did all the time. Colds. The flu. Headaches. Fever. But she was a type-A personality and she always pushed through it. She'd take paracetamol to stop the pain or bring down her fever. She'd push through a cold and take decongestants. She never let illness stop her doing what she was meant to be doing.

But today she felt a little...

It was difficult to pin down exactly how she felt. She'd felt tired a lot just lately. She'd had a few headaches, but had put it down to her workload over recent weeks. They'd been a surgeon down, and waiting for the hospital to employ a replacement, so in the meantime she'd been working extra-hard, extra-long hours, long days, completing the work of two neurosurgeons, with two neuro lists, and it had been a real struggle.

But she'd felt on top of it, and she'd even received a pat on the back from the chief of neurosurgery for the way she'd been handling the workload.

Sam looked down on the patient's shaved head—he'd barely even begun to grow thick hair—and made the first incision. Sure. Precise. There was nothing wrong with her hands! She was as steady as a rock.

'How are we looking, Aarav?' she asked the anaesthetist.

'All good.'

'Excellent.'

She was hoping to place a ventriculoperitoneal shunt into little Dante, which would work by taking the extra fluid out of his brain and shunting it down to his belly, where it would be absorbed.

'Drill, please.'

She held out her hand for the instrument and as she did so suddenly felt nauseous. That wasn't something she usually experienced—and most definitely not in Theatre. In Theatre, the rest of the world ceased to exist until the battle was over. This new sensation, in a world that was usually under her total control, threw her.

'Could someone get me some water?' she asked, feeling all eyes suddenly on her.

Sam never asked for water. She never asked for music. She liked the silence. The reassuring rhythm of the machines was all the tune she needed to hear. This odd diversion was something that would be noted, and with all the attention she felt herself grow a little hot.

Nerves, that's all it is. You've had a lot on. This is normal. Natural. Ignore it. Besides, you want to be on top form today.

The new surgeon would be arriving this morning. Was probably already here. Filling in paperwork, most likely, getting an ID card sorted, being given the welcome pack from the chief of neurosurgery, Elliot Parker. Elliot liked to give his new recruits a welcome meeting—liked to talk them through what he expected, what his vision for the department was and all that jazz.

Sam had passed Elliot in the corridor earlier and told him that when he'd finished terrorising the new surgeon he should send him to her theatre to join in. She might even let him assist. Get his hands dirty straight away and make him feel part of the team by showing trust in regard to her patient. Besides, this shunt surgery was simple enough. It was something Sam could do in her sleep. And it would be a good excuse to assess her new colleague. Make sure he was right for Barney's.

A team couldn't run smoothly if there was someone on it who couldn't pull their weight. They each needed to know that they could trust and rely on each other. Especially in a place like this, where it was life and death every day. This new neuro was a good guy, too. She'd heard of his work. David Emery had recently published a paper on burr hole techniques that had been absolutely fascinating, and she was looking forward to working with him.

She took a steadying breath as she placed the equipment and drilled a small hole through the skull, determined to ignore the churning in her stomach. She carried on working. Steady. Sure. Each movement a practised piece of perfect choreography. It helped her to focus... the familiarity, the sequence of steps needed to place the shunt.

A nurse arrived with a glass of water, equipped with a straw, and lowered her mask slightly so Sam could take a long drink. That felt better. Her mouth was no longer dry and that weird taste in her mouth had gone, if only for a moment.

Refreshed, she continued to work, aware of the theatre door behind her opening, of someone approaching the table opposite her. She looked up to welcome David Emery.

'Good morning! Glad you could join me...' She stopped as her eyes met those of someone she hadn't expected. Someone she remembered all too well. They were unmistakable. Icy blue, framed by long, dark lashes.

Was it really him?

It couldn't be!

Could it?

What had happened to David Emery? Was he still coming?

'Yanis?'

'Bonjour. How are you?'

She saw his eyes crinkle, saw them gleam in amusement at how shocked she was. For a moment she struggled to gather her thoughts, trying to push aside the memories she had of Yanis. Of them together in her hotel room. Making love in the dark. Her mind felt as if it had been cast into a raging storm. She needed to ground herself.

'This is Dante. Four months old and in for a ventriculoperitoneal shunt. Have you ever done one of these before?'

Sam was aware that her voice sounded shaky. She couldn't meet his gaze. Couldn't look at anyone. It was as if her body *remembered*. Their last encounter, such a passionate one, had ended in such a state of confusion when, after their lovemaking session, she had practically kicked him out of her hotel room, afraid that she had exposed too much of herself to him. Given away too many secrets.

'I have.'

She needed to get control of this situation! This was *her* theatre. Her patient. Dante was the most important person in the room, not him. And this was not the place for second guesses and doubts. But she could feel her reaction to Yanis. The trembling in her body.

'Then let's see what you can do.' She passed him the tools, feeling that it would put her in a stronger position and would not alert anyone to how he had affected her by just walking into the room. Would not let anyone see how her hands had begun to shake.

Damn him!

'Water, please.' The nurse presented her with the straw again and briefly lifted her mask for her, so that she might drink. 'Thank you.'

When she turned around again to face Yanis, he was already at work. His face was a mask of concentration as he perfectly placed the shunt and attached the valve. He checked to see that there was correct drainage of the cerebrospinal fluid and then began his preparations to close. The scrub nurse assisted him as Sam watched, maintaining a careful eye on everything.

'I wasn't expecting to see you today,' she said.

'*Non?* It was a last-minute change. Elliot's first choice turned down the post at the last minute. I did not.'

Yanis, as she already knew, was an exceptional neuro-surgeon and would be a brilliant fit for the team here at Barney's. She'd watched this man in action many times. He worked the same way she did. Had the same instincts. He strove for perfection in every surgery he undertook. She had no doubt that Dante was in excellent hands.

'Aarav? Everything all right at your end?' she asked, trying to establish a modicum of control in the room.

'BP is running steady. He's dealing with the surgery very well.'

'Good.'

As Yanis closed, she felt a wave of heat wash over her and she swayed slightly on her feet. What the heck was *that*? It startled her, worried at her, and she turned to the nurse so she could dab at her brow with a cloth.

Sam never sweated like this in a surgery. Even when something went wrong and she had to leap into emergency protocols to fend off a bleed, or administer CPR. She remained steady and sure, reliant on her knowledge and her training being at their peak. She felt adrenaline rushes, sure, but this heady mix she was feeling right now was all because of *him*.

When the last stitch was in and Yanis turned to thank everyone, Sam knew she had to get out of the room before his gaze turned on her. She couldn't stand there a moment longer.

I need some fresh air.

Yanking off her gloves, mask and then her gown, she pressed the treadle foot for the bin and threw them all in, then headed to the scrub room to clean up. Maybe she could get in and out of there before Yanis followed and caught up with her. If she could just get some time to think this over…think this through.

How was she going to deal with having him here? She had opened herself up to this man. Had allowed him to see her body. Her soul. She had exposed herself to him and he knew things. She knew he did. Even if he didn't know what they meant, he had seen her scars and she had allowed that to happen thinking that she would never see him again. Thinking that, believing that, it was a safe thing to do. She had allowed herself to find comfort in his arms, but it had only been meant to be a one-time thing!

Now he was her colleague. Permanently.

Sam scrubbed at her hands and nails, eager to get done, keen to get away from the way she was feeling, from the warmth of her body, the light-headedness that was affecting her, the churn of her stomach. Her legs felt weak, her whole body felt drained, and what with the shock of his arrival, it was all—

'Samantha.'

That voice! Velvety… Soft liquid richness with a French accent tempering and sweetening all his words. It was as if his voice was an actual caress. A balm to her tortured soul. Yet it was also the cause of its discomfort right now. It was a confusing juxtaposition.

She closed her eyes and paused in her scrubbing for just a moment. She had to get control! She turned to look at him, knowing she needed to create distance between them after their last intimate, close-up encounter.

'Mr Baptiste.'

He'd taken off his headcover and mask, and now she was reminded of the true impact of the man. He was exactly as she remembered. It hadn't been a dream, or an exaggeration. He truly was as stunning as she recalled.

But just because we've slept together once, it doesn't mean anything. It wasn't a connection. It wasn't lust. We just comforted each other—that's all and he's probably with someone now.

Surprisingly, that last thought did not bring her comfort. Only awkwardness.

'I didn't know you were planning on coming to Richmond.'

'I wasn't. But the opportunity presented itself, along with a raise in salary and a chance to perform some research, and my brother said I could live in his flat until I found my own place.'

'Your brother lives in *Richmond*?' How had she not even known he had a brother? What on earth had they talked about back in Paris?

Oh, that's right, we talked about patients and surgeries because I was panicked by how stunning he was and it seemed an easy way to keep my mind on task.

'*Oui*. Well, he did. Now Luca is off trapping and radio-tagging rhino in South Africa.'

She turned off the water and grabbed at some paper towels to dry herself. 'Rhino?'

'He is a veterinary surgeon.'

'Is everyone a surgeon of some kind in your family?'

Yanis smiled, and it did strange things to her tummy. Why was her heart racing? Why did she feel so shaky? Why couldn't her stomach settle? And what was that strange roaring, rushing noise in her ears?

She saw Yanis answer her, but it was almost as if noise had been muted. The rushing sound in her ears became louder and she found it hard to focus. She looked up at Yanis, tried to focus on his features, tried to use him as some sort of anchor. But everything was beginning to blur, and the world had begun to darken at the edges, and she realised much too late that she was going to pass out.

The last thing she saw was Yanis frown and reach for her, before everything went black and her world became blissfully peaceful once again.

He caught her before she hit the floor and in one rapid movement scooped his arm under her legs and carried her out of the scrub room. He had no idea why she had fainted like that, but he wondered if maybe she hadn't eaten that morning and had low blood sugar.

He determined to check. Surgeons often thought they were machines and could carry on for hours, putting their patients first, but if they didn't look after themselves then what use were they to the people in their care?

A scrub nurse carrying a surgical pack stopped and stared. 'What's happened to Sam?'

'Fainted. Tell me where I can lie her down.'

She was getting heavy in his arms, but that didn't matter. He would carry her as long as she needed. He knew how driven Sam was. He'd seen it. Watched her. He had sometimes been amazed by her, and clearly she'd been trying to pursue her goal of becoming chief of neurosurgery one day by working herself into the ground.

She needed to rest. To eat. To drink. And then he would run a blood test to see what she might be deficient in.

'In here.'

The nurse opened a door, allowing him into the room where pre-operative patients sometimes waited, before being taken into Theatre. Right now it was empty, and he gently laid her down on a bed, then grabbed the bed control and raised the lower end, so that her legs were higher than her heart. He placed an oxygen mask over her face and turned on the air flow at the wall.

He stared at her face. At the fine arches of her natural eyebrows and her high, rounded cheekbones. The spread of her flaming hair against the whiteness of the pillow reminded him of that night together.

'Can you get me something to test her blood sugar with? And the kit for a basic blood test?'

The nurse nodded and hurried from the room.

Alone with Sam, he leaned over her, close to her face, and made his voice soft and soothing. 'Samantha? Wake up.'

She was so pale. Paler than normal. Normally her alabaster skin looked perfect against those long locks of auburn flame, but right now her skin had an ill tinge to it that he did not like. *Had* she been working too hard? Trying to fulfil the hours of the surgeon they'd not had until his arrival? Had she taken on too much? Doctors did it all the time. He'd seen them burn out. He sincerely hoped that this wasn't the case here.

He'd been thrilled to accept the post at St Barnabas's. Although, unwilling to leave his own department in the lurch to travel to Richmond for interview, he had asked Elliot to interview him by video call. Since Covid, the world had adapted, and people had discovered that so much that used to be done in person could just as easily be done online. He was grateful for it. He'd worried about finding a place in London, but then Luca had come to the rescue there, and everything had fallen into place.

Discovering that Sam was still here had been thrilling to hear, after their friendship and intimate connection in Paris, though he was still a little perturbed as to why she had thrown him out afterwards the way she had. As if she'd been embarrassed. He couldn't understand why. She was perfect. Beautiful.

He'd thought about her often since that night, but told himself that she was off-limits to him, what with the way she'd thrown him out. Such a clear message that she had regrets. Maybe she didn't date co-workers? He'd decided he would respect her boundaries and offer friendship only.

But now? He had almost been amused at how shocked she'd been to see him in her theatre. And glad that he'd affected her so. That he'd made an impression. He'd even enjoyed it.

But fainting? That he was not so pleased about. It told him that she hadn't been looking after herself lately, and he suspected she'd already had some past health concerns.

He'd not been blind that night. He'd seen all those scars. Surgical scars. Laparoscopic marks on her abdomen. An appendectomy scar. She'd been through something. A long time ago, judging by the silvery nature of the marks—they were almost invisible. But surgeons noticed those things the way phlebotomists noticed good veins. They were trained to. And although he'd said nothing that night, perhaps now that he was here and working with her he could keep an eye on her to make sure she took care of herself?

Sam groaned softly.

He reached for her hand and squeezed her fingers. 'Hey…that's it. Open your eyes.'

He saw her frown, then blink, before opening her eyes wide and pulling the oxygen mask off her face. 'What happened?'

'You fainted.'

'Fainted? No.'

She tried to sit up, but he gently pushed her back down against the pillows.

'Stay there for a moment. You have not been looking after yourself, Samantha.'

She glared at him.

It was his turn to frown. Why was she being so hostile? Was she embarrassed about having passed out? He'd only been trying to make a light-hearted joke.

At that moment the scrub nurse returned with the equipment he'd asked for. He smiled a thank-you. *'Merci.'*

'What's that for?' Sam asked.

'To check you over.'

'I'm fine.' She tried to sit up again, and swung her legs out of the bed, but when she sat up she paused and went a little green-looking. 'Ugh…'

'Lie back, *mon amie.* Let me take care of you.'

'I feel sick.'

'That is normal after fainting.' He turned to the scrub nurse. 'Could you wet some paper towel for her head?'

The nurse nodded and brought over some wet blue paper towel and draped it on Sam's forehead.

'Thank you.' She laid her head back against the pillow. 'What tests are you taking?'

'Blood sugar. Vitamins and minerals. A basic blood test.' He glanced at her, thinking for a moment about a possibility he would ask any young woman about if she had fainted in front of him. 'And HCG. Do you consent?'

She raised a sardonic eyebrow. 'Are you going to let me off this bed if I say no?'

He smiled at her. *'Non.'*

'You can't force me to do anything against my will.'

He continued to smile, knowing he would win this small battle. 'That is true.'

'So I could just sit up and wait for you to go. Or wait until I get beeped to take care of a patient.'

'Yes. But then I would have to go to Elliot with my concerns.'

'You wouldn't…'

He met her gaze, deadly serious now. 'Try me. I take patient care very seriously indeed, and I'm sure Elliot would not be happy if his best neurosurgeon fainted in Theatre over an open brain.'

Sam glared at him, then closed her eyes again, pressing the wet towel against her head. 'Fine. I consent. But I never expected you to be the sort to tell tales.'

She held out her arm.

Smiling at his small victory against this very stubborn woman whom he admired so much, he prepped her fingertip first, to take the blood sugar sample. As he'd suspected, her blood sugar was very low.

'You need to eat.'

'Right now, I think it would come straight back up.'

'You still feel sick?'

'It's just tiredness. I've felt that way for a while. It's what happens when you work too hard.'

'Perhaps.'

'Well, what else could it be?' she asked irritably.

As he slid the needle into her arm, and began applying tubes to the Vacutainer system, he considered his next words very carefully. 'Well, you've either not been taking care of yourself very well, or you have an illness, or...'

She looked at him. 'Or what?'

'Or you're pregnant.'

She seemed to stare at him for an age, before laughing nervously. 'Pregnant? That's ridiculous. I...'

She stopped talking and looked away. He saw her do some rapid period maths.

'No. It can't be...'

'When was your last period, Sam?'

He felt a frisson of something ripple through his own body at the way she'd just reacted. This might not be his problem. Just because they'd slept together nearly three months ago, it did not mean she could be pregnant with *his* child. She could have slept with someone else after him. Eight weeks ago, maybe. Six weeks ago. Who knew? Besides, it might not even be pregnancy!

But the look on her face unnerved him a little.

'They've always been irregular. I'm on the pill. I told you...'

The pill was good. Could he relax, then? 'You take it regularly?' he asked.

'Yes. I try to.'

He removed the needle from her arm and pressed a small cotton wool ball into her antecubital fossa. 'Press here.'

He turned to label the tubes and then slipped them into a bag to send them off to Pathology, his mind whirring like a cyclone.

'Did you take it regularly when you were in Paris?' he asked quietly.

She met his gaze. 'You think I'm pregnant with your baby?'

He shrugged. 'I have no idea. Have you slept with anyone else since?'

'That's none of your damned business!'

'Okay. Let's see what the results say.'

He was not offended by her defensiveness. He understood it. If pregnancy *was* the cause of her fainting and feeling ill, Sam would be greatly affected. Her life changed in an instant. It was no wonder she was getting upset with him. Though if she'd been taking the pill properly they should be fine.

She nodded. 'It'll be negative. I'm sure of it.'

But she didn't *look* sure of it, and inwardly he was worried. Worried that the test would come back and show that Sam's HCG levels were raised. Worried that she could be carrying his child in her womb.

Because if that was the case then his new start, the new life that he'd hoped to begin when he arrived in Richmond, would soon be destroyed.

CHAPTER TWO

LITTLE DANTE WAS doing well after his surgery. Sam had checked on him and her other post-operative patients before a quick trip to the hospital cafeteria to get something to eat. She'd stood over the counter, looking at the various hot and cold offerings, not sure what she wanted to eat that she would keep down, and opted for a large chocolate chip cookie to help her blood sugar and a small bottle of fresh orange juice. Because, well… Healthy stuff would balance out the sugar-laden cookie. Plus, they were both quick to consume.

She hadn't even sat. She'd simply bought them and now stood in the corridor, quickly eating and drinking.

She didn't want to stay in any one place, even for a little while. It was better, she felt, to keep moving, because she was trying to avoid Yanis and those questioning eyes of his.

Yanis Baptiste. Here. *Permanently!* In *her* hospital.

Bewilderment was a fine word to explain how she was feeling. Never in a million years had she ever expected that he would come back into her life, and it was a complication that she didn't need right now.

She'd fainted. *Fainted!* Sam had never fainted in her entire life, and she'd been through some pretty harrowing stuff. To faint in front of Yanis, of all people… And now he had this ridiculous idea that she could be pregnant. It was impossible, wasn't it? She was on the pill and she'd slept with Yanis three months ago. There'd have been signs…there'd have been—

Sam let out a breath as her mind helpfully provided the evidence that she had dismissed as just being overworked. Tiredness. Today's nausea. Headaches. The bloating which she'd put down to eating a few weird food combinations…

But all that had to be coincidence, right? Doctors worked odd hours… They grabbed what they could, when they could. It didn't always make sense, but sometimes you just wanted the calories, no matter where they came from. And a bowl of cereal was fabulous at any time of day or night.

She rubbed at her abdomen through her scrubs. Was it rounder? Had she put on weight? Maybe a little. It was hard to tell when you lived in scrubs for most of the day. Those things were elasticated or had a pull-string around the waist. Nothing was fitted.

And I had that tummy bug in Paris.

She couldn't be a mother. Absolutely not—no way. It wasn't in her life plan. It wasn't on her to-do list. There wasn't a maternal bone in her body. Sam's own mother had seen to that.

But she didn't want to stand here ruminating on *her*. There were things to do, and she couldn't stand idle whilst she waited for her blood test results to come back. A part of her didn't want to know the results. Living in blissful ignorance sounded great right now.

Thankfully, at that very moment her pager went off. She was needed in A & E to assess a trauma patient.

She threw the cookie wrapper and the juice bottle in the nearest bin as if she was playing basketball, applauded herself for getting them both in first time, and headed for the stairwell.

The patient was a middle-aged man who'd had a fall from a height of six feet onto concrete, just over a week ago. Max Winshaw had presented to A & E then, via ambulance, and initial scans of his head and neck had been clear. But now he had been brought in again by his wife, Cara, who was concerned that there was something more going on.

'He's not right, Doctor.'

'In what way?'

Sam was observing her patient carefully. He lay back on the cubicle bed, one arm over his eyes as if he had a headache.

'He's been really irritable from this pain in his head, which he says is getting worse, and paracetamol doesn't touch it. He's got no energy, and he says his vision is weird.'

'Explain "weird".' She pulled out her pen torch and examined the pupilar reaction in Max's eyes.

'Blurry...out of focus sometimes. But it's the pain in his head that's most worrying, and this morning he's been sick.'

Sam nodded. 'His last scans were clear, but considering the mechanism of his injury and the symptoms, I suggest we do another immediate scan to be on the safe side—just to make sure he hasn't developed a slow bleed.'

'Into his brain?' Cara covered her mouth. 'Oh... You think it might be serious?'

'Let's see what the CT scans say. I'm going to order

one right now, okay? A nurse will come and take you through. Max? I want you to stay on this bed.'

He nodded and groaned. He didn't look good.

Sam ordered the scan and then had a thought. If Max needed surgery, she would take him into Theatre. That would be a good way to pass the time until her blood results came back in. But then again, she had just recently fainted. Perhaps doing surgery herself right now wasn't the best idea? If she called Yanis, she could give the case to him—no matter how much that would grate on her nerves—and the patient would be in secure hands. *And* she would know exactly where Yanis was, and wouldn't have to worry about running into him unnecessarily.

She turned to a nurse. 'Could you page Mr Baptiste from Neurosurgery for the Winshaw case, please?'

'Of course.'

'Thanks.'

Sam hated giving over any surgery she considered her own, but right now it seemed the sensible thing to do. Even though she felt better since eating, and she didn't think she would faint again. She'd simply been hungry, and then there'd been the shock of seeing Yanis. Somehow she'd passed out, but she was fine now and felt perfectly well, if a little tired. But patient care came first for Sam, no matter how much she wanted to claim this patient as hers.

When Yanis finally strode into the emergency department, Sam watched with mild amusement as the female staff and a couple of the patients watched him pass with a look of admiration. Sam smiled. He certainly could have that effect if you weren't used to such fine features, and those eyes and cheekbones were a sight to behold indeed.

'Hi. Thanks for consulting on this case with me,' she said.

'No problem at all.'

'I hope I didn't tear you away from anything important?'

'I'm good. How can I help?'

Sam filled him in on the case as much as she could, showing him the previous scans on the computer. As they talked, the second set of scans appeared, and they instantly saw the problem.

'Subdural haematoma.'

'With marked midline shift.' Yanis pointed. 'He needs immediate surgery.'

'I think you should take the lead on this one,' said Sam.

He nodded. 'My pleasure. Do you want to assist?'

No. That was what she intended to say. The whole point of this was to put Yanis in Theatre, so she knew where he was and could move unencumbered around the hospital until her blood results came back and exonerated her. Then she could go back to being normal.

But the one thing she hadn't bet on was her own personality and drive, and her need to be involved and in control. She loved Theatre. It was difficult to give up an opportunity to be in one.

'Sure,' she said, but inwardly she was berating herself, figuring she'd now have to spend an hour or two with Yanis in a very small space indeed.

With nowhere to run and nowhere to hide.

Yanis stepped forward. 'Are we all ready?' he asked the theatre team.

There were nods of assent.

'Do we have any classical music?'

A nurse nodded and turned on the player.

Something soothing and lyrical began to issue softly from the speakers and Sam smiled beneath her mask.

She'd forgotten he liked classical music. When they'd first met in Paris, and she'd shared her first theatre with him, she'd expected someone like him to prefer heavy rock blasting from the speakers, but she'd been wrong. And watching Yanis operate, his hands and his fingers expertly and delicately operating on a brain whilst heavenly music played, was a sight to behold. His focus was a thing of beauty, and those intense eyes of his, when they were all you could see above the mask, were...hypnotic. It was like watching a craftsman.

She admired his skill and abilities, and knew she found them attractive. So why on earth had she agreed to come into Theatre with him?

He began the craniotomy. The part of surgery that temporarily removed a bone flap from the skull, to allow access to the brain. He worked steadily. Surely. With no hesitation.

Sam liked watching him work. Liked watching his hands. The way he manipulated the tools. She found herself stealing glimpses at his face, wondering what he was thinking.

There was no sign of apprehension on his face. No hint of worry of any kind that he might have got her pregnant. That he might be facing fatherhood.

But perhaps normal people didn't fear becoming a parent?

Sam knew she was different. The idea that she might become a mother was almost impossible to get her head around. She had a career. A vocation. She planned on becoming chief in a few years! Nowhere in her ten-year plan was there a gap created for maternity leave! It simply wasn't going to happen.

The blip she'd experienced today was simply that. A blip. She'd worked too hard, hadn't eaten right, hadn't looked after herself properly having worked so hard to show Elliot what she was capable of. He'd marvelled at her ability to get through her surgical lists, even clapped her on the back a few times, and each time she'd received praise from him she had felt so proud. So noticed. So marvellous. It had made her feel *good*.

Approval was something she craved. There was no way in hell she was going to walk away from something she had fought so long for. She couldn't be pregnant! Her body was playing tricks on her. Acting up. And God only knew she was used to that. It was all a lie. Worries manifesting themselves as symptoms that Yanis had simply imagined could be something else.

Of course the blood test would come back negative.

Max's bleed could now be seen through his dura. Sam hoped it would be a simple case of Yanis opening the dura and removing the clot with suction. However, she knew that though the operation might be simple enough, Max's recovery would be anything but. There was a high mortality rate with this kind of damage. They could fight all they wanted to get rid of this clot and get him through surgery, but anything could take him down afterwards. Brain oedema. New bleeds. Infection. Seizures. An increase in intercranial pressure. They'd have to monitor him closely in the ICU afterwards...

'Suction.'

Yanis slowly and carefully began to remove the clot, and they were all able to quickly see where the bleed had originated. Sam worked quickly to take control of the bleeding and repair the site. She and Yanis had done this before in Paris, and they worked well together. Staying out of each other's way but knowing exactly what the other was doing, knowing what they needed to do, what angle they required to work from, and then adapting their own position.

There was something beautiful about this surgery. About the way they worked. It was as if the rest of the world had slipped away and all there was left was the patient, Yanis and Sam, operating in some kind of bubble. She forgot the music, forgot the other staff, didn't hear the beep of the machines or the clank and clink of instruments as they were placed back on trays. It was like a dance. A tango. Two people working independently to create something beautiful.

'Bleeding has stopped. Good work, Samantha.'

She smiled at his praise and met his eyes. She wanted to say something. Anything. But it was as if her throat had stopped working. All she could feel was the pounding of her heart in her chest and the dryness in her mouth. His gaze made her feel all aflutter, and she had to look away in an attempt to try to regain control.

What was happening to her? Why did he have the ability to affect her like this? It hadn't happened in Paris.

But you hadn't slept with him then. Not until that final night.

And she'd only done so then because she'd known she would never have to face him again.

She'd thought she could let her barriers down, accept his comfort, enjoy what he offered.

She'd wanted him. She couldn't lie about that.

And now temptation was back in her life, and maybe

her body was telling her it would like to get to know him again, because it knew how good it could be with him?

Yes, well... My body used to say a lot of things, and look where that got me.

Yanis replaced the bone flap and closed up, and they both stepped away from the table to go and scrub down.

'I think that went very smoothly,' he said.

She nodded. 'We'll need to keep a close eye on him in Recovery.'

'I always keep a close eye on my patients. Speaking of which—how are you feeling?'

She laughed. 'I'm not your patient, Yanis.'

'Whilst we're waiting for those blood results, technically you are. Until I discharge you from my care.'

'They'll be negative. I'm fine. Just a little overworked, that's all. Now you're here I can sit back and relax a bit more.'

'Doctors always make the worst patients.' He smiled as he dried his hands with paper towel.

At that moment a nurse arrived with a brown manila folder. 'Those urgent blood results, Mr Baptiste.' She laid them down on top of the metal sink and walked away.

Sam suddenly felt her blood pressure rise and she grew hot. Her stomach was churning now. They'd be negative, right?

She reached for the folder to read them herself, but she was too slow—Yanis already had them in his grasp. He gave her a look. *Are you ready?*

And then he opened the folder.

CHAPTER THREE

'YOU'RE PREGNANT.'

The words fell from his mouth in disbelief. He'd considered it a possibility, but hoped he was wrong. Now there it was in black and white, and he was stunned.

His past flashed before his eyes. Those moments in Sonography with Giselle. The tears. The pain. The grief. The isolation. The rejection. The accusations.

'What? No. Give me that.'

Sam snatched the slip of paper from his hand and scanned it, frowning as she read everything. The beta HCG numbers, her name, her date of birth, checking it was *her* result and not someone else's.

Yanis watched her silently, his mind whirring with fears and thoughts that he hadn't had for a long time. Sam was most definitely pregnant.

'Is it mine?'

He had to know. Had to know if she'd slept with someone else after him. Had to know whether or not he was going to be let off the hook. Even thinking it, hoping for it, he felt bad. Because even if it wasn't his, Sam was still going to be left pregnant, and he could tell from what he knew of this woman that having a child and being a mother were not part of her life plan.

He could even remember them talking about such things back in Paris. They'd chatted about where they saw themselves in the future. What they wanted to achieve. All Sam had talked about was work. Maybe starting up a clinical trial, with all that entailed, and really putting herself and St Barnabas's on the map as *the* leading neuro-surgery centre in the UK.

Were there tears in her eyes? Seeing her look so shocked made him want to comfort her and pull her close, but he just couldn't do it.

Sam glared at him and then stalked past him, blasting the door open with her palm and striding off down the corridor.

She didn't want this either.

He followed quickly. He was not going to allow her to shut him out on this. He needed to know.

He caught up with her by the lifts. 'Sam?'

'We need to run the test again. It's got to be faulty, or it's got mixed up in Pathology.'

'They're your results.'

'Stuff gets mixed up all the time—'

'Sam. Look at me. Is this baby mine?' he said urgently, making her meet his gaze, wanting her to focus, but not wanting to cause a scene in the busy hospital. He needed her to accept what was printed on that slip. There'd been no mistake and he was not going to waste time by pretending that there had. Facts needed clarifying.

The lift doors pinged open and she stepped inside. He went with her. 'I need you to answer me.'

'I didn't sleep with anyone else!'

Yanis sucked in a breath. So it *was* his. She was pregnant with his child. They'd slept together three months ago—that meant she'd had no antenatal care in that time.

They had no idea if this baby was healthy. And with *his* history he needed to know and he needed to know now.

'We need to organise an ultrasound. Right now.'

Sam shook her head. 'No.'

By God, this woman was stubborn! 'We need to check on the baby!'

'I don't want to see it! If I see it, it'll be real, and then—'

'It *is* real! You cannot stick your head in the sand on this one, *mon amie*!'

The lift opened at the neurology floor and Sam gave him one last withering look before stalking out of it. She headed to the main desk, where she took a seat and angrily punched her password and code into the hospital computer. She started to write up her part of the surgical notes on Max. Then she paused, her hands over the keyboard stopped, trembled, and her whole body sagged.

He couldn't see her face. Her long auburn locks hid it from view. But by the shake of her shoulders he knew she was crying.

He had done this to her. And she didn't know the worst of it yet. His heart ached for her. He was wishing he could protect her from all that was to come. He'd never wanted this to happen. Not again. And to think that he could be about to put Sam, of all people, through something so terrifying...

'*Ma chérie...*'

He reached out and tucked her hair behind her ear, draped his arm around her shoulder. She leaned into him and he wrapped both arms around her, just held her for a minute.

She didn't seem to mind that someone might see her crying, but knowing how sad she'd been after losing Emmeline, back in Paris, he wondered if the staff here were maybe used to her getting upset after losing a patient, and that was what they thought this was?

A nurse who passed them by silently mouthed *Is she okay?* He gave a quick nod to indicate that he had this, and that Sam was fine and she could carry on with her job.

It was nice that the staff here looked out for one another. That was the best thing about working in healthcare. Everyone usually had each other's backs. They were a family.

But as he held Sam in his arms, he wondered how much hurt he might put her through. She didn't know what had happened between him and his ex-wife, Giselle, and he knew that at some point he would have to tell her. Warn her. Yet now was not the time. He knew he had to let Sam accept the fact that she was pregnant first. And until they got a scan to see exactly how healthy this baby was, there was no point in worrying her unduly.

On the desk was a box of extra-large tissues, and he reached for one and passed it to her. 'Dry your eyes.'

She wiped at her eyes and sniffed. 'Thank you.'

'For what?'

'For not freaking out on me.'

He smiled. 'That's okay. You were freaking out enough for both of us. If I'd got involved with that, too, we both might have been sent to the fourth floor.'

The fourth floor was Psychiatry.

Sam hiccupped a laugh and let out a long breath. 'What are we going to do?'

Yanis sighed, glad that she was now co-operating. Asking for his advice. He knew how much it must be taking her to rely on someone else. The woman he'd known in Paris had been a tour de force and had relied on *no one*.

'We're going to get information. Organise an ultra-sound. Get your dates. Measurements. Make sure that *bébé et maman* are both okay.'

She looked at him then, seemed reassured by his kindness. 'At least one of us knows how to behave,' she said. 'And this baby will need it. Because I don't have a single clue on how to be a good *maman*.'

He smiled again, his eyes full of affection. 'I'll buy you a manual.'

Sam was a woman who could endure surgeries lasting an entire day. She had the patience to endure complicated and delicate operations, knowing that at times she would have to work at a snail's pace, so as not to do harm to any important areas of a patient's brain as she worked to remove tumours and clots or clip aneurysms. She could sit by a patient's bedside, waiting for them to wake, and not mind if it took hours, but this forty-minute wait she was having to endure for an ultrasound scan of her womb seemed interminable.

'Why are they taking so long?'

'It's a busy clinic. And don't forget we've not done this like all the other women here, who saw their family doctor first. We've used the privilege of being colleagues and they've fitted us in. We should be patient.'

'I'm not sure I know how.'

Becoming the patient and sitting in a hospital waiting room was terribly familiar to Sam, and it was bringing back memories that she had tried to forget many years ago. Of course, back then, she had been much smaller, and she'd not had a handsome man by her side but her mother, who would sit there reminding her quietly about what to say and what *not* to say.

That had been easy enough. Sometimes she'd felt so ill it had been simple to stay quiet and let her mother act the part of a distraught parent who '*just knew*' something was '*terribly wrong*' with her daughter. She would let them prod her, poke her with needles, examine her wherever her mother had said there was a problem, because she herself had wanted to feel better, and she'd known that the doctors had the power to make that happen.

In a way, she had been in awe of them, and it was where her own love of medicine had come from. Its seeming ability to make miracles happen. But she'd also known, from all the times before, that even if she got better she would fall ill again soon after, and sometimes the treatment would hurt. Sometimes she would be left in pain.

Technically, she knew this was not the same. She was not about to be used like a human guinea pig. This was a simple ultrasound. It would not hurt. If anything, it would be slightly uncomfortable as they pressed down upon her full bladder—they'd asked her to turn up with one. And this scan would give them the answers both she and Yanis needed.

But as she looked around the room at all the women, some with bumps that were barely there and others full and wholesome, with rounded, swollen abdomens, she couldn't help but imagine what that might be like. Becoming a mother...

Mothers were supposed to be loving and kind. They were supposed to be a child's soft place to fall. But Sam was convinced she could never be that. Surely she was all hard, sharp edges? Her broken pieces mangled together with the glue of time?

I simply don't know how to do this. What if I can't? What then? Do I fail this child? Doom it to years of therapy?

She shifted in her seat at the discomfort of her thoughts.

Yanis turned to look at her and she gave him a reassuring smile, but she was feeling anything but. His life was changing, too. This wasn't all about her. How was *he* feeling about this? He hadn't said much.

'What are you thinking?' she asked.

He shook his head. 'I don't know.'

'This must be as much of a shock to you as it is to me.'

He smiled. 'It certainly is.'

'It's going to mean us both having time off and parental leave. That's going to be really challenging.'

'We'll work something out.'

'I'm not giving up work. What I do is my life. It's what I live for,' she said, making sure he understood that she was not going to become a stay-at-home mother.

Neurology *was* what she lived for! It was all she'd ever lived for. She'd always been fascinated by medicine, and had known she would become a doctor, but specialising in neurology was her passion. It had been ever since her mother, and then her doctors, had suspected she had a brain tumour as a child.

The idea of someone working in her head... Sam had begun doing her own research. That had been hard back then—there hadn't been any books on neurology in her school library, and when she'd asked the librarian to order some... Well, she'd got a few strange looks. But the workings of the brain had fascinated her. And had gone on doing so for most of her adult life.

It was one of the largest and most complex organs of the human body. It contained over a hundred billion nerves and created trillions of connections every day through the synapses. It was who you were. How you reacted to things. How you loved. What made you laugh and cry. It was where the emotions came from, where memories were stored.

To think that all that passion for her job might fade, that this pregnancy was about to sideswipe everything she knew...

It was terrifying.

'I don't think I can do this, Yanis.'

He turned to look at her. 'You can.'

'How do you know? You don't really know me... You don't know anything about me! We're colleagues, thrown together by circumstance. I don't think you want this either—this *situation*.'

He sighed. 'It's certainly a surprise. But if we can excise tumours and clip bleeds and bring people back from the brink of death or a lifetime of disability, then I think we can do this, too. Millions of people worldwide do it, and they all do so without formal training. We're intelligent. Capable. I believe in us.'

She was envious of his certainty. Where did it come from? She wanted to believe his words. They made sense—of course they did. But her fear was impinging on every thought she had. What if she failed? What if she ruined this child's life the way her mother had almost ruined hers? Sam always tried to be the best she could be in anything. In her job. As a friend. Could she be a brilliant mother?

Her fear and her doubt told her no.

'Samantha Gordon?'

A lady dressed in pink scrubs stood in the doorway with a clipboard.

Sam and Yanis glanced at one another and he reached for her hand, giving it a quick squeeze.

'We can do this.'

She gave him an uncertain look and allowed him to lead her by the hand into the darkened room.

The sonographer introduced herself as Marta. 'You can take a seat on the bed, Ms Gordon.'

'Thank you for fitting us in. We both appreciate this very much,' Yanis said.

He felt it was important to say that. To show gratitude. It had been a long time since he'd been in an ultrasound room like this one and he could feel his apprehension growing.

Rooms like this either brought brilliant news or horrendously bad news. There never seemed to be any in between, as far as he was concerned. His last visit to a room like this had been with Giselle, his ex-wife, and the news then had been devastating. Their son's heart had stopped beating at thirty weeks' gestation.

Showing a little gratitude might win him some good luck points. It was worth a try.

'I just need to ask you a few basic questions,' said Marta, and ran Sam through them.

She wanted to know when her last period was, whether she had a regular cycle, her GP details, her medical history. All standard stuff. But he could hear the nervousness in Sam's voice as she responded and he put what he hoped was a soothing arm around her shoulders as he watched her fiddle with the blue sanitary paper that covered the bed.

She glanced up at him and gave him a brief, grateful smile. He saw fear in her soft blue eyes. A need to be protected. He wished he could protect her from everything, but that was not a power he had. Instead, he gave her another little squeeze, wanting her to know that they were in this together for the baby's sake, if no one else's.

'All right—so if you could lie back for me? That's it.' Marta tucked some more of the blue paper into the top of Sam's underwear. 'And this will feel cold.'

She squirted gel onto her belly and he watched her flinch. She gave him a look of such sheer terror that he reached out and took her hand.

'It's going to be okay.'

He had no true way of knowing, of course, but he felt it was important to say it. That she should hear it. And, no matter what the health of the baby, he wanted her to know that he would help her through whatever was to come. He would not abandon her. That was not the type of man he was.

He had supported Giselle as much as he could, but at the end of the day, even he hadn't been able to help, and they had separated. It was something that had made him feel a failure for such a long time and the reason why his work had become so important. At work, he could help. He could make a difference. He could control things.

This was not an area in which he had any control. Nor did Sam. So he knew how she felt in this moment.

Marta placed the probe on Sam's abdomen and began to move it around. Neither he nor Sam could see the screen. The sonographer had it turned in her direction only. He knew they all did this to check everything was all right before they turned the screen to show the ecstatic parents-to-be. It was a shield until it was a gift.

Her face gave nothing away as she moved the probe.

'It's bad news, isn't it? It's okay, you can tell me. It's a chemical pregnancy? A molar pregnancy?' Sam asked.

He was surprised that she was already assuming it was going to be bad news. He'd thought he was the only one. But then, she was a realist, and he liked that about her. There were no fluffy rainbows and unicorns in Sam's life—just cold, hard facts. Maybe that would help them deal with whatever was to come.

At that point Marta shook her head, then smiled. 'Is there any history of multiple pregnancy on either side?' she asked, and turned the screen.

Yanis's mouth went dry as he stared at the image. Was he seeing right? Was he reading this correctly?

'Twins?'

Two babies. They were having *two babies*. Two!

He squeezed Sam's hand tighter and she looked at him in shock.

'What? Twins? No, it can't be!'

'It can and it is.' Marta smiled some more as she showed them in detail. Baby A, and then she morphed the image to Baby B. 'And they're both good sizes, too, according to these measurements.'

Yanis almost didn't know what to say. Was this really happening? Everything he'd been through…everything he'd lost… His dream of starting a family had been torn from his tight grasp and destroyed—was it suddenly a possibility again? It almost didn't seem real.

His initial feelings of surprise and joy suddenly dived down into the deep, dark pits of fear. This could all still go horribly wrong. Was he about to send Samantha through something he never wanted to see a woman he cared for go through again? There wasn't just the risk of losing one baby here—there was the risk of losing *two*.

'Want to hear the heartbeats?'

Marta pressed a button and there it was. Two healthy heartbeats—*pow, pow, pow*—thudding rhythmically through the room. They sounded strong. They sounded steady. Exactly as they should be.

But then, that was how it had been with his son. He'd seemed healthy. Nothing wrong on the scans. He'd simply died in utero. Just as he and Giselle had been beginning to believe that they were on the home stretch. That everything was fine…that *this time* they could start decorating the nursery and buying a cot.

'Twins… I don't believe it…' Sam's voice trembled with awe and shock. 'And they're both healthy? All looks good?'

Marta nodded. 'At the moment. They're sharing a sac, so they're identical twins. They're also sharing a placenta and blood flow, so we'll need to keep an eye on that.'

'TTTS. Right…' Sam nodded, sounding more sure, for some strange reason, now that she was talking about something grim.

TTTS stood for Twin-to-Twin Transfusion Syndrome. In a twin pregnancy, abnormal blood vessels could form in the placenta, allowing blood to flow unevenly between the two babies, causing one to get too much and the other to get too little. It could make them very sick, and in some cases it could be fatal.

'Your placenta is quite low at the moment, though that could change. As the uterus grows with the pregnancy, it can move higher up and not cause a problem.'

'You're talking about the risk of placenta praevia?' Sam said.

It was a condition that could cause severe bleeding and lead to a medical emergency during the pregnancy or at delivery.

'We'll monitor you regularly.'

'Right.'

Again, he thought how Sam sounded strangely okay about the risk of these complications. As if she'd expected it. Was it because it grounded her? Didn't allow her to get overwhelmed by the *'twin'* news in all of this?

Because all Yanis heard was *Risk. Danger. Complications.* Real reasons as to why this pregnancy might not be successful. He blamed himself. But he could not let it show for Sam. She would need him to be strong for her, the way he had tried to be strong for Giselle.

'Would you like pictures?' Marta asked, the bright smile back upon her face.

Sam nodded and let out a heavy breath. She looked up at him. 'Yanis? You okay?'

He forced a smile. 'I'm good,' he lied, feeling sick with fear.

Back in the lift going up to Neurology, Sam continued to stare at and study the ultrasound photos she held in her hand. It felt a little unreal, but there they were. Two babies. And they were in her womb, growing like weeds.

What a day this had been.

She rubbed at her abdomen, as if making a physical connection between the scan pictures and her body. Twins… And she had the risk of placenta praevia and twin-to-twin transfusion syndrome. Of course she did. She wasn't surprised about that at all.

'What do we do now?' she asked Yanis.

Yanis looked as if he was in another world, and it was strange to see him like that. Usually he was the quintessential confident Frenchman. Stunning to look at, as always. But now he looked as if he wasn't present. As if he were somewhere else. He certainly didn't look happy.

'It's a bit of an odd situation we find ourselves in and this is a surprise to me,' she said. 'So God only knows what you must be feeling. A quick hook-up with a colleague and wham, bam, thank you, Sam—it's *twins*.'

She folded the pictures and slid them into the chest pocket of her scrubs. No point in telling her colleagues until she was ready.

She sighed. 'If you want to bow out, that's fine. I'm wishing I could do that myself.'

The lift doors opened and they stepped out into the corridor.

He met her gaze then. 'What are you saying?'

His quick, sharp reaction surprised her. 'I don't know! I don't *know* what I'm saying. All I know is that I find myself in an impossible situation and my brain is telling me that I can't do this. Be a mother, that is. I don't know how.'

'Of course you can. Anyone can,' he said irritably.

'Anyone?' she scoffed. 'You should meet some of the parents I see in A & E. Some of them don't have a clue.'

'You do. You're intelligent. A doctor.'

'Yes, well, sometimes too much knowledge can be a bad thing.'

She thought of her own mother and her extensive knowledge. Thought of all the medical books her mother had pored over at home. The second-hand textbooks on medicine and physiology she'd managed to score, almost as if the books themselves were drugs. They had been her mother's heroin. Her cocaine. Her addiction. They'd meant more to her than her own daughter. And she'd used them to create the situations she'd craved and needed. She'd deliberately harmed Sam, so that she would receive the attention she craved from doctors and the nurses and consultants.

It had been something she'd thrived on. Something that had put Sam in harm's way. Sam believed it had begun years before, though. That craving for attention. When her mother had fallen pregnant with her and her father had left her, not wanting to be a parent. It had been triggered then.

How could Sam be sure she wouldn't be the same way? Look at her own medical knowledge! It was hard enough looking after one baby, but two… Think of the stress! What if she snapped? What if she couldn't do it?

All of this and more flooded through her brain in an instant, but she let none of it show on her face.

'I just… I just don't know if I can do this. Finding out I'm having one baby is stressful enough, but twins…'

'I know it's hard, but let's not have any jerk-knee reactions.'

'It's knee-jerk. And you still haven't told me how you feel about all of this.'

He pushed himself away from the wall and ran his hands through his hair. It sprang perfectly back into place and she found herself inordinately annoyed by that small thing, wishing her own hair behaved as impeccably. But then she realised she was allowing herself to be distracted from the elephant in the room. Which, as it turned out, was *her*.

'I think… I think we take this day by day,' he said.

She nodded. 'You mean ignore it until we have no choice? Seems like a good plan. Except the sonographer made it clear that this is a risky pregnancy and will most likely go very wrong indeed. One baby could become a giant leech. The other will be tiny—like Alice when she took the *Drink Me* potion. Or, hey, I could bleed out at any point! Won't that be fun! Perhaps we should take notice of it then?'

She realised even as she said it that her hysterical sarcasm probably wasn't the best response, but she couldn't help herself. It was easy enough for him to say they should take it day by day, but he wasn't the one growing new life! Two new lives! He wasn't the one who would have to face the medical issues, the doctors looking her over as if she was some strange specimen, poking and prodding her, sticking needles in her, doing internal examinations. She was the one who would have to give birth. Twice!

Sam didn't want to feel bitter, but this situation seemed grossly outweighed in Yanis's favour. Not hers. He wouldn't have to watch and feel his body change. He wouldn't have to go through cravings or bloating or cramps. Or stretch marks or heartburn or labour. This was *easy* for him.

He might say that they were in this together, but were they? She had no proof of that. He could walk away at any time. She would always be the one left holding the baby.

The *babies*! Plural!

'That's not fair,' he said.

'Nothing about this is fair!' she argued, turning away from him.

At that moment her pager went off, distracting her from her upset, pulling her back into her other world, in which she was a highly respected neurosurgeon and she was *needed*.

'My next patient is being prepped. I've got to go.'

'What is it?' he asked.

'Private patient. He's got a benign tumour impinging on his spine and affecting leg movement.'

'I'm free. Let me assist you in Theatre.'

'I don't need you babysitting me, Yanis. I'm fine.'

'I'm sure you are. But it's always good to have an extra pair of hands. And you've had a shock today.'

'So have you,' she challenged.

Lewis Kozalski was an internationally acclaimed canoeist, who had first noticed a problem with his back and legs after a twenty-four-hour canoe race he'd done for charity. At first he'd put his problems down to having been in the canoe for such a long time, but when the problems had persisted beyond a reasonable time, he'd begun to worry.

'There's this thing we do called a roll,' he explained to Yanis now. 'I was teaching a class of students in a swimming pool, and when I went under the water I didn't have enough strength to roll up again. The pain in my back was horrendous. I had to undo the canoe skirt so that I could get out, and for a minute there I thought I was going to drown.'

'Must have been scary,' Yanis said.

'Not as scary as this.' Lewis was on the bed, waiting for Anaesthesia to do their thing.

'You're in excellent hands. Ms Gordon is very confident that she can excise this tumour.'

Lewis nodded. 'I hope so.'

'You ready?'

'Yes.'

Yanis gave a quick nod of his head to the anaesthesia team and they got to work, putting Lewis under. He then went to scrub in and found Sam fastening the back of her scrub cap.

'He's nervous,' he told her.

'Aren't we all?'

'You're not nervous about this surgery?'

She smiled. 'No. In this, I know *exactly* what I'm doing.'

'Good. And you've had something to eat?'

She began to scrub. 'I'm not going to faint, Yanis. Relax.'

'I'm allowed to worry.'

'Are you?'

'I think so. Besides, last time I could catch you. This time I'll be on the opposite side of the table, so if you go down you're going to hit the floor hard.'

'It's never going to happen.'

'Good.'

'But it's nice to know you care, I guess.'

'I do.'

She smiled. 'The twins thing hasn't scared you off? You sure you don't want to run? I wouldn't blame you. In fact, I think I'd understand it.'

Yanis turned on his own faucet and began to scrub. 'Because you want to run?'

'Yes. But it's hard to run from your own body, so I'm kinda stuck with it.'

'Whatever this pregnancy throws at us, I'm sure we'll be able to handle it.'

'You don't sound sure.'

No, he didn't. He'd only said it out loud as a way to convince himself.

When did he tell her? When did he tell her that Giselle hadn't lost one pregnancy, but three?

Sam already seemed to be expecting the worst. The warning today about the risk of TTTS was bad enough. What had *he* passed on to their babies? Were there genetic errors in his make-up that determined every pregnancy he fathered wouldn't last? If this pregnancy didn't make it, would Sam blame herself, or him? And if she did blame him, would he be able to cope with it?

He'd told himself after Giselle that he would never try for a family ever again. It was too risky. Too heartbreaking when your every hope and dream dissolved into cramps and clots.

He could hardly believe that only a few days ago he'd been so excited for this new start in Richmond. Thrilled to find that Sam was still there, believing that the two of them could help make Barney's neurosurgical centre one of the leading lights in UK medicine. And now this?

He liked Sam. He more than liked Sam. That night they'd spent together had been magical, and he'd felt a connection with her he'd not felt for a long time. He'd hoped for friendship, for fun and laughter and joyful times. Instead, he was going to put a woman he cared for through the most difficult time of her life.

He'd tried so hard to be there for Giselle, but he'd needed someone to be there for *him*. And although his family had tried to understand, none of them had truly known how he felt. His brothers and sisters had had their own family without a single problem. How could they know how he'd felt? How hopeless...helpless.

No matter what he'd said or done, none of it had seemed to make anything better for Giselle. He hadn't been able to take away her pain, or his own. The idea that he might have to go through all that heartbreak again was just too horrible for words.

They both walked through into Theatre and the scrub nurses helped them on with their gowns and gloves.

'Let's run it,' said Sam.

The scrub nurse went through Lewis's details and his exact surgery. He watched Sam examine the scan images one last time. She muttered something under her face mask, then said out loud, 'Let's make a difference, everyone. Scalpel.'

Let's make a difference.

He pondered those words. He'd heard her say them in Paris and thought it was just part of her ritual. But now he realised they were proactive. Not reactive. They suggested that the team were doing something to force a positive change.

Maybe he could learn something from that? Maybe he should stop fearing the worst and waiting for something bad to happen and instead imagine only the good— assume that only good would come from this situation he and Sam found themselves in?

He would make sure she accessed all the right healthcare, make sure she took good care of herself, eating and resting properly, and make sure that he was there to support her, to show her that he was an active partner in all of this and that they weren't helpless in this situation.

He could make a difference.

He could show her that they could do this scary thing. Show her that they could support one another and be there for one another and, most importantly, that they could get on with their lives and stop feeling as if they were in a canoe, being hopelessly propelled through some rapids.

They could weather this. They had oars. They could steer, they could take back control, manoeuvre themselves out of the rough water and into the calm. Maybe even get their feet back on dry land.

Okay, their lives were changing even now, but it didn't mean that they were only passive witnesses to it all. They could tackle their fears and their doubts by taking back control. By making a difference to their thought patterns, they could show this pregnancy who was boss and refuse to cower in fear.

Sam made the first cut, and the focus in her gaze made Yanis feel a little better about his decision. He allowed all his previous worries to disappear as the surgery began. What mattered right now was this man on the table. His spine. His tumour. His future. If Sam could push the turmoil of her life to one side and focus, then so could he. He could learn something from her.

He took a deep breath and concentrated.

The rest of the world and all its associated concerns soon melted away.

This was why he loved surgery so much.

CHAPTER FOUR

THE ATRIUM WAS such a calm, soothing place. Real trees, bushes and flowers grew there, in what felt like a tropical glasshouse. The walkways twisted and turned, providing small pockets of privacy, and it was dotted with benches and water features. In the largest of these, koi carp swam serenely beneath the water. It was a good place to think. A perfect place to try to clear your head.

Sam sat there now, staring at the fish in the water, almost hypnotised by their movements.

'Earth to Sam.'

The voice brought her back to the present and she looked up to see her good friend Gil Alexander, the head of neuro rehabilitation. Sam smiled and patted the bench beside her.

Gil sat down. 'You okay? You looked miles away.'

Sam let out a sigh and gave a cynical laugh. 'I'm not and I was.'

'Oh. Anything I can help with?'

She looked at him and shook her head. 'I don't think this is your area of expertise.'

He frowned. 'So it's nothing to do with work, then? Hmm… Interesting. Do you finally have a personal life? What's that like?'

She smiled. It was a long-running joke between them. 'Complicated,' she said.

She'd first met Gil at the hospital, but not as a colleague. Sam had been called down to the emergency department to consult on a patient. She'd done her consult and was just dropping off some paperwork into the tray by the receptionist when she'd spotted him, sitting on a chair in the waiting room, squinting, talking nonsense, obviously waiting to be seen.

Sam had laid a hand on the receptionist's shoulder and asked, 'What's his story?'

The receptionist had shrugged. 'Oh, I don't think he's checked in yet.'

'He's not been triaged? You're sure?'

'I'd have remembered him coming to the desk.'

Sam had known something wasn't right, so she'd gone right out there and knelt in front of him to ask a few questions. His confused answers had concerned her, and after performing a FAST stroke test, which had been negative, she'd felt sure she was dealing with a brain injury. Then he'd seemed to indicate that his head was hurting him intensely, and she'd sent him for a scan and discovered he had a slow brain bleed and needed emergency surgery.

He'd been her first 'catch', and Elliot had been so impressed he'd allowed her to assist in Theatre. Afterwards, he'd been able to tell her what had happened. Gil had had a nasty collision with some other players during a rugby scrum, and although he'd thought at the time he maybe had a mild concussion, he'd rashly assumed he was fine. Though as the day had worn on, he'd begun to feel awful, and that day had somehow made his way to hospital.

The surgery had changed Gil's life, and though he'd been an A & E doctor, he'd changed careers after going through rehabilitation and physiotherapy. He'd retrained and now he ran the neurological rehabilitation centre at Barney's, helping to look after many of her patients. Helping them readjust to life after traumatic brain injury.

'Do tell,' he said now. 'You never know—I might have some wise words.'

Sam let out another sigh. 'You know I went to Paris a few months ago, for that work exchange?'

Gil nodded, sipping from his coffee cup.

'I kind of met someone.'

He raised an eyebrow. 'You didn't say anything when you got back.'

'No... Well, I thought it was nothing.'

'Only it was *something*?'

'Yeah.' She gave another sigh. 'He consoled me after we lost a patient on my last day. A young girl.'

'I'm sorry.'

'I felt so bad... I knew that the girl was scared of the surgery, even though she'd had counselling.'

Gil knew of Sam's past. He'd understand how much that would have hurt.

'I'm sure you did it for the right reasons,' he said.

'Yeah, well... Yanis and I ended up sleeping together.'

When Gil said nothing, she knew she had to say more. If there was anyone on this planet she trusted as a friend, it was Gil. She knew he wouldn't spill her secrets. The friendship they had struck up after his surgery was strong. She was proud of her first catch, her first save, and he was grateful to her for changing his life and making him re-think what he wanted from it.

Medicine could cure, but it could also impact on doctors' lives to such a degree that they had no life outside of the job. It was something that they'd both been guilty of. Only

Gil had changed, whereas for Sam, Gil's surgery had just made her even more sure that this was the life she wanted. She was dedicated to her work. Driven by her passion to help save lives.

'And now he's here,' she said. 'Yanis Baptiste?'

Gil nodded. 'I've seen his name on a couple of patient charts. And a few nurses might have drooled over him at break time. Apparently he's *"a looker"*.' Gil raised his hands to make air quotes and smiled.

Sam laughed. 'He is what they call "easy on the eye".'

'And I assume he wants to carry on the relationship you started back in Paris?'

'Not exactly.'

'Then what?'

Sam sucked in a big breath and then let it out again, biting her lip, grimacing. She turned to him and whispered, 'I'm pregnant.'

And then Gil proved exactly why he was her friend. He didn't let out a low whistle, he didn't laugh, and he didn't smile or offer forced congratulations. He looked directly in her eyes and got straight to the point.

'And how do you feel about that?'

He was such a good man. Empathetic. Kind. She hoped he'd find someone to be with one day. He deserved to have that.

'I'm terrified.'

He reached out and laid his hand on hers, before squeezing her fingers. 'Which bit scares you the most?'

'All of it.'

'Motherhood?'

She nodded and wiped away a tear.

'You won't turn out like her. You're different. You're not the same person.'

'Children deserve the best parents, Gil. Parents who love one another. Parents who are there for each other. We barely know each other. We had one night and now this. And it's hard enough looking after one child, but two...'

'It's twins?'

'Yeah.'

He was silent for a moment, looking out across the atrium, waiting for a couple of patients to pass, dragging their IV poles behind them. When they were alone again, he said, 'I'm not going to lie: parenting will be hard. And you're being thrown in at the deep end. Will this Mr Baptiste be there to help you?'

'He says he will. I think so.'

'You need to make sure.'

'But what if it all goes wrong? A twin pregnancy is a risky one, and my body hasn't exactly done the right thing in the past.'

'There's nothing wrong with your body. Not now. You're strong. Any faults it had previously were deliberately put there by your mother.'

'But when you're told that you're broken *every single day*...'

'You're not broken. Look at you. You fix things. You're one of the top neurosurgeons in the country. When were you ill last? That cold last summer? Everybody gets those. There's no reason why you can't continue in this pregnancy and do so without a single issue rearing its ugly head.'

'I knew you'd talk some sense into me.'

'I like getting to save *you* occasionally. You brought me back from the brink—it's only fair you let me think I'm doing the same for you.' Gil smiled.

'Thanks...' said Sam. 'I best be getting back. I've got

an outpatient clinic list to get through. Are you okay? Everything fine with you?'

'Don't you worry about me. I'm good.'

'Okay.' She dropped her hand on his shoulder as a physical thank-you, and then headed off back into the hospital.

Gil was right. She needed to think positively. It had been proved in many research papers that having a positive mindset could be very beneficial to overall health, and if there was anything she could do to make this pregnancy go well then she ought to do it.

This wasn't just about her any more.

She had a family to think of.

'I thought you'd like to know that Lewis is doing well.'

Yanis popped his head around Sam's door just before she started her outpatient clinic. He'd checked on her patient in the ICU and, although it was early days, Lewis seemed to have homeostasis—was maintaining his blood pressure, temperature and respirations within normal parameters.

The first twenty-four hours after surgery were always crucial. Anything could happen. The body might throw a clot from the surgery, there could be a fluid build-up at the operative site, a drainage tube could block, or an infection could set in. Patients were closely monitored whether they were private, like Lewis, or not.

'Good. Thanks for letting me know,' Sam said. 'Is he on half-hourly obs?'

'*Oui.*'

'That's good.'

She smiled at him then, as if she wasn't sure of what to say next, so he slipped into her room and closed the door behind him, before walking over to her desk and sitting on the chair across from her.

'I want you to feel that you can come to me at any time,' he said.

'All right…'

'I feel that this is something that we should be able to get through by relying on one another.'

'Okay… Though I might have difficulties with that. I've never relied on anyone in my entire life. That's going to be strange for me—just so you know.'

He smiled. 'Strange is okay. Impossible I would have a problem with.'

Sam nodded. 'Noted. Anything else?'

'*Oui*. Let me take you out to dinner.'

'Dinner? Why?'

'Because we need to eat—and why not do that with each other, to help build our bond?'

'You want to build our bond?' she asked uncertainly.

'Don't you? We're going to have children together.'

'Dinner. Right. Okay. What time?'

'I could pick you up at seven?'

She smiled. 'You could.'

'I would need your address.'

She reached for a notepad and scribbled her details down on it, then passed it over, her cheeks flushed with heat. 'It's a date.'

Now it was his turn to look at her intensely. 'It most certainly is.'

Sam was struggling. She didn't normally do *dates*.

Dates involved getting to know people and placing your trust in them. She wasn't able to do that easily, so whenever she felt like male company, she'd sort out the convenient kind that involved a quick tussle under the bedsheets and leave it at that. No getting to know one another. No finding out what their favourite breakfast cereal was or whether they preferred cats to dogs. It was all about scratching a physical itch and then moving on.

She hadn't done it often. Why would she when it meant exposing herself to scrutiny? Showing someone her scars? To them they might mean nothing, but to her they were glowing beacons that revealed how much she'd let someone else control her.

Those days were over. She was her own person and she'd got used to only having herself to look after. It was easy. Less chance of screwing up. Less chance of losing control.

But dating...? That was a different kettle of fish.

Her last real date had been her prom date, and she'd chosen someone who'd been no physical threat to her whatsoever—a geeky young man who had been very Clark Kent and president of the chess club. He'd turned up at her aunt's house and presented her with a corsage, and that was as far as their physical contact had gone.

So why had she agreed to this?

Because he caught me off guard. Because I didn't know what else to say. Because... Because I'm curious and getting to know Yanis seems like a sensible thing to do.

A sensible thing. Gil had suggested that they would do a better job if they supported one another and that made sense. Why fight it?

She kept telling herself, as she curled her hair with curling tongs and put on make-up, that it had absolutely *nothing* to do with the fact that she still felt incredibly attracted to the man, and absolutely *everything* to do with her trying to hold out an olive branch and become a sensible adult.

In simple terms, they were going to have to parent together. Which meant, if they were going to do it right, they would need good communication. And that meant actually liking the guy and getting on with him. So if they needed to go out to dinner to do that then she would give it a go. For the babies' sakes.

She still couldn't quite believe it! Twins... It was crazy...

On the dot of seven, her doorbell rang. Her stomach felt like a knot of nerves, but she sucked in a deep breath, headed for the front door and opened it.

Yanis looked incredible. The kind of incredible that made her ovaries ache and her heart pound.

She was amazed she was having such a reaction.

I mean, he wears a shirt and tie to work, for God's sake.

But without the addition of stethoscope and ID lanyard, he looked a different kind of edible.

Dark trousers moulded his strong legs, and a fitted navy shirt emphasised the bright blue of his eyes, the narrowness of his waist and the broadness of his shoulders. And what was that scent he wore? She wanted to just stand there for a moment, close her eyes and breathe him in, allow the aroma to caress her senses and make her go all warm and gooey inside.

'Wow. You look...nice.'

Yanis smiled. *'Et tu as l'air belle.'*

She tried to dredge up her secondary school French. *And you have...something-something...*

She must have frowned, because he translated for her. 'And you look beautiful.'

'Oh.' She blushed, hoping she was blushing in a pretty kind of way, and not in a blotchy I'm-having-a-hot-flush kind of way. 'Thanks. Where are we going?'

'To Le Chef.'

'French food? Sounds great. Let me just grab my bag.'

She slipped it off the back of a chair, placed her keys and mobile phone inside, and then set off down the path towards his car. She could feel the light touch of his fingers on the small of her back and it reminded her of the last time his fingers had touched her that night in Paris.

She felt herself grow hot, and was glad that he didn't know what she was thinking about. She'd spent many a night since Paris thinking about that encounter, wishing she was someone else so that she could go back to him again and again. He was a skilled lover—someone who knew what he was doing and knew how to pleasure a woman.

How many lovers had he had? Looking the way he did, she had to assume that he'd had many. Was she just one of many notches on his bedpost? Did he resent her for trapping him into fatherhood? He wasn't acting as if he was, but could anyone say they truly knew one another? He wore no ring, and she knew nothing of his past, though she did recall hearing something about the ending of a long-term relationship that he'd been involved in. Had he celebrated his freedom from that with multiple lovers? Most men would. Wouldn't they?

As Yanis drove them to the restaurant, she was trying her best to think of something casual to say. It was easy at work, because they could discuss their patients, but in this instance, what sort of things did people talk about? She knew she wasn't skilled in this arena, and they had so much riding on them getting this relationship right—

even if it was just a parenting one. She was terrified of screwing it up.

Hey, kids...well, yes, I did know your father, but I said something really stupid and now you'll never see him ever again. Soz.

'So, what do you think of Richmond? How does it compare to Paris?'

Yanis smiled. 'They cannot be compared. Paris is Paris. It holds a certain style and *feel*. It has a beating heart that no other place has. Richmond is quiet, compared to my home city. Greener. I like Richmond Park. I go running there most mornings.'

'You run?'

She tried to imagine him in tee shirt and shorts, his powerful leg muscles flexing and burning, sweat running down his forehead, darkening his tee. Yanis in the shower afterwards, naked and hot...

She cleared her throat.

'I try to,' he said. 'Do you run?'

'Me? No. I do the occasional spin class when I feel I ought to be doing more exercise, but I figure I walk enough miles when I'm at work, so...'

'You should come running with me sometime.'

'In my condition?' She laughed.

'Maybe afterwards, then.'

Afterwards.

After the pregnancy.

So he *was* thinking of sticking around for a while, then. The idea of having Yanis Baptiste in her life for ever was...disconcerting. Nice, but strange. What would they be to one another? Two people who just happened to co-parent? Or something more? Friends with benefits? Until Yanis found someone better?

Even though Sam was aware that to some people she was a great catch, in herself she knew that she wouldn't be able to persuade herself that she had anything she could offer another person. Not like that. Not long term. Long-term relationships meant give and take, trust and respect, and though she could do all those things, her distrust of people ran deep.

Her own mother—the woman who was meant to have loved her and protected her to the ends of the earth—had been the one to harm her and hurt her, the most. If her own mother could do that, what might someone else do? Someone who didn't have that familial connection?

Yanis seemed great. Of course he did. He was handsome and intelligent and caring. But what lurked beneath the surface? Who was the real Yanis?

'Maybe,' she said.

'You could be one of those mothers who runs whilst pushing those off-road strollers I keep seeing.'

'Or you could be one of those fathers who push the stroller,' she countered.

He nodded and laughed gently. 'I could. You see? We can do this. Two mature adults…discussing how to parent.'

She didn't know how to answer that. Technically, he was correct. And if they kept it that emotionless and simple then, sure, it wouldn't be a problem. But life wasn't like that, was it? Emotion was wrapped around everything. Every decision you made. Could it be that black and white? She doubted it.

Le Chef had its own small parking area, and Yanis managed to find a spot quite easily. The evening was cool, and she was glad she'd brought a coat. Once again she felt Yanis's hand on the small of her back as they walked in and he confirmed the reservation in his name.

The waiter took them to a nice little table for two, by the terrace, so that they could look out upon the small garden there. It was beautiful. Intimate. A potted garden of bushes and small fruit trees, herbs and flowers, lit by the most gorgeous Victorian-style lamps.

They took their seats and the waiter poured water into both of their glasses.

'This is nice. Have you been here before?' she asked.

'*Non.* But it was on my brother's list of recommendations.'

'Oh. Okay… Is this the brother who tags rhino?'

He smiled. 'Yes.'

'Do you have other family? Any more Baptistes I should know about?'

'My sister Yvette. She is a schoolteacher.'

'And your parents?'

'My father was also a teacher. My mother is a critical care nurse.'

'Is that where your passion for medicine came from?'

'Perhaps. I know I was always fascinated by her stories of life and death. It may have had an impact on my decision making. What about you? What made you choose medicine?'

She didn't feel she could tell him the truth about that yet. She was too ashamed. So she decided to go with a half-truth. 'My mother had a passion for health and medicine, too. The way she talked about doctors and the nurses, how they made her feel… I wanted to be like them, I guess.'

How could she tell him that she'd wished that she alone could have been enough for her mother? That she alone could have provided her mother with enough love so that she hadn't done what she had? So that her mother hadn't looked to medical professionals to provide her with the attention and care she'd so desperately sought?

She took a sip of her water, just as the waiter brought over the menus. Sam was glad of the distraction and for a moment to hide as she allowed her gaze to travel over the unfamiliar words. Most of it was in French, but thankfully there were English translations underneath each item.

'This all sounds wonderful.'

'Have you told your mother about the pregnancy?'

Sam bit her lip behind the menu. What to say? That she only called her mother once a month? That a lot of their phone calls were harrowing and Sam often had to put the phone down on her? That telling her mother she was going to become a grandmother would make her want to get back into Sam's life and she'd spent years without her in it?

'Not yet.'

'Any reason why?'

'It's just…early days, that's all.'

He looked at her strangely, and she knew what he was thinking. Technically, she was out of the first trimester, so the risk of miscarriage was less, but she was very aware that her pregnancy could have complications— so, no, there was no way she would tell her mother any of that. It would reopen old wounds.

'Have you told *your* family?' she countered, throwing the focus back onto him.

He smiled. *'Oui.'*

'How did they take it?'

'They were surprised, but happy.'

He looked away then, as if he was also only telling a half-truth. So they'd been happy...but what else? Yanis wasn't saying.

Then she realised he was signalling for the waiter.

'Are you ready to order, *monsieur...mademoiselle*?'

Yanis looked back at her then, and she nodded.

'I'll have the potted crab with sourdough toast to start, and the confit duck leg with dauphinoise potatoes for main, please.'

The waiter scribbled her order into his notebook. 'And for you, *monsieur*?'

'The salmon gravadlax to start and the marinated chicken for main, *s'il vous plaît.*'

'Excellent choice. Would you like to see our wine list?'

Yanis looked at Sam.

'I won't, but you have some, if you want.'

'I'm driving. No, thank you,' he said to the waiter.

'We do some excellent mocktails, *monsieur*, if you are looking to avoid alcohol.'

'A Shirley Temple would be nice,' she said.

'Make that two.' Yanis nodded and the waiter bowed and hurried away to fulfil their order.

She liked it that he was talking in English here. It would have been so easy for him to converse with the staff in his native language, but he'd kept to English so that she knew what was being said. It was nice. Considerate.

But she'd already known that about him. Even in Paris, when they'd been surrounded by native French speakers, if she or one of the other English doctors had been there he had automatically spoken in English. She'd been so grateful that he knew her language well, because she certainly couldn't manage the French language, and that had been a real worry for her, going over to Paris for that work exchange.

After their mocktails had been delivered, Sam smiled at Yanis over the table. He really was the most delectable-looking man, and the candlelight made him even more so. It was hard to believe that they were in this situation, but here they were, and she didn't know what she was going to do about the fact that she was still highly attracted to him.

Did he feel the same about her?

Would it be dangerous to add attraction to this situation?

Would it be better to keep their relationship as just friends?

She wasn't sure she had it in her to get involved in a relationship, because what if they fouled it up before the babies were born? What then? If there was hostility between herself and the father, that wouldn't be good, right? If her body had the capacity to fail her, did she really want her emotional state to screw this up, too?

Their starters arrived, looking delicious.

'Bon appetit.' The waiter smiled and then made himself scarce.

Sam knew she needed to keep herself and Yanis as friends. That she knew she could do. They'd done it in Paris. Why not here in Richmond and at Barney's, too?

She tucked in, feeling ravenous despite her nerves. Something weird had happened since the discovery of her pregnancy. It was as if now it was official, and she *knew*, her body was letting her know in no uncertain terms what it wanted—and that was plenty of food. As a surgeon, she often went without food or drink for hours, especially if she had a busy clinic or was operating, and this new territory was making her wonder if she'd be able to get through those ten-hour, twelve-hour, twenty-hour surgeries without stopping to refuel halfway through? It was a good thing she now had Yanis, because if that was the case then she would need someone she trusted to step in and pick up the scalpel, if necessary.

'This is gorgeous. How's yours?'

'Wonderful. Would you like to try?'

He held out a forkful of beautifully pink rock salmon and she leaned forward to try it. It was quite an intimate moment, letting him feed her. Opening her mouth, gazing into his intense blue eyes as she took the food from his fork. She could feel her cheeks heating up and was grateful for the subtlety provided by the candlelight.

'Try some of mine.'

She tore off a small corner of her sourdough crust and loaded it with crab. Then she hand-fed Yanis, intensely aware of his lips enveloping her fingers.

Oh, my...

Her fingertips felt alive. Each nerve ending was tingling and fizzing with the need to be kissed by Yanis once again.

Her heart thudding in her chest and her mouth going dry, she suddenly wasn't sure if she'd be able to eat another bite! So she had a long drink of water and took a moment to just breathe and not meet Yanis's gaze.

I just need a second or two...

She kept her eyes on her plate, but all she could think about as she tried to calm her runaway heart was that night in Paris, stretched out naked beneath Yanis as his soft lips and gentle fingers explored her body. Arcing up towards him, her own hands hungry for the feel of him, needing him to fill her. Those lips...

'I…er… Excuse me. I just need the bathroom. Do you know where it is?' She stood up, her whole body thrumming with heat.

Yanis stood, too, placing his napkin down on the table. 'Are you all right?'

'Yes…yes. Just need to…erm… Where is it?'

Yanis pointed to a small dark door at the back of the restaurant that she could clearly see now had a silver *Ladies* sign on it.

'Thanks. Do carry on eating. I won't be long.'

And she hurried as quickly as she could to that door, opening it up, slipping inside and letting out a strangled breath or two as she gazed at her flushed reflection in the mirror above the sink. She turned on the cold tap and splashed water on her face, gazing at herself once again.

'What are you doing? Feeding Yanis? *Hand*-feeding him? Friendship, Samantha! *Friend. Ship.*'

Behind her, someone flushed the toilet and opened the cubicle door. A little old woman came out and smiled at her as she went to wash her hands.

'He's a lovely young man you're with this evening,' the woman said.

Sam recognised that she'd been seated at a table close to them. She nodded. 'Yes, he is.'

The old lady used the dryer to dry her hands and then, as she grasped the door handle to go out, turned once more to Sam and said, 'If I was fifty years younger I'd jump his bones so hard they'd shatter beneath me.'

She winked and left the room.

Sam stared after her, mouth agape, and then laughed.

Yanis felt guilty for not having told Sam the whole truth about what his family had said when they'd learned he was going to be a father. Of course there'd been surprise, exactly as he'd said, but then their voices and faces had filled with concern over the video link.

'Do you think the same thing could happen again?' his mother had asked.

He'd tried to remember that losing the babies with Giselle had not just happened to him and his wife, but to his family, too. They'd looked forward to becoming *grandmère* and *grandpère* or *oncle* and *tante*. They'd looked forward to seeing Yanis become a father and they'd all been broken-hearted by what had happened. Even more so when Yanis and Giselle had split up after so many years together.

They had loved Giselle. Adored her. Welcomed her into their homes. And now they had lost her, too, as Giselle couldn't bear to see them any more feeling as if she had let them all down. It wasn't true, of course, but grief and pain distorted things.

He'd wanted to tell Sam that his family would like to meet her, to put a face to her name, but he knew he wasn't ready. They were hardly in a relationship. He had no idea what this thing was that they had between them, and he didn't want to break the fragile nature of it.

Because he knew that it was breakable. Early days. Anything could go wrong.

And what if he introduced her to his family and they mentioned Giselle? Sam hadn't yet been told. She would feel she had been lied to. That he had deliberately kept important information from her. But how could he tell her about all that had gone wrong for him when she was already dealing with the possibility that their twins might develop TTTS, or that she might bleed out at any point if the placenta broke away from the lining of her womb?

So many things could go wrong. Not just physically, but mentally and emotionally. He knew he shouldn't allow his thoughts to linger on the doubts and fears, but it was something he associated with pregnancy now and it was a difficult habit to break.

As he waited for Sam to return from her bathroom break, he reminded himself that his relationship with Sam was different. Just because he'd lost his babies with Giselle, it did not mean the same would happen with Sam. There were issues, yes, but those could happen in any twin pregnancy. And there were plenty of identical twins out in the world. He needed to focus on positivity for the future, rather than the regret and pain from his past.

As Sam made her way back across the restaurant, he stood and pulled out her chair for her. 'Everything all right?'

She nodded. 'Everything's fine.'

CHAPTER FIVE

'LET'S MAKE A DIFFERENCE.'

Sam stood by the table in Theatre and made an incision in the leg to locate the femoral artery. Today she was hoping to use endovascular coiling to solve the problem of Maureen Bowman's posteriorcerebral aneurysm. It was an aneurysm that Maureen had lived with for some time, but as its size had remained static for many years, they had left it alone. In the last few weeks, however, the aneurysm had grown to just over seven millimetres and now was at greater risk of rupture.

'Guiding catheter, please.'

Her scrub nurse for the day, Sarah, passed it over and Sam gave a nod to the radiologist to move the fluoroscopic imager into position.

The adrenaline buzz she always got from surgery thrummed throughout her body. She was feeling good. Positive. And she knew it was down to the fact that nothing terrible had happened to her yet, and that she and Yanis were getting on quite well.

These last few weeks with Yanis had been enlightening. Yanis had been attentive and considerate, but not pushy with his opinions. Every day he saw her at work he checked to make sure she was feeling all right, and they'd spent a few hours in each other's company after work, too. Nothing heavy. Just walks in Richmond Park.

And once, he'd done her supermarket shop for her, because she'd been so tired. He'd come into her flat carrying all the bags and even unpacked everything for her. She'd been so grateful, and a little bit gobsmacked. Not used to anyone taking care of her like that.

Though she'd lived with her aunt for a while, after everything had come to light about her mother and her battle with Munchausen's by Proxy, she'd very much felt that her aunt was only doing her a favour. That she was tolerated. It had been almost as if her mother's sister had *blamed* Sam for what had happened to her mum. Having someone be kind was strange.

Once Yanis had dropped the shopping off, he'd asked her if she needed anything else before he left. Although she'd been absolutely desperate for someone to give her a shoulder massage, she'd simply shaken her head, said she was fine and then walked him to the door.

That had been awkward. Just like the night they'd gone out to that restaurant and he'd taken her home at the end of it. They'd had a really good chat. Got to know one another a bit more. And then there'd come the moment when she'd assumed most normal people would have kissed each other goodnight.

'Well, I've had a lovely evening, Yanis. Thank you,' she'd said. 'The food was delicious and the company was…enjoyable.'

He'd smiled at her, and in the evening darkness his eyes had twinkled. She'd almost felt that she should just kiss him and get it over and done with, but she'd known it wouldn't end there. She wanted him. Yearned for him. And if she'd leaned in for a kiss and pressed her lips to his she would have stopped thinking straight. She would have thrown caution to the wind and her clothes to her bedroom floor and they'd have been right back where they'd started.

So she'd let him lean in and drop a gentle kiss upon her cheek. She'd blushed and said goodnight, and with a great amount of self-control had closed the door, her heart pounding, her insides screaming at her that she could have had more than just delicious *food* this evening.

But maintaining his friendship and support through her pregnancy mattered more to her than anything else. At four months now, she was doing okay. Her belly was most definitely showing, and she'd had to tell her colleagues that she was expecting.

When they'd discovered that Yanis was the father, they'd all gaped, or gasped, and she'd received a range of comments. From *'You go, girl! Wow, lucky you!'* to a rather more amusing one from Judy, a junior doctor who was hoping to specialise in neurology, who had said, *'Well, of course you're expecting! I wouldn't get any sleep with him beside me either!'*

The support and care she was getting from her colleagues now was eye-opening. She'd spent so much of her life in a vacuum, feeling separated from everyone, feeling she could never connect with people, and yet here she was, and it seemed *everyone* was keeping an eye out for her.

It was nice. It was strange. And it made her see her relationship with Yanis with new eyes. No longer a secret. No longer a shameful hook-up she'd had in Paris. This relationship had become something more. Was it possible she could have a happy ending? Her work colleagues seemed to think that they made a good couple. Could it really be true?

She concentrated hard as she guided the catheter all the way up from the femoral artery to the posteriorcerebral artery, where the aneurysm was located.

'Micro-catheter, please.'

Slowly, and with great care, she inserted the smaller catheter directly into the aneurysm. Then the first coil went in, along the aneurysm's wall, to begin creating the frame. Once that was done, more coils were inserted, each progressively smaller, until she felt that she was done.

'Contrast dye.'

The radiologist inserted the dye to see if any flowed into the aneurysm, but there was no flow of dye to be seen, which was excellent.

'Okay, we're almost done.'

Sam withdrew the catheters and closed up. If all went as expected, Maureen would go home in a day or two and live the rest of her life as if this had never happened. It made Sam feel good to know that she had helped this poor woman. She'd been living with a time bomb, and Sam was having personal experience of how that felt right now.

Something could go wrong with her pregnancy at any minute. But so far she'd been okay, and she had an appointment this afternoon with her obstetrics consultant, Mr Meyer. Hopefully he would be able to reassure her.

She came out of surgery and went to get changed, and found Yanis just arriving for his shift.

'Hey,' she said.

'Good morning. *Ça va?*' He bent and laid a kiss upon her cheek in greeting, and once again she had to bite her bottom lip, to stop herself from reaching out and pulling him close.

'I'm good. You?'

'Very well. You're glowing.'

His eyes were bright and amused, and she liked it that she could make him look that way.

'Yes, well, aneurysm surgery first thing in the morning always gets my blood pumping.'

'No, it's more than that. How are the babies?' He laid his hand upon the swell of her abdomen and she had to fight not to lay her hand on his, too.

She met his gaze, smiled. 'They're good, as far as I know. They're telling me they want waffles with chocolate sauce.'

'Then you should give it to them.'

He turned away to open his locker, placing his rucksack inside and slipping off his jacket, revealing the almost skintight waistcoat he wore over his shirt beneath. He really did look yummy this morning. She found her gaze roving up and down his long body, remembering how it had felt that night in Paris.

What the hell is wrong with me? Hormones?

'I will.'

She opened up her own locker and grabbed her clothes from earlier, then went into a changing area to slip off her scrubs. She had rounds to do, to check on her post-operative patients from yesterday. Once dressed, she pulled her long red hair up into a twist and secured it with a clip.

When she came out of the cubicle, Yanis was waiting for her.

'I have some news,' he said.

'Oh?'

'I have rented a flat of my own.'

She raised her eyebrows. 'Whereabouts?'

'Near the park. It has two bedrooms. I'd like you to

come and see it. I thought it was important that I put down some roots here.'

Seemed sensible…

'I'd like it if you could help me choose which room should become the nursery.'

She hadn't even thought about that. It was almost as if she had a mental block. But these babies might survive… She would actually have to think about where to put them after giving birth. Her own flat had two bedrooms, but the second one was loaded up with boxes and books. It would need a clear-out.

'Oh. Okay,' she said.

'Fancy coming round tonight?'

'You've moved in already?'

'I have.'

Going to Yanis's flat? Was that a risk? It was one thing to be at work together, and it was one thing to sit in a restaurant together—they were in public, after all—but in a private place… The last time they'd been in a private place together she'd got pregnant.

Well, I guess there's no risk of that happening again.

'What time?' she asked.

'I can pick you up at seven?'

'That's fine. Are you coming with me to see Mr Meyer today?'

'The appointment is at three?'

She nodded. If he didn't want to come, that would be fine. She'd do it on her own.

'I'll make sure I'm free, and if I get called into a surgery, I'll text you and let you know.'

He hadn't got called into a surgery. So here he sat with Sam and all the other expectant mothers at Mr Meyer's clinic.

Mr Meyer was apparently the go-to guy here at Barney's for multiple births. Sam knew he was good because she'd already researched him online. Just as she'd researched TTTS and placenta praevia and a whole host of other pregnancy complications that she didn't actually have.

It didn't hurt to be prepared.

Her mother had taught her that, at least.

When they got called through, they entered his room, shook his hand and sat down.

'So, you're expecting identical twins, it says here. Congratulations. How are you feeling, Mum?'

Sam blinked. It was the first time someone had called her *Mum* and it made her heart thud to realise that he was referencing *her*.

'Okay... No, I'm good. Hungry all the time.'

'Well, that's to be expected.' He smiled and tapped at his keyboard, bringing up the images from her first ultrasound. 'The babies were both a good size...what, four weeks ago? They were each measuring the size of a singleton baby. I guess it would be a good thing to check on them again today, especially as they're sharing a placenta.'

She nodded.

'I'm sure you know the risks of that?' he said.

'We do,' she said.

'No prior pregnancies I should know about?'

Sam shook her head.

'Okay. I'll get that arranged in just a moment. Want to hop up onto the couch? I can check how you're measuring.'

Sam glanced at Yanis. He looked nervous. Anxious. Perhaps because it was here they would find out any bad news, whereas out in their real lives they could just pretend that everything was fine. Mr Meyer seemed to be the type of man who looked for issues so that he could treat them ahead of time.

She lay down on the couch and undid her trousers.

Mr Meyer had cold hands, which he apologised for, and then he palpated her abdomen slightly, smiling before reaching for a tape measure.

'Perfect. Exactly what I'd expect at this stage. Just lie there for a moment and I'll prep the ultrasound.'

He pulled the machine over and asked Yanis to kill the lights. The room went dark, except for the glow emanating from the screen.

Sam felt nervous. Sick. Just because she felt fine, it didn't mean that everything would be fine. It made her feel as if she was a little girl again. Lying there on a doctor's couch, waiting to be poked and prodded, oohed and aahed over… waiting to be told she would need surgery.

This is not the same. If I have surgery this time, it will be because I really need it.

Did that help her at all?

No.

She was so lost in her thoughts, Sam almost didn't feel the gel being applied, or the probe being placed on her stomach, until Mr Meyer turned the screen to show them the babies.

'Both looking very well. Again, both measuring as if they were singleton babies. Baby A is ever so slightly bigger than Baby B, but only just. Nothing for us to worry about yet.'

'Good.'

The machine pumped out some more scan pictures. Mr Meyer passed a couple to Yanis. 'Any questions?'

'Is there anything Sam should be doing? Taking it easier? Maybe not doing long surgeries?'

Sam bristled inside. How *dared* he ask those questions? Hadn't Mr Meyer just said everything was fine?

Mr Meyer smiled at Sam. 'Whilst you're feeling good and the babies are happy you can carry on as usual—though obviously you'll need to take adequate rest breaks and make sure you stay hydrated and fed.'

She gave Yanis a look as if to say, *You see? You don't have to wrap me in cotton wool!*

'Do you have any questions, Sam?' Mr Meyer asked.

'How often will the babies be monitored from now on?'

'I'd like you to have a scan every two weeks. But if you have any concerns in between—if you don't feel them move, or something just doesn't feel right to you—you get in touch, okay?'

She nodded. She hadn't felt the babies move yet, but she'd read somewhere that mothers in their first pregnancies didn't normally feel movement until about eighteen or nineteen weeks. But the babies were measuring more than that. Why hadn't she felt them move? She knew nothing was wrong, because she'd just had the scan.

'How will I know that I feel them moving?'

Mr Meyer smiled. 'Oh, you'll know. It might feel like little fishes swimming at first, but eventually you'll feel kicks and the babies stretching. Pretty soon, too. Don't be surprised if you feel it by the end of the week. At the rate they're growing, it's pretty imminent, I'd say.'

Sam smiled. 'Okay.'

But she was nervous.

When Yanis arrived at her door that evening, she was still feeling pretty annoyed with him. 'Are you happy after trying to pull that stunt today?' she said, after she'd opened the door.

He frowned. 'I don't understand.'

'Trying to get my consultant to say I needed to slow down. You don't get to take charge of my life like that, do you understand? *I* decide how I work. *I* make the choices.'

He held up both his hands, as if surrendering. 'I'm sorry. I just wanted to make sure it was safe for the babies if you keep working at the rate you do.'

'I'm perfectly capable of making that decision myself.'

'I understand. And I'm sorry. But I'm allowed to worry. They're my babies, too.'

He gazed down at her growing abdomen with such a look of fear and concern that she felt awful for yelling at him. He was only trying to look out for them all.

'I know. Look, let's forget today. Why don't you just show me this flat of yours?'

'Deal.'

He drove her through Richmond and she allowed herself to enjoy the luxury of kicking back and having nothing to do. No patients. No surgeries. No stress. She could just enjoy the trees breaking into bloom, the signs of spring bursting forth in everyone's gardens. The shop windows with their Easter offers, and bunny rabbits and eggs and chicks in their displays.

This time next year I'll have two kids! If nothing goes wrong.

It still scared her. It seemed such an insurmountable task. How did parents do it? How would she mix motherhood and working? How would that work? Sure, they would get childcare, but what if she was in a very important surgery and she got a call from her child's nursery to say one of her children was sick with a fever? What if she got a call from their school to say she needed to come and pick them up that instant?

There were other surgeons who were parents. Perhaps she ought to ask them? They were best placed to give her answers. But would they think less of her for worrying about such a thing?

Who came first? The patient on the table? Or your child? Surely her own child should come first, but she couldn't possibly leave someone on the table. That was a life! It would mean playing tag with another neurosurgeon, but what if they weren't free either? And what if Yanis was in surgery, too?

'You're very quiet,' he said.

'Just thinking about things, that's all.'

'About the babies?'

She nodded.

'I think about them all the time, too.'

'You do? What sort of things do you think about?' She was intrigued.

'How we parent them. How we share them.'

She'd not thought too much about that. But he was right. How *would* they share them? Was she going to be a Monday-to-Friday mother and then Yanis got them weekends?

'Thanks,' she said.

'For what?'

'For giving me something else to worry about.'

He smiled and laid a hand upon hers. 'We will be okay.'

'Will we? Can you promise?'

He lifted her hand to his mouth and kissed the back of it. 'I can do my very best.'

* * *

Sam was very impressed with Yanis's flat. It was a decent size, with a large living area, a medium-sized kitchen, a bathroom that had both a shower and a bath, and the two bedrooms.

'Which do you think should be the nursery?' he asked. 'The room that faces the town, or the room that faces the park?'

It seemed a no-brainer to Sam. 'The room that faces the park, I guess. What do you think?'

He smiled. 'I agree.'

The room that faced the park had been painted by the previous tenant in a dark shade of green.

'It'll need a coat or two of paint. Brighten it up a little,' she said.

He nodded. 'Something neutral until we know what they are. Do you want to find out the sex of the babies?'

She'd not given that too much thought either. Her mind would briefly land on thoughts and ideas about the babies, but her unconscious was so busy telling her that everything could go wrong, and she could lose them at any point, that she'd spent a lot of time trying not to get attached to the idea of them actually existing.

Of course, she'd *wondered*. What it might be like to learn she was having two sons, or two daughters. Blue or pink?

But if she found out, if Mr Meyer told her what she was having, wouldn't that make them seem more real? Wouldn't that make her feel she was getting attached? If they found out what sex the babies were, then Yanis would want to start suggesting *names*, and that would make it really difficult. It would give them identities. Make them real people.

And if she lost them after they had names…that would hurt. It would hurt terribly even if they didn't have names. She couldn't imagine what it was like to lose a child. How did you get through something like that?

'I think I'd like it to be a surprise,' she said, thinking that was the diplomatic answer, rather than telling Yanis her fears.

'Oh. I'd hoped to find out.'

'You want to know?' she asked.

He nodded.

'Why?'

Yanis shrugged. 'I think it would make them more real. More solid. We could decide on names.'

She smiled. 'Maybe they could tell you, but not me?'

'You think I could keep a secret like that?'

Sam laughed. 'Maybe not. You don't seem like the kind of man who keeps huge secrets. I think you're an open book.'

He gave a strange smile and walked over to the window that looked out over the park. 'Just think…one day we could be out there, walking with them through the trees. Playing with a kite or a football, or on bikes. Does that seem strange to you?'

It did. Sam hadn't had the kind of childhood that revolved around fun and normal childhood things. Her childhood had revolved around temperature spikes, sitting in doctors' offices, being made to eat and drink strange things that tasted funny, having blood drawn… There were fuzzy memories of a mask being held over her nose and mouth to send her off to sleep. Her friends had been nurses. Kindly ladies in colourful scrubs with teddy bear pins on their lapels.

How would she know what her child wanted?

'It does,' she said.

She rubbed at her abdomen, then stopped. What was that? That feeling? That weird sensation?

She must have frowned, because Yanis was instantly at her side.

'Sam, what's wrong?'

He was pulling his phone out of his pocket, ready to ring for God only knew what. An ambulance?

She grabbed his hand and laid it on her belly. 'Can you feel that? It's like little fishes. It's exactly what Mr Meyer said!'

A smile had formed upon her face without her realising. This was the joy of new life. The surprise of actually feeling these new lives *inside her*.

She'd spent years having doctors look for things to remove from her—tonsils, appendix, a rogue piece of cartilage that had actually been in her shoulder. There had been scans looking for tumours and growths, things that shouldn't have been there, things that were alien, and now she had this. Real life growing within her.

'I can't feel it...' Yanis sounded incredibly disappointed.

She tried to get him to press more firmly, but he couldn't feel what she could.

'Maybe the movements need to be stronger. Proper kicks before you'll be able to feel them.'

He nodded. 'But this is good. This is a good sign that they are strong. Healthy. Growing.'

'Yes.'

She looked up at him with tears in her eyes. She wasn't sure where the tears had come from. Were they tears of happiness for the babies? Or tears of happiness because after all these years of thinking she was broken and needed fixing, her body still knew how to do something right?

'I've changed my mind,' she said.

Yanis frowned. 'About the pregnancy?'

'No, about finding out what sex they are. I want to know, too.'

Suddenly it seemed vital.

His frown turned to a hopeful smile. 'You do?'

'Yes. I think I *need* to know now. I didn't before, but it's almost like...like they've persuaded me. Like they're saying, *Hi, we're here... You can't ignore us.*' She laughed. 'Does that make any sense at all?'

'*Oui, ma chérie.* It does.'

She felt the movements again, and laid a hand upon her abdomen. Yanis put his hand on her belly, too, and for a long time they just stood there, marvelling at the new lives they'd created, enjoying the knowledge that, for now, everything was perfectly all right. Nothing was going wrong. That there was hope of a bright and wonderful future.

Sam looked up at Yanis with joy and happiness in her eyes and saw the same emotions in him. *They* had done this. They had created these two new people together. She felt a connection with Yanis that she had never felt before. Something deep. Something meaningful. She knew that no matter how their future played out she would remember this moment for ever.

Yanis reached up and stroked the side of her face. His finger trailed down the side of her cheek and along her jaw.

She almost stopped breathing, staring up into his beautiful blue eyes and seeing his intent there and not wanting to stop it. Of course she had yearned for his touch—ever since he'd walked into her Theatre. But she had told herself he hadn't followed her here to pursue that, and then... then the pregnancy, the twins, the connection they had...

Why not do this?

As he moved closer, she lifted her hands to clasp him at the waist—a physical sign that he should proceed.

He lifted up her hair and his lips found her ear and the length of her neck, nibbling and kissing.

Her heart began to pound and she allowed herself to sink into the sensations he was creating, closing her eyes in ecstasy.

Oh, she needed this! All the stresses and strains of the last few weeks were melting away beneath the pleasure of his caress. It was as if all the tensions she'd been holding in were beginning to fade away into oblivion. Her skin felt electric, each nerve ending waiting for his caress, and when his lips found hers she moaned and threaded her fingers through his hair, holding on to him as if she never wanted to let him go.

He scooped her up and took her through to the main living area, where there were stacks of boxes, but also soft furnishings, and there he gently laid her down upon a pile of pillows, as if she was a precious jewel.

But Sam didn't want to be precious and she didn't want delicate. She'd waited for this for so long, denied herself the pleasure of him for too long, and so she reached for him and began to undo his shirt. She needed him. Needed to feel the heat of his skin, the hardness of his body. Needed to feel him against her. *In* her. If she filled herself with him...

I would feel complete.

She didn't stop to analyse that thought. It came and

went in a single second, and she was too busy fiddling with buttons and his belt.

'Slow down, Sam. There's no rush,' he whispered as he stared into her eyes. 'This is not like before. You have no plane to catch. No need to run. We have all the time in the world.'

She smiled and let out a sigh.

She was used to making this a hurried thing. Something she did with a stranger to answer a need, making sure to leave before questions could be asked, before commitment could be implied. She'd always just satisfied her need in the moment. It had never been part of something more.

But whether she chose to like it or not, what she had with Yanis was something much deeper. It had a commitment to it. This wasn't going to be some flash in the pan. This wasn't going to be some quick hook-up and she'd never see him again. He was in her life permanently now. He had seeded two babies into her womb and she worked with him. They shared patients and a place to be. He understood her world and her passion and her needs.

He was right.

What would it feel like if she took this slowly? It had been mind-blowing the last time, because they'd both been feeling hurt and lost and had sought comfort in each other. This time it was going to be different.

'Okay.'

She smiled and rolled him over onto his back, so that she sat on top of him. His hands held her hips as she slowly began to undo the buttons of her blouse. She liked him watching her. Liked seeing the pupils of his eyes dilate as she revealed more and more of herself.

'Tu es si belle.'

'What does that mean?'

'It means you're so beautiful.'

She blushed and reached around her back to undo her bra.

'Non,' he said. 'Let me.'

And he sat up and stared hungrily into her eyes as he reached around and expertly undid the clasp.

'You've done that before,' she said.

He smiled at her. 'Not my first time.'

She laughed and tossed back her hair as his hands moved to her back, supporting her as his lips trailed across her chest and his fingertips tickled her sides before coming forward to her breasts. The heat of his breath and the scrape of his teeth against her skin was exquisite, and when he lay back she went with him and pressed her mouth to his, her tongue exploring the depths of him, dancing in a tango with his.

This was all such a delicious delight but she needed more. Wanted more. She was hungry for a man in a way she had never been before.

Yanis gently turned her onto her back and his expert fingers made swift work of the zip of her skirt, pulling it down to reveal her lacy underwear. His lips kissed her belly button, the swell of her abdomen, and his fingertips gently traced the curve of it, this fascinating development of new life that he had helped create.

And then his lips went lower.

It was exquisite agony through the lace. She wanted direct contact. To feel his tongue upon her swollen, hungry flesh. But he teased her mercilessly, until she began to beg him.

'Yanis…*please*!' She'd never begged for anything in her entire life, but she was begging now and she didn't care.

Slowly, with a wicked smile, he began to peel down her underwear, removing them from her legs and tossing them to one side. And then, just when she thought that, *yes*, she would get everything of him that she wanted, the pleasure that she sought, he stood up.

She almost thought he was going to leave her in that state, which was cruel. 'What are you doing?' she asked.

'Taking off my clothes.'

'Oh...' She smiled, lying there naked and wanton. 'Want some help?'

He held out a hand and she clasped it, and then he pulled her upwards into a standing position. She kissed him, mouth to mouth, her fingers unfastening his belt, finding the button of his trousers, the zip, feeling the hard swell of him beneath the fabric and wanting the gift inside. She reached into his trousers and caressed him, making him gasp at her touch, and then she was kneeling in front of him, pulling down his trousers, helping him step out of them and stroking his erection through the fabric of his boxers.

She would tease him the way he'd teased her. It seemed only fair.

She brushed her lips over the taut fabric and looked up at him. Yanis was breathing hard. He was magnificent. All of him. Clothed and unclothed.

Was this really happening? For most of her life, all Sam had thought was that people only needed her medically. That her only use was to be picked over for information, or to use her professional skills to heal someone. On a personal level, she had always kept herself and her heart and soul remote from others. It had just seemed easier. Safer.

And now she found herself in strange territory. Dipping her toe into unknown waters. But she felt *good* about it—and that was the oddest and most surprising thing. Was that because *she* had changed? Or was it because this was Yanis, and with him she felt that it was safe to do so?

Either way, right now it didn't matter...

Afterwards she lay in his arms as he lazily stroked the skin over her hips.

'Sam?'

'Yes?'

'I notice you have laparotomy scars.'

She tensed, swallowing. 'Yeah.'

'What were they for?'

She shrugged. 'Something I had done as a child. Exploratory stuff. They weren't sure what was going on.'

She'd known, though. Sam had known well enough what was going on. There had been nothing physically wrong with her except for what her mother was doing. Starving her so that she would have *'unexplained weight loss'*. Making her drink weird concoctions to give her *'unexplained stomach pains'*. All so that her mother could act the angst-ridden parent who was just so terribly grateful to all the doctors for looking after her and comforting her while Sam was in surgery.

The laparotomy had been the final straw for Sam. She'd had enough. She'd finally spoken out. After the doctors had gathered around her bed to tell Sam and her mother that they'd found nothing conclusive and her mother had gone home—no doubt to plan her next medical move—Sam had asked to speak to one of the doctors and told him everything, fearing that he wouldn't believe her. Only he had. He had listened. And when her mother had turned up for her next visit, the police had been waiting.

But to tell Yanis that...? Even though they'd just shared something so intimate she should be able to tell him anything...? It wasn't just about entrusting him with that information, it was whether she would be able to cope with the horror and pity she would see in his eyes. That she would never be able to stand.

'And the appendectomy?'

'Same. Done as a child.'

'You spent a lot of time in hospitals when you were younger, then?'

'You could say that.'

'Is that where you found your passion for medicine?'

She thought for a moment. 'It made me want to understand the human body. What it was capable of. What it could create. What diseases it could fight. Its strengths, its weaknesses.'

'You are strong—you know that, right?'

'Am I?'

'Of course. Two new lives you carry within you. That's a marvellous and wondrous thing.'

'It's a scary thing. I have a whole new respect for mothers.'

'You didn't have respect for mothers before?'

'Yes. I just never really *knew*, if that makes any sense?'

'What about your own mother?'

'We don't really talk.'

'Why not?'

'It's a long story. If you don't mind, I'd really rather not sully this perfect moment by speaking about her right now.'

Yanis had nuzzled into her neck. 'Okay.'

Lying there, sated, was everything she needed in that moment.

CHAPTER SIX

'YOU'VE GOT A SURGERY?'

Yanis was scrubbing in for a surgery on a private patient when Sam found him.

'I have.'

'On who?'

'A private patient.'

'Oh, right. Anything interesting?'

'Craniometaphyseal dysplasia.'

It was a rare condition that presented as a thickening or overgrowth of bones in the skull. It was something that would continue throughout life.

'Is it her first surgery?' Sam peered through the viewing pane at the patient, already laid out on the table.

'No, it's her fourth.'

'Poor kid. Need an assist?'

'I'm good. I've got a resident and a student in with me, so it might be crowded.'

'Okay. It's my twenty-week scan later, at two p.m. Are you going to be free for that?'

Yanis glanced at the clock, clearly doing some mental maths. 'I should be.'

'I don't want to go in on my own.'

He glanced at her, hearing the fear in her voice. She

looked well. Even though she was only technically five months pregnant now, she actually looked more like six or seven. If there was an issue, surely she would have said?

'Is there a problem?' He hoped not. Not now that they were so close! If they could just get to twenty-four weeks, then they'd stand a good chance.

'No, I just don't want to go in by myself in case there's bad news.'

'Why would there be bad news?'

'Things like that just happen to me.'

And to me.

But he had to be strong for both of them. Be there as he had tried to be before. Remain positive.

'You'll be fine. The babies will be fine. I promise.'

He knew it wasn't a promise he should make. He didn't know they would be fine. How could he? No one would know until the scan. And this time, hopefully, they would find out the sex, too. At the last scan, a couple of weeks ago, the twins had been positioned in such a way it had been impossible to be sure. The sonographer had said she could make a guess, but neither of them wanted to rely on guesses. Certainty was what both of them needed.

'I'll be there, *ma chérie.*'

She nodded. 'Good luck with your surgery.'

He smiled. *'Merci.'*

When she'd left, the smile dropped from his face as he concentrated on scrubbing properly, but his thoughts worried away at him. He was dreading this scan. He dreaded all of them. Each time they went, he tried to remain focused and positive for Sam, but inside he was being torn apart.

What if this was the scan that showed a problem?

What if this was the scan where they saw they'd lost one or both of the babies? What if this was the scan when he would have to come clean with Sam and tell her everything? He couldn't imagine upsetting her like that, scaring her like that, but didn't she deserve the truth?

He wanted to tell her *so badly*! But each time he thought about discussing with her what had happened, he saw her own doubts, her own fears, her own certainty that something terrible was going to happen, and he didn't want her thinking that way. He'd seen it tear Giselle apart and he couldn't watch it tear Sam apart!

He'd not been able to save his relationship with his wife after that, and right now he and Sam were doing well. He was beginning to have some hope of happiness again. If he told her everything, would he ruin it all? He didn't want to ruin anything. Being with Sam was... almost indescribable. She was such a strong woman. He could see it, even if she didn't. He admired her. Not just as a surgeon, but for her bravery in the face of uncertainty. An uncertainty that hung over him every day like a dark cloud.

The pressure was immense. To be the one with broad shoulders so others could lean on you. Being the one to provide one of those shoulders to cry on, or a soft place to fall, a safe place in which they could vent their fears and worries.

It was a load he was happy to carry, but sometimes—just sometimes—he wondered if there was a place *he* could go to vent? He wanted it to be Sam, but she needed him to be strong right now, so he kept all of his fears and worries tightly bound up inside.

Yanis moved into Theatre and checked with Aarav, the anaesthetist, that the patient was good to go.

Aarav nodded. 'Ready to rock and roll.'

'Okay, let's do it.'

The babies were kicking and she was finding it hard to concentrate. Sam rubbed at her abdomen, pushing down on what felt like a foot and smiling as she reviewed a patient's notes.

'So, your GP has referred you to me because you're having some dizzy spells, is that right?'

Molly Jacobs was a woman in her early forties. Slight, pale and fidgety. 'Yes, that's right. They just come out of nowhere.'

'And how long does each of these dizzy spells last?'

'Not long. Minutes…or just seconds. But the after-effects last a week or two. It takes me ages to be able to stand up, and when I do, I have to lean on things, because the world seems tipped on its axis. It's like being drunk, when I've not had the joy of a night out.'

Sam smiled. 'And how long have you been having these episodes?'

'Three to four months. They're debilitating. I've had so much time off work.'

'What do you do?'

'I'm a preschool teacher.'

'And it says here your GP first suggested it was labyrinthitis?'

'Yes.'

'Any hearing loss?'

'I don't think so, but I've developed tinnitus. I can hear sounds inside myself.'

'Any headaches? Blurred vision?'

'Headaches for sure. And my eyes get tired.'

'Hmm… Okay. Well, I'm going to send you for an

MRI, just to make sure you haven't got anything going on that shouldn't be.'

'Like what?'

'It could be all manner of things. It could be something as simple as Ménière's disease, which affects the balance, but with symptoms like these, we like to perform a scan just to rule out other conditions.'

'Such as?'

Sam smiled. 'Let's not worry about what it might be until we know what it's not. Deal?'

Molly nodded. 'When do I get the MRI?'

'Today. You're already booked in.' She handed over a slip of paper. 'Take that to Reception and the lady there will direct you. You can go home afterwards, and if everything's fine, your GP will let you know. But if we find anything, then I'll get in touch to arrange further treatment, okay?'

'All right. Thank you, Ms Gordon.'

'No problem. Best of luck.'

Molly left and Sam stood to stretch and gaze out of the hospital window. From her office, she could see down into the atrium, and across from there to the older rehabilitation buildings, where her friend Gil worked. She hadn't seen him for a while and hoped he was okay. Normally they met up once a week, just to check in, but what with her pregnancy and spending time getting to know Yanis, that had fallen a little to the wayside.

Feeling guilty, she sat down again and picked up the phone, dialling the extension for Gil's office.

He picked up almost immediately.

'Hey, Gil, it's Sam.'

'Hey! How's tricks?'

'Good. Haven't seen you for a while... Just wanted to check in and make sure you're okay?'

'Busy, as always. How about you? Everything going all right?'

'Yes. Got my anomaly scan this afternoon.'

He must have heard the tension and the worry in her voice, because he said, 'You'll be just fine. The babies have been doing okay so far. How's Yanis holding up?'

'He's good.'

'I like him. I've met him a couple of times when he's come over to the unit to follow up on a patient.'

'He gets your approval, huh?'

'He does. He really cares for you, you know?'

'What makes you say that?'

'The way he speaks about you. It's this look he gets in his eyes... I don't know. Don't ask me to name it. I'm no expert in the human heart.'

The way Gil's Australian accent drew out the word *heart* cheered her soul.

'You almost sound poetic.'

Gil laughed. 'It's the new me.'

'We should meet up for lunch one day. In the atrium.'

'We should. I'll call you another time. Right now, I've got a patient waiting. You'll call me and let me know how the scan goes, right?'

'Sure thing.'

'Bye.' And he put down the phone.

She felt better for having checked in with him. She had done her duty as his friend and colleague. She didn't have many close friends, and he was the only one who truly knew what had happened to her.

Sam knew she would have to tell Yanis at some point—but when? After the babies had been born? Before? She wasn't sure. It was such a huge thing to share. So deeply personal. And right now they were creating something new. Not just new life, but a relationship of sorts, and she kind of wanted to see where that was going. She would have to trust him one hundred per cent before she could tell him everything.

Sam picked up the phone and called through to the receptionist. 'Can you send my next patient in, please?'

The patient came in alone. Perry Lombard. A forty-eight-year-old man who had been referred to her by his GP for trigeminal neuralgia. TN was characterised by sudden, severe and extremely sharp lasting pains in the side of the face. The attacks could be so debilitating and so awful that patients reported that they were unable to do anything until they had passed.

'Hello, Mr Lombard, I'm Samantha Gordon. How are you today?'

'All right for the moment.'

'I see you're here because of your trigeminal neuralgia. Why don't you tell me about how it's been affecting you?'

'I've had it for over a year. It came on suddenly. We couldn't work out what had triggered it. Now I get multiple attacks every week.'

'How many attacks a week, would you say?'

'Sometimes every day. Sometimes every other day. It depends… But it's really beginning to affect my mental health now, and I don't think I can keep going on if the rest of my life is going to be like this.'

That, unfortunately, was something she heard a lot regarding this particular condition, when it affected someone so brutally.

'Your doctor gave you carbamazepine? How did that work out?'

Mr Lombard sighed. 'Initially it seemed to work. It didn't get rid of all the pain, but it lessened it for a while. Still enough to damn well hurt, but I could do things. I could go out with my wife. I could work in the garden. I could stay upright, for God's sake. But after a month or two of taking it I began to suffer side effects.'

'What kind?'

'Dizziness. I felt like I couldn't think straight. Like my head was all woolly. And it made me feel sick to my stomach, I could barely eat, and I've lost weight because of it.'

'It says here in your GP's letter that he then tried you on gabapentin. Was that any better for you?'

'It helped me eat. But it gave me problems in other areas.'

'Such as what?'

Mr Lombard looked uncomfortable. 'Sexually.'

Sam nodded. That sometimes happened. The ability to reach orgasm could be a struggle. 'And what do you hope to gain from today?'

He shrugged. 'I don't know. Some ideas, I guess, on what I can do next. Medication seems to just add problems, and the neuralgia is problem enough! I guess I asked to be referred to you to see if there were any other options. Surgical, or not.'

'There are a few things we can try if medications aren't working. There are percutaneous procedures that can offer some relief. There's radiosurgery and decompression procedures we could try, all done under a general anaesthetic.'

'What's the easiest one?'

She smiled. 'Well, of the percutaneous procedures, we could try a glycerol injection.'

Sam brought up an image on her computer screen that

showed a cut-through slide of the human head, highlighting the branches of the trigeminal nerve.

'This here is called the Gasserian ganglion—it's where the three main branches of the trigeminal nerve join together. We inject glycerol directly into it, in the hope that it will disrupt the pain signals that travel along it.'

He nodded. 'How long would I be in hospital for?'

'Just the day. You could be home in the evening.'

'What other options are there?'

'There's a procedure called radiofrequency lesioning, where we use a needle to apply heat directly to that ganglion, or we could use balloon compression. We pass a tiny balloon along a thin tube through the cheek. Then we inflate it around the ganglion and squeeze it.'

'So, basically, you think it's this ganglion thing that's causing all my issues?'

'Applying treatment to that area seems to have good outcomes.'

'Is it dangerous?'

'All surgeries have an element of risk, of course, but these are the more basic procedures we'd carry out before we'd consider anything else.'

'And if they worked, would that be for ever?'

'That can depend on each case. For some people the pain relief lasts for years, for others it's months or weeks, and in some cases there's no relief at all.'

Mr Lombard sighed. 'It's a lot to take in, isn't it?'

'It is.'

'Would I be a candidate for these procedures?'

'I would be happy to put you forward for treatment. Clearly you've tried medication, and that's not working for you, and if the condition is beginning to affect your mental health then it's time to do something.'

'But if these procedures don't work, we could still try something more radical?'

She nodded.

'Okay. Well, I'd like to think it over. Talk about it with the wife, you know?'

Sam understood. 'Of course. Here's a printout of all those procedures I've mentioned. Take it home, discuss it, and then contact my secretary on the number at the bottom to let me know what you decide. There's no rush. All right?'

She stood up and reached over to shake his hand.

Mr Lombard smiled at her. 'You've been a great help—thank you very much.' He looked down at her belly. 'Will you be around to do my surgery?'

She laughed. 'I've still got a few months to go, so yes, I will.'

'All right. Well, it was nice to meet you, Ms Gordon.'

'You too, Mr Lombard.'

She watched him go and rubbed at her abdomen. The babies were kicking a lot today. She liked that. It reassured her in ways she hadn't expected. She was getting used to the idea that she was going to become a mother now. It had been so scary at first, and knowing that she had Yanis supporting her had become important. It was good to have someone in her corner. Someone who truly meant it. Who genuinely cared for her.

She saw it in her patients. If they had support, had someone sitting by their bedside, rooting for them to get well, it impacted on their healing time. Those who had a good support network healed faster and better, with fewer residual side effects, than those who had no one.

She'd thought at the start of this that she'd have no one.

But she was beginning to see that that wasn't true at all.

His dysplasia case had overrun, but finally he was out of Theatre. Yanis scrubbed and dried off his hands, then checked the time. Fifteen minutes late for the anomaly scan.

His phone showed four text messages from Sam and two missed calls.

Cursing under his breath, he rushed to the lifts that would take him down to the floor he needed and punched the button. The lifts seemed to be taking an age, so he headed for the stairwell and ran down the stairs instead, bursting into the waiting room for the antenatal clinic all out of breath and causing everyone to turn and look at him.

He scanned the faces and saw Sam over in the far corner. Her frown disappeared and a relieved smile crossed her face.

'I'm so sorry I'm late!' He dropped a kiss on her cheek and sat down next to her. 'Have I missed it?'

'No. Thankfully, they're overrunning, too. What took you so long? I thought I was going to have to go in on my own.'

Whispering to her, to avoid being overheard, he said, 'The dysplasia case had a few complications. Her BP dropped multiple times and we were having problems with anaesthesia.'

'What kind of problems?'

'It seemed way too light. She needed more and more. I was beginning to think we would have to stop the surgery to give her body chance to recover.'

'Did you finish?'

'*Oui*. Thank goodness. How are you doing? How are my babies doing?' He laid a hand on her belly and smiled at a well-timed kick right in the centre of his palm.

'We're all fine. Let's hope they tell us the same when we go in.'

'I'm sure they will.'

He pressed his lips into her hair and breathed her in, trying to savour this moment. Everything was fine right now, and it felt good to just revel in it with her.

The closeness they'd been creating between them was to be cherished, knowing that she felt something for him, too. Ever since they'd had sex in his flat, their relationship had gone in a different direction from just colleagues and friends to something more...intimate. He liked it. Liked her. Liked the way she made him feel. Liked sneaking glances at her. Watching her smile, or flip her hair, or laugh.

Sam could be very intense at work. Dedicated. Driven. It was nice to see her take her foot off the pedal occasionally and relax and be herself.

'Samantha Gordon?'

They both stood up, and once again Yanis felt his stomach twist in a familiar fear. He'd been to every scan so far with Sam, and they both kept an eye on the blood flow and amniotic fluid around the twins, and each time he knew they could go in and hear something devastating.

He'd spent far too much time at home researching TTTS and he knew the awful risks—had read some terribly upsetting blogs from parents who had been in the same situation as them. Parents who had lost one or both of their babies.

He had felt their pain and wept, and he couldn't believe he was walking that same tightrope once again.

He told himself that he had to draw strength from Sam. From how she was acting. How she was telling him how she felt. How much the babies were moving. All of these were positives.

Sam lay down on the couch and bared her growing abdomen. She was a good size now, and looked healthy.

The sonographer began moving the probe over her abdomen.

'How does it look?' asked Yanis. He could see two heartbeats, so that was good. That made him relax somewhat.

'Twin A is measuring at just under twenty-seven centimetres and is about thirteen ounces, and Twin B is measuring at about twenty-four centimetres and eleven ounces.'

'That's good, right?'

'They're doing well. But there's less fluid around twin two, so we'll want to keep a closer eye on that. Up till now they've both been measuring about the same, according to your records, and now we're beginning to see a difference.'

'Is it TTTS?' asked Sam.

'You'll have to speak to your consultant. He'll probably want you scanned weekly, instead of fortnightly.'

'Oh…'

'But the babies are healthy for now?' asked Sam.

'Their heartbeats are strong. You've noticed plenty of movement?'

Sam nodded. 'Yes.'

'That's good. Do you want to know the sex?'

Yanis squeezed Sam's hand. 'We do.'

'You're expecting identical girls.'

'Girls?' Sam let out a breath.

Daughters.

He was going to have two daughters.

Something welled up deep inside him and his desire to protect them all intensified. He lifted Sam's hand to his mouth and kissed it, fighting back the tears that threatened to show. Now the babies were even more real, and they needed their *papa* to be strong for them.

'I'll send copies of the scan and my report straight up to Mr Meyer,' said the sonographer.

'Thank you.'

Everything else checked out. Their brains, their bladders, their lungs, the length of their femurs... All the things that were checked showed that the babies were doing okay. The placenta was still low, though...

Sam and Yanis walked out of the scan room on a muted high. Elation at finding out they were expecting girls, but also caution because of the difference in size and the suggestion that now they'd be on weekly scans instead of fortnightly.

'It could get worse, Yanis.'

'But it might not be. Twin A might have just had a growth spurt and her sister will have caught up the next time you're checked.'

She nodded, but her face showed that she wasn't sure. 'Her sister... I can't believe it's going to be girls.'

'I know. We'll have to think of some names.'

Sam shook her head. 'No, we can't. Not yet. It'll be too awful if we name them and...' Her voice trailed off. 'And the worst happens.'

He sucked in a breath and then let it out slowly. He'd been through the worst happening. They'd named Jacques before they'd lost him. Had that made it worse? Surely losing a child at this stage would be terrible even if they didn't have a name?

Could this happen to him again? Was it always going to happen to him? The idea of watching it happen again was just too awful to contemplate. Her reminder that it could all still go wrong was just too much.

'I'm sorry. I have to go check on my patient.'

Sam watched him go, feeling suddenly hurt. Had she upset him by suggesting that they might still lose these babies? She was only being practical. He needed to know the risks. He needed to know that not everything was straightforward when it came to her body, though thankfully her womb was one of the areas her mother hadn't deliberately set out to injure, and Sam had been living with her aunt by the time her periods began.

Perhaps he was fed up with her worrying constantly and wondering why she couldn't just be happy and embrace the joy of carrying their children.

She wanted to. She wanted to be like a normal pregnant mother-to-be. She wanted to delight in her blooming belly, in every kick. She wanted to decorate nurseries and spend ages flicking through baby name books, looking for the perfect name. Only she couldn't. She'd been on fortnightly scans and now it would be weekly.

Every other mother only got two scans. Two! One just after the first trimester and a second one at around twenty-one weeks. But, oh, no, not Sam. She had 'issues'.

Twins could develop life-threatening TTTS, where the donor baby became small and weak and the recipient twin became huge and suffered heart problems, or even worse. She also had a low-lying placenta that looked as if it wasn't going to move, and that meant she could begin to bleed out at any time, so they had to keep an eye on that, too.

If the likelihood of TTTS increased, she might have to have laser ablation, to try to sort out the blood flow for the twins, and that procedure carried risks, too. The twins could die. It might not work, or only work for a short time, and she was only twenty-one weeks pregnant. Nowhere near the safety line after which her babies might try to survive if they had to be delivered early.

The idea that she might only be mere weeks away from delivery startled her and made her feel sick....

She wasn't ready. Nothing was ready. Yanis had bought a few things and she'd told him off for doing that. But otherwise they had nothing. No cribs, no car seats, no nappies, no bottles, no clothes. Should she start preparing? Preparing for them to live?

Sam headed up to the neurosurgery floor and went straight to the doctors' station. She booted up the internet and in a fit of optimism started buying baby things. Basic things. A place for them to sleep. Some clothes for newborns, some nappies, a double buggy, two cots... She arranged for them to be sent to her home. Once it was done, she felt marginally better. It might show Yanis that she was looking ahead. That she was hoping for a good outcome, no matter how much she worried out loud.

But she couldn't silence the small voice in the back of her head that told her she'd somehow tempted fate.

The post-operative ward was usually a nice, quiet and peaceful place where patients recovered from surgery. Having already spent some time in the ICU, the post-operative ward was a positive step forward for them. It meant that they were out of the danger zone of that crucial first twenty-four hours post-op and could start thinking about either going home or heading to the neurological rehabilitation suite.

Sam waited for Yanis to be free after talking to his patient. 'Could I have a quick word?' she asked.

'Of course.'

He followed her over to the nurses' station, a look of enquiry on his face.

'I wanted to apologise,' she began.

He frowned. 'For what?'

'For being me. For always thinking the worst is going to happen. I get that you're not like that. I get that you're the optimist here. It's just that I'm used to thinking the worst, especially when it comes to my health, and...' she paused for a moment, debating '...I'd like the opportunity to tell you why I'm like that.'

'Okay...'

Sam looked around them. 'Not here, though. My place? Tonight? I could cook. Pasta or something.'

Her heart was racing at the thought of what she was going to do, but she knew she would have to do it. Yanis was going to find out sooner or later. He had to know. These were his children she was carrying—he had a right to know just who he'd got involved with. This wasn't just about her any more, and now that everything was getting scarier she felt that if anything were to go horribly wrong and he found out *afterwards*, she wouldn't be able to live with the guilt. Knowing that she should have been upfront with him from the very beginning.

'I'll be there,' he said.

She nodded. 'Great. That's great. Thank you.'

He reached out, took her hand. 'You do know you don't have to apologise to me, don't you?'

'Don't I?'

'*Non.* Your worrying…it just goes to show how much you care. It shows how much you love the twins already, so why would I complain about that?'

She shrugged, not knowing what to say. He was being so nice to her. So kind. But then, he always had been, ever since they'd met. Maybe she had to accept that that was just how Yanis was? That she had to let him be that way with her, and that maybe not everyone she allowed to get close was out to hurt her?

When the doorbell rang, she still wasn't sure she was ready to do it. But when he came in and kissed her on the cheek, and presented her with a bottle of non-alcoholic wine and a small bouquet of flowers, she knew that she must.

Yanis had to understand where she was coming from. He had to know who she was. He was possibly about to become a father and co-parent with her, and that sort of relationship didn't deserve secrets.

She served up the food—a basic pasta dish, made with a jar of sauce and some Parmesan cheese grated on top—and poured the non-alcoholic wine into their glasses.

'Cheers.' She held hers up. 'To healthy babies.'

'To healthy babies.' He clinked her glass with his, smiled and took a sip.

The wine did nothing to make her feel more confident, of course, but it did help settle her churning stomach, which was making it difficult for her to eat.

'I need to tell you something, Yanis. Something about

me and my past and how it's made me the person that I am today.'

'All right.'

'I'm telling you because I think I can trust you—and, well, because we're having babies together, hopefully, and I'd like to think that you will always be in my corner.'

'Of course I will. What is it, Sam?'

She took in a deep breath and laid down her fork. 'You remember I told you about when I was a child? About how I spent a lot of time being ill?'

He leaned forward, resting his elbows on the table, his eyes intense as he listened to her. *'Oui.'*

'Well, the bit I left out was the fact that I wasn't really ill. At least not really.'

He frowned. He didn't understand.

She knew she had to plough on. Get it out. Tell him everything.

'My mother made me sick,' she whispered. Saying the words out loud somehow cemented the truth of it once again, and the shame she felt almost swallowed her whole. 'My mother suffered from Munchausen's by Proxy.'

Yanis closed his eyes in dismay, then reached out and held her hand, clasping it in his strong, firm fingers. 'What did she do to you?'

'You've seen my scars. She convinced doctors to do several exploratory laparoscopies, and I had my appendix removed, my tonsils removed. I had endoscopies, blood tests, stool tests, urine tests... I was poked, prodded, scanned. She used to give me salt water to make me sick, so she could take me to the doctor. She would sometimes starve me, only feeding me small amounts of soup, so that I would suddenly lose weight.'

Yanis shook his head in silence.

'I think it started when my father left. When my mum discovered she was pregnant he didn't stick around, and she was bereft. She had a difficult pregnancy with me, and kept going into premature labour, so they kept her in hospital on bed rest. It started there, her therapist told me. With the attention she got from the doctors and nurses. She had no one else, so the caring they showed her in making sure that I was all right seemed to get confused in her head. She believed that their caring natures actually showed her the love she craved. When I was born and she was sent home, things were all right for a while. She would take me for walks and complete strangers would stop her and coo over me, ask her how she was doing and if I slept through the night. She flourished under their praise. But then I got older, and the attention disappeared. She craved it. And that's when she started doing things to me.'

'Oh, Sam…'

She smiled and squeezed his hand tight, glad of his reassurance. Glad that he hadn't withdrawn, appalled.

'The doctors would see her sitting by my hospital bed and think that she was the most attentive mother, constantly talking to me, trying to keep me cheerful, but she wasn't doing that. She was just whispering instructions. *"Lie still. Don't move. Try not to eat the food. Don't speak. Don't answer their questions."'*

Sam shook her head.

'When I was in hospital for that last laparoscopy, she was already planning my next "illness". She was trying to convince the doctors I had a brain tumour. She told them I was having seizures, that I'd said my vision was blurry, that I had headaches. I was even already booked in for an MRI. But after that laparoscopy I was scared, and I told the doctors everything. They waited for her to come in on her next visit and had the police and social services waiting. When I recovered, they took me away from her and placed me with my aunt.'

'Thank God that they did. And you were all right?'

'Apart from the scars she'd left me with. Apart from the fact that for years I'd been brainwashed to think that I was faulty. That I was broken. That I needed fixing. I had a lot of therapy afterwards, and I struggled to trust people because of what she did.'

'I'm glad you've trusted me enough to tell me.'

'You needed to know. I'm pregnant. We're having two babies and you need to know why I always think the worst. Why I always suspect that something is going to go wrong. It's my defence mechanism, if that makes any sense. If I assume things are going to go badly, then when it happens it hurts less.'

'Does that really work?' he asked, sounding really interested in the possibility.

She shrugged. 'I tell myself it does. I thought I'd escaped before things got too bad, but still I find myself in this situation: pregnant with problems. My mother had a difficult pregnancy and nearly lost me—what if the same happens to me?'

'How do you know your mother didn't cause the pregnancy problems herself?'

She shook her head. 'I don't know.'

'From what you've told me, it's possible that she did. Your mother's pregnancy should have no bearing on your own.'

'But it doesn't stop me from worrying, Yanis. What if I'm like her?'

'That's impossible.'

'How do you know that?'

'Because you're a healer. A doctor. You make people better... You've never caused anyone harm. Do you attention-seek? *Non*. You're not like her and never will be.'

'But I worry in case I'm broken for real. What if I'm not meant to have children? What if my womb is so terribly faulty that it won't get to the end of these nine months? What if my mother was right all along?'

Yanis got up from the table and came around it to her side. Kneeling down in front of her, he laid his hands on her swollen belly, kissed it. 'You're scared. I get that. I am, too. But the Samantha Gordon I know is *nothing* like the woman you've just described. You're strong. Beautiful in heart. Your love and concern for these babies shine through. You could never harm them. I believe that more than I believe anything.'

She smiled. 'Thank you.'

'Thank you for telling me. For trusting me enough to tell me. That's a big step, Sam. A *big* step.'

She nodded. Hoping that he wouldn't prove her wrong.

CHAPTER SEVEN

'WHERE ARE WE GOING?' Sam asked, when Yanis turned up at her home, told her to put on her jacket and get ready for a walk.

'Richmond Park.'

'Why?'

'To remind you that there is happiness and life to be found *outside* of the hospital.'

'Oh.' She smiled, then laughed, and grabbed at the lightweight jacket that was hanging over the balustrade.

Yanis drove them through the busy streets, away from the centre of town and out towards the park, finding a nice parking spot down a small road. As she waited for him to lock up the car, he went to the boot, opened it and pulled out a picnic basket.

'We're having a picnic?' she asked.

'We are.'

'Okay…'

It was entertaining for him to watch the strains of the day slowly ease away from Sam's face as they walked through the park. Yanis reached for her hand and clasped it in his, and with the early summer sun beating down upon their faces, he felt the cares of the world begin to dissipate. This was nice. This time away from the hospital.

It would be all too easy for them to allow their entire lives to revolve around work and patients. Their jobs were intense. Too intense. It was extremely important that they had downtime. Time to relax. To shake off their worries and their cares and just enjoy being in each other's company.

'Look, Yanis...the deer!'

He looked across the landscape and over to a small clump of trees where there were some fallow deer. About twelve that he could see. A few of them were alert and keeping an eye out, whilst the others munched on grass. They were beautiful creatures. There were even two younger ones. Babies. What was the word? *Fawns?* They looked so sweet, with their large dark eyes.

To see them made him hopeful. Hopeful that he would get to see his babies soon. See their eyes. Gaze into them. Adore them.

'You're smiling,' Sam said.

He laughed. 'Thinking happy thoughts.'

'Want to share them?'

'I was thinking of our babies. Holding them in my arms. Looking down at them. Falling in love with them. Do you ever think of that moment?'

She nodded. 'I do. Sometimes. When I allow myself to hope that everything will be all right.'

She stretched out her back, rubbed at it. He hoped she wasn't too uncomfortable. Carrying two babies, she was already the size of a singleton pregnancy at term, and it was affecting her centre of balance. And standing for long hours in surgery, slightly bent over an operating table, was doing nothing for her backache or her sore ankles.

'You okay?' Yanis asked.

'Fine—just stretching out a bit.'

'Want to sit for a bit? I've got a blanket.'

'Let's choose a good spot.'

They walked for about another ten minutes, just taking in the scenery. The quiet. The blue skies. The sparrows and blackbirds and thrushes singing in the trees. Occasionally they heard a dog bark as it chased a Frisbee or a ball, a child's laughter. It was nice. Different from the beep of machines and the clank of instruments that they were so much more familiar with.

Eventually they found a spot near the Isabella Plantation, and Yanis laid out the blanket and opened up the basket of goodies. Once he and Sam both had plates of tiny sandwiches, strawberries and triangles of watermelon, they settled in to talk.

'How are you feeling regarding the possibility of ablation?' he asked.

She sighed, swallowing a bite of ham-and-cheese sandwich. 'I don't know. If it needs to be done, then it needs to be done, but... I don't enjoy the idea of being a patient under anaesthetic, increasing the risk of losing them and submitting my body to doctors again.'

'I understand that.'

'I think I'd feel better if you were in the theatre, too. Observing.'

'They wouldn't allow that. In this case, I'm just the father. Being staff won't get me in the room.'

'It's the lack of control, I think, that worries me the most. What happened to me as a child made me feel powerless, and I vowed to never feel that way again.'

'There are moments when we all feel powerless. I feel it all the time just lately.'

'You do?' She looked at him almost hopefully, as if it reassured her to hear that.

'Of course! I can't do anything to help you. I can't stop the twins from being at risk of TTTS. I can't stop the fact that your placenta is low. That weighs on me more than you know.'

She smiled. 'Thank you.'

'For what?' He was confused.

'For confiding in me. For worrying. For trusting me enough to tell me.'

'We need to be honest with each other. You were honest with me about your past, about what happened to you. I can only hope to be the same.'

'You have something in your past you want to share?' He smiled. *'Non.'*

He hoped he sounded convincing.

Since she'd told Yanis about her past, he'd been even more attentive—and she'd allowed him to take care of her. She was getting past the strangeness of someone being kind, and she was now trying to embrace the care and attention. And she found that even though she enjoyed it, she didn't want to take advantage.

She tried to look after him, too. Massaging his shoulders after a long surgery. Cooking him a meal most nights. Asking him out to see a movie. Bringing him hot drinks when he was busy and hadn't stopped to take a break.

She'd hoped he might expand on their conversation in Richmond Park. It had sounded, for a moment there, as if he had something in his past that he'd hoped to share, but then he had diverted the conversation. There was something. She was sure of it. But what? She had opened up to Yanis. Exposed herself. Made herself vulnerable in the attempt to bring them closer together. Why couldn't Yanis do the same? What was he hiding?

Otherwise the relationship they were developing was growing as quickly as her abdomen—and the weekly scans she'd been having were growing more and more concerning.

Her latest scan this morning had shown that there was beginning to be a sizeable difference between Twin B, the donor twin, and Twin A, the recipient twin. After her last surgery she had an appointment with her consultant, Mr Meyer, to see what he wanted to do. She knew laser ablation was an option, but she'd researched it and found that although it did work in a lot of cases, in some it didn't work at all, and in others, mothers lost one or both babies. It was a small minority, but it did happen, and that concerned her greatly.

But she had reached the magical twenty-four weeks of pregnancy now, so technically, if the twins had to be born early—even with all the possible complications of early delivery—they had a chance of survival.

She rubbed at her abdomen absently, smiling as the babies kicked, and hoped that she'd get to keep them inside her for a lot longer.

It was one thing to be a surgeon and be in control, knowing absolutely that what you were doing was right for your patient. It was completely another to be the patient and give yourself over into someone else's hands and hope that they knew what they were doing.

Of course, she'd researched Mr Meyer. She had done it the second she'd been assigned to him. He was a good doctor. A renowned obstetrician with a specialty in multiples and neonatal surgery. But it didn't matter how many gold stars he had against his name—this was *her* body, *her* babies. She might have thought that she felt scared as a child, submitting to all those procedures, but now she was terrified.

She was normally so great at hiding it, but now, with the TTTS getting worse, putting her babies at risk, she truly felt that maybe her mother had been right all along. Maybe her body couldn't carry babies without something going wrong. Maybe she was faulty and this situation was somehow all her own fault.

Yanis had told her she had to stop thinking that. Kept telling her it was simply bad luck. But what if it wasn't? She was terrified and the fear was all-consuming. She needed to know she could rely on Yanis, and she thought that she could, but there was something niggling away that she just couldn't put her finger on. Maybe he would tell her soon? Maybe he just needed a bit more time to feel that he could open up to her the way she had to him?

She wanted him to feel that he could tell her anything.

Because that way, when the worst happened—*if* it happened—then they'd both be able to get through it.

Mr Meyer looked grim.

Yanis did not like the look on his face at all, and he knew that significant news was coming.

'Your latest scan shows a significant difference developing between the donor and recipient twins. My advice is that we schedule you for immediate laser ablation.'

Every word he delivered sank Yanis deeper and deeper into fear. He'd hoped that this day would never happen. That it would not have come to this. But here they were, sitting in the consultant's office, being told that surgery was the only way forward if he and Sam wanted to keep their daughters inside the womb and healthy for a little while longer.

No one wanted to deliver these babies at twenty-four weeks. Not if they could help it. So surgery was the only option.

Yanis reached out and grasped Sam's hand, knowing that this news would terrify her. 'What will that entail exactly?'

But Yanis already pretty much knew. Like Sam, he had researched the surgery and knew the basics, but he wanted to hear from Mr Meyer just exactly how he hoped to approach the situation.

'Laser ablation is a minimally invasive surgery that will offer you the best chance at having two healthy babies. We perform it endoscopically, entering into the uterine sac of the recipient twin. We identify the cord insertion and follow the vessels that connect to the donor twin. This is where we bring in the laser and coagulate the vessels to ensure that there is no blood flow between the two twins. Next, we return to the sac of the recipient twin and drain fluid levels back to normal. Within about two weeks the urine output and fluid levels around both twins should have stabilised. We'll need you to rest afterwards. No working, Ms Gordon. No twelve-hour surgeries. I suggest you stay at home for three weeks.'

Sam nodded, but she seemed far away, in a world of her own. Yanis knew she had to be scared. Preparing herself to go under the knife once again. Something she hadn't done since childhood. It would most definitely bring back all those feelings of being helpless.

He felt helpless himself. In a situation in which he had no power. In which nothing he did would help at all. All he could do was support Sam and be strong for her and make sure that she followed doctor's orders. He would make sure of that.

'When will you do it?' he asked.

'First thing tomorrow morning. If you can get to the hospital for six, we could have you in Theatre by eight o'clock—how does that sound?'

They both nodded.

'We'll be there,' said Yanis, and looked to Sam. 'You go home, get ready, pack a small bag. I'll take care of your patients today and see if Ms Gupta can take over the scheduled surgeries for tomorrow.'

'Sure.'

He squeezed her hand tight and then looked at Mr Meyer. 'What are the risks of the procedure?'

'As doctors, you know that there is a risk with any surgical procedure. You need to fully understand that one or both of the babies might not survive. However, there are studies that show that babies treated with laser ablation are more likely to be free of neurological deficits than those who had only been treated with fluid reduction, and those who have the laser ablation generally remain in utero for longer than babies who don't have any surgical interference.'

'And the risk of the TTTS returning?'

'One study showed that the condition returned in fourteen out of a hundred and one pregnancies.'

'But *not* having the surgery puts the babies at risk?' Sam said.

'Unfortunately that is so. You also need to be aware of the risk of early rupture of the membranes. Having ablation might mean the rupture will happen within weeks of the surgery. There's also a risk of miscarriage and vaginal bleeding.'

'And the risk of infection,' Yanis added.

Mr Meyer nodded. 'It all sounds terribly grim, and I'm aware that it's not a wonderful choice that you're having to make. But in my opinion, if you want to have one or more babies by the time this pregnancy is over, then laser ablation is your best option. Despite all the risks.'

There seemed to be so much doom and gloom. They'd just have to hope that both babies made it through. That there were no complications. No infections. No loss of life.

Yanis turned and looked at Sam, knowing that if she got through this surgery he would do his damnedest to look after her and their girls. 'We'll do it. And I'll move in with Sam afterwards to make sure she rests.'

Sam opened her mouth as if to say something, but he stopped her.

'You have no choice in this matter. I'm going to look after you and you're going to like it. Okay?'

She seemed to think about that for a moment. Then she smiled and nodded as tears welled in her eyes. 'Thank you.'

Yanis sat next to Sam as she lay in her hospital bed, waiting to be taken down for her procedure. It was half past seven in the morning. As instructed, she'd had nothing to eat, only sips of water, after eight o'clock last night.

Sam had asked him to stay with her overnight at her flat, telling him that she didn't want to be alone the night before her procedure. That she needed someone to talk to her and keep her mind occupied whilst she waited.

But although they'd chatted about a variety of things, all Yanis could think about was those two girls inside her. His daughters. And the risk they were at. The risk Sam was at.

He'd got used to her. Used to having her by his side… used to the idea that they could be a family and that all his dreams just might come true. This hope that he felt welling inside, rising up out of his core, spreading throughout him, was agonising—because alongside it all was the doubt. The second-guessing. He couldn't lose them. Any of them.

Yanis struggled to internalise his feelings. Was this love? It was all frighteningly familiar. But although he desperately wanted to tell Sam what had happened in his past, he knew he couldn't do it right before this surgery. He couldn't put that extra worry on her—not right now.

If everything went well with the procedure and the babies were fine, then he'd say something. Because by then the TTTS would be fixed and they'd be in safer territory, knowing that even if their twins were born early they should be okay. Babies could survive if born after twenty-four weeks. It would be hard and a difficult road, but it was doable.

He'd tell her when she was recovered. When she was stronger. Because she *was* strong. Sam was strong. With all that she'd been through, look at how she'd come out on the other side of it. He admired her. More than she knew. For some people, stress and upset and heartache destroyed them, and they never recovered, but Sam…

He'd never realised the stress of holding in such a secret as his. And as he smiled at this woman he had come to care for a great deal, he wished he could take it all away for her. He'd happily take on that burden if it meant that Sam could be carefree again. He liked seeing her smile. He liked seeing her laugh. She'd not done much of that lately. She always seemed to be somewhere else. Distant. Her gaze unseeing, as if she was imagining the worst.

'It will be all right,' he said now, taking her hand and stroking it. 'Mr Meyer is the best and he knows what he's doing.'

She nodded. 'But this is *me*. Things tend to go wrong for me.'

Me too.

'We must be positive.'

'I know, but it's hard to be.'

'Maybe we should think of some names?'

She turned to look at him. 'Wouldn't that be tempting fate?'

He shook his head. 'No. It would be showing the world that we're not afraid to look forward. To plan. To hope for a good outcome. These girls—and you—are so precious to me. They're people already, no matter what happens, and I think they should have names.'

She smiled. 'I couldn't do this without you, Yanis.'

She reached up and stroked his face, and he leaned in for a gentle kiss.

'What about Yvette?' he asked.

She scrunched up her face. 'After your sister? What about Darcy?'

'It's a possibility. We should make a list.'

He got out his phone and brought up his notes app and typed in the name. 'Estelle?'

'Esme is nice. What about Addison?'

He smiled, relaxing somewhat. 'Charlotte? Isabella?'

He liked this. This moment of hope. He was lifting her. Supporting her. Showing her that what they were facing was possible. They could conquer it and come out on the other side. They only had to choose to believe it.

'Ms. Gordon? We're ready for you now.' A nurse stood at the end of the bed with a smile.

Sam turned to look at him. 'If anything happens…'

He got up, pressed his forehead to hers, holding her face in his hands. 'It won't.'

'You promise?'

He couldn't do that. He knew he couldn't. It was the one thing he couldn't promise and the one thing he wanted to promise more than anything.

The pain of keeping it in overrode logic. 'I promise.'

He dropped a kiss onto her lips and stood back as the nurse took hold of her bed and began to wheel her away.

He felt sick. Awful.

Feeling as if his future were being taken away from him, he stood there and watched.

Being helpless was the worst feeling in the whole entire world.

She dreamed she was young again. Lying in a hospital bed, her gown up over her stomach, while her mother sat by her bed, telling the doctors terrible things. Sam had something growing in her stomach—her mother was sure of it. She'd seen something move.

Sam was lying there frozen, unable to move, as the doctors stuck in big metal probes and moved them about. She could feel them doing something to her, but she couldn't stop it, so she began screaming and—

She woke slowly, blinking her eyes open to the sight of white ceiling tiles and fluorescent lights. There was the sound of a heart monitor…

Hospital. Right. She gazed down at her abdomen. *Still*

pregnant. Okay. At the side of her bed sat a nurse, writing things down on a clipboard.

Sam licked her lips. Her mouth felt dry. As if she'd not had a drink for hours. What was the time? She felt her voice would be croaky. 'Hey...'

The nurse looked up and smiled, putting the clipboard down on her chair. 'Hi. Your surgery went well and you're doing great.'

'It did? I am?' She felt relief surge through her—and then she fell asleep again. This time, thankfully, there were no bad dreams.

Much later she woke again, and this time she stayed awake.

The dark-haired nurse was smiling. 'Good, you're awake. We're about to take you back down to the ward.'

'Did everything go okay?'

She smiled. 'It went fine. Babies both doing very well.'

Sam felt reassured. At least for now. If the surgery had gone well, then that meant all she had to do was rest for a day or so in hospital, to recover from the surgery, then take bed rest at home for a couple of weeks. She could get back to work for a little bit longer before the babies arrived if all went well.

I hope so.

As the nurse wheeled her back onto the obstetrics ward, she saw Yanis get up from a chair and beam a smile at her. She felt her heart swell with happiness and joy to see him, and as she was wheeled into her bay, he took her hand and pressed his lips to it.

'Sam.'

'They say it went well, Yanis. We're all okay.' She felt so sleepy.

'I heard.' He bent over her and kissed her on the lips. 'How do you feel?'

'Bit tired…but I'm all right.'

'That's to be expected.'

'How long was I gone?'

'Too long. But you're back now, and it's good news, so all you need to do now is make sure you rest.'

Sam nodded. 'I'll try.'

'You will do more than try. And I'll make sure of it. Do you need a drink?'

'If there's any water, I'd love some.'

He passed her a plastic beaker with a straw in it and she took a few sips of iced water. The drink felt beautiful and cool upon her sore, dry throat, and she smiled her thanks afterwards.

'Are you okay?' she asked.

'I am now you're back. That was the longest wait of my entire life.'

'You don't have to stay with me now if you need to go. I'm just going to be lying here for the next day or two.'

'I'm fine exactly where I am. I'll go when visiting is over—move some of my stuff to your place, so that I can look after you properly when you're out.'

'You're sweet.'

'Sweet?' He smiled. 'I'm sure you meant devoted. Or courageous? Or heroic? *Heroic* is a good word.'

They were very good words. But she had another one, too. 'Well, I'm thankful. Thankful that I have you. If I'd had to go through this on my own, I don't know how I'd have done it.'

He smiled, gazing softly into her eyes. 'You'd have rocked it. But you're not alone. Not with me. Do you understand? I will always be here for you. Always.'

It meant so much to her to hear those words, and the fact that she and the babies meant so much to him made her feel as if she wanted to say something similar back to him. But the words *I think I might love you* got stuck in her throat. She was too afraid to say them.

He'd probably think she was just strung out on anaesthetic, anyway, and that she wouldn't remember saying it. She wanted the first time she said that to someone to mean something. To be clear. To have no doubt about how much she meant it.

Besides, she was afraid to say it. She'd never said it to anyone. Never come close. And they seemed such huge words, with such power and intensity and meaning... She hesitated, because what if what she was feeling *wasn't* love? It could be infatuation, or something else. How would she know? She'd never experienced it before. She could just be confused.

And what if she said it and Yanis didn't feel the same way? That would be mortifying. Especially if he didn't say it back. Yanis might be saying all these wonderful things now, but what if he was just saying them because he was worried about the babies? About his two little daughters? And there was still the matter of Yanis holding back on something. Keeping something of himself back from her. She couldn't say *I love you* unless she felt she had every single part of him.

I'm racing ahead here.

Sam closed her eyes and allowed herself to drift in the fog of anaesthesia. It was easier there. She didn't have to face her feelings...her doubts, her fears, her confusion over Yanis. She didn't have to lie there thinking about how she was in hospital. A patient again. After surgery. And that something had been truly wrong with her this time.

Drifting was kind of blissful.

It meant she didn't have to face up to anything and confront it.

CHAPTER EIGHT

'Oh, my God, what's this?'

Sam laughed as Yanis walked into her bedroom carrying a tray. Upon the tray was a small vase with a mini bouquet of pink and purple flowers, a saucer with croissants and butter curls, a pot of strawberry jam, a plate of scrambled eggs and crispy bacon and a bowl of fresh fruit. Two glasses of freshly squeezed orange juice and a large cafetière of coffee.

'I can't eat all of that!'

'It's for both of us. I thought we could have a bed picnic for breakfast.'

'You're quite the picnic man, aren't you? I could get used to this.'

She let him plant a kiss upon her lips as he set the tray down on the bed and clambered on beside her. This last week or two at home with Yanis had been wonderful. He'd truly been the perfect carer. Bringing her breakfast every morning. Bringing her a cup of tea when she needed one and even when she didn't. Making her a fresh lunch or popping out to get her something she was craving. Cooking a homemade meal every night. He took care of the laundry, the shopping... He'd even assembled the buggy, when it arrived, and built the cots and sorted the nursery in her spare room at her exacting instructions.

He was considerate, caring, empathetic. He truly was the most wonderful man she had ever met. And every day her feelings for him became stronger and stronger.

The more time she spent with him, the more that they talked, and the more she wished she could say the words she was too scared to say. Three little words. But three words with such import, such deference, such power... She knew that, once said, they would change everything. They would move her and Yanis's relationship forward into territory where maybe Yanis did not want to go.

She believed that he felt the same way. At least, she hoped so. Why else was he here, looking after her so well?

And yet every time she had that thought, asked that question, she heard her mother's voice in the back of her head telling her, *It's not you he's caring for... It's those babies.* Why was it that every time she had a doubt, that doubt spoke in the voice of her mother?

It couldn't be true, could it? Yanis seemed so genuine. So kind. She had never got the impression from him that he was caring for her only because of her role as incubator for his children.

But doubt still remained. The only time Sam had been important to other people was when she could give them something. To her mother, she had been a conduit for attention.

What if Yanis was only attending to her because he wanted the babies? More than he wanted her? What if he was leading her to believe that she was important so that he got what he wanted? His daughters. And then, once they were born, would she see less of him? Would he create a distance between them?

Sam was used to being used for other people's sakes. Her mother had used her, had even caused her harm, to get what she needed emotionally. And if her own mother could do that...

She bit into a croissant, ignoring the flakes of rich, buttery pastry that fell to the bedspread.

'Mr Meyer said you can start getting up today,' said Yanis. 'Moving around. I thought we could take a walk around the block...get you some fresh air?'

'That would be great. Being waited on hand and foot is wonderful, but cabin fever is not.'

He smiled. 'Why don't you freshen up and get dressed, whilst I clear all of this up?'

She nodded, and heard him clanking around in the kitchen as she got washed and dressed.

The sun was shining and summer had arrived. It would be nice to be outside.

He met her by the door, gave her a long, slow kiss that had her wishing they were heading back into the bedroom, rather than outside, and then took her hand and led her out.

They didn't go far. Just enough to do a bit of window shopping as she gazed adoringly at a shop filled with baby clothes, imagining dressing her own girls in all the pretty dresses she could see. Then they stopped at a small café and chose a table outdoors on the pavement.

A waitress came to get their order and they asked for lattes, still too full from breakfast to ask for anything to go with them.

'This is nice,' Sam said, sipping at her milky coffee.

'We should bring the girls here when they're older,'

said Yanis. 'There's a children's area inside, filled with toys and books and a small ball pool.'

Sam smiled. 'It's nice to think of the future like that.'

'It is. And now you're through the surgery, there's no reason why we shouldn't think of it more often.'

'Do you think we're ready?'

'I hope so.'

She nodded and put down her mug. 'We haven't really spoken about the future. About when they're here. About how we'll share them.'

He looked away, across the road, watching a mother push her child in a buggy. 'We'll find a way,' he said.

'We've got so close. You don't think that we ought to…?'

He glanced back at her. 'Ought to what?'

She shrugged. Embarrassed. *Move in together?* They were practically living together now, and it was *so good*.

She sucked in a breath and made a less risky suggestion. 'Think about how we're going to fit in parenting around our work schedules.'

'I'm sure Elliot will be willing to work with us both.'

Sam nodded. 'He's a good man. And so are you.'

He smiled. *'Merci.'*

'You do know that if there's anything you want to tell me, you can? I want you to feel that I'm here as much for you as you seem to be for me.'

'I know.' He looked at her, as if thinking about saying something else, but then obviously decided against it.

She wondered what had passed through his mind, but said nothing as he got up and held out his hand to help her to her feet. As they continued their walk down the street, she wondered what it was that bothered him. Something did, and she was terrified that it was something huge—that she had read him wrong.

Because she was really falling in love with Yanis, and if it wasn't reciprocated, she could see herself getting very hurt indeed.

'I just think it's time I faced the truth head-on. I can't keep going like this.'

Martin Merriweather, Yanis's private patient, sat in front of him, his tremors plainly visible. It was clear that he had reached his limit, and from his movements, Yanis felt sure that Mr Merriweather wouldn't even be able to sit and hold his own cup of tea without a spillage occurring. And the tremors weren't just in his hands. His bottom lip quivered, and he walked with a hunched gait, as if he couldn't lift his feet off the floor properly.

'Surgery is a big step, Martin. You're definitely sure you want to proceed?'

His patient leaned forward. 'My wife and I want to renew our vows. We've set the date for next year. We're going to have a big ceremony. Make up for the small registry office thing we had forty years ago. Our children are going to be there. Our grandchildren. And I, for one, would like to walk my wife down the aisle without looking like I'm being electrocuted.'

Yanis nodded. 'I understand.'

'These tremors are getting beyond a joke, Doctor. They affect everything. Surgery has always been my last resort option, and I'm there. I want to try the deep brain stimulation. I'd like to have my last few final years with control of my body. Is that too much to ask?'

'Of course not. But before we allow you to have DBS, we have to assess you for a period of months, both on and off your medication. You'll also need an MRI. It's procedure. But if we find you're a suitable candidate, we can proceed.'

Yanis typed on his keyboard and then turned the screen around so that Martin could see a diagram of what happened during surgery.

'Okay. So, if you meet the criteria, what we do is this: we insert a pulse generator—it's a bit like a pacemaker—under the skin in your chest area. That generator is connected to some very fine wires that are inserted into specific areas of your brain that allow motor control. Do you see here?'

Yanis pointed out the various parts on screen.

Martin nodded.

'We switch on the generator and the electrodes deliver high-frequency stimulation to the area that is targeted. This stimulation changes the electrical signals in your brain that cause the symptoms of your disease.'

'Like jump leads for a car?'

'Sort of. But if you definitely want to proceed down this path, I must reiterate the fact that this surgery is not a cure, and it won't stop your Parkinson's from progressing.'

'I know.'

'But it should give you better control of your movements.'

'Good. That's good. You don't realise what you miss doing... I can't even sign my own name. Can you imagine how that feels?'

Yanis nodded. 'I can imagine the difficulties. But, as with all surgery, there are risks involved. Bleeding. Stroke. And you'll have to consider whether you will be able to cope with the part of surgery when we wake you to check your movements.'

'I'd be *awake* for the surgery?'

'Oui.'

'With my skull open?'

Yanis smiled. *'Oui.'*

'Okay… What else?'

'You'll need to stay in hospital afterwards for a few days—to recover, and also so that we can monitor your stimulator settings and adjust your medication so that you get the most benefit from your surgery.'

'Okay, Doc, so how do I proceed?'

'You definitely want to go ahead?'

'I do.' Martin smiled, as if already imagining himself at the altar next to his wife.

Yanis nodded. 'All right. So, I shall write to your GP, instructing him on how we wish to do the assessment first. You're currently on your medication, so I'll want you to keep a diary for a couple of weeks, detailing what your tremors are like, what difficulties you're having, what things you are able to do by yourself. After that we will discuss how to safely take you off your medication. Obviously at this point your wife will have to keep the diary for you, if you have difficulty writing or typing. Then we'll schedule your MRI and look at all the results. If you're a candidate, we'll make an appointment for surgery.'

'Thank you, Doctor.'

When his patient had gone, Yanis found himself thinking about Martin Merriweather. The man had been through enough and decided he needed to face the truth of his situation and try to make it better. Medication had helped mask his symptoms for a while, but the truth of a situation always came to the fore.

Yanis knew that he had to do the same thing with Sam. He'd kept his secret for far too long and she was doing well now. The babies had made it through the ablation surgery and Sam was looking forward to returning to work. Surely they were all safe now? Surely now he could tell her about his past? About Giselle and the babies he had lost before?

He cared for Sam deeply. More than cared. It was possible that he loved her.

She was difficult sometimes, prickly on occasion, but he understood her. Worried about her. Enjoyed being with her. Looking at her smile lit up his life. Seeing her happy made him happy. When he wasn't with her, he found himself thinking of her and wondering what she was doing. He liked waking up with her. He liked going to bed with her. She was carrying his twin daughters and he could foresee a wonderful future for them all.

He'd missed being a part of something. Part of a family. Being with Sam gave him that feeling back, and he didn't want to lose it.

But he couldn't go into the future with his secret, and if he was going to give all of himself to Sam then she had to know him.

All of him.

Including his sad history.

Resolute, he decided to head for home.

Sam had laid the table for two. Ideally, she would have liked to go all out and really decorated the table—looked for a tablecloth, hunted down some long candles, maybe a small bouquet of flowers...

But instead of heading out to the florist's and picking up something special, she'd reused the small bouquet that Yanis had included on her breakfast tray that morning.

And, unable to go out and hunt down a fabulous lunch, she'd opened a couple of tins of soup and warmed some part-baked bread in the oven.

He would be home soon, and Sam was hoping that she could take the opportunity to talk about them and where they were heading, what their future would look like. By sounding him out on those issues, she'd be able to gauge where he was, and if she could finally say to him those magic words she dreamed of saying.

She pictured the look on his face when she said it. The way his eyes might light up...the way a smile might creep across his face. The way he might reach across the table to take her hand in his and whisper *I love you, too*.

If that happened... She couldn't imagine how happy she'd be. To have found someone like him. Someone who knew her history. Who really understood her, and loved her, and wanted to be in her life for ever.

They could have the dream. And why shouldn't she wish for it? Hadn't she already been through so much suffering? Eventually someone like her had to have some good luck, right?

She heard his key in the lock and felt her heart race at the thought of what she was going to say. She simply couldn't allow the thought that he might say nothing back.

These last couple of weeks since the surgery had shown her how much he cared. A man simply didn't do as much as he was doing for a woman if he didn't care deeply for her. She meant something to him—Sam was sure of it. And now she really wanted them to move forward, towards the birth of the twins, knowing exactly where they stood with one another.

Turning down the heat on the soup, she sat at the kitchen table, a smile upon her face.

He came in, carrying a folder or two, and put them down on the hall table. 'Something smells nice. Have you been cooking? I told you not to do anything,' he admonished gently as he came into the kitchen and saw her sitting there.

He walked over and cupped her face, kissing her lightly on the lips.

'It's just some tinned soup. Hardly a roast dinner. How did it go with your patient?'

'We're going to do the assessment to see if he's a candidate for DBS.'

'Well, fingers crossed he is. Why don't you sit down and let me look after you for a change?'

Yanis shook his head. 'No, you stay seated. I'll finish it off. Is that bread in the oven?'

'Yes. It should be ready, if you're hungry.'

'Starving. What drink do you want with your meal?'

'Just tea would be great.'

Butterflies were swirling in her stomach. But they were so good together. The domestic set-up worked for them both. She was happy to have Yanis in her home and he *fitted*. They were perfect together.

The urge to blurt out what she wanted to say was incredibly strong, but she thought they should eat first.

Yanis served up the meal, and soon they were both tucking into French onion soup. It was beautiful with the warm crusty bread and, despite her nerves, Sam devoured everything.

As she sipped her tea, she decided to broach the subject. 'So, I can go back to work soon. Things are moving on... There haven't been any problems with the twins... I feel great. Strong. I guess we really need to start looking towards the future.'

He nodded. 'I guess we do.'

'I've really enjoyed having you here with me, Yanis. I wouldn't have been able to do it without you.'

'It's been my pleasure. It's been good for us.'

'It has.'

Was this her moment? The now or never?

But Yanis spoke first. 'I've been wanting to talk to you, actually.'

'Oh?'

Perhaps she wouldn't have to be the one to put herself out there. Perhaps Yanis was going to do it first?

Relief flooded through her and she beamed, looking at him. Trying to show him that she was ready to hear it. Ready to hear what he had to say and that she'd *welcome* it. She was encouraging him to say what he needed to say. She'd told him before that he could tell her anything.

'I've been wanting to do it, but I wanted to wait for the right time.'

He seemed nervous. She could understand that. She was nervous, too. So she did what she'd expected *him* to do. She reached out and took his hand.

'You can tell me anything,' she said.

This was it. She felt it. The crucial moment when he would tell her what had been bothering him, and then she would know, and it would be nothing at all, and they could skip into the future as a happy couple.

At least, she hoped so.

Yanis gave a quick, nervous smile. 'Okay. I guess I can, now that you're better. Now that you're stronger. Now that everything has gone so well.'

She laughed. He was making her nervous now. 'What is it?' she asked.

He bit his lip, squeezed her hand and let out a breath. 'I used to be married.'

What? She heard the words, but they were so unexpected, so out of the blue, that at first she didn't quite understand them.

'Married?' She pulled her hand free of his. Shocked.

'*Oui.* Giselle and I had known each other since school. We were great friends first, before we fell in love.'

Sam's stomach churned. *Giselle.* The name itself sounded so beautiful and exotic—as if she was someone Sam could never, ever dream of comparing herself with without losing.

'We got married as soon as we could. It seemed silly to wait. We had already been together all those years— we wanted to get married and start a family as soon as we could.'

Start a family?

A deep, dark sense of dread began in Sam's stomach and she suddenly wished she'd not eaten all that food.

Yanis had been married before.

'Giselle got pregnant just as I got into medical school…'

Yanis's gaze was fixed on a distant object. As if it was safer for him to look somewhere else other than into Sam's eyes. As if he didn't want to see her reaction. As if the act of her pulling her hand free of his had told him that they weren't as close as he'd hoped.

'We were both ecstatic and we told everyone we knew. But then she lost the baby a couple of weeks after.'

Sam stared at him, imagining that loss. 'I'm sorry,' she whispered. They were the only words she could squeeze out of her tight, locked-down throat.

'We were both hit hard by the loss, as I'm sure you

can imagine, but we knew that miscarriage was unfortunately common with first pregnancies, and so after some time we decided to try again.'

Sam's heart was thudding hard. Every beat was a painful knock inside her chest. She could feel herself growing hot. Could feel her legs becoming shaky and was not sure she wanted to hear any more of this.

'She got pregnant again, and this time we were more cautious. We decided not to tell anybody until she'd got to twelve weeks and we'd had a scan. She seemed fine. We thought everything was going well. Until they told us at the scan that they couldn't find a heartbeat.'

Sam closed her eyes, imagining the horror of that sort of thing happening to them. How did you get past something like that?

'She had a D&C and both of us were broken into pieces.'

Sam rubbed at her belly with her free hand, glad that she could feel her own babies kicking and moving.

'We were hit hard, and we dealt with it in different ways. I worked harder. Giselle retreated into herself. She saw doctors who told us that we weren't exceptional, that we just needed to keep trying.'

'What happened?'

She didn't want to hear the answer, but she *needed* to hear how this ended.

Now he looked at her, imploring her with his eyes to understand.

'We'd had all these dreams of becoming a family. Dreams of what that might be like. I wanted us to try again, but I knew I had to wait for Giselle to want the same thing and not put pressure on her. Eventually she began talking about trying for one last time. But she said that if this one didn't work out, then she didn't know what we'd do. We began trying and she fell pregnant once again.'

Sam realised she was holding her breath and had to force herself to breathe.

'Once again we were quietly cautious, quietly happy. We didn't dare to hope. But at the first scan everything went well, and we finally began to believe that we would be okay. We told everyone and, like us, they were cautiously optimistic.'

Sam saw the grief in him, saw it so openly laid bare, and realised that all this time with her he must have been so scared that they were going to lose the babies. Suddenly her heart melted into a puddle at his pain. She wanted to scoop him up into her arms and hold him tight and never let him go. But she couldn't.

'Then, at thirty weeks, she realised she couldn't feel the baby moving. We rushed to the hospital and they told us that the baby had died.'

'Oh, Yanis…' She couldn't stop herself. She got up and went around to his side of the table. He stood and she took him in her arms, shocked to feel him trembling.

'I so wanted to tell you!' His voice broke. 'But I couldn't. I didn't want to terrify you—not when you were already so scared about what might happen. I kept it inside…to protect you.'

Now she understood. How scared he must have been! And all this time she'd thought that only she could truly imagine how it might all go wrong for them.

She took his hand and walked with him over to the couch. Sat him down. 'What happened then?' she asked.

'Giselle had to give birth. They induced her, and she had to go to a special suite for mothers whose babies were stillborn. But we could still hear other mothers with their perfectly healthy babies in other rooms. And every time we heard a baby cry out, it broke us.'

'I don't know what to say...'

'We had a little boy. We named him Jacques. We got to be with him for a while, but eventually we had to let him go. Then we went home and tried to grieve.'

Sam wiped her eyes. This was unimaginable. To think Yanis had held all this inside him... He must have been so scared. No wonder he hadn't told her.

'But losing Jacques broke us apart. I tried to be there for Giselle, but whatever I did was not enough. I wanted to be with her, talk to her, comfort her. But every time I tried to touch her she'd flinch. She dealt with her grief by retreating. Every time I went near her she turned away from me. Like she didn't want me near her...like she blamed me.'

'I'm so sorry.'

'We split up eventually, and I knew I could never go through all that again.'

She nodded. 'Until *I* got pregnant?'

'*Oui.*'

Sam felt awful for everything he'd been through. She wanted to comfort him, but she was reeling from all this information.

The conversation had not gone as she'd been expecting, but now was not the time to say what she'd wanted to say. Plus...she wasn't sure if she even could now.

This was a huge secret. Something Yanis had kept to himself throughout the entire time she had known him. What else might there be? What else didn't she know about him? Were there any more secrets lurking in his past?

It made Sam feel that maybe she didn't know Yanis

as well as she'd thought. Maybe she'd had a lucky escape in not saying anything. Maybe she needed to take some time to get to know Yanis more.

She wished that he had told her before—but she was also glad that he hadn't told her. If she'd known about it in advance, she would have been even more terrified about something going wrong with the pregnancy.

The dilemma was confusing.

All of this was confusing.

And now she didn't know how to feel.

But she did want to be there for him the way he had been there for her throughout all this.

Sam laid her head upon his shoulder. He'd said he hadn't ever wanted to go through all this again and look what had happened. Did he just mean the pregnancy? Or becoming a father? Or did he mean more? Becoming a husband? A 'significant other' in a relationship?

'I felt like I'd failed my wife. That I hadn't been able to protect her. That I hadn't been able to stop her from getting hurt. I blamed myself after she left.'

'It wasn't your fault. You weren't to know what would happen.'

'I was so scared when you went in for surgery. I wasn't sure I could stand it. It was one of the most terrible waits in my entire life.'

'But we got through it.' She lifted her head and turned to look at him, tears in her eyes. 'We're okay. We're good.'

He raised her hand to his lips and kissed it. 'I know. Do you see now why I needed to be here to look after you?'

'I do.'

'I want to be here all the time, Sam. I know I have my own place—I know that. But being here with you every day… To go back to my own place now, after all of this, would make me feel…lost.'

'What are you saying? Are you asking to move in permanently?'

She almost didn't dare to think about it. The Sam she'd been before his revelation would have welcomed it, but the Sam she was now had some reservations. She loved him, yes, but he'd blown her out of the water with this. She needed time to think. She needed time to take it all in. He'd kept this massive secret from her and…

She felt ashamed for her next thought.

What if Giselle hadn't left him but he'd left her? To find someone who could give him the family he wanted?

She shook her head to clear the thought from it. No. That couldn't have happened.

'I want to be with you,' he said.

Sam nodded. Unsure what else to do. She could hardly kick him out and say no right now.

'Let's take it one day at a time, huh?'

Yanis smiled and kissed her. 'One day at a time sounds perfect.'

Standing in the car park, looking up at the hospital, Sam felt that her stomach was full of butterflies.

'Nervous?' Yanis held her hand.

Yes. And not just about this.

'Yeah, it feels strange to be back. I want to work—I do. I just feel like there's going to be a lot of questions. Maybe I can hide out in clinic all day.'

Yanis laughed. 'You don't have to go in if you don't want to. You could start early maternity leave. I'd support you in that.'

He'd said that before. But his need to wrap her in cotton wool seemed overpowering to her now, rather than nurturing. She couldn't get the thought out of her head that he might only be interested in the babies.

'We've already discussed this. Me staying at home would be a nightmare solution. I'd go crazy without a scalpel in my hand. Without being in Theatre. Being a neurosurgeon is who I am.' She turned to look at him. 'I'm fine. Mr Meyer has given me the all-clear and I'm back now.'

'Just remember to take it easy. You're nearly eight months pregnant with twins. I want to see you eating and drinking and, most importantly, sitting down whenever you get the opportunity.'

'You don't have to babysit me, Yanis. I'm a grown woman.'

Was Yanis just desperate to start a family? To replace what he had lost? Maybe he'd never expected to start a family with her, but it had happened, so he was making the best of it?

She hated having these invasive thoughts. Because everything about him screamed that he was nothing like that. Only he'd lost so much... And she could imagine that if she'd been the one to lose three babies, having another baby would be the only thing on her mind.

'Indulge me,' he said.

He kissed her, and she allowed herself to sink into it. To enjoy the pleasure of his touch. Because what if all this was fleeting? What if it went away the second the girls arrived?

She hated feeling needy, but she was hormonal and scared. And she was feeling enormous now. Nothing fitted very well, she always felt her ankles hurting by midday, and if she ate anything she got heartburn.

But she knew that if she got the chance to get inside Theatre, then all of that would go away. With a scalpel in her hand, she could make the outside world disappear while she fixed someone's brain or spine. She needed that much more than she needed to be sitting at home watching cookery shows, waiting for her contractions to start.

She'd come such a long way. It was hard to think that at the beginning of this she'd hated the idea of becoming a mother. Had feared it. But with Yanis at her side, she had grown. He had helped her see that she could be anyone she wanted to be. They'd both been through some terrible times, but the future looked bright for both of them now. All they had to do was keep it together.

Maybe the babies arriving would make everything better? Maybe the doubts would go away and she would see Yanis as the perfect partner again?

Because he was. He'd shown her no reason to believe that her fears were real. This was all coming from inside her own mind. Her own suspicions. Because she'd been used before. By her own mother. The finishing line for them both was so close now…she could soon have everything she wanted!

Yanis seemed brighter since sharing his burden. He smiled more. Laughed more. He really seemed to be enjoying the time he spent with her and she loved being in his company. But there was still something… An edge. A sharp edge that cut her if she tried going near it. The babies weren't here yet. They weren't completely out of danger. Anything could happen. Who knew? Yanis had thought his son Jacques was out of danger and look what had happened there.

Since he'd told her, Sam had been almost militant in ensuring she could feel her babies moving. She took the time to notice. She counted movements. Made sure she felt more than ten every day, panicking whenever she only felt kicks in one place, thinking something had happened to one of the twins, but not the other.

Yanis had had such awful luck with pregnancies in the past. What if there was something fundamentally wrong with both of them?

Would she relax once the babies were born? Maybe. All she'd have to worry about then was SIDS, or meningitis, or a whole host of other terrible things.

Wow. Parenting is one long worry.

She saw her friend Gil talking to a patient in a wheelchair over by the entrance and gave him a wave. He waved back as they went over to the lifts and pressed the button that would take them up to the neuro floor.

'You've got your outpatient clinic first?'

Yanis's question brought her thoughts back to the present.

She nodded. 'Yeah. It's a light day—half as many patients as usual. Sonja has followed my instructions not to fill my diary this first week, so I should be done by midday if any emergent surgeries happen.'

Sonja was her secretary.

'And if there's any problem you'll call me—for anything.'

She smiled. 'I will. You're in surgery?'

'*Oui.* Pituitary tumour removal up first, I believe.'

The lift doors pinged open and they walked their separate ways.

'Sam?' Yanis turned around.

'Yes?'

'Take it easy.' He grinned and blew her a kiss.

Automatically she reached out to catch it, then felt

silly. But who cared? No one else was around, and she actually quite liked the way he looked out for her.

Sam pressed the kiss to her face and, determined to think good thoughts, headed to her morning clinic.

As Yanis successfully removed the pituitary adenoma on his patient, he let out a sigh of relief. Hopefully now his patient would suffer fewer headaches and get back the peripheral vision that he was losing.

'You wouldn't think it would matter, Doc. Not being able to see the stuff that you wouldn't normally notice. But when it's gone...when you don't have it any more... you realise how important it was and how much you want it back.'

He sympathised. Of course he did. He was missing so many of the simple things in life whilst he was worrying about Sam. Not being able to tell her his secret, fretting all the time, needing to know she was okay, making sure she wasn't having any weird symptoms. He was so focused on Sam he couldn't see anything else. He had tunnel vision. Only making sure Sam and the babies were okay.

Having told her everything, he felt as if a weight had been lifted a little. Not totally. Since telling Sam, she'd been...a little different towards him. Not hugely different, but it was almost as if he felt she was looking at him in a strange way...a considering way—as if she was trying to make her mind up about something.

He'd been so scared of telling her about Giselle, hoping she wouldn't freak out. She hadn't done that, but still something was off and he couldn't work out what it was. He didn't want to smother her with his feelings for her, so he was trying to give her space. Time to process all that he had told her. But it was hard to take a step back.

He liked being with her. *His Sam.* Beautiful, wonderful Sam. He liked her delicate hands. The way she moved, even heavily pregnant. She looked *good.* Those things had always been there, but his mind was focused so intently on keeping Sam and the babies safe that he'd almost stopped noticing them.

It had happened with Giselle, too—especially with that last pregnancy. Of course Giselle had pushed him away, accused him of suffocating her, of not giving her a moment's peace, and he'd tried to learn from that. He'd tried not to suffocate Sam and give her space and opportunity without constantly being there...hovering. It was hard, but he was doing it. Giving space to the woman he loved when all he wanted to do was be there for her and protect her and keep her safe. When all he wanted was to be stuck to her side like a limpet?

He smiled. They'd get through it. They were stronger than they'd ever been, and although he'd not really wanted her to return to work, he'd known he had to take a step back and let Sam make the choice. It was her body. Her life. And she was a grown woman, intelligent and creative and beautiful. He had to show her that he trusted her.

After all, she would be in the right place—a hospital—if help was needed, and at work he could keep an eye on her still. Not because he didn't trust her. He did. Implicitly. It was just that she was so near the end of her pregnancy now, and labour could start at any time.

It was difficult at night time, when they lay in bed together. He would spoon her, inhale her scent, his nose nestled in her hair. He'd hold on to her, and his body would want to do all the wonderfully delightful naughty things he could think of. But sex had been taken off the agenda since the ablation. It had seemed the safe thing to do and neither of them wanted to break that, no matter how turned on they got.

He missed that intimate connection, but he knew they'd get it back.

He just had to be patient.

He just had to wait.

And if this pregnancy had taught him anything, it had taught him to be patient.

CHAPTER NINE

HER MORNING CLINIC went smoothly. She was able to sit for most of it and just talk to her patients—check to see how they were doing post-surgery and post-rehabilitation. These were the clinics she really enjoyed, seeing the progress her patients had made, how their lives were different—how much she and her entire team had helped change a life.

On occasion there were patients who still had some difficulties, but they were getting there, adapting to a new situation and accepting a new normal. They inspired her. Made her see that if they could overcome great individual barriers and move beyond them to complete things they'd never thought possible, then so could she.

This pregnancy had changed her so much, and beyond that, Yanis had helped her grow, too. She was contemplating being a mother without fear, feeling that she had the power within her to do it, and that together they were strong. And now they were *so close* to the finishing line.

They met for lunch in the hospital cafeteria, and she was just contemplating going home early when she was paged by Accident and Emergency to consult on a case.

'Let me take it,' Yanis said. 'You go home and get some rest.'

'It's fine, honestly. I've been sitting all day. It'll do

me good to waddle down there. Let me go and see what the case is, and if it's surgical then I'll let you take it.'

He nodded. 'All right.'

She headed down to A & E and was directed to Majors, where she was told about an elderly gentleman called Edward Forster. She went to see him and found him lying in bed with a middle-aged woman sitting beside him.

'Hello, I'm Samantha Gordon. You must be Mr Forster?'

The man just looked at her.

'He can't speak. We think he's had a stroke,' said the woman.

'Are you family?'

'No. I'm Sylvie. I work at a dog rescue centre and Edward is a volunteer with us. He walks the dogs.'

'And can you tell me what happened today, Sylvie?'

As Sam performed her examination on Edward, Sylvie explained what had happened.

'He'd just come back from walking Duke and was putting him back into his kennel when he suddenly seemed a bit unsteady. When I got to him he was slumped on the ground and his face looked odd. I did that FAST thing you see on that advert on television, and it seemed to show he'd had a stroke.'

Sam agreed. Her own FAST assessment on Edward—checking his face to see whether it had fallen on one side, seeing whether or not Edward could raise both arms and keep them there, what his speech was like—had made it clear that Edward was experiencing an event.

'What time was this exactly?'

'About twelve-thirty.'

Sam nodded. Edward's face had a slight droop to the left side, his left hand could not be raised as high as the right and seemed weaker in its grip, and he had aphasia. She needed to get him to a CT scan immediately. It would tell them if Edward had had an ischaemic stroke, caused by a blocked artery in the brain, or a haemorrhagic stroke, caused by a burst blood vessel.

'Do you know if he has any other medical problems?' she asked.

'I don't... Sorry.'

'I'm going to get him to CT. If you've got any contact details for his family, you should call them—or give the numbers to the nurse and she can do it for you.'

Sylvie nodded. 'Will he be all right?'

'We'll do our best for him.'

She could never promise that a patient would be one hundred per cent recovered, because she just didn't know. Sam could operate on hundreds of stroke victims and the results would all be different. There would be successes and failures. And although relatives and friends just yearned to have confirmation that everything would be all right, she could not promise anything except to do her very best.

Sam left to order the CT, and then asked a nurse to page Yanis. She wanted him available if surgery was needed.

When the CT scan results came in and showed that Edward was having a haemorrhagic bleed in his brain that would need surgery, she phoned Neurosurgery and told them to prep Theatre for a craniotomy.

Then she called Yanis. 'Are you free to complete the surgery?'

'Sure. No problem. I'll be there in a minute.'

'I'll meet you there.'

Yanis was gowned and gloved and ready when she saw him next.

'Look after him,' she told him. 'He's a good guy. Volunteers at a dog shelter. We need people like him.'

'I will. Are you going home?'

'I thought I'd wait and see how the surgery goes. You'll come find me when it's done?'

'*Oui.*' Yanis headed into Theatre and for a brief moment she watched him from the scrub room, wishing that she was in there. Maybe she'd do the next surgery that came along? She ached to get back to it.

Sam went to her office and caught up on a bit of paperwork, dictated a couple of letters to be sent to GPs. Just when she thought she ought to check on how Yanis was getting on in surgery, her pager went off. She was needed yet again in Accident and Emergency.

She headed down in the lift, rubbing at her abdomen as her girls happily kicked and stretched as if they were doing some sort of twin yoga workout, and arrived in A & E to find the doctors swarming around a teenage girl.

From the doctor leading the case, she discovered that the seventeen-year-old had been cycling on her way home from college, without a helmet, and had been hit by a car and flung over the bonnet, landing on the road head-first. She was unconscious, and bleeding from multiple contusions.

Sam pushed to the head of the table to do a neuro exam and it was soon clear that there was some head trauma. Not just from the gaping gash that had been bandaged by the paramedics, but also from the evidence of a blown pupil.

'Let's get her to CT—stat.'

Sam stepped back and allowed the team to rush the

young girl—Jahira Stevens—to the scanning department. They needed to get her into surgery quickly. Every second counted, but she couldn't afford to operate blind. She needed to know what was going on.

'Page Mr Baptiste and find out how much longer he'll be in surgery, then tell him to meet me in Theatre Two.'

As the scan images came in, Sam could see that Jahira had a massive bleed on the right side of her brain and that they would need to go in and evacuate the clot.

She'd not planned on doing any surgery today. By rights, she should be at home by now, resting. But she was glad that she was here to help this young girl, who still had all her future in front of her and, if Sam was quick, would hopefully get through this trauma with all her faculties. Her neck was clear, so they didn't have to worry about paraplegia. All Sam had to do was fix this girl's brain.

As she scrubbed in the scrub room, she felt the adrenaline begin to surge, as it always did when she was about to do a surgery. The feeling was familiar, and welcome, and it made her feel as if she was truly back. Back to being the Samantha Gordon she knew she could be.

Confident. Clear-headed. In control.

Yanis pulled off his scrub cap and mask, signing the chart for a nurse as he did so. 'Let's get Mr Forster to neuro ICU. I want hourly obs—all right?'

'Yes, Doctor.'

As he started to scrub, his pager went off, and he pulled it from his pocket and frowned. A page to A & E?

He grabbed the nearest phone and discovered that another neuro case had come in and Sam had taken the patient to Theatre Two. He was to scrub in, when he could.

He quickly washed his hands. This other case meant that Sam must have gone into Theatre, which was slightly worrying. He hadn't wanted her doing any surgeries on her first day back. Surgeries were stressful and exhausting, even if at the time they felt as if they were energising you. He'd hoped that Sam would be resting by now. That she would be sitting with her feet up, sipping a hot cup of tea.

He should have known she would have taken this case straight away.

In Theatre Two, he rescrubbed and put on a fresh gown and mask. A nurse helped him on with his gloves as he walked through.

'What have we got?' he asked.

'Seventeen-year-old cyclist versus car,' said Sam. 'Blew her pupil, so I got her straight in. I've performed a craniotomy and I'm currently evacuating the clot.'

'Like me to assist?'

Sam looked up at him and her eyes creased, indicating a smile. 'Yes, please.'

He stood opposite her and helped provide gauze and suction. 'Nasty. Was she wearing a helmet?'

Sam sighed. 'No, unfortunately.'

'She could have saved herself a whole heap of trouble if she had been.'

'I'm sure everyone will tell her that when we get her into Recovery. This might just have been a one-off. Maybe she was in a rush and forgot to pick up her helmet. Maybe she usually wears one but something today made her forget. We can't judge her. We don't know.'

'Well, I'm going to damn well make sure that *our* girls wear helmets,' he said with passion.

Sam looked up at him. 'Oh, so you're going to be one of those fathers? Overprotective. A helicopter parent.'

He'd never heard that English phrase before. 'What does that mean?'

'It means you'll hover over them, paying close attention to their every move.'

He smiled at the image. 'You say that like it's a bad thing.'

Sam laughed. 'No. In fact, I like it. I love the fact that you want to protect them so much. It's nice. It's refreshing…'

'I hear a "but" coming…'

'But we won't be able to protect them from everything. At some point we'll both have to let go and trust them to do the right thing.'

'That's years away. For now, let me be a helicopter dad.'

She laughed. 'Okay.'

With the clot fully evacuated and the bleed stopped, Sam sighed and bandaged up the patient's head. 'Her brain has significant swelling. We can't put the skull flap back until it goes down a bit. Let's give her twenty-four hours and then we can bring her back in to complete the surgery.'

'All right.'

Sam had suddenly gone very still.

'Sam? Are you okay?' he asked.

She didn't look at him. She just continued to stare down before calmly handing her instruments to the nurse at her side. Then she took a step back and sucked in a breath.

Something was wrong. He knew it. All his instincts were aroused. 'Sam?'

'Er... Ms Gordon?' A scrub nurse spoke from behind Sam. 'I don't want to alarm you, but...you're bleeding....'

Yanis rushed around to the other side of the table to look at Sam. She stood there in pale blue scrubs and gown, but the bottoms were stained with red. A bright, alarming red that continued to spread as she bled actively.

'Nurse, take Jahira to recovery,' he said frantically.

And then he rushed to catch Sam before she fell.

'Yanis, what's happening?'

Sam lay on a trolley, being pushed rapidly through the corridors towards another theatre. Her heart was pounding so hard, so fast, she thought she might pass out. And she felt so weak. So fragile. And the look on Yanis's face was one of the utmost fear.

'Are the babies okay?'

She had to know. Had to know that she hadn't done anything wrong. Was this placenta praevia? Was the placenta tearing away from the uterine wall? Because if it was, then she could lose the twins, and she'd come too far to lose them now.

'I don't know. I've paged Obstetrics.'

'We need Mr Meyer.'

'I've paged whoever is free.'

'Yanis, we can't lose them. This isn't fair! I had the surgery. I did everything right. This isn't my fault!'

'It's no one's fault.'

'You told me we could do this. You said we'd be okay!'

'We will be.'

They turned a corner and her trolley bashed its way through the double doors that led into the pre-theatre room. It was normally where they anaesthetised their patients and made sure they were stable before taking them through to surgery.

Were they going to put her out?

They couldn't do that!

She needed to know they were okay.

Sam tried to sit up, but Yanis pushed her down.

'What are you doing? I need to—'

'Sam! Lie down! I need you to stay still.'

But she couldn't. Panicking now, she remembered going in for all those surgeries as a child. When they'd wheeled her through and her mum had had to let go of her and leave her in the hands of the doctors. She'd been so scared. She'd always tried to get up, but hands had pushed her back down, a mask had been placed over her face...

She'd felt herself losing control. Felt the fear, the horror of what was going to happen... She was about to be cut open... Someone would be rummaging around inside her when she didn't want it, didn't need it. There had been helplessness, hopelessness. No power to stop what was happening...

It all came flooding back now and Sam struggled, fought to get off the trolley. But she was too weak, too ineffectual to stop the hands that were holding her down. Yanis was holding her down. She wanted to stop him. Wanted to make him let go.

'This is *your* fault! I can't believe you're doing this to me. *You* made this happen. This is all your fault!'

'Sam—'

'I never wanted this. I never felt I could do this. But you told me! You told me I could do it. I knew I was broken, I knew I was faulty, and so did you! We were doomed from the start—both of us!'

'Sam!'

She pulled herself free of him. 'Admit it! You've only stayed because of the babies. Giselle didn't walk away from you—you walked away from *her*! When she couldn't give you a child!'

Yanis stared at her, shock written across his face.

Did that mean it was true?

Behind her, she heard the doors open and a familiar man's voice. Mr Meyer? And then he was there, pushing forward, past Yanis, who stepped back and out of sight.

The consultant began examining her, and through the muffled sounds as she began to fade into unconsciousness, she heard him say something about her placenta, about blood loss, about losing them all.

She tried to fight. She tried to stay awake. She tried to hold on to whatever shred of control she had left. But it was to no avail. Her eyes closed, and all the pain, the fear, the blood and the panic began to drift away until it did not exist at all.

Yanis sat in the waiting room, his head in his hands, utter despair washing through his body. Was it true what she'd said? *Had* he made her do this? Had he forced her to do something she hadn't wanted?

He didn't think he had.

But what if he'd done it without realising? What if he'd made her feel she *had* to do this? What if his own desire to have healthy children after his losses had made him push her into a choice she wasn't ready for? Had he put her life at risk just so he could have children?

If he had, then he would never forgive himself if he lost her. The idea of losing her was...unbearable. Inconceivable. Heartbreaking.

And that other thing she'd said—that last thing about

Giselle. Did Sam truly believe that of him? He felt sick at the thought. It had never been like that between him and Giselle. He had done what he could. What she had allowed him to do. She had been the one to push *him* away!

What was happening? Was he going to lose them all? Why wasn't anyone coming out to tell him what was going on?

Whenever he performed surgeries and knew there was family waiting outside, he would periodically send out a nurse to keep them updated. Why was no one updating him? He hoped it was because they were so busy saving Sam and the babies' lives that no one was free to take a quick stroll outside and let him know what was happening.

If that was the case, then so be it. He'd rather they were doing that. But… He sighed, letting out a long-drawn breath. It would be nice to know *something*.

He couldn't quite believe he was in this position. Sitting there. Waiting to hear whether Sam and the babies were okay. Whether they were even *alive*. Whether he would even have the chance to explain to her that she was so terribly wrong about him and Giselle.

After the ablation had gone so well, he'd imagined he'd finally get to be a father, sitting at Sam's bedside, holding her hand and mopping her brow as she laboured and gave birth. He'd dreamed of that moment. Fantasised about it—about how beautiful it would be to see his children come into the world.

But even that was being denied him now. All these physical things were going wrong…

Why was she trying to blame him?

Because she's scared, and scared people lash out.

He'd never even made it out of the starting gate as a

father. Ever. There had always been a problem, always a fault, always something devastating waiting for him around the corner. They should never have gone ahead with this. The risk was too great. It wasn't worth it.

Was Sam right? Was there something so fundamentally broken in both of them that they couldn't have children without risking their lives? He'd already lost three babies. He'd already been through hell. He'd already been left alone and broken. Was he doomed to have the same thing happen? Could he go through that devastation again?

No. I have to believe that Mr Meyer is saving them all.

He had to believe it. But he didn't know how. Didn't know how to sit with the guilt and the fear and the worry.

Yanis's pager suddenly went off, and he grabbed a phone and dialled the number.

Jahira's parents were still waiting for an update on how the surgery had gone. He'd not had a chance to speak to them—he'd rushed straight here with Sam.

He went over to the receptionist and told her that he'd be in Neuro, talking to the young girl's parents—reassuring them—and that they should page him when they had news. He wouldn't be long.

Yanis couldn't help Sam right now, but he could help that girl's worried parents. They had to be going out of their minds, wanting to know if the surgery had been a success, and he had let them down. He had put his personal feelings for Sam and the babies over his patient's family.

There's a pattern showing here. I'm selfish. Selfish beyond belief. Maybe Sam is right in that.

No one could hate him more in that moment than he hated himself.

* * *

Jahira's parents stood as he approached them in the neuro ICU. Yanis shook their hands and introduced himself.

'How is she doing?' asked her father.

'She's doing very well. The surgery went as expected, though we were unable to replace the bone flap due to some swelling, which we hope will go down in the next day or so.'

'What happens then?'

'Then we take her back into Theatre and replace it. For now, as you can see, she is all bandaged up, and there's a marker there for all staff, to remind them to be careful.'

'When will she wake up?'

'It could be any time. Surgery on the brain affects people differently. Plus, she has the trauma of the accident to deal with, so it may be a little while longer.'

'She's a good girl. She always wears her helmet. I don't understand why she didn't have it on.'

Yanis nodded. 'People do things sometimes that don't make any sense.'

'Will she be okay when she wakes up?'

'We don't know for sure. She received quite a severe knock to her brain, and it was injured. We removed the clot and repaired what we could, but we'll only know when she wakes up.'

'And if there's a problem?'

'Then she'll need to go through some physio. Some rehabilitation work. We have a very good department here at Barney's.'

'She has her whole life ahead of her, you know...?'

He nodded. He did know. He felt that way about his babies. He'd already lost three. Extinguished before they could even begin. Life wasn't fair.

'Jahira was our miracle baby,' said her mother. 'A complete surprise. I'd been told I couldn't get pregnant and... Well, she's our whole world.'

'I understand. Do you have any other questions?'

'No, thank you. You're busy. I'm sure you have other patients to worry about.'

He nodded and walked away towards the reception area, where he sank down into a chair and held his head in his hands before checking his bleeper, to make sure that the battery hadn't gone flat and that he hadn't missed anything.

These twins were *his* miracle babies. A complete surprise. Unexpected. Was it possible that he'd got so close to the finishing line, but wouldn't make it across? Had he somehow failed Sam in his duty to look after her? *Was* this all his fault? If it was—if he lost any of them—he would never forgive himself.

At that moment his bleeper sounded and he almost jumped out of his skin. Checking the number, he saw it was Theatre. He had to take a moment to steady his hand and take some deep breaths to slow his heart rate, before he picked up the phone and dialled through.

'This is Yanis Baptiste.'

Sam woke reluctantly. She'd been having a lovely dream. Something about riverboats and lying back in the sunshine with her fingertips trailing in the water, creating ripples that made music. It had been relaxing. Peaceful... But as she came back to awareness and blinked open her eyes, she heard the beep of monitors, smelled the familiar aroma of hospital and suddenly remembered what had been happening before she was put to sleep.

Tilting her head, she looked down at her abdomen.

The mountain she was used to seeing was gone. Her belly was substantially less domed than it had been the last time she'd seen it.

The realisation that her babies had been delivered hit hard. But they weren't in the room. There were no cots. Then she realised that someone was holding her hand and she saw Yanis, saw his tear-stained face, and her heart broke into a million pieces. She must have lost the babies.

'No!' She sobbed, hiccupping in great breaths.

'Sam... Sam, it's okay.'

'It's not okay! They're gone! They're gone and it's all my fault!'

'No, no, they're not gone. They're okay. They're in the NICU. They're alive!'

She stopped to stare at Yanis. Had he really said what she thought he'd said?

'What?'

'They're alive, Sam. They're doing great. We're parents.'

'We are?'

Yanis let go of her hand to reach inside his pocket for his mobile phone. He tapped at the screen to bring up his gallery. 'Look—I have pictures.'

She took his phone, noting a cannula in the back of her left hand that she hadn't noticed before, and gazed in sheer delight at the photos Yanis had taken of their two girls, lying side by side in incubators.

'How long have I been out?'

'All this happened yesterday. They had a little difficulty breathing when they came out, but Mr Meyer said it was just the shock of sudden delivery. They're going to be fine!'

'They are?' Sam burst into tears again. 'I want to see them.' She tried to sit up.

'You need to recover a bit more first. You lost a lot of blood. When your transfusion is done you can go up there.'

'What happened?'

'The placenta happened.'

'It came away?'

'*Oui*. I thought I was going to lose you all…'

'You could have.' She wiped her eyes. 'I shouldn't have blamed you. I was frightened. I thought I was going to lose the babies, and I thought that if that happened then I'd lose you, too.'

'You would never have lost me,' he said, with such certainty that she just had to stare at him for a minute.

'No? You lost Giselle. I thought…' She looked away, ashamed of her thoughts, ashamed of admitting her feelings. 'I thought that maybe you'd told me Giselle had walked away to save face—that *you* might have left *her*. To find someone who *could* give you a child.'

'You thought that of me?' He looked shocked. 'That I could be so cruel and selfish?'

She shook her head, wiping away more tears. 'I didn't believe it, Yanis! Honestly, I didn't. But it crossed my mind. Briefly. I'm not proud of it. And once I'd thought it, I couldn't get it out of my mind! I've always been used by other people. Used to get things that *they* want. When you told me about what had happened, all I could think was that you'd do anything to have a child. Anything to have a family. She couldn't give that to you.'

'So you thought I'd walked away from her?'

'Maybe… I don't know! I was scared. Afraid of being alone. I thought that if I prepared for it, if I justified it in my mind, then I wouldn't be so shocked if you *did* walk away. But it was because I didn't want to lose you. Because I thought that maybe you were with me just because of the babies.'

'Sam!' He shook his head. But then he looked at her, imploring her with his eyes. 'I *love* you. I've loved you for a long time. If the worst had come to the worst and we'd lost our girls, you still would have had me. I promise you that.'

'You love me?' His words seemed impossible.

He nodded, smiling. 'I do. And there is nothing in the whole wide world that will change that. I've been so scared, Sam. Scared of losing you all. Not just the babies. The idea of losing you... I could never have coped with that.'

Sam smiled back, reaching out for his face, stroking it, feeling the fear and the shame drift away. 'Can you ever forgive me for thinking all that?' she asked.

'There's nothing to forgive. You were scared. People do and say strange things sometimes when they're scared.'

He thought of Jahira. The girl who'd always worn a helmet but hadn't yesterday. Had she been scared? Had she set out in a rush because something had scared her?

'The surgery I did. That last patient. Jahira. Was she okay?' asked Sam.

Yanis nodded. 'She's fine. I'm going to go in tomorrow and replace the skull flap. The swelling has come down.'

'That's good. That's very good.'

'This is what I love about you.'

She smiled. 'What?'

'How much you care for other people. Even when you're at risk yourself, you still worry about others.'

'I'm not at risk any more.'

'Thankfully.'

'I have you. I have my girls. It all ended okay.'

'It ended more than "okay". It ended perfectly.'

She reached out and took his hand. 'You've been so patient. So strong. You've been there for me despite all my fears, as well as carrying a burden of your own. I love you so much. *Je t'aime*, Yanis.'

He raised an eyebrow. 'You've learned French?'

'Un peu.'

Yanis laughed. 'We might have to work on your accent!'

Yanis wheeled her into the NICU, and even though her heart was already full of love, it overflowed at the sight of her two girls, lying next to each other in one incubator.

'We had them in their own incubators to start with, but they wouldn't settle. I think they missed each other, so we put them together,' said a nurse.

Her two girls were identical. The same dark hair, the same noses, same mouths. They were beautiful, lying facing one another.

'Would you like to hold them?' asked the nurse.

'Can we?' Sam asked.

The nurse nodded. 'Let me get you a pillow.'

She gave Sam a pillow and then opened up an incubator to get out the first baby, laying her in Sam's arms within her open top, so that they could be skin to skin.

'And one for Dad?'

Yanis nodded, smiling, ripping off his tie and opening up his shirt, too.

'I'll leave you to it. I'll be just over at the nurses' station if you need me.'

'Thank you.'

Sam and Yanis both sat holding a baby, their gazes taking in everything about their daughters.

'Look at how they hold their hands the same way,' said Sam.

Both babies held one arm across their stomach and the other up by their face.

'We need to choose their names,' she said.

'We do. What do you think of Charlotte?' Yanis suggested.

She nodded. 'I like that… Charlotte Emmeline?'

Yanis looked up at her and, remembering their patient in Paris, nodded. 'I like it.'

'And this little one… What about Aurelie? Or Camille?'

'Or both? Aurelie Camille… That's beautiful.'

'Charlotte and Aurelie Gordon-Baptiste.' She laughed. 'That's quite a mouthful.'

'It could just be Baptiste.'

Sam frowned. 'What do you mean?'

'You could marry me.'

Sam held her breath.

Had he really just suggested marriage?

Could she imagine herself married to Yanis?

Yes, she could!

She laughed. 'I could…'

'Is that a yes?'

She thought back to the beginning. To that night when they'd first got involved and how she'd told herself always to be sure of her decisions. This one was easy to make.

'It is. *Oui.*'

Yanis leaned forward and kissed her. Softly. Gently. His eyes were full of love.

'You can still keep your surname, though. You don't have to take mine.'

'Are you kidding me?' She leaned forward and stroked his face. 'I want the whole world to know that I'm yours.'

* * * * *

THE DOCTOR'S REUNION TO REMEMBER

ANNIE CLAYDON

MILLS & BOON

CHAPTER ONE

IT WAS A brisk uphill walk from Richmond Station, and Dr Clemmie Francis was a little out of breath by the time she got to St Barnabas's Hospital. The large modern building sparkled in the sunshine, and Clemmie turned left at the main entrance as she'd been instructed, walking towards the older building that stood next door.

The neurological rehab unit was an example of a previous reincarnation of Barney's. Grand in quite a different way, with high arched windows and fancy brickwork, that would have been a state-of-the-art example of a modern hospital in Queen Victoria's reign.

Clemmie was a little early, so she crossed the road and sat down on a bench that was placed on the border of Richmond Park. She imagined that the windows of the neurological rehab unit afforded a magnificent view of the park, and that it would be possible to see for miles from the top floor of the building. A smile found its way from her heart to her lips. Seeing for miles was exactly what she wanted to do.

For too long now, she'd taken each day as it came, facing each new challenge as it presented itself. It had been a matter of self-preservation, a way to ignore a future that seemed to hold only jarring reverberations from the past. But slowly she'd made a new start. Found a place to live, scraped old paper from the walls and made it home. Found a new job, at a neurological rehab unit attached to a central London hospital. She'd been determined to shine, and she had.

And now she was on a fast track to promotion. The head of the unit was due to retire in six months, and Clemmie would be his successor. Spending six weeks here at Barney's, which was recognised as one of the best neurological rehab units in the country, was an opportunity to learn and prepare herself for her new role.

Clemmie filled her lungs with air. The future really did seem to be waiting for her, sparkling in the early morning sun. She took a moment to appreciate the feeling of anticipation, and then got to her feet. Turning up early on your first day was never a bad thing, and she just couldn't wait any longer.

The entrance of the older building gleamed in quite a different way from the main hospital complex. No vast sheets of glass or shimmering automatic doors. Here the pace seemed a little slower and quieter, and it was the polished wood of the lobby that caught the light. Beyond that, a large, bright space, where Clemmie could see a woman sitting behind a reception counter.

'Dr Clemmie Francis. I'm here for the director of the unit…' Clemmie handed over the letter from her hospital's administrator, who had dealt with her placement here at Barney's, and which instructed her to be here at nine this morning.

'Ah! Yes, we're expecting you.' The receptionist grinned. 'You wouldn't *believe* how many people have turned up here this morning instead of where they're supposed to be.

You're in the right place though. I'll give Dr Alexander a call. Sit down right there.'

Dr Alexander? A name from the past, which even now had the power to send shivers of agitation down Clemmie's spine. She turned, obediently walking over to the seat that the receptionist had indicated and sitting down.

It was nothing. How many Dr Alexanders were there in this world? More than one, clearly, and this one would probably be middle-aged and avuncular, if the welcoming style of the reception area was anything to go by. Or a woman, maybe…

Clemmie took a deep breath, going through all the reasons that this *couldn't* be the Dr Gil Alexander that she knew… Scrap that, the one she'd met seven years ago, had a brief fling with and clearly hadn't known at all. He'd be somewhere in the fast lane, getting his kicks from emergency medicine. That, or sitting back in a comfortable leather seat with private patients hanging on his every word. Maybe back in Australia…

Enough. Wherever Gil Alexander was, he was part of her past now. She'd moved on and she didn't need to wonder about him every time something happened to remind her of *that* mistake. The first domino to fall in a succession of others that had brought her world crashing down.

'You'll be with us for a while…?' The receptionist's voice came to her rescue and diverted her attention.

'Yes, six weeks. I work at the Princess Victoria Hospital in north London.'

'Ah. Nice.' The receptionist shot her a blank look. 'You'll like it at Barney's. Everyone's very friendly. And if there's anything you need, just come and ask me. I'm Maggie.'

'Thanks…' There was one thing. 'Could you tell me where the ladies' is, please?'

'Back there, turn left, and the lockers and the ladies' room are right in front of you.' Maggie jerked her thumb, pointing behind her. 'If you want to pop there now, Gil said he'd be five minutes.'

Dr Alexander. Gil. *Dr Gil Alexander.* Shock must have impaired Clemmie's reasoning ability, because she was already on her feet and halfway over to the door that the receptionist had indicated before she put it all together. And even then she was groping for some reason not to believe it. Maybe *this* Dr Alexander was Dr Gillian Alexander... No, Maggie had said *he*.

By the time she got to the washbasin in the ladies' room, her hands were shaking, and she turned on the cold tap, dangling her fingers in the stream of water.

A warm summer, much like this year's. Sticky heat. Sweat. Gil doing things with her body that she couldn't forget, however hard she tried. She'd met him at a two-week conference and liked him...a lot. Fallen into bed with him with embarrassing speed, and then believed him when he'd said that he couldn't wait to see her again. That business with the photo booth, where they'd had their pictures taken and written their telephone numbers on the back, had been just cruel. He'd never called her, and when Clemmie had called him, excited to hear the sound of his voice, he hadn't picked up. She'd been embarrassed and belittled, as well as hurt.

She stared at her reflection in the mirror above the basin. What if he recognised her?

What if he didn't? That could cut both ways: it would be a blow to her pride, but it would make things easier. She could pretend that it had never happened. If he started to make her nervous, she could employ the old interview trick of imagining him naked...

Which wasn't going to work. Imagining someone naked was supposed to empower you. The Gil she'd known was far more powerful naked than he was clothed.

Imagine him as a liar. Someone who breaks his promises.

That wasn't going to be so difficult—Gil *was* a liar. Clemmie splashed a little cold water onto her cheeks, drying her hands carefully. She had to think clearly. Gil had made her feel so miserable, so humiliated, that her work had suffered. She'd pulled herself together and resolved that would never happen again. Now more than ever it was important, because this six-week placement meant so much to her.

If she was just one in a long line of forgotten lovers, then it was simple. Clemmie would pretend it had never happened. If he did recognise her, she'd play dumb and pretend she didn't remember him.

She picked up her bag and opened the door of the ladies' room. The reception desk was still hidden from view, but the sound of a man's voice made Clemmie stop in her tracks.

She was sure now. Even after all these years, Gil's voice sent shivers down her spine. An Australian accent, softened by years living in London. The sound of a smile in his tone.

'That philodendron's looking a bit sad, Maggie. Aren't you going to water it?'

Maggie chuckled. 'I thought *you* were the gardener around here. And I can't leave the desk…'

Clemmie heard him laugh. She'd liked that laugh so much…

She should probably breeze back into Reception as if nothing were amiss, but that just wasn't possible. If seeing Gil had as much effect on her as hearing his voice, then she needed a moment to breathe. She tiptoed forward and caught sight of him.

Gil was standing with his back to her, examining the large plant that stood by the entrance doors. Still broad-shouldered and slim-hipped. His hair was a little different from the neat crew cut he'd had when Clemmie had known him, and had grown out into a mass of dark curls. Just that brief glimpse of him left her breathless with shock.

'I'll go and get some water. I've got some plant food in my office—that'll give it a pick-me-up.'

'I'm sure it could have waited until lunchtime, Gil.' Maggie reached under the reception desk, producing a glass jug and putting it on the counter. 'And stop insinuating that I'm trying to murder the poor thing. It'll turn against me.'

'Actions speak louder than words...' Clemmie ducked back as he turned to fetch the jug, peering out again to see Gil walking back out of the reception area as Maggie waved her hand dismissively at him.

Actions *did* speak louder than words. Gil had told her how much she meant to him, and then his actions had proved him a liar. Clemmie tried to swallow down her anger. The dazzling future she'd imagined for herself had suddenly shrunk into a tremulous hope that she would be able to just get through today. Gil had no right to take away her hopes and dreams, or to damage her career. Taking a deep breath and squaring her shoulders, Clemmie walked back over to the reception desk.

'Gil won't be a minute. He's gone to fetch some water for the plants.' Maggie smiled up at her, then squinted over at the philodendron. 'It looks perfectly fine to me...'

Clemmie turned, surveying the plant. It did look a little sorry for itself, but maybe Gil could sweet-talk it into reviving. Poor thing. Even a plant didn't deserve Gil's brand of loving care...

'He's given me a form for you to fill out. Contact details for while you're here.' Maggie slid a sheet of paper and a pen towards her.

'Right. Thanks.' Clemmie picked up the pen, grateful that she didn't have to talk to Maggie about Gil any more.

She couldn't help glancing up at the corridor that led into the reception area every few seconds, though. If she saw him coming, before he saw her, then maybe it would give her some advantage. Maybe her heart would stop beating so ferociously, and she'd manage to get her knees to stop shaking. Clemmie scribbled down her name and address.

'Here he comes.' Even Maggie's murmured words made her jump. Clemmie forced herself to look up, and saw Gil, exchanging a few words with a cleaner who was working her way along the corridor with a mop.

Don't stare. Clemmie dragged her gaze back to the form in front of her, her mind blank with panic. Telephone number. She wrote the first four digits down and then jumped again as a loud crash sounded from the corridor.

'Oh, for goodness' sake...' Maggie was on her feet, hurrying towards Gil, who was surrounded by water and shards of broken glass. The cleaner was bending to pick up the glass, and Gil stopped her before she cut herself. Maggie began to fuss and was clearly receiving assurances that he was all right. Gil appeared to be attempting to brush the water from his soaked shirt.

She shouldn't laugh. But Gil's obvious embarrassment

made her feel a great deal more in charge of the situation. Sometimes, just sometimes, there was a little justice in the world.

Sometimes there wasn't. Gil looked just as delicious wet through as he did dry. More so. He hadn't changed in the last seven years and that male magic was still there, pulling her towards him despite everything she knew and all that she felt.

And... Clemmie looked around. You'd think that in a hospital there would be a doctor or nurse around somewhere, who could rush to his aid. But there was no one, and Gil had snatched his hand from his shirt as a pinkish red stain started to spread across it. Blood could go a very long way when mixed with water, but he'd clearly cut himself. Two of his fingers were curled awkwardly, and Clemmie wondered if he'd done any real damage to his hand.

There was nothing for it. She was going to have to go and check on him. Just standing here, watching a person bleed, wasn't anywhere in her remit as a doctor, and she was a *good* doctor. She'd hung on to that, building her life back up around it.

She heard her heels clack on the floor as she walked towards him. Concentrated on that, and not Gil's sudden stillness when he saw her.

'I'm Dr Clemmie Francis...'

'I know. Gil Alexander.' He held out his hand as if to shake hers and then saw that he had blood on his fingers, from having inspected the cut, and pulled it back again.

'Are you all right?'

He didn't even think about his answer. 'Yeah. I'm fine.'

Take charge. All of Clemmie's professional instincts

were screaming at her to do so, and it seemed a good personal strategy, too.

'You're bleeding. Let me take a look.'

'Thanks, but it's nothing. I snagged my hand on some glass.' Gil stepped to one side as the cleaner, armed now with a dustpan and brush, waved him away so she could deal with the mess.

Typical doctor/reluctant patient exchange. Clemmie could work with that, far better than the conversation that was going on in her head, where she demanded to know why he'd written his number down and begged her to call, when he'd had no intention of ever speaking to her again. There was no possible answer to that question that wouldn't tempt her to slap him.

'The wound needs to be irrigated and dressed.' She looked up at him.

Gil shot her a querying glance. Somewhere, deep in his dark eyes, there was a hint of tenderness that couldn't entirely be accounted for by her offer of medical assistance. Then it was gone. If Gil recognised her, he was clearly keeping quiet about it, which meant that Clemmie could, as well.

'Uh…yeah, thanks. I've got a medical kit in my office.' He turned suddenly, walking briskly along the corridor, and Clemmie followed him.

It was a nice office, light and just tidy enough to inspire confidence. Just messy enough to make someone feel at home. Gil didn't seem over-interested in making Clemmie feel at home, walking directly to the washbasin in one corner and reaching into the cupboard below it to take out a soft bag.

'Let me do that.' Gil was trying to unzip the bag one-handed and Clemmie took it from him. Inside, there were a number of colour-coded bags.

'Blue for cuts.' Gil turned on the cold tap, wincing slightly as he held his hand under the stream of water.

'Can you straighten your fingers for me, please?'

Gil smiled suddenly. 'No. But that's nothing to do with the cut. It's an old injury.' He opened his hand, the little finger staying obstinately curled, and Clemmie watched carefully as he pulled it straight. 'I had a brain bleed, some years ago. I was treated in this hospital.'

So *that* was the reason for Gil's sudden change of course. The last seven years had obviously been no more straightforward for him than they had for Clemmie. And Gil had been the victim of something he couldn't control. Clemmie had made her own mistakes, walking into them with her eyes blurred by tears over him.

She couldn't think about that now. She was having difficulty thinking about *anything* other than that she was too damn close to him and his scent was just the same as it had been before. But inspecting a cut and dressing it were difficult to do at arm's length.

'This hospital?' Clemmie seized on the one detail that didn't send shock waves hurtling through her.

'Yes. Funny how things turn out, sometimes.'

'Funny?' Clemmie swallowed hard.

'I meant strange...'

Suddenly his gaze caught hers. It still held the silent suggestion that she was the only person within a two-hundred-mile radius that Gil was interested in. Even now, it sent shivers along Clemmie's spine.

It was an effort of will to break away from it and look back down at his hand. For a moment Clemmie could see nothing, and then her medical training came to her rescue. That compartmentalisation that allowed her to set everything else aside and concentrate on a patient.

'I can't see any glass in there...' By some miracle, her tongue was still working and her voice sounded vaguely normal. And she couldn't see any splinters lodged in his palm, which was a relief because Clemmie wasn't sure how she would manage to tweeze shards from a wound while her heart was still beating so fast.

'There's nothing. I had a look myself.'

Clemmie nodded. That was Gil all over—he didn't leave anything to chance. Finding that his control had been wrested from him must have been a cruel blow.

She should stop this. She could feel sympathy for Gil when he wasn't so close, and she could look at everything more objectively. Clemmie busied herself with cleaning the cut and applying three wound-closure strips, then carefully covering it with a dressing.

But she couldn't help it. She'd fitted everything together so neatly in her head, and now this. The one piece of information that didn't fit and was careening around in her brain, tearing everything else apart. She *had* to ask.

'How long ago was your brain bleed?' She tried to make the question sound casual, a matter of professional interest.

Gil was silent for a moment, and she glanced up at him. 'If you don't mind my asking.'

He shook his head. 'Of course not. It'll be seven years at the end of next month.'

Next month. Clemmie couldn't even work out what *this* month was at the moment. Today must be a Monday, because it was her first day here...

Suddenly she couldn't stay still any longer. Springing

to her feet, she made a grab for her handbag, and then inspiration hit her.

'I've just remembered… I have to make a call.' Gil was watching her steadily, his eyebrows slightly raised. 'A patient of mine… I need to just check on them.'

He nodded. 'Go and do whatever you need to. I should get changed.' He gestured towards his soaked shirt.

That was the last straw. The thought of Gil unbuttoning his shirt, and the smile that had accompanied it, was altogether too much to bear. Clemmie flung a *thank you* over her shoulder, practically running out of the room.

CHAPTER TWO

Gil sat motionless for a moment, staring after Clemmie. Then he got to his feet, shutting his office door and flipping the lock. The click as the bolt slid home was comforting, even if it was unnecessary.

Everyone knew that when his office door was closed he wasn't to be interrupted. Perhaps the lock was a matter of keeping something in. Now that Clemmie was gone and he had no need to keep them in check, his emotions seemed to be bursting around the room like a tornado, threatening to lay waste to everything in their path.

Clemmie. Her name was Clemmie. Gil allowed himself to savour the name for a moment.

He pulled his wallet out of his back pocket, flipping it open on the desk. His cuff dripped onto the leather and Gil shrugged off his shirt, letting it drop to the floor. One-handed, he fished the photograph carefully from the hidden compartment at the back of the wallet.

It was her. The same dark hair, coiling down around her shoulders, the same oval face and flawless skin. He'd recognised Clemmie as soon as he saw her, and the shock had been so profound that his fingers had tightened around the thin sides of the water jug. It had practically burst in his hands, showering him with glass and water. Everyone had assumed he'd dropped it and it had smashed on the floor, and he hadn't corrected the notion. Clemmie hadn't appeared to recognise him, and he'd allowed that to go unchallenged, as well. He'd thought about this moment for so long, and now it was here he had no idea what to say to her.

Seven years.

It seemed like a whole lifetime ago. To all intents and purposes it was, because he was so different from the man in the photograph, smiling at Clemmie.

Raised in a family of overachievers, Gil had graduated top of his class from medical school and decided that even Australia was too small for him and he wanted the world. Fourteen countries later, he'd come to rest in a busy London A & E department, earning the nickname of 'Stress Eater', because he'd take any amount of pressure without buckling. He'd worked hard and played even harder.

Life had been good. And then he'd woken up in a hospital bed, a stranger amongst strangers.

Slowly he'd begun to reorientate himself. Friends and colleagues had visited, some of whom he'd recognised and some who'd had to remind him who they were. He'd learned how to put a sentence together, and how to hold a cup to his lips when he was thirsty. Taking two steps forward and one back, he'd slowly put the pieces back together again.

But there were still gaps. Some of them inconsequential, and most of them shrinking by the day, but four weeks remained obstinately blank. The two weeks after his injury didn't hold much interest for him, and the nurses who tended him were able to answer all of his questions. The two weeks before were more problematic, largely because there was no one to ask about them.

Gil knew he'd been at a conference, because he remembered packing his case and checking the train times for Manchester. That he must have come back to London on the Saturday, and then gone to play rugby with his club in Richmond on the Sunday. He remembered nothing of that, but his teammates had told him that there had been a collision and that he'd got up and continued playing, seeming none the worse for it. Four hours later, Sam Gordon, one of the surgeons in the neurological unit at Barney's, had found him sitting in the waiting room in A & E, and realised how ill he was. Sam's quick action had probably saved his life.

Then he'd found the photograph in his wallet. He was in a photo booth, sitting close to a beautiful woman, whose face he no longer recognised and whose name he didn't remember. Gil had looked into Clemmie's dark eyes for what felt like the first time, although he knew it couldn't have been. The two of them looked happy, and there was an intimacy there that never failed to send shivers down his spine.

One of the things he'd had to learn was patience. Gil had watched the door, waiting to see if the woman might walk through it at visiting time. It was almost a relief when she didn't because, however much he wanted her smile, he knew that he couldn't compare with the man in the photograph. It had been months before he could pluck up the courage to call the number written on the back of the photograph.

Too long. Gil had been too late. The number was unobtainable, and so was she. She'd stayed that way until this morning, when Clemmie had found her way back into his life. Still as beguiling, but she'd given no clear indication that she recognised him.

Gil pulled some paper towels from the dispenser, shakily dabbing himself dry. Unwrapping the clean shirt he kept in the office, he pulled it across his shoulders, buttoning it clumsily.

He had to get a bit of perspective. He couldn't have known Clemmie for more than a week or so. They must have met at the conference and gone their separate ways. Gil had stared at the photograph, willing himself to remember, so many times that he'd felt he knew the sweet curve of her face better than he knew his own reflection. Clemmie had probably let him go a long time ago, submerged in the sea of faces that she did remember.

He reached for an apple from the bag on his desk. Clemmie had seemed a little jumpy, but who wouldn't in the circumstances? And when he'd responded to her questions, she hadn't taken the bait and searched her memory for him. Maybe he'd lost whatever it was that had ignited the chemistry that the photograph showed so clearly. When she'd looked into his gaze, Gil had thought he felt it again, sizzling between them, but maybe that was just his own reaction and not Clemmie's.

He really wasn't sure that he wanted to know, right now. Gil had confided all of his hopes and fears to the photograph, and her smile had remained the same, whatever he said. The real Clemmie might not be so accommodating; she had no reason to be. Expecting her to know him, the way he felt he knew her, was ridiculous.

Gil sank his teeth into the apple, reaching for his phone and dialling Reception. When Maggie answered the phone, he could hear a hum of activity in the background.

'I hear you've been patched up. Unlike my jug...'

Maggie's no-nonsense approach was like a breath of fresh air.

'Sorry about that, Maggie. I'll get you a new one.'

'That's all right. I have a plastic one at home. I'll bring that in and you can throw it around to your heart's content. Dr Francis has popped out. She said she might be half an hour. She said she had a call to make.' The sound of someone demanding Maggie's attention sounded in the background. 'Right you are. Sorry, Gil, got to go...'

Maggie hung up on him, and Gil sat back in his chair, savouring the taste of the apple. If Clemmie's call was going to last for half an hour that wouldn't be such a bad thing; it would give him time to get his head straight. Fate had given him the chance to get to know the *real* Clemmie, and even though the thought was daunting, it set his pulse racing.

Gil tucked the photograph back into his wallet. If Clemmie didn't remember him, that was probably all for the best. He had the opportunity to forget about the man who'd turned to a photograph for comfort and encouragement, and to start again with a clean slate.

She'd been about to suffocate. Or throw up. Or both. All Clemmie knew was that she had to get away from Gil. She hurried past Reception, remembering to tell Maggie that she'd be back in half an hour, then through the main doors and out into the sunshine. That was no relief at all, because she couldn't run away from herself. But at least she could try to deal with what she'd just heard, without the awkwardness of feeling that her new co-workers might be looking on.

The bench outside the unit was out of the question— far too public. She could go for a coffee in the main hospital building, but she really did feel sick now, and it was always possible that someone from the unit might see her. Clemmie crossed the road, walking into Richmond Park, past the seat she'd sat on this morning to a more secluded one that was shielded from view behind a tree.

Think. *Think!* The conference where she'd met Gil was an annual event, and they must have a website. She took her phone from her pocket, and a search got her to a page that listed out previous conferences and speakers. Tapping on the link for the one that she and Gil had attended, she scanned through for dates.

September the thirteenth to the twenty-seventh. Gil had almost missed his train, because he'd kissed her goodbye one more time at the station. She'd watched him run along the platform and then he'd turned, calling to her that he couldn't wait to speak to her again tomorrow. It was August now and everything fitted. There were only four possible days when he could have sustained the TBI.

Or Gil was lying. He'd recognised her, and had fudged the dates to give himself an excuse for not having called, so that the next six weeks would go a little more smoothly.

The thought was almost comforting. A desperate attempt to hang on to the world as she'd seen it for the last seven years. But there was very little chance that Gil was lying. He was no fool, and it would be easy enough to check the dates in the hospital records. Anyway, who on earth could possibly make this up?

Seven years next month. There had been a vulnerability there when he'd said it, quickly hidden. No one could fake that. Gil wasn't lying and that meant that Clemmie had to adjust her assessment of him. Which meant adjusting a lot of other things, as well.

The thought made her feel physically sick again. Clemmie took a few deep breaths and the hot flush of nausea began to recede. That was a *big* relief. She might not be able to handle what was going on in her head, but at least her body was a little more under control. She sat for a moment, her head in her hands, concentrating on keeping her breathing slow and steady.

What had just happened? She'd found out why a man she'd known for less than a week hadn't picked up the phone, when she'd hoped he would. Seven years ago. That wasn't such a big thing; she should be able to shrug it off by now. Maybe even laugh about it.

But however short-lived their relationship, Gil had been a breath of fresh air. Clemmie had still been living in the shadow of her childhood, when the only person who had seemed to notice her existence was her gran. Then dementia had robbed her grandmother of the ability to notice her, as well. Gil had given her his undivided attention, and, when you added his charm and looks to the mix, it was irresistible. It had been a whirlwind romance, the love at first sight that she'd never believed happened in real life.

And then he hadn't called. Her calls to him went unanswered. Everything her childhood had taught her, that she was the girl who was unseen and unheard, came back to slap her in the face.

Her broken heart had made mistakes. It had been so easy for her to believe that Gil could just throw her away. Not to expect more from him, because she hadn't thought herself worthy of it. She'd hated Gil, for showing her that life could be different and then taking that all away again.

Clemmie had clung on to what she knew. Married the

wrong man and accepted his efforts to belittle and control her for too long before she'd had the self-confidence to break free. She'd concentrated on her career, mending all of the damage that had been done by her turbulent personal life. And now—just as she was getting on her feet again—she'd found that Gil might not have left her after all. That the whole of the last seven years was founded on *her* lie, and not his. The thought brought another wave of nausea, this one stronger than the last.

Deep breaths. Wait until the trembling stops.

It wouldn't do to cry here, when some kindly passer-by might see her and stop to ask if she was all right. Clemmie kept her head down, staring at her phone while the cold shivers subsided. Then she blew her nose, wiping her eyes.

A ten-minute walk, brisk enough to get her a little out of breath, was what she needed. Then she could go back inside and face Gil again. Remembering that if what she suspected was true, and she'd been calling his phone while he lay critically ill in hospital, he was the one who was vulnerable.

This was something she could understand. She would have jumped at the chance to help him through the dark days that everyone experienced after a TBI, either as a friend or something more, but he would have had so many other things to think about. Maybe he hadn't felt as much for her as she'd felt for him, but it wasn't a calculated act of rejection.

Time to step up, Clemmie.

She'd found her strength. If Gil didn't recognise her, it would be easy. There was no conflict—she could protect him and herself, along with her career, by never letting him know how much he'd hurt her. She might not be able to change the past, but she could change the future.

CHAPTER THREE

GIL JUMPED FROM the seat behind his desk, ushering Clemmie into his office. She'd walked for longer than she'd thought, but he didn't ask where she'd been. He apologised for his clumsy welcome this morning and waved Clemmie to a seat, his face betraying nothing.

'Apple?' He pushed the bag on his desk towards her. 'They're home-grown.'

That was unexpected. Gil was the same in many ways, and that one long look they'd shared had reminded Clemmie that she wasn't so different from the young woman who'd fallen in love with him. But he'd changed, too.

'Um… You grow apples?'

'Yeah. This variety fruits early and I've had a real glut of them this year.' He smiled suddenly. 'Gardening is my way of winding down.'

Right. The only horticultural aspect of Gil's so-called winding-down process that Clemmie had been introduced to was strawberries. With champagne and seduction. On balance, it was probably better to stick to apples. She leaned forward, taking one from the bag and rubbing it against her sleeve. It was shiny and she could smell the apple scent that proved it was home-grown.

'Right, then.' Gil shuffled the papers on his desk.

'Down to business, I suppose. What do you want from your time here with us?'

That was typical of Gil. Asking questions first and listening to the answers. Clemmie avoided his gaze, in case it made her tongue-tied.

'The neurological rehab centre here at Barney's has a reputation for excellence. I want to see all aspects of your work and learn from you.'

'And teach us something?'

Clemmie risked meeting his eyes. 'Learning is always a two-way process.'

He nodded. 'I'm told you're in line to head up your own department at the Royal Victoria Hospital.'

'Nothing's been decided yet. The head of Neurological Rehab there is due to retire at the beginning of next year, and he's hoping for a smooth handover and someone who can build on all the good work he's done. We're working together on a few new initiatives that can be fully developed after he's gone, and...hence my watching brief here.'

Gil's lips curled into a lazy smile. 'In other words, *yes*.'

Clemmie's heart beat a little faster. When they'd last met, he'd told her that she didn't give herself enough credit, and that she shouldn't undersell herself. But now she had the confidence to push back a bit.

'In other words, that's the official position.' Even if Gil was exactly right and she had already been promised the job.

He nodded. 'Well, I'm flattered that you chose to come here.'

Was he fishing for information? Maybe he *did* recognise her, and the idea that he might think she'd come here on purpose rang a shrill alarm in Clemmie's mind.

'My boss suggested it. He was the one who made all of the arrangements.'

Gil didn't miss a beat. 'In that case, we'll have to see if we can justify *his* confidence in us. There are three main aspects to my job...'

He smiled, holding up his hand to count on his fingers. He'd done that once before, when they were discussing one of the conference sessions they'd been to, only he'd counted on her fingers. And the look in his eyes had been so delicious that the only conclusion they'd come to was that work could wait and they wanted to play a little. Clemmie would do well to remember that work was now all-important and play was out of the question.

'First and foremost, as a doctor, I oversee all of our patients' medical needs. There are two other doctors on the unit who work with me, but I have ultimate responsibility for everyone here.'

Clemmie nodded.

'Second... Rehab carries with it a very strong element of motivation, and we're working *with* people in a very real sense. Our counsellor does a great deal in helping patients come to terms with the emotional aspects of what's happening to them, and it's my job to help her to consolidate that.'

'You talk to people.' Clemmie reckoned that Gil's charm helped to inspire no end of confidence.

'In a nutshell, yes. I do a bit more listening than talking, generally. I find I learn a lot more that way. Thirdly, there's the organisational side. It's my job to support all the staff here in being the best they can be. Give them the framework that best allows them to inspire our patients.'

'So you'll be showing me all three of those things?'

Gil nodded. 'Along with anything else you're curious about…?'

Clemmie didn't take the bait. If she'd thought it was hard to be professional with Gil when she hated his guts, now that she'd warmed to him it was letting in all the old memories. She had to be careful.

Gil paused, waiting for her answer, and then shrugged. 'Right, then. We also value our close links with the surgical unit, over in the main building, in terms of continuity of care. Sam Gordon's a neurological surgeon and I usually meet with her for lunch at least once a week, as well as liaising with her closely on a day-to-day basis, but she's on maternity leave at the moment. Maybe we can organise a lunch meeting sometime in the next few weeks. I'm sure it would be helpful for you to have a chat with her.'

'I don't want to break in on her maternity leave…' Gil's eyes had softened momentarily, and it occurred to Clemmie that this Sam Gordon might be his partner. That the baby might be his… She tried to clear the lump that had formed in her throat.

'That's okay. I mentioned it to her the other day and she'd be very happy to see you. She's already interrogating me about how things are going at work whenever I see her. I dare say you'll bump into her fiancé at some point. Yanis is also a neurological surgeon. Sam's just had twin girls, and it'll be a great excuse for me to play godfather while you two talk business.'

Perfect. Trying to concentrate on holding a sensible conversation, while Gil was playing with two newborns. Clemmie had once dared to imagine a future in which he might be the father of the children that she so wanted. That she *had* so wanted, before life had set in and destroyed her confidence in ever being able to make a good relationship with someone she loved. But the instinctive tug still pulled at her.

But she'd made up her mind not to show any fear. She could watch Gil holding a baby and come out of it unscathed.

'That would be very helpful. Thank you.'

Gil nodded, turning his attention to his phone, which had started to vibrate urgently on his desk. He glanced at a message, and suddenly his relaxed demeanour changed.

This was the Gil that Clemmie knew. The gleam in his eyes as a challenge presented itself. Ready to face anything.

'Someone's fallen.' He didn't waste words, turning to the glazed double doors behind his desk, which looked out into a garden behind the unit. He opened them, moving outside swiftly.

Clemmie got to her feet and followed. Participating in conference sessions with him had made it clear that Gil was an excellent doctor, and the kind of person that everyone wanted around in an emergency, but she'd never seen him deal with a real situation. This was the aspect of his job that she was the most curious about.

He was hurrying across the lawn, towards a group of greenhouses, and Clemmie caught him up at the door of one of them. He quickly ushered her inside. Between the long row of benches, covered with trays of green seedlings, she saw an elderly woman lying on the ground, a young woman in a nurse's tunic beside her, holding her hand and urging her to stay still.

'Elaine...?'

The nurse looked up at him. 'Jeannie slid off her seat. I didn't see her hit her head...'

'I think I could get up now, if someone would just give me a hand. There's no need for all this fuss.' The elderly woman frowned up at Gil and he smiled, squatting down beside her.

'We can't be too careful, Jeannie. Elaine did exactly the right thing in asking you to stay right where you were until I got here.' Gil glanced at Elaine, nodding his approval, and some of the tension lifted from her face.

He was good. Very thorough. He examined Jeannie's head and neck, carefully gauging her reactions and level of alertness. Gil's serious intent was masked by relaxed jokes and encouragement for Jeannie.

'This is Clemmie.' He introduced her as he worked. 'She's a doctor and attached to the unit for six weeks, and so you'll be seeing her around a bit. She may be wanting a chat to see what you think of the place.'

'Oh. And I suppose you'll be wanting me to give you a good report.' Jeannie was quite clearly a match for anyone, including Gil.

'Of course I do. But I'll settle for firm but fair.' Gil's attention had moved to Jeannie's hip and legs, to check there was no injury there. 'Does that hurt at all?'

'No.' Jeannie shot him an impatient look, and then turned her gaze onto Clemmie. 'Now, don't you take any old nonsense from him, will you?'

Best advice she'd had all morning. The more she found to forgive, the more difficult it was to resist Gil's charm.

'Thanks. I won't.'

Gil finished his examination and sat back on his heels. 'Since I've failed to find anything wrong with you, I think we'd best get you on your feet, eh, Jeannie? Elaine, can you bring the wheelchair over, please? And call someone to take Jeannie back to her room, as well.'

'About time. I'll be late for tea if you don't hurry up.'

'You'll get your tea, even if I have to make it myself.'
Gil grinned.

'I don't think I'd want you to do *that*.' Jeannie's teas-
ing was clearly the result of liking Gil a lot, the kind of
easy doctor-patient relationship that all good practitioners
tried to cultivate.

'Clemmie…?' Gil turned to her. Elaine was a member
of staff, and the obvious person to ask for help in lifting
Jeannie, but the girl seemed very shaken by what had
happened. Clemmie nodded.

His eyes, again. Checking that they were both bal-
anced and ready to lift Jeannie upright. Clemmie felt
herself flush, and ignored the touch of his fingers behind Jeannie's shoulders. On his count, they lifted her
smoothly to her feet and then into the wheelchair that
Elaine had positioned next to them.

'See you later, Jeannie.' Gil gave her a smile as another
nurse arrived to take Jeannie back inside.

'Don't fuss…'

'It's my job. I get paid extra for fussing,' Gil retorted.
Jeannie flapped her hand dismissively as she was wheeled
away.

'Elaine…' Gil quietly stopped her from following.

'I'm so sorry.' Elaine was obviously blaming herself
for the fall. 'I'd followed all the guidance, but I turned
away for one minute to fetch something for her, and she
just slid out of the chair.'

'It's okay,' Gil reassured her. 'We'll need to make out a
patient incident report, but what I want you to remember
is that the aim of it is to improve patient safety, not find
someone to blame. They help me to do my job better.'

Elaine nodded, biting her lip.

'Go and ask Maggie if she'll give you a form, write everything down straight away while it's fresh in your mind and then come and see me this afternoon so we can have a chat about it. And don't look so worried, eh?'

'Okay. Thanks.' Elaine gave him a relieved smile and hurried away.

Gil stood silently, watching her go. It was a difficult balance; his patients' needs were paramount, but at the same time he must support his staff. Clemmie would need to consider that same balance if she took on the running of her own unit.

'What happens next?'

Gil pressed his lips together, turning to pick up one of the plant trays that had fallen onto the floor, and collecting the seedlings that had been uprooted. Carefully smoothing the soil and replanting them seemed to figure somewhere in his thought process.

'Accidents happen—we'll never be able to prevent that. Elaine's very new, but from what I've seen of her, she's very conscientious about safety and patient care. We have to discuss what happened honestly, and look to correct any mistakes that were made. And reassure Elaine about the things she couldn't have prevented. She seems pretty eager to shoulder all of the responsibility for this.'

Clemmie nodded. 'And Jeannie?'

'The nurses will keep a close eye on her. I'll let her have her tea and then go and have a word, get her version of what happened. Confidence is always an important issue to address, after any fall.' He smoothed the earth around the seedlings carefully, making sure they were all upright. 'Have I missed anything?'

'No, I don't think so.' His approach was fair and constructive. Clemmie bent down to pick up a small plant that was still on the ground. 'Apart from this.'

His fingers touched her palm as he picked the plant up, and Clemmie shivered, even at this momentary contact. Gil replanted the seedling, and then brushed the soil from his fingers.

'That'll do for now...' He reached for a broom, clearing the scattered earth from the walkway and setting the chair that Jeannie had been sitting on back on its feet, checking that it was stable. Moving slowly and deliberately, as if still deep in thought.

'This flooring...?' Clemmie reckoned that the slight give in the tiles that covered the floor in the greenhouse would have cushioned Jeannie's fall.

Gil smiled suddenly. 'You noticed. The tiles are made of a rubber compound similar to what's used in children's playgrounds. They're non-slip, and if anyone does fall, they make for a softer landing. We keep everything tidy in here, and try to eliminate hard corners.' He ran his hand along the rubber lip that was fixed along the edges of the bench.

'It's impressive. I'll be wanting to take another look in here.' Everything was well organised and done with care. Colourful too, the space bright and attractive.

'Be my guest. We're lucky to have this space. Gardening's the most popular of all our therapies. And the garden's nice for patients to come and sit outside, as well.'

'A larger area for you to monitor.'

Gil grinned suddenly. That delicious, loving-the-challenge smile. 'Yeah. It would be a great deal easier to make them all stay in their beds. That's not really what we're here for, is it? Our job is all about widening people's horizons.'

That was exactly how Clemmie saw it. She confined herself to a brief nod and followed Gil out of the greenhouse.

It had seemed like a long day, although in truth it had been only nine to five. But it had been eight hours of intense concentration, trying to analyse Clemmie's every word. Her every move. Sometimes Gil thought he saw recognition in her eyes, and sometimes not.

He'd left her to her own devices while he went to see Jeannie, and then given her the standard tour of the unit, introducing her to everyone. Clemmie had accompanied him on his afternoon rounds, and he'd watched her carefully. She was great with his patients, confident and friendly, listening to what they had to say as if she had all the time in the world. No wonder she was on a fast track to promotion—she seemed to have all the skills that were required to run her own unit. All she needed was a little more experience.

Gil wished her a good evening and went back to his office, puffing out a breath. When he took the photograph out of his wallet again, he could better understand the look on his face as he stared at Clemmie. She wasn't just beautiful. She was clever and kind and had all of the qualities that would make a man want to sit and listen to her, all evening and late into the night.

He propped the photo up against the phone, leaning back in his seat and putting his feet up on the desk. It seemed that much more precious to him now, but he still couldn't fathom a way of asking Clemmie if she remembered having met him before. It was a risky excursion into the unknown, and if Clemmie *did* remember and was keeping quiet about it, then that raised all kinds of awkward questions.

A knock sounded on his door and he looked up. Anya Whitehead breezed into his office, a gauzy purple scarf trailing in her wake.

'You called?'

Gil smiled. 'And you came.'

'Of course I did. You're looking very deep in thought.' Anya fixed him with one of those searching, perceptive looks that she was so good at.

He'd met Anya when he was a patient here, after his own brain injury. She'd been assigned as his counsellor and had done everything to encourage him to talk, despite Gil's dogged resistance. They'd come to an understanding, Gil acknowledging that he had difficulty in admitting that he *had* any problems, and Anya challenging him to go away and think about that. When Gil had started to recover, and was considering the idea that maybe his future career lay in Rehab rather than emergency medicine, Anya's listening ear had helped him make the right decision.

'I'm just considering a few awkward questions.' Gil grinned at her, taking his feet off the desk and flipping the photograph face down.

'Goody. You know I like awkward questions.' Anya sat down.

'It's nothing…' Gil shrugged. It wasn't nothing, but if he had something to say, he should say it to Clemmie first.

'Of course it is. Well, you know where Miss Purple is when you want her.'

Gil chuckled. When he'd first known Anya, he'd still been struggling with expressive aphasia and the simplest words would elude him. Names were a particular problem, and he'd called Anya 'Miss Purple' because it was unusual for her not to include the colour somewhere in her outfit. It had become a standing joke between them.

'What I'd really like is if you could spare some time to talk to the doctor I'm working with at the moment, Clemmie Francis. She's here for six weeks, to see how we do things, and it would be great if you could give her an overview of your work in the unit.'

'Ah yes, I'd heard you had a visitor. Of course. Give her my number and we can sort out a time.' Anya gave him another searching look. 'Anything else?'

Gil knew that ruse, and he wasn't going to fall for it.

'I don't think so. Want an apple?' He pushed the bag towards her.

'Can I take two? My kids love these. They're so sweet.'

'Take the bag. Please. I have a lot more at home.'

'Thank you. Oh, and by the way, Jamie's bike's back from the repair shop, so he's up for Sunday if you're not too busy.' Gil and Anya's husband often met on Sundays for an early morning ride around Richmond Park.

'Sure, I'll give him a call. Anything else?' Gil pulled a face to exaggerate the joke.

'Hm. I'm sure there must be. Your fingers don't lie, Gil.' Anya nodded to his hand and Gil realised that he'd been massaging his curled fingers. It had been a stress reaction, constantly massaging his fingers and arm in the hope that they might respond a little quicker, and he and Anya had talked about it when he was a patient here. He hadn't done it in years.

'I cut my hand.' And he'd met Clemmie.

Anya knew it was an excuse, and let him get away with it, because she and Gil had fought that battle before, and she knew he wouldn't talk about things he didn't want to. She gathered up the apples and got to her feet.

'Okay. Don't stay too late, will you? I dare say the awkward questions will manage on their own for a little while—they don't need your constant supervision.'

'You mean the world's not going to collapse if I take my eye off it for a moment?' He shot Anya a look of mock horror and she laughed.

'Go home and pick me some more apples. Smell a few flowers while you're at it, Gil.'

It wasn't a bad idea. Gil supposed he'd reverted to the old habit of massaging his fingers because Clemmie's arrival had brought back the last piece of unfinished business from his brain injury so vividly. Or maybe it was just that he felt so confused about this situation, the way he'd felt back then.

But he had a few things to do still, if he was going to have time available for Clemmie tomorrow. And his determination to make the day run more smoothly than today had done was all he had in the way of control over what happened next.

He couldn't let this break him, the way he'd been broken before. And he wouldn't allow his own feelings to complicate matters. Gil heaved a sigh, picking the photograph up from his desk and putting it back out of sight in his wallet.

Clemmie had made the long journey home, through the evening rush hour. Dropping her bag in the hall, she made a cup of tea and then threw herself down on the sofa. Today hadn't gone entirely as planned, but then, who could possibly have planned for something like this?

Gil was doing it all over again. No...actually *she* was

doing it again. Liking him. Wanting to hear his opinion. Watching the way he moved, which only brought tantalising flashbacks of how she had once responded to his caress. It was beyond unacceptable.

Gil was a little different from the way she remembered him. More measured and thoughtful, not quite so keen to squeeze everything from the moment. Maybe that was because this time she was working with him, rather than indulging in a whirlwind of romantic gestures, which inevitably led to wild and wonderful sex.

She couldn't imagine that the Gil she'd known would bring a bag of home-grown apples to work, or stop to rescue seedlings that had been tipped onto the ground. But he was still the kind of man that any woman could make a fool of herself with. That Clemmie *had* made a fool of herself with. It wasn't enough to simply accept that she'd been wrong in thinking so badly of Gil and then move on. She had to protect herself, and him, too.

She reached for the tapestry cushion that sat beside her on the sofa, hugging it tightly. It was about the only thing she had left of her grandmother, and Clemmie really needed her now.

She'd spent most of her time at her gran's house when she was little. Her parents had worked hard, and never had much time to spend with their daughter, but that had never mattered to Clemmie because Gran was there. Until the unrelenting slide into dementia had taken her away.

Her gran had gone into a nursing home when Clemmie was thirteen, and the loss of the only place that had ever really felt like home was profound. She visited every afternoon, after school, watching the light slowly fade from her grandmother's eyes. Time took its toll, and when her grandmother had died, she hadn't known that the young medical student, sitting by her bed and holding her hand, had been her granddaughter.

In the years that followed, Clemmie had felt herself disappearing, with no one left who would see or hear her. Gil had shown her that she could no longer live in the shadows, and then he'd been taken from her. There was no way back now; too much had happened in her life and she couldn't just flip a switch and make it un-happen. And Gil couldn't know how much she'd invested in their brief relationship. He'd had every reason not to call her, but the Gil she knew hadn't cut himself a great deal of slack and probably wouldn't see it that way.

And Gil was still dangerous. Every time she saw him she felt herself falling under his spell again. Wanting him even more than she had before, because now she knew how hard-won his success was. He'd been crushed, and he'd built his life back up again, piece by piece.

There was only one thing for it. She'd take a leaf from Gil's book—the old Gil—and squeeze every professional opportunity she could from the next six weeks. And then she'd leave. She wouldn't look back and he'd never know just how special he'd been to her.

CHAPTER FOUR

THE MAN WHO held the door open for her to enter the rehab unit the following morning had an unmistakable spring in his step. As Clemmie stopped to greet Maggie, she saw Gil hurrying out to meet him.

'Yanis...' Gil shook his hand vigorously. 'What are you doing here? Tired of waiting on Sam?'

Yanis grinned. A bright smile that said life was treating him well. 'I'm never tired of that. She insisted I come into work this morning.'

'She must be feeling better, then. And how are the twins?'

'Beautiful.' Yanis's French accent made the word sound special. 'Sam heard that one of her patients was coming over to Rehab from the surgical unit, and sent me to make sure the handover went smoothly.'

Gil chuckled. 'I'm surprised she didn't demand you brought her over here to do it herself.'

'She tried.' Yanis gave a smiling shrug and his blue eyes sparkled. 'I promised her I'd ask you over to dinner tonight and I'm under instructions not to take *no* for an answer.'

'That'll be a *yes*, then, thank you. I haven't had my

fill of baby-holding yet. I'll bring some fresh-picked strawberries…'

The two men were still talking, but the image of strawberries and champagne was blocking everything else out. How did that work, that four short days and three long nights could overshadow everything else so completely?

Clemmie wondered if she should slip past the two men and find something else to do, until Gil was free to chat about the sessions he'd promised to arrange with all the key workers in the unit. But Gil had seen her now, and he and Yanis were walking towards her.

'Clemmie, this is Yanis Baptiste. I mentioned Sam Gordon to you yesterday, and Yanis is her fiancé. He works over in the main hospital in the surgical neurology department.'

Clemmie turned to Yanis, feeling her shoulders relax. He was handsome, the blue sparkle in his eyes evidence that Sam Gordon was a lucky woman. But that was all it was—evidence. Something she could think about rationally without feeling every nerve ending explode the way they did when she looked at Gil.

'Pleased to meet you.'

Yanis nodded, shaking her hand. Not a trace of the inappropriate electricity that had sparked in response to Gil's handshake yesterday.

'I'm standing in for Sam at the moment.' Yanis grinned brightly. 'Have you heard that we've just had twins?'

Gil chuckled quietly. 'If there's anyone in Richmond you *haven't* told yet, I'll help you get round to them this evening…'

Yanis was laughing, and Clemmie kept her gaze studiedly on him, ignoring Gil. 'That's news worth sharing. Congratulations to both of you. Do you have a photograph?'

Yanis took his phone from his pocket, swiping through images and then handing it to Clemmie. At the mention of photographs, Maggie shot to her feet, rounding the reception desk with breakneck speed.

'You walked straight past me with *photographs* in your pocket, Yanis? How *could* you?' Maggie leaned in close to Clemmie, and she held the phone between them, flipping slowly through the pictures.

A woman with red hair, her face aglow. Clearly Yanis had been spending most of his time recently capturing as many images as possible of his partner and their two tiny babies. It was heart-warming. An echo of what Clemmie had wanted for herself, before she'd realised that finding herself meant being alone.

'Gorgeous!' Maggie delivered the smiling assessment that Clemmie probably should have voiced. 'Anna, come here. Yanis has photographs.'

The young nurse who was passing through Reception stopped suddenly and hurried over, craning to see the pictures over Clemmie's other shoulder. This was nice. Being part of something that was full of warmth and happiness and didn't focus on Gil.

But out of the corner of her eye, she could see Gil and Yanis discussing something. Probably to do with their new patient, and Clemmie really ought to be a part of that. Reluctantly she handed the phone over to Maggie, and joined the two men.

'Your photographs are wonderful, Yanis, thank you.'

Yanis nodded, smiling. 'I'm actually here to deliver some notes. I'll be bringing your latest patient over in a moment. It's one of Sam and Gil's little traditions. Sam's there to say goodbye and Gil's waiting to welcome them.'

'It's a good idea. I imagine it makes the transfer much

less stressful for your patients.' Clemmie addressed Yanis, ignoring Gil completely.

'Yes, it does. It's one of the things that impressed me when I first came here.' Yanis seemed just as determined to include Gil as Clemmie was to exclude him. 'Both Sam and Gil have busy schedules, but they try to make time for the little things, too.'

'Now you mention little things… I'm just going to check on the room we have ready. Perhaps you'd like to go with Yanis?' Gil avoided Clemmie's gaze, even though his question was clearly aimed at her.

'If that's okay…?' Clemmie directed hers in Yanis's direction.

'Yes, of course. As soon as I can get my phone back…'

Yanis had managed to wrest his phone from Maggie's grip by promising she could have it back again later. Clemmie walked beside him, over to the main hospital building, feeling a little calmer now that she was out of Gil's range. For the moment, he could get on with whatever he was supposed to do, and she could spend her time doing what she was supposed to do, watching and learning.

The building was even more impressive inside than it was from the outside. Not just clean and functional, it was built to include soaring spaces and light, too. A place to lift the spirits, as well as meet patients' medical needs. As Yanis led her through the atrium, Clemmie couldn't help glancing up towards the glass ceiling, eight floors above her head, and he stopped for a moment so she could take in her surroundings. The greenery, twisting walkways and benches lent a sense of peace to the space, even though it was right at the heart of a busy hospital. This was somewhere that staff and visitors alike could catch their breath. At either side were slender-trunked giant ficus trees in huge containers, their spreading canopies reaching up into the atrium and providing dappled shade for those who sat beneath them.

'This is just as important as the technology we have here,' he murmured quietly. 'In a different way.'

Clemmie nodded. 'Yes. The Royal Victoria is really nice, and everyone does their best to make it welcoming, but this place is…something different altogether.'

Yanis led the way to the lift, and then back out into Neurosurgery. When he ushered her into a private room, it seemed that their patient was all ready to go. A nurse was helping a young girl into a wheelchair, talking to her as she did so.

'This is Jahira.' Yanis smiled at the teenager. 'Jahira, this is Clemmie. She's one of the doctors who'll be looking after you at the rehab centre.'

Jahira eyed Clemmie silently. There was a trace of caution in her face, which was only to be expected, and Clemmie stepped forward.

'Hi, Jahira. We're looking forward to getting to know you.'

'Thanks.'

One word, but Jahira had clearly been through a bad time already, and her wariness was more than understandable. The left side of her head had been shaved, and her dark hair was swept over to one side of her face, flat and lifeless. One hand lay in her lap, and she was massaging her fingers with the other hand, as if she needed urgently to bring them back to full working order. Clemmie realised that she'd seen Gil display that same stress reaction yesterday.

'Your mum and dad will be coming soon. They'll help you settle in.' Yanis added the information.

'They know where to find me?' Jahira's speech was a little slurred and panic showed suddenly in her eyes. 'Cos I don't know where I'm going…'

'They know exactly where to find you. Your mum's been over there already, to check on your room and bring some of your clothes,' Yanis reassured her.

'Uh… Maybe she said…' Jahira shook her head.

This was hard for Jahira. Out of control, relying on other people for everything. Clemmie had seen this so many times before. Yanis seemed to be in no rush, and she sat down in the chair beside Jahira's bed.

'Before we go, is there anything you'd like to do here?'

'Sarah. Does *she* know how to find me?'

Clemmie glanced over her shoulder at Yanis, who nodded towards a brightly coloured card that stood on the cabinet next to the bed. She reached for it, handing it over to Jahira.

'Is this from Sarah?'

Jahira nodded, opening the card and staring at the rounded writing inside.

'It's a lovely card. What does it say?' Clemmie waited, giving Jahira some time to focus.

'She says she's coming to see me. In Rehab.'

'That's really nice. I'll bet you've been missing everyone. Sarah sounds really special.'

Jahira nodded. Her eyes were still on the card, and Clemmie took it from her hands, tucking it into the blanket across Jahira's legs. 'You'd better take good care of this—you don't want to lose it. Is there anything else you need to bring?'

'My photographs…' Jahira looked around the room and Yanis gestured towards a bag that lay at the end of the bed.

'We packed those already, along with your other things.'

'You're sure?' Jahira frowned and Yanis bent down, unzipping the bag and taking out a photo cube. Jahira reached for it.

There was a photo of her with another girl, their arms around each other. One of Jahira with two dogs, and another of a man and woman together, who must be her parents. She looked at each one, turning the cube awkwardly in her hand, her fingers stroking the smiling faces in an expression of longing that tore at Clemmie's heart.

'Yeah. This is right.' Jahira looked up.

'Would you like me to take care of that for you?' Clemmie volunteered. 'It'll be the first thing we find a place for in your new room.'

'Yes, please.' Jahira gave Clemmie the cube, and Yanis zipped up her bag, looping the straps over his shoulder.

'Ready to go?'

'What happens if I don't like it?' Panic flared again in Jahira's eyes.

Yanis grinned. 'You like it here?'

Jahira looked around. 'No. Not really. It's nice and everything but…'

'It's not home, is it?' Yanis clearly understood where Jahira really wanted to be. 'But the rooms at the rehab unit are much nicer. You'll be able to have things the way you like them and a few more visitors. After that you'll be going home. How does that sound?'

Jahira sighed, clearly resigning herself to the inevitable. 'Yeah. Sounds okay.'

* * *

Yanis had pushed the wheelchair, taking his time and stopping to let Jahira say her goodbyes to the staff in the surgical unit. Clemmie had carried the photo cube, making sure that Jahira could see that it wasn't being left behind. When they entered the rehab unit, Gil was waiting in the reception area.

'Hi. You're Jahira? My name's Gil.'

'Gil…' Jahira stared at him, clearly making an effort to connect the name with the face. 'What do you do?'

'I'm a doctor, so you'll see me every day. I'm also in charge here, so if there's anything you're unhappy about then I want you to tell me about it, and I'll do my best to fix things for you.'

Jahira nodded thoughtfully. Gil was reaching out, trying to get through to her, and he was saying all the right things. He'd just given Jahira a hotline to the man in charge, and that was important for someone who felt unsure and out of control.

'My photos. And my card…' Jahira pulled the card out from under the blanket.

'You're going to need somewhere safe for those. Come with me and we'll fix that up straight away.'

Gil clearly knew how important those little things were to Jahira, and that they connected her to her home and the people she loved. He straightened up, waiting while Yanis said his goodbyes, and then wheeled the chair out of the reception area and along a corridor. One of the doors at the far end was open, and Clemmie followed them inside.

Jahira silently looked around the room. The rooms here still had the trappings of a hospital, a hospital bed and a power-assisted easy chair. But every effort had been made to make them homely, with curtains at the window, a wardrobe and a small writing table. And there was a bright bedspread on the bed, with some cushions that Jahira's mother had obviously brought from home.

'Hot in here…'

'Yeah, you're right.' Gil strode over to the window, opening it. 'Better?'

Jahira nodded.

'What about your card, and your photos? Where would you like those?'

'There.' Jahira pointed towards the cabinet next to the bed and then handed her card to Clemmie, who arranged the photo cube and card so that they could be seen from the bed and the easy chair. Clemmie then turned to Jahira.

'How's that?'

'Yes. Thank you.'

'Would you like to try the chair out?' Gil motioned towards the easy chair.

'My gran's got one like that.' Jahira turned the edges of her mouth down. 'It helps her get up.'

'Yeah?' Gil grinned. 'Well, I guess you'll know what to do with the controls, then. It's not going to be for ever, just to help you for a little while.'

Jahira's hand gripped one of the armrests of the wheelchair, and her dark eyes filled with tears. Clumsily she tried to wipe them away with her other hand. Clemmie moved to comfort her but Gil was already there, pulling the chair that was tucked under the desk around to face Jahira and sitting down on it.

'What's up?'

'You're going to fix it?' Jahira's question sounded a lot like a challenge. Always a red rag to a bull where Gil was concerned. Clemmie froze as the memories of all the challenges she'd thrown at him, and which he'd met so deliciously, assailed her yet again.

'There are some things I can't fix. But if I can, I will fix it for you. Try me.'

'Want to go *home*.' Tears started to course down Jahira's cheeks.

'I want you to go home, too. I don't want you here.' Gil handed her a tissue, waiting for his words to sink in. When they did, Jahira stared at him uncomprehendingly.

'Here's the thing. You're going to leave that wheel-chair behind and walk out of here yourself. Reach out with that arm...' Gil motioned towards Jahira's left arm, which lay uselessly in her lap '...open the door and go.'

This was tough love. And it was risky. Clemmie felt the back of her neck prickle with alarm.

'I'll do it at home... The...things... Exercises.' Jahira was pleading with him now, and the look in her eyes was enough to melt anyone's heart.

'Maybe you would. I can help you recover better and faster, though. We'll be asking a lot of you here, and sometimes you won't see the point of it. But it works.'

'You don't *know*...' Jahira's lip curled. Maybe an attempt to smile, but from the scorn in her eyes, Clemmie didn't think so. She hoped that Gil knew what he was doing, because he seemed to be pushing Jahira awfully hard.

'I know that you're scared, and wondering if anything's ever going to be the same again. You're busy pretending that everything's all right, but really you just want to run.'

Gil's voice was tender, and Jahira was staring silently at him now. He was getting through to her.

'I've done this before. I know I can help you to run if

you'll let me. Your mum tells me that you want to go to veterinary college. I'd like to help you make that happen, too.'

Silence. 'Do we have a deal, Jahira? You don't have to like it, and you probably won't like me too much when I ask you to do things that you think you can't. But I promise I'm not going to give up on you.'

Jahira nodded. 'Okay. Deal.'

Gil smiled. 'All right. What's next, then? The first thing on your list of things to do, to get you on the road home and then off to veterinary college.'

Jahira looked around the room. 'My stuff.' She nodded towards the bag of belongings they'd brought with them.

'Sounds good. Your mum will be here soon. Would you like me to send one of the nurses to unpack your things so you can be settled in when she gets here?'

'I'll stay.' Clemmie broke in quickly. Gil had obviously decided that Jahira had taken about as much challenge as she could manage right now, and that he should leave her alone to settle. Clemmie could do with some time away from Gil, as well. 'If you'd like, I can help you arrange everything the way you want it, Jahira.'

'Yes. Thanks.'

Gil's gaze flipped towards Clemmie for a moment, and then he stood.

'Okay. I'll leave you to get on with that, then.' He pointed to the call button, which lay on the bed. 'There's your hotline, Jahira. Make sure you use it if there's something you need.'

He'd done a good job. Clemmie knew that feeling helpless and unable to communicate was common in patients with traumatic brain injuries, and Gil had given

Jahira some much-needed control. She wasn't going to think about how he'd managed to get inside her head, or whether Jahira's reaction to him was because she saw that he understood. Clemmie was here to learn, and part of the learning curve was going to be resisting the temptation to fall for Gil all over again.

Gil helped Jahira take a few slow, hesitant steps, and settled her into the armchair. Then he folded the wheelchair, taking it with him when he left. Clemmie lifted Jahira's bag, putting it on the floor at her feet, and bent down to unzip it.

'Right, then. What goes where?'

Gil walked back to his office, flexing his fingers. Clemmie was doing exactly as he'd wanted her to do, getting involved and using her own expertise to become a part of the process here and see how it worked. He wasn't as pleased about that as he'd wanted to be.

He'd decided to keep the photograph under wraps today, and stop staring at it so obsessively. But before he could stop himself, he'd taken it out of his wallet and propped it back up against the phone.

How could anyone look at someone the way that Clemmie was looking at him, and then forget all about them? Gil had gone over it time and time again, trying to recall people he'd met seven years ago. There were the blanks, caused by the brain injury, but apart from that, he didn't think that anyone had just dropped out of his head like that.

But he'd had the photograph. It had been something more than just an enigma. It reminded him of his past, the ways in which he'd changed, and the ways in which he was the same. He was still ambitious and still wanted to be the best at what he did. He'd just learned to deal with that in different ways.

Stop and smell the flowers.

It was ironic that this had literally become one of his ways of coping. The slow process of preparing the ground and watching things grow had started here, when he'd managed to beg some tools from one of the hospital's gardeners and gone out to attack a piece of rough ground. It had been a difficult, painstaking process, and he'd fallen more than once. Clawed at the earth, raging at his own inability to transform it as quickly as he wanted to.

But the staff had stood back and let him do it. Allowed him to push himself to the limit and take out his frustrations on Mother Nature. And he'd learned to love it, to take sustenance from the slow pace and pride in the new green shoots he had nurtured.

And now Clemmie. The woman he'd been afraid to call, because he'd been raging against his own weaknesses. When he'd finally plucked up the courage, it had been too late. When he thought about it now, he wasn't even sure he wanted her to recognise him. He'd worked so hard to leave the man that he was then behind. Even if he couldn't help looking at her now and hoping she'd remember that wide-eyed expression she had on her face in the photograph.

'Stop it.' He muttered the words to himself under his breath. It was seeming more and more likely that Clemmie didn't *want* to remember and he had to respect that. Do what he could to make these next six weeks work for her, and then learn to say goodbye to the image

that had sustained him and kept him honest for the last seven years.

Gil was only just beginning to understand how hard that was going to be.

CHAPTER FIVE

CLEMMIE HAD SPENT time arranging all of Jahira's belongings, plumping the cushions and folding the bedspread just the way Jahira liked it. When her parents arrived, they found their daughter bubbling with excitement and wanting to explore the rest of the unit with them. Clemmie fetched a wheelchair, settling Jahira into it, and left them to it.

Gil had lost no time in fulfilling his promise to set up sessions with the therapists who worked in the rehab unit, and Maggie had several messages for her. Anya Whitehead, one of the hospital counsellors who took care of the unit's patients, had some free time this afternoon and Gil was nowhere to be found, so Clemmie left a message on his desk telling him where she was, and walked over to Anya's office in the main hospital building.

Her own work had taught her the importance of counselling, but here the service seemed more integrated with the other therapies the unit offered. Anya spoke about the many and different issues that patients in the neurology units faced, and then went on to talk about the way she'd worked with Gil to help make a supportive environment for his patients.

'From what I've seen, he seems to understand what's

needed, very well.' Clemmie supposed that the compliment was okay, since Gil wasn't actually around to hear it.

'Yes, he does.' Anya smiled. 'There's something to be said for having seen both sides of the process.'

'Gil said he'd suffered a traumatic brain injury himself. I imagine that must help him a lot in his work.'

Anya pressed her lips together. 'Yes and no. Gil has an extraordinary way of empathising with his patients, but I'm sure you're aware of how difficult it is to recover completely from a traumatic brain injury.'

'He mentioned his fingers.' Despite herself, Clemmie was seized with a wish to know more.

'Yes. I'm thinking more about the psychological effects.' Anya shot her a thoughtful look. 'Gil makes no secret of it—everyone here knows what happened to him. He suffers from retrograde amnesia.'

What? Clemmie felt herself stiffen. Generally speaking, if retrograde amnesia was present, it covered a time period immediately before an injury.

'Retrograde amnesia is something that particularly interests me. I've seen it in some of my patients.' Clemmie neglected to mention that the thing about Gil's retrograde amnesia that really interested her was whether it covered the two weeks at the conference they'd both attended.

'Yes, it's an interesting phenomenon. You should definitely ask Gil about it. He always says that it was one of the more difficult things to come to terms with.' Anya smiled. 'I'll leave him to tell you about our little struggles over it.'

'You were his counsellor?' Clemmie could imagine that there *were* struggles. The Gil she'd known didn't seem very good at biding his time and staying within his limits. He'd taken her way beyond *her* limits…

'Yes. He's usually generous enough to say that he learned a lot from me, but I actually learned a great deal from him.'

Mutual respect. Learning a lot. This was getting more interesting by the minute. But it wasn't really fair to ask Anya about it; she had her own confidentiality to maintain. She'd told Clemmie the things that Gil had obviously made clear were for public consumption, but asking any more of her would be wrong.

She had to know, though. And somehow she had to find out without betraying too much to Gil. If he didn't remember her then it was best to let sleeping dogs lie. Her placement here meant a lot to her, and the last time she'd got involved with Gil on a personal basis, her work had suffered. She couldn't let that happen again.

'I'll bear that in mind when I ask him.' Clemmie took a deep breath, wondering how on earth she was going to broach the subject.

'Do.' Anya looked at her watch. 'I have a patient in half an hour. Have you been to our wonderful coffee bar yet?'

'No, I haven't had the chance. I must make the time to take a look around here. It seems like a very well-thought-out building.'

'It is.' Anya got to her feet. 'I'm very interested in the role of environment in healing—it's something Gil and I have endless discussions about. Let me buy you a coffee and we'll appreciate the architecture together…'

Knowing that Clemmie was in the main building with Anya had allowed Gil a moment to breathe. He had shoehorned himself back into his usual routine, and that was surprisingly restful, as well.

And then, just when he thought it was probably time for her to go home, and he wouldn't see her again today, Clemmie walked into his office. Bringing with her all of the conflict and the agonised pleasure that being in the same room with her always engendered.

'Hi. Sorry I've not been around. Anya introduced me to one of the other counsellors. They were both really helpful.'

'Don't apologise. This is what you're here for. I'm not expecting you to follow me around all the time.'

She nodded, hovering between the door and the visitors' chairs, clearly making her mind up which she was going to choose. 'I…um… Anya mentioned something that I'd like to ask you about. At some point…'

'Now's as good a time as any.' Gil waved her to a chair. 'Sit down.'

Clemmie sat, taking her time in hanging her handbag over the back of her chair, and then stowing the note-pad she was carrying into it. Obviously this conversation didn't require pen and paper, but it did seem to be taking its time to get started. Gil waited.

'Anya said that you've suffered from retrograde amnesia.'

A knot tightened suddenly in his stomach. He'd decided to follow Clemmie's lead, and that was what he'd do.

'Yes, that's right.'

'It's something I'm interested in. I was wondering if I could know a little more about what happened to you.' The tips of her ears were glowing red now. This meant something to Clemmie, as well.

'Of course.' Gil leaned back in his seat, trying to collect his thoughts. He should just start at the beginning and find out where that went. That went a little against the grain; he liked to be prepared in these kinds of situations.

'I was injured playing rugby. I don't remember what happened, but I'm told I collided with one of the other players, and then got up again and continued playing. I left the club after the match and four hours later Sam Gordon found me sitting in A & E, here at Barney's. I hadn't checked in and no one knew I was there, until Sam found me.'

'You were just sitting there?' Clemmie gave him a horrified look and Gil felt himself flush with embarrassment.

'Admitting I needed help wasn't my strong point and I was probably on autopilot by then. I imagine I was looking pretty grim by that stage, and since Sam's a neurosurgeon, she was well aware of the symptoms. It was my good luck that she happened to be there at all—she had been called down to see a patient. I'm told I didn't express much gratitude at the time, and objected very vociferously when she tried to examine me.'

'She probably saved your life.' Clemmie was staring at him now, and it was Gil's turn to look away. He knew how close he'd come...

'She did. Sam used to say that I was her first diagnosis in the wild, and she assisted in my surgery. After that she took a particular interest in my case and that's how we first became friends.'

'And you don't remember any of that.' Clemmie seemed to be homing in on what he did and didn't remember.

'The first thing I remember is waking up in the neurosurgical unit, two weeks later. I was very disorientated, and hardly even knew who I was. I regained most of my memories pretty quickly, but there's a complete blank starting two weeks before my injury and running through to two weeks after it.'

'And you have no memory at all of what you were doing for any of that time?'

'Nothing. I've been told about the circumstances of my injury and what happened after that, but no one can tell me about the two weeks before.' Gil carefully omitted a few salient details.

'Why not?'

'I was at a conference, in Manchester. Away from home, and none of my friends could tell me anything about that.'

'Do you have any theories? About why you might have forgotten just that two weeks?' Clemmie looked up at him quickly and then back down at her hands. But that one glance spoke volumes. This meant something to Clemmie and there was a reason behind her questions.

'Stress is often thought to be a contributing factor to retrograde amnesia. I had a high-stress job and my way of dealing with that was not giving myself the time to think about it too much. That's not a healthy way of living.'

Clemmie was nodding slowly, weighing every word he said. And she was giving nothing back. Gil couldn't keep this up, and it didn't bode well for their working relationship either. Knowing that she must remember him, but was deliberately not saying so, wasn't any kind of basis for the trust that was needed when dealing with patients.

Gil waited for her to reply. Then he took his wallet from his desk drawer.

'As I said, I don't remember much about the conference I went to. But I found this photograph in my wallet, about a month later.'

He laid the snapshot on his desk and Clemmie leaned forward, examining it. He'd waited seven years to find out what this photograph meant, but these moments seemed far more agonising than all the rest. When she finally looked up at him again, Clemmie's eyes were glistening, as if she'd just blinked away tears.

'I thought I recognised you. I wasn't sure.'

'I'm a little different now.' Not *that* different. 'If there's something I have to apologise for, Clemmie…'

She shook her head quickly. 'No. Nothing.'

'I wasn't sure whether I should say anything about it or not. I don't remember anything about that week, and…' He shrugged. 'You might have thought I was a real pain in the neck.'

Clemmie's eyes softened suddenly. 'No. No, I didn't think that. We were friends.'

It was quite a leap from thinking she recognised him, to their having been friends. Gil decided not to mention it.

'That sounds nice.' The regret at what had been lost felt as fresh and new as if it had all happened last week. 'I'm sorry that we didn't stay in touch.'

He would have left it at that, but then Clemmie gave herself away. She reached for the photograph, flipping it over as she did so and glancing at the back before she put it back down on the desk again, face up. She knew what was written on the back…

'I called you.' She pressed her lips together as if even that small detail was too much. 'I know now why I didn't get an answer.'

Then it hit him. Meeting someone, making friends or

maybe something more. Then ignoring their calls. She must have thought that he'd ghosted her.

And...when Gil thought about it, that was exactly what he'd done. It had been weeks before he'd asked one of the nurses to help him retrieve his phone from the locker by his bed and charge it, and Gil had clumsily deleted the missed calls and messages, barely looking at them. Those who knew of his injury wouldn't be expecting a reply, and those who didn't... He couldn't bring himself to explain that the man who was calling them back wasn't the one they were expecting to hear from.

Two more *if onlys* to add to the list. If only he'd realised that there would be a time when he could recognise himself again. If only he'd kept those call records and compared them with the number on the back of the photograph. He might have called Clemmie sooner and been able to speak with her.

'I'm so sorry, Clemmie.' It was all Gil could think of to say.

'What for?'

For the way she was kneading her hands together in her lap, the knuckles showing white with tension. For the pinched look on her face. For everything and anything that he might have done, which he couldn't remember.

'I don't know.'

'You've nothing to apologise for, Gil.'

Gil wasn't too sure of that. But whatever the rights and wrongs of it, Clemmie seemed determined not to share, her lips pressed together tightly. Since fate seemed pitted against them, maybe letting the conversation run its course had been a bad idea.

'I should let you go. You must have a train to catch.'

She glanced at her watch, and then nodded. 'Yes, I'll

catch the five-forty if I hurry. Perhaps we could talk a bit more another time.'

She was trying to pretend that nothing was wrong. Gil could identify with that—he was making the very same effort. Maybe it was best to leave things here and see how they both felt in the morning.

'Go and catch your train. Have a good evening.'

'Thanks. You too.' Clemmie was suddenly a blur of activity, jumping to her feet and almost running out of his office.

Gil stared after her, wiping his hands across his face. It had been a long time since the world was this out of control, jumbled thoughts dancing in his head like strangers at a party that he'd wandered into by mistake.

He'd cleared the air between him and Clemmie—or at least he hoped he had. Time would tell. But it still nagged at him that he was sure there was something she wasn't telling him. Something that had hurt her, and which she hadn't been able to brush aside and forget.

Something that she remembered, and he didn't.

CHAPTER SIX

IT WOULD GET EASIER. Clemmie told herself that each morning when she dragged herself out of bed, and each evening when she got home, flung her bag down in the hallway and filled the bath, in the hope that steaming, perfumed water would wash away the ache she felt.

And it did get easier. Making sure that her personal issues didn't get in the way of her work meant avoiding Gil as much as she could. That wasn't difficult. He'd drawn up a list of people that she should spend time with during the first week of her stay here. Physiotherapists, counsellors, the head of the nursing team, and the administrators. The two hours that she spent with Maggie learning how she juggled calls, sign-in sheets and people who had every kind of question were a revelation. She even spent a couple of hours in the early morning with one of the cleaners, listening to an interminable stream of chatter about the little quirks of her job. Clemmie had *thought* that she knew exactly how all the different cogs in the hospital day fitted together, but she was finding out that she really didn't.

She had time to sit down and speak with the patients here too, and was learning just as much from them as she was the staff. Jeannie's bravery, in setting aside her fear of falling again. Jahira's bubbly nature, which was breaking through her difficulties in communicating. Everyone was special and had something to contribute.

At first it was a relief that her communication with Gil had dwindled to a succession of notes, left with Maggie, who voiced her exasperation with the situation and asked Clemmie a couple of times if she couldn't contrive to actually *speak* to him. But even passing him in a corridor made her heart jump, flooding her head with memories of his touch. Watching him approach her was a pure and delicious experience, where every line of his body seemed traced with joy. And then seeing him walk away allowed the resentment back in. How could he have forgotten that he'd fallen in love, when that was supposed to be an experience that changed every fibre of your body?

And then it happened. Clemmie was standing at the reception desk, talking to Maggie, when Gil came hurrying through. He shot his usual brief smile in Clemmie's direction and kept going, despite the fact that Maggie had reached for his messages and was waving them at him.

'Sorry, Maggie. On my way to see Jahira...'

Maggie nodded, stowing the messages back on her desk. Before she could weigh up the advisability of it all, Clemmie followed. If Jahira was having problems, then she wanted to be there for her.

'What's happening, Gil?'

'It's Jahira. Something's upset her.' He didn't slow his pace. 'Shouldn't you be going home?'

'No, I'm supposed to be watching and learning. Even helping out if that's not too much of an imposition.'

He flashed her a querying look. She could have left out that last part; the fact that she hadn't exchanged more than two words at a time with Gil over the last few days was just as much her responsibility as his.

'Of course not. I'm sure I remember giving you access to everything we do here.'

'You did.'

They were agreed on that, at least. Maybe it was time to back off a bit now and show him that she knew how to work as part of a team. As they neared Jahira's room, Clemmie could hear the sound of raised voices, and Gil's pace slowed. It wouldn't help for them to rush in there as if they were the cavalry.

Jahira was sitting in the chair beside her bed, tears rolling down her face. One of the nurses was trying to calm her, but the girl seemed inconsolable. She raised her arm, banging it down hard onto the wheeled over-bed table.

Gil moved swiftly, catching up a pillow from the bed and plumping it down onto the table before Jahira could bang her arm down a second time. Then he backed off, giving the girl some room.

'If you want to let off a bit of steam, you can bang a lot harder than that without hurting yourself.'

Jahira glared at him at first, but then seemed to calm a little in response to the relaxed tone of Gil's voice.

'It doesn't even hurt all that much.'

He nodded. 'Just when you're not banging it, yeah?'

'Yes. That's when I get the shooting pains and the pins and needles.'

Gil nodded. 'That's pretty much the way of it. I can explain exactly why that's happening if you're interested.'

Jahira shook her head. 'Not really.'

The atmosphere in the room was calmer now. The nurse had melted away, and Clemmie had taken one of the visitors' chairs from the stack in the corner and sat down, assuming that Gil wanted her to keep out of the way but determined that she wanted to be here for Jahira. Gil reached for the second chair.

'So what's going on, then?'

'Everything's...different. *I'm* different.'

'Different how?'

Silence. Gil tried again.

'You know, it's pretty easy to feel that you're different when you can't rely on your arms and legs to do the same things they used to. I'm not sure that makes you a different person, though.'

'You don't understand...' A tear rolled down Jahira's cheek.

'Try me. You're right—I don't understand everything, but I'll listen.'

'Sarah came this afternoon. You know she's my girlfriend?'

Gil nodded. 'Yeah, your mum told me. Were you pleased to see her?'

'I hated it when she came to the hospital. I didn't want her to see me like this but... Here it's not so bad.'

'It's good that you're spending so much of your free time together. Sarah's always welcome here, and she can bring a drink or some sandwiches with her from the café. Call in to my office for an apple.'

Apples again. Clemmie was tempted to roll her eyes, but it made Jahira smile. 'How many apples have you got?'

'Far too many at this time of the year. I'm always on the lookout for someone to help me with them.'

Jahira heaved a sigh. 'Well, I don't know if Sarah's

even coming back. We had a hug and a kiss and...she said I was different. Not like I was before...'

'We've talked about feeling different.' Gil floated the idea.

'Yes, but... I didn't think *that* would be different. Was it different for you?'

Gil turned his mouth down in what looked like regret. 'I wasn't in a relationship when I had my brain injury.'

Clemmie had been. With him. It had taken a long time for her to accept that Gil had gone. But then, the complications of that situation weren't really what Jahira needed to hear right now, and he was understandably cautious about giving a seventeen-year-old girl relationship counselling.

'Gil might not be the person you need to ask.' She heard her own voice, and Gil swung round suddenly towards her. From the look on his face, he was grateful for the intervention, and Clemmie reminded herself that she was doing this for Jahira, not him.

'S'pose not.' Jahira shrugged. 'You're going to tell me to talk to Sarah, aren't you?'

'Talking about how you feel is always a good idea, if you feel you can do it. Sometimes it's difficult.'

'I don't even know what to say to her. I love her, and...' Jahira's eyes filled with tears. 'She asked me if I still fancied her. Suppose I don't...'

'I don't think...' Gil lapsed into silence again, probably realising that whatever he did or didn't think wasn't going to help.

'Let's talk about this a bit, shall we?' Clemmie wished she hadn't sat back here now, because Gil's large frame was partly obscuring her view of Jahira. 'Why don't I get us something to drink?'

Gil was on his feet before she could move. 'I'll get the

drinks and leave you two to talk.' He waved his hand in an indication that Clemmie should come and sit where he'd been sitting.

'Thanks.' Clemmie gave him a smile that wasn't totally for Jahira's benefit. Leaving now was an expression of trust that she hadn't done a great deal to earn.

'I'll bring some biscuits, as well…'

Jahira grinned at him. 'Those chocolate ones are nice. No apples.'

'Right you are. No apples.'

The last few days had been like walking on eggshells. Gil had recognised the need to give Clemmie some space, and maybe take a little space himself, but he'd yearned for her. Every note, every time he'd caught sight of her, had been precious.

All the same, he was aware that he'd given her a little too much rope, and that their own personal needs were beginning to interfere with his professional goals of giving Clemmie a full understanding of how the unit worked. He'd noticed that she'd missed the staff meeting yesterday, and that was an integral part of communication within the unit. She really should have come to that.

He waited outside Jahira's room for almost an hour, managing to pretend that he was doing something for part of the time, but largely just waiting. It reminded him of when he'd been a patient here, and much of his time had been spent waiting. It had been the polar opposite of being an A & E doctor, where his main aim in life had been to get around to everyone as soon as humanly possible.

He could hear laughter coming from behind the closed door and guessed that what his mother and sisters termed as 'girl talk' was going on. Whatever. If it worked, it worked.

And apparently it had. When she left the room, Clemmie had a broad smile on her face, which slipped a little when she saw Gil.

'Jahira's okay?' That was what Gil really needed to know.

'Yes. It's hard enough working out who you are when you're seventeen, without having a brain injury to deal with. We talked it all over and I've convinced Jahira that her circumstances might have changed but she's still the same person she always was with all the same wants and needs.'

And the same desires. He felt that his desire for Clemmie must have been born seven years ago, and had only lain dormant, waiting for the moment he laid eyes on her again. Such was the force with which it had burst back into his life.

'And Sarah?'

Clemmie shrugged. 'From what Jahira says, it sounds as if Sarah wants things to be back the way they were, and she's just going through a few difficulties over knowing exactly what to say. We talked about some ways that Jahira might ask for what she needs, and I said that I'd talk to them both the next time Sarah visits.'

That all sounded good. Clemmie was looking at him expectantly, and he should say something.

'Thank you. I'm glad you could spare the time to come and talk to her.'

Clemmie nodded. 'Always. She's a good kid.'

And Clemmie was a good woman. He tried his best to be a good man, and this couldn't go on. Clemmie's advice to Jahira had been spot on.

'I think *we* need to talk, too.'

'That would be good. Your office?'

'It can wait. Don't you have a train to catch or something?'

'There's always another one.'

She turned on her heel and started to make for his office. Gil followed her, retreating behind his desk and waving her into one of the visitors' chairs. He supposed that this was a work conversation, even if he had a strong suspicion that whatever was bugging Clemmie had very little to do with their work.

'I...um...have the impression that you've got a few issues about working with me. If it's because of our conversation the other day...'

Her eyes darkened. There was something there, in his forgotten past, and he wished that Clemmie would just say it.

'If I've done something wrong, I need you to tell me about it because I don't remember.'

She shook her head. 'There's nothing. We were acquaintances.'

Now he was sure. First it had been a half-forgotten encounter. Then a friendship. Now it was back to an acquaintance, and every nerve in his body told Gil that it was more. If his conscious mind couldn't remember, then maybe his instincts did.

'There's something, Clemmie. I feel it. We're allowing our personal feelings to get in the way of our jobs, and that's unacceptable. I'm to blame, but you're not helping—you didn't even come to the staff meeting yesterday.'

'I was...' Clemmie reddened, shaking her head. 'It doesn't really matter what I was doing. You're right—I know the staff meeting's important and I should have come.'

'It's okay. I'll forward the meeting notes to you.' Gil gave a little in return.

'Thanks.' Clemmie heaved a sigh. 'That's not really the issue, is it?'

Gil shook his head. 'No, not really.'

The room suddenly seemed very quiet. None of the bustle of a busy hospital. He fancied he could hear the sound of birdsong, floating through the open doors in from the garden. This was nice. Even Clemmie's silences seemed to feed his soul.

'All right. We met at the conference and we talked a lot. We became friends and...there was a connection there. You seemed to get what I was saying.'

Gil felt a lump form in his throat. He got what she was saying now; it all seemed to make sense to him. 'A meeting of minds?'

'Yeah. I'd really hoped that we could continue our friendship, and when you didn't answer any of my calls or messages, it felt as if you'd brushed me away. I thought I deserved a bit more than that and I was very angry with you.'

He'd come to terms with not remembering, but suddenly it felt like a terrible loss. Gil chose his words carefully. 'You did deserve more.'

'I know now why you didn't pick up the phone, and I'm sorry that I was angry with you.'

'It's okay. You came to the obvious conclusion. Did I say that I'd call you?' Since Clemmie was in the mood for honesty, then Gil could risk a little of his own.

'Yes, you did. Obviously you couldn't...' She blushed a little. Clemmie *had* been angry with him.

He took a deep breath. This was so hard to finally say. 'I deleted all of the missed calls from my phone without looking at them. I had your number on the back of the photograph, but I didn't know who you were and it took me a long time to pluck up the courage to call you.'

'Why?'

Gil wanted to shrug and tell her that he didn't know, but the warmth in her eyes stopped him. This might be the only chance he ever had to tell her how he'd felt, and it seemed to be important to Clemmie.

'I wanted to call. But I had nothing to offer you, or anyone else who had contacted me. I wasn't the same man as the one in the picture.'

'You felt the way that Jahira does now?' Clemmie gave him a look of gentle reproach.

'Yeah. Quite a bit like that, actually. I wondered sometimes if I'd ever be able to get back to what I was before the brain bleed. Reckoned I was just the guy with slurred speech and a useless hand, who fell over quite a lot and forgot everyone's name.' Gil shrugged. 'I had my share of self-pitying moments.'

'It's human.' Clemmie shot him a reproving look. 'And I would have understood.'

'I know you would. I'm the one who didn't understand, and I'm sorry.'

'Apology accepted. I'm sorry that I was angry with you, and that I allowed that to cloud my thinking...' Clemmie fell silent as Gil frowned at her.

'Apology *not* accepted. My mother wasn't much of a one for advice, but the one thing she told my sisters was that if you call someone three times and they don't get back to you then you give up on them.' The advice had been if they called a *guy* three times, but Gil wasn't comfortable suggesting that he and Clemmie had been anything more than friends. Even if her admission of anger told him one thing very plainly. That she'd been hurt.

But Clemmie seemed to know what he meant. 'That's good advice. Something everyone should know. Can I say that I regret what happened, then?'

Gil nodded. 'That's fair enough. So do I.'

He already felt that maybe he'd said too much, but it was unexpectedly good to talk. A great weight seemed to be lifting from his shoulders, and maybe one last admission on his part would take away some of Clemmie's hurt anger.

'I… I did try to call you. Much later. Your number was unobtainable.'

She stared at him, the tips of her ears going a deep red. 'When?'

'I don't remember exactly…' Gil thought hard. 'It must have been in the new year. I'd made a resolution.'

She shook her head suddenly. 'I had a new phone for Christmas. My number changed…' Her cheeks were red now, and she was biting her lip.

'Nice present.'

Clemmie shook her head. 'Not so much… My old one turned out to be better.'

The implication that she would have kept her old phone had she known he would call warmed Gil. That Clemmie would have been there for him, despite his having hurt her and taken nearly six months to pluck up the courage to call. It seemed inconceivable that he could ever have been just friends with Clemmie, but Gil had nothing concrete that he could rely on to suggest otherwise. Just a feeling, which could have been the result of staring at Clemmie's photograph for the last seven years, and a lot of wishful thinking.

'Are we good?' Clemmie's voice broke into his thoughts.

'Yes. We're good.' Gil hoped they were. Maybe saying it would make it so.

Clemmie nodded, getting up out of her seat. 'I really should be getting my train.'

'Yeah. Have a good evening.'

He watched her go, and then sank his head into his hands. There had been so much new information in the last couple of days, and he imagined that Clemmie was finding it all as difficult to process as he was. And there was still the nagging feeling that he didn't know everything yet. Maybe he never would. Gil wondered whether the protocol regarding not kissing and telling applied to the person you'd kissed. There probably weren't many precedents for that particular situation.

Would they ever really get past this? They'd talked before, and then retreated into silent avoidance. Maybe this was just too much for either of them to ever really be friends, and the best he could hope for would be Clemmie not seeing him as the enemy.

A knock sounded on the door and he jumped. Clemmie was standing in the doorway, holding a peach.

'I didn't eat this at lunchtime. Swap you for an apple?'

Suddenly the world felt a happier place. Clemmie's bright smile was all he needed to revive his belief that nothing was impossible. He grinned at her.

'Thanks. Don't tell anyone, but I'm in danger of getting a little sick of apples.'

CHAPTER SEVEN

THAT DAMNED PHONE! Harry had given it to her for Christmas, a top-of-the-line new smartphone. Clemmie had been touched by the gesture; he'd known that she was thinking of getting a phone that did a little more than just make calls, and this was a really nice one. He'd said that the line rental was paid up for two years…

Clemmie shivered at the thought. She'd used that phone a lot, talked to her friends on it and texted them. When the two years were up, she'd wanted to keep it and decided to renew the contract. Harry had been away for the weekend with his friends, and Clemmie had known he didn't like to be interrupted, so she'd gone onto the website and got a new password for the account sent through to her by text.

Then she'd realised. There were numbers that had been blocked. Texts sent. The friends who'd seemed to melt away after she'd got engaged to Harry had been calling her and she'd never known. And Harry would have been able to see who she'd called and when.

That phone had been her worst enemy and now it was her best friend, because it showed her the truth about Harry. Clemmie had searched the house and found a list of all her internet usernames and passwords hidden at the back of his wardrobe. The subtle control he'd exercised over her became suddenly clear. The way he trivialised how she felt and made her doubt her own judgement and memories. The way being around him when he was in one of his moods was like walking on eggshells. These weren't just the symptoms of a marriage that could have been better if she'd tried a little harder. They were all part of a deliberate and systematic violation.

Clemmie had spent the whole afternoon changing her passwords. Then she'd packed her bags and left the following morning, stopping off at Tower Bridge. Wheeling her suitcases to the centre of the bridge and waiting until the water beneath her was clear of boats had felt like a private and overdue ceremony. She'd taken the phone out of her pocket, holding it over the parapet, and as she'd dropped it, she'd said goodbye to Harry for good.

And now Gil had told her that he'd tried to get in touch with her. His call could have changed everything, her past and her future. Maybe it still could.

Clemmie wasn't sure what to expect when she arrived at work the following morning. She'd spent much of the night awake, and when she'd slept she'd dreamed of Gil. Yesterday had left her feeling that there might be a way forward with him, despite all her fears and doubts, but that might change.

But Gil had clearly abandoned any uncertainties he had, in favour of action. When she reported to his office, she found him sorting sheets of paper into piles and stapling them together.

'It's Budget Review time.' He didn't bother with anything as mundane as a *good morning*.

'I can see you're busy. Do you want me to leave you

to it?' Perhaps this was Gil's way of making sure that they didn't have an opportunity to spend too much time together.

'No, I'm hoping you'll help.' He collected the stapled bundles together in a pile and dumped them on the far side of his desk, opposite the visitor's chair.

'But I've no experience of doing budgets.'

'Exactly. It's why you'll need to learn. You may want to get yourself some coffee before you get settled.'

Clemmie surveyed the pile of papers. 'Yes, I think I will. You want some?' He'd obviously been here for a while and the mug on his desk was empty.

'Thanks, that would be great.' Gil went back to his sorting and stapling, and Clemmie picked up his cup and made for the coffee station.

She'd always imagined that budgets were deadly dull. But she had to admit that Gil's smile, and his dark eyes, added a heady arithmetic to the mix. And *his* budgets were all about what might be done if you thought outside the box, rather than what couldn't be done. The staffing and equipment costs were pretty standard, but exigencies were a world of their own, touched by Gil's ingenious charm.

'You do all this.' She scanned the list of activities. 'On *this*?' The figure at the bottom seemed very small.

'That's the essence of good budgeting. Making it stretch. So, for instance, the figure for the library…'

Clemmie ran her finger down the list. 'Yep. Got it.'

'That figure's for bookshelves only.'

'Okay. So where did all the books come from?'

'There's a bin where patients can put books that they've already read and don't want to keep, and a lot of visitors can be persuaded to bring in whatever they have spare at home. There's an advantage in being a relatively long-stay unit, because we get to know patients and their families, and they're often very willing to help out.'

His grin made Clemmie feel she was about to melt. Pure sex on wheels. It did make rows of numbers seem far more enticing. Maybe she could just sit back and enjoy it. She'd made her decision—work came first—and she wasn't going to go back on that.

'All right. So if we're talking about squeezing as much as we can from as little as possible...' She could have phrased that better, but Gil didn't seem to mind. 'How do you manage the gardening therapy on so little? I would have imagined the garden would be very costly to maintain.'

'We rely on a little help from the landscaping crew here at the hospital, but we also have a team of volunteers who come in to help once a month. They do the bulk of the work. The greenhouses were free, although we had to spend a bit of money on the flooring and other safety elements.'

'Where did you get free greenhouses? They look pretty smart.'

'They were display models that were given to us by a local garden centre. We dismantled them and brought them here and put a notice up saying who'd donated them, and everyone was happy.'

'And someone just knocked on your door and offered you a greenhouse?' Clemmie imagined there had been a bit more to it than that.

'Um...no. I spent a couple of days driving around until I managed to find someone who was willing to help us.'

Clemmie allowed herself a smile. Two whole days, before Gil found someone who would succumb to his charm by giving him a greenhouse. These garden centre proprietors must have hearts of steel. Gil's obvious enthusiasm for stretching a tiny budget far further than she could have imagined had already made her pulse beat a little faster.

'So what do you think? If you'd like, we could do these together and it would give you an insight into what's required. Or if you'd prefer, you could work with Kami in the physiotherapy suite, while I work on the budgets.'

Clemmie had already chatted with Kami, the head physiotherapist in the unit, and although she wanted to spend some more time seeing how she put theory into practice, Clemmie could do that later. Gil had given her a means of escape, but she didn't want to take it.

'I'd like to get a feel for how the budgets work, if you don't mind. It'll stand me in good stead for the future. I can come in a bit earlier tomorrow to give us more time together.'

'Good.' Gil seemed pleased with the outcome of his morning's work so far. 'Then I suppose the best place to start is to take a look through these together.' He turned his computer screen to face her and walked around his desk to sit down next to her. When Clemmie leaned in to see the screen, she caught a hint of Gil's scent. Soap and sex really did go well together.

'Right, then. What am I looking at?'

Gil liked to think that when he applied himself to a problem, he could generally find a way to work through it. That was Clemmie's approach too, she was always looking for ways to say yes instead of reasons to say no, and that made for a great team. Working through things together was more pleasurable than he could have imagined, but maybe he shouldn't be so surprised. Clemmie had said that they'd understood each other when they first met, and that hadn't changed. Why would it? Chemistry was chemistry, and the whole idea of it was that you put two of the same elements together, and they always reacted in the same way.

Clemmie was going to have the best of him from now on. He would give her every insight into the running of the rehab centre that he could, every last piece of experience that might help her to advance her own career. He owed her that, after the way he'd let her down.

And it was working. Clemmie had taken him up on the challenge with such enthusiasm that he was in real danger of being outdone. He wasn't sure if she'd forgiven, and he doubted that she'd forgotten, but her smile told him that she was making as much of an effort as he was to come to terms with the way he'd hurt her and move on.

Two days later, she bounced into his office, looking as fresh as a daisy, even though she must have got up very early to get here at this time. The sombre suits that she'd worn to work until now appeared to be a thing of the past. Yesterday she'd worn a bright top, and this morning Clemmie was wearing a dress, her hair swept to one side and rippling over her left shoulder. The asymmetry really suited her.

'I added up all of these numbers in three ways last night, and they still don't balance.' Clemmie laid the printed spreadsheet down on his desk and Gil tore his gaze from the soft folds of the fabric that covered the tops of her arms, focussing on the pencil ticks beside each total.

'Good morning.'

She gave him a smile. 'That too.'

He loved the way that just a few words between them were enough to set the day running on its intended course. A few words and a smile.

'You haven't added in the contingency.'

'Ah! Yes, of course. I forgot that the last time, as well. Always expect the unexpected, eh?'

That was one of Clemmie's wry jokes, and it was heartening to find that she finally found some humour in their situation.

'Sometimes the unexpected isn't so bad.'

She reached for an apple from the bag on his desk and sank her teeth into it. Those little signs of friendship were coming to mean so much to Gil. Because Clemmie meant so much to him. She was the reality behind the photograph, a living, breathing woman who was unpredictable and fascinating. Each day she asked more of him, expecting him to forgive himself for the way they'd parted, and put aside his doubts. It was challenging, but her smile gave him the strength to achieve the impossible.

They worked for two hours, and then Clemmie threw her pencil down onto his desk. 'Everything adds up now. Shall we stop here?'

'Yeah, it's time for my morning rounds. Do you have to meet with anyone this morning, or are you coming with me?'

'I'll tag along with you if that's okay.'

Gil nodded, gathering together the papers they'd been working on, and closing down his computer. 'We've made some good headway. I don't suppose you'd like to pop back and help me with the accounts next year, would you?'

She laughed. 'Maybe. But only if you bribe me with apples.'

That was definitely a deal. 'I'll be pruning for an

extra-large crop next year. And throw in some straw-berries for good measure.'

Clemmie laughed. 'You know I can't say no to straw-berries.'

He actually didn't know anything of the sort. Suddenly it didn't matter all that much. If Clemmie was comfort-able enough to access the memories that he couldn't, without even realising she was doing it, then that had to be a good portent.

He rose from his seat, stretching the knots from his shoulders. 'Let's go and do the rounds, shall we?'

Gil's rounds of the patients in the unit generally con-sisted of checking on the results of any tests that had been done, reading through therapy reports and medication charts, and, most importantly, going to see people. Clem-mie knew that there was a lot to be gained from a five-minute conversation with someone, and Gil was one of those doctors who watched carefully and noticed every-thing. It was one of the things she'd liked about him, and which she was rediscovering now.

'That's it.' He closed the door of Jeannie's room be-hind them. 'I'm glad to see that Jeannie's confidence is growing, after her fall. Well done on that.'

'Thanks.' Gil always seemed to notice the things that Clemmie did too, and it was gratifying. She shouldn't get too carried away with that, though; it was just some-thing that Gil did with everyone, however special it made her feel.

'I told Kami that I'd drop in on her physiotherapy ses-sion with Dave Newman. He's been experiencing cramps in his leg and Kami's a little concerned.' Gil's list of people he had to see and things he had to do was never-ending, and although he never seemed to rush, he got through an enormous amount in his working day.

His phone rang, no doubt someone else wanting to see him. But instead of his usual promise to be there at such-and-such a time, his face darkened.

'We're needed. Reception.'

Gil turned, hurrying along the corridor, and Clemmie followed him. Maggie was kneeling down beside an elderly man who was sitting in one of the easy chairs, and Clemmie recognised Joe, Jeannie's husband. Joe was here every day to see Jeannie, and everyone knew and liked him.

'I can't rouse him, Gil. And he looks awful...'

'Okay. Thanks, Maggie. Let's take a look at him.' Gil bent down beside Joe and Maggie backed away.

'Oh, dear. I hope he's all right. He said he just wanted to sit down for a few minutes before he went in to see Jeannie.' Maggie shook her head. 'Isn't there anything I can do?'

'The phone...' The phone on the reception desk was ringing insistently, and Gil could do without that distraction. Maggie would probably feel better if she had something to do, as well.

'Oh. Yes, of course.' Maggie hurried away, and Clemmie turned her attention to Joe.

Gil had managed to wake him up, and Clemmie could immediately see what Gil's initial diagnosis was.

'Can you hold your other arm up, Joe?' Joe was holding his left arm above his head, but his right arm lay limp at his side.

'Nah.'

'All right. That's fine, no worries. You can put your arm down now.' Gil's gaze flipped towards Clemmie. Joe was exhibiting the three principal symptoms of a stroke: the right side of his mouth was drooping downwards, he couldn't raise his right arm, and his speech was slurred.

She nodded. 'Should I call for a porter?' Joe clearly needed to be taken over to the main building, where there were facilities to scan and treat him.

'No, it'll be quicker if I wheel him over myself. We need to get someone to keep an eye on Jeannie. She'll be expecting Joe.'

'You stay here. I'll organise that.'

No conflict, no second-guessing. That happened when professionals trusted each other, working together to do what was needed. How ever had she managed to get to that place with Gil after everything that had gone between them?

There wasn't time to think about it, just act on it. Clemmie could heave a sigh of relief later.

Speaking to the head nurse and fetching a wheelchair only took a couple of minutes, but by the time she got back, Joe had a lot more colour in his face. It seemed that he was feeling better, because he was arguing with Gil.

'There's no need. I really should go and see Jeannie. I'm late already and she'll be wondering where I am.'

'We should get you checked out first, Joe.'

'But I'm feeling better now.' Joe seemed about to try to get to his feet.

'I've just spoken to James, the senior nurse. He's with Jeannie and he's going to tell her that you've been delayed.' Clemmie smiled down at Joe. 'She'll be okay, and we can make sure that you are, too.'

Joe shook his head. 'It's just one of my turns… I've had them before and I'm always okay afterwards.'

Concern flashed in Gil's eyes. Clemmie knew exactly

what he was thinking. If Joe had been experiencing this before, then it was likely he'd been suffering a series of mini strokes. Gil knew all too well about the consequences of ignoring warnings and keeping going.

'We're going to go now, Joe.' He spoke quietly, but very firmly.

Joe clearly didn't much like the idea, but he nodded. Clemmie and Gil helped him out of his seat and into the wheelchair, and Clemmie wheeled him towards the covered walkway that ran between the rehab unit and the main hospital, while Gil walked ahead of them, phoning through to the A & E department.

They were waved through the reception area, and a doctor came to see Joe immediately. All he really needed to do was to sign a few forms and pick up the phone to get Joe an immediate slot for an MRI scan, because Gil was watching Joe carefully, talking to him and gauging all of his reactions.

They stepped outside the cubicle, while a nurse got Joe into a medical gown, and the A & E doctor came to speak to Gil.

'A porter will be along soon, to take him up for the MRI.' The younger doctor was clearly aware of Gil's senior position at the hospital, and had been deferring to him in everything.

'Good, thank you. I'll stay here with him and explain what's happening. You get on to your next patient.'

'Thanks. We've been busy this morning.' The young man hurried away.

'Would you like me to stay? You can go and talk to Jeannie and let her know what's going on,' Clemmie asked.

Gil nodded. 'Do you mind?'

'Of course not. Jeannie trusts you and it's a lot better if the news comes from you.'

Something kindled in his eyes. That word again. Two weeks ago, it would have been unimaginable that she could use the word *trust* in any sentence that referred to Gil, but now it had slipped from her lips without a second thought. And Gil had heard it, the way he heard everything that she said.

'Thanks.'

He could have said more, but Clemmie knew exactly what he meant, and he wasn't thanking her for staying behind here with Joe. She shot him an embarrassed smile, and then the nurse appeared at the entrance to the cubicle.

'We'd better…go and talk to Joe.'

'Yeah.' His gaze held hers for a moment longer than necessary. The warm feeling that flooded through her felt suspiciously like the way she'd felt before all the mistakes had ruined the precious bond between them. And then he turned, walking back into the cubicle. Clemmie followed, her knees shaking a little from the force of the realisation. She and Gil were rewriting the past and building a new friendship together.

'This is all a lot of fuss over nothing. I feel fine now.' Joe was frowning. 'At my age it takes a bit longer to wake up.'

'Joe, when I first saw you, you were really unwell. You've been showing all of the symptoms of a TIA, which is a transient ischemic attack. Some people call it a mini stroke. It can pass very quickly, and you feel fine afterwards. We do need to check you out, though, and make sure that we prevent it from happening again.'

'Leave me here, then. I'll sort things out…' In Joe's estimation, sorting things out clearly involved persuading everyone that he was fine, so that they'd discharge him. He wouldn't succeed, but it would be good if he devoted his energies to something a bit more constructive.

Something softened in Gil's eyes. Maybe he was feeling the same as Clemmie did, that it would be special to have someone who cared as much about you as Joe did for Jeannie.

'I get it, Joe. We've all seen how well you look after Jeannie, but it's time for you to let us take the weight for a little while. Stand down, will you?'

There was sense in Gil's words, but it was the conviction behind them that made them so convincing. Joe puffed out a sigh.

'I suppose it won't do any harm to get this checked out.'

'No, it won't. Clemmie's going to stay here with you and I want you to tell her how many times this has happened before, and any other symptoms you've been having. I'll go back to the unit and keep a close eye on Jeannie for you.'

'Yes. Thanks.' Joe stretched out his hand, and Gil shook it.

He left, shooting Clemmie a smile, and with a reminder for her to call him as soon as she knew anything, which was probably for Joe's benefit. She turned to Joe, picking up the notes from the end of the bed and sitting down to address the question of just how many of these TIAs he'd already experienced.

Joe was wheeled up to the MRI suite twenty minutes after they'd found him in Reception. A swift and appropriate response that stood a good chance of preventing the catastrophe of a full stroke. Clemmie allowed herself a smile. Maybe friendship with Gil wasn't so hazardous to her work after all.

CHAPTER EIGHT

SOMETHING HAD HAPPENED. Perhaps the same thing that had happened seven years ago. Clemmie seemed to understand it in a way that Gil didn't.

But he trusted her now. The idea of putting his destiny in someone else's hands had never gone down too well with Gil, but if he was going to do it, then Clemmie's hands were the ones he wanted.

Jeannie had shed a few tears over Joe, but Gil had made sure that she knew that he hadn't suffered the same devastating after-effects of a stroke that she had, and that he was going to be all right. Clemmie had stayed with Joe until he was transferred up to a ward for observation, and Gil had wheeled Jeannie across to visit him after lunch.

'What's this?' Joe smiled at her. 'You're visiting me now?'

'You silly sausage.' Jeannie took his hand. 'I should be giving you a piece of my mind.'

It was obvious that she'd be doing no such thing. Gil reached into the pocket at the back of the wheelchair and handed her the bag that contained the purchases that Jeannie had made at the hospital shop on the way over. Jeannie propped it on her lap, withdrawing her gifts one by one and giving them to Joe.

'Grapes. Just the thing. Are you going to peel me one?' Joe teased his wife.

'That's enough of that, Joe. I've got you those gardening magazines you like. They should keep you quiet for a while.' Jeannie passed him the magazines, smiling as Joe picked them up, flipping through them.

Clemmie rose from her seat, glancing at Gil. By wordless agreement, they left Joe and Jeannie alone.

'Nice.' Clemmie was smiling. 'I'm glad you stopped at the shop.'

'Jeannie wasn't going to arrive empty-handed.' The sudden wish to put his arm around Clemmie's shoulders was almost irresistible. Just to turn the closeness of this morning into physical reality.

'I need to get back to the unit to see Sally. She's one of our volunteers—she brings her dogs in once a fortnight. You want to stop by the coffee shop on the way and get a takeaway?' He started to walk towards the main lobby of the ward, waving to the senior nurse who had promised to keep an eye on Jeannie and call him when she was ready to come back to the rehab unit.

'Yes. That sounds good.'

They strolled through the atrium together, joining the queue for coffee. Then walked back to the rehab unit, enjoying the sunshine of a bright, warm day.

'Do you miss it? A & E?'

'You think I'd be better off working there, still?' Clemmie must have seen what Gil had felt. The rush of adrenaline that made him feel suddenly that bit more alive.

'You've made the rehab unit into one of the best in the country. It would be crazy to suggest you should be anywhere else.' She paused for a moment, sipping her coffee reflectively. 'But you told me that you loved the buzz of emergency medicine.'

He had. But it was the kind of love that had done him no good at all. 'My brain bleed forced me to reassess a lot of things. I thought that I was thriving on the stress, but in fact, it almost killed me.'

'You think that stress had something to do with your injury?'

'No, probably not. I don't remember what happened, but I know that I always played to win, so I wouldn't be surprised if I made a bold tackle—' Gil raised one eyebrow as Clemmie snorted with laughter.

'A bold tackle, eh? You were known for that kind of thing?'

'Always. Didn't I tell you that before?' Gil ventured the question.

'No. But my impression of you was that you had a lot of…momentum.'

It was nice that they could talk about the first time they'd met. There was so much that Gil wanted to know about and now it wasn't quite so much of a no-go area between them.

'I had a bit too much momentum back then. I didn't even know how to stop…' Gil shrugged. 'I often wonder if the stress wasn't a contributing factor in my memory loss.'

Clemmie raised her eyebrows. 'So you think that something stressful happened at the conference.'

It was interesting that she should jump to that one conclusion, when she must know as well as he did that wasn't always the way stress worked.

'No. I think that the way I was living my life was putting me under constant pressure.' Gil slowed his pace, hoping it would give them more time. The conversation was beginning to get very interesting. 'Did I seem stressed at the conference?'

Clemmie considered the question and then shook her head. 'No, you seemed happy. Quite relaxed at times.'

There was something she wasn't telling him, but Gil let it go. They were her memories and Clemmie seemed to be more comfortable with sharing them one piece at a time.

'Then you must have caught me at one of the better times in my life.'

She seemed pleased with the idea. 'So you were under a lot of stress with your job?'

'I was, but stress was already a way of life for me. I come from a family of overachievers.'

'What does that mean?'

Gil took a sip of his coffee, thinking about the question. 'It means…my parents worked hard and had good, fulfilling jobs. They taught their kids to do the same. When I was growing up I only saw the rewards—we lived in a nice house and my dad had a boat. I wanted to be just like them, someone who could go out and get anything I wanted. But what my parents didn't teach us was how to handle the fallout from that attitude.'

'Did they know?' Clemmie asked the all-important question.

'No, I don't think they did. My uncle died from heart failure when he was only forty-seven, and Mum began drinking too much because she couldn't sleep without it. She got help eventually, but none of it was ever talked about, and I didn't know how to deal with weakness or failure. I couldn't admit to it.'

'They pushed you too hard?'

Gil shook his head. 'Nah. That would be the easy answer, but they really didn't. They just set an example and I followed it without question. When I had my brain injury I simply didn't know how to tell them, because I couldn't admit to feeling that I was somehow less than what I'd been before. I didn't call them for months.'

Maybe he shouldn't have said that, because he hadn't called Clemmie either. He could see the shock on her face, but then she pulled a regretful smile.

'The way you didn't call me? That's almost reassuring. I don't feel quite so singled out now.'

The consequences of his actions began to sink home. 'Don't ever feel that way, Clemmie. It was all me, and nothing to do with you. I can't say how sorry I am—'

She reached up, putting her finger against his lips. It was all Gil could do to stop them from forming the shape of a kiss. 'You've said sorry already. Apology accepted, so we can move on now, eh?'

Gil nodded. 'I won't make those mistakes again.' He meant it. An apology didn't mean much unless it was accompanied by change.

'So was it your decision to move out of emergency medicine?'

Gil smiled. 'If you're wondering whether I changed course for medical reasons, then no. I could have gone back to my old job, but I realised I was there for the wrong reasons. At work they used to call me a Stress Eater, but in truth, I was only internalising the stress. I was proud of the fact that I didn't need to talk about it and couldn't see that the colleagues who did were the ones who were really coping.'

'Everyone needs to talk.' Clemmie pressed her lips together thoughtfully.

'Yeah. It took losing the very basic things, like being able to feed myself and walk across a room, before I realised that.' It had taken Clemmie's arrival to make him realise that he still had a few outstanding issues and that he didn't talk enough, even now. 'Pride's a hard thing to let go of.'

'You're not proud of what you've achieved here? You should be.' She raised her eyebrows.

Gil chuckled. 'Well…yeah. It's different, though. I handle stress differently, as well. I've learned that I can't work every waking hour and then blow it all off with a game of rugby at the weekend. That kind of machismo doesn't do me any favours, and it doesn't do my patients any favours either.'

Clemmie nodded, smiling suddenly. 'You've found the place that's right for you, then.'

'Yes. I think so.'

They were nearing the path that ran around the back of the rehab unit, and Gil wondered whether Clemmie would turn to go into the building. But she followed him as he walked to the small walled garden to one side of the greenhouses.

This was one of his favourite places. Donated by an elderly lady who had spent time here after a stroke, it had an air of peace and quiet, away from the activity of the hospital. Raised beds on three sides meant that patients could reach to touch the scented flowers and herbs that grew here, and the central paved area was shamrock-shaped, giving three separate areas where groups could sit and talk.

Sally was already here, along with her two dogs. The gentle animals were used to being stroked and petted, and the giant Bernese mountain dog lay sprawled in the sun, while Zaffie, the golden retriever, was sitting with Jahira and Sarah, enjoying the fuss that both girls were making of her.

'Everything all right, Sally?' Gil addressed the dogs' owner.

'Yes. I dare say a few more people will be coming out soon. I've let the nurses know I'm here.' Sally lowered her voice. 'How's Joe?'

Gil knew that the unit was a close-knit community, but was constantly surprised by how far and how fast news travelled. 'He's doing well. I've taken Jeannie over to see him, so she won't be coming out to sit with you today.'

'Well, give her my love, won't you? Tell her I'm glad that he's okay.'

'Will do. Thanks for being here today, Sally.'

'My pleasure, Gil. Particularly on such a lovely day.'

Gil turned, pleased to see that Clemmie was still with him, despite all of the opportunities she'd had to go and do something else. He hadn't finished his coffee yet, and so he walked over to the bench outside the greenhouse, sitting down there. Warm pleasure enveloped him when Clemmie followed him, sitting down next to him.

'So how about you? What made you go into neurological rehab?' It was the kind of question that she could answer at almost any level she liked, but Gil was hoping that she might tell him a little more about herself.

'My reasons haven't changed.'

'Uh. We've had this conversation before, haven't we?'

'Yes, but that's okay. I don't mind repeating myself.'

Again, he got the feeling that she was reaching back. Maybe testing out each memory before she shared it, to see if they were still tainted by those unreturned phone calls. Gil hoped that Clemmie was finding that they weren't.

'It'll be the last time. I'll make sure I don't forget *this* conversation.' How could he? The warmth of a scented afternoon, with Clemmie sitting by his side.

She smiled. That made the afternoon complete.

'I spent most of my time with my gran when I was little. Working parents…' There was a hint of wistfulness in her tone.

'A lot of people work and still have time for their kids.'

Clemmie chuckled. 'That's new. You didn't say that last time.'

'We're breaking new ground, then. Maybe I've changed a bit more than I think.' That would be down to Clemmie. Having to re-examine himself so that he could connect with her.

'Maybe you have.' She nudged him gently, in a sign that she liked the change. 'You're right. A lot of parents work, but mine were…absorbed. They didn't seem to have much interest in me, and I didn't feel they really saw me.'

'Their loss.' Clemmie's as well, growing up with that kind of neglect.

'Well, my gran made up for all of that. But she developed dementia and had to go into a nursing home when I was thirteen. I used to visit her every day after school, and I got to know most of the residents there.'

'And you got used to speaking with people who have those kinds of challenges?'

'Yes, I did. I learned not to worry when Gran couldn't remember something, or she didn't know who I was. She knew I was someone and that I was there, and that was enough. And when she *did* recognise me it felt like a really good day.'

'Not everyone has the patience to wait for those good days. Particularly teenagers.' It sounded a lonely way to live, particularly for someone so young who didn't seem to have much parental support.

'When they came they were worth it. Gran was always the one who saw me for who I was.'

Clemmie had said something like that before. That they'd clicked, and she'd felt he understood her. Gil was beginning to realise just how important that would have been in her life. And how much she must have been hurt when he'd seemed to abandon her.

Not just then, but now, too. He'd allowed her to go her own way, spending most of her time talking to everyone else in the unit apart from him. Gil had thought that it was what Clemmie wanted and gone along with it, but maybe it was just what she feared the most. She'd hung on to her anger like a shield, and taken herself out of his orbit, before he could reject her again.

He resisted the temptation to apologise again, because he knew Clemmie wouldn't accept it. 'So you decided to specialise in neurological issues.'

'Yes. I wanted to help give people a chance to get back into their lives again. Society tends to turn its back on those who can't communicate the way everyone else does. Or who don't remember. You understand that, don't you?'

'Yes, I do. For a long time I felt that there was a barrier between me and everyone else, and that I was too slow and couldn't remember the right words. The world was going too fast for me, and a lot of people don't stop and wait.'

'Unseen and unheard.' A melancholy smile hovered around her lips. If only Gil could kiss it away...

'You should never be either of those things.'

She smiled suddenly. 'I've learned that sometimes you have to make a little more noise.'

He cupped his hand behind his ear, hoping that the gesture might tell her that he was listening now. And that he'd listen for as long as Clemmie would allow him to, because time with her was becoming more and more precious, with each day that passed.

She got it. Clemmie laughed, a look of sweet knowingness dancing in her eyes. Gil was becoming more and more sure about the time they'd spent together at the conference. That he'd felt the way he felt now. That when they'd talked it had been more than just a pleasant way to pass an evening. It would have been like food and drink to him. And if he'd been the one who was guilty of smashing all of that to pieces, he could be the one to mend it, as well.

Clemmie had said more than she'd meant to. But that didn't seem so bad, because Gil understood, and coming to an understanding with him had become important to her.

They sat in silence as she finished the rest of her coffee. It was almost cold now, but she didn't want these moments to end too soon. Then she saw James, one of the senior nurses, wheeling a patient along the path that led to the walled garden.

'Ah, good. I'm glad that Edward's made it out here. I told him that there would be dogs here this afternoon.'

Gil laughed softly. 'You've been passing the time of day with my patients again, haven't you?'

'No more than you do.'

'That's okay, then. Edward likes dogs?'

'Yes. He's a volunteer dog walker for his local rescue shelter. He was grilling Jahira about her plans to become a vet the other day.'

'Really?'

'Yes. They've struck up quite a friendship. As unlikely as that might seem.'

Gil nodded. 'Brain injury's a great leveller, sometimes. It's good that Edward is making friends. He's finding the after-effects of his stroke very hard to deal with.'

Clemmie nodded. Edward was in his seventies, a widower and career soldier. She knew that it irked him that his back wasn't as straight as it had been, and that he had to be pushed from place to place in a wheelchair, but he bore it with a quiet resignation. When none of the nurses was able to knot Edward's tie in quite the way he liked it, it had been Jahira who had come to the rescue, insisting that Sarah give it a go. It had taken a few attempts and a stream of advice from Jahira before Sarah achieved the desired effect, but Edward had been pleased that his appearance was finally back up to scratch.

They both got to their feet at the same time. Clemmie knew that Gil was seldom too busy to greet a patient, and Edward waved cheerily at their approach.

'How are you feeling today, Edward?' Gil asked.

'Much better, thank you.' That seemed to be Edward's stock answer, irrespective of how he was actually feeling. 'Can't complain at all.'

'You're going to the walled garden?'

'Yes. Jahira tells me that I should come and help with the dogs.'

Clemmie saw Gil suppress a smile. Since she'd sat

down with Jahira and Sarah, and talked through how they both felt, their relationship had improved. Jahira was still struggling, but she was beginning to settle in and become a force to be reckoned with. She'd obviously realised that Edward liked to make himself useful and had asked him to come and help.

'I'm going that way. May I walk with you?' Clemmie asked Edward.

'That would be my pleasure.' Edward's blue eyes twinkled with old-fashioned charm.

'I'll leave you both to it, then.' Gil gave her a smile and then turned to James. 'I'd like to review a couple of the medication sheets with you, if you have a moment...'

James nodded, and the two men headed back to the building together. Clemmie pushed the wheelchair into the walled garden, and when the girls caught sight of them, Sarah jumped to her feet, making room for Edward in between her and Jahira. Sensing the possibility of some attention, the Bernese mountain dog got to its feet, ambling over to him, and Edward smiled, holding out his hand to greet the animal.

CHAPTER NINE

CLEMMIE HAD STAYED in the garden, talking to Sally about the dog visiting schemes here and at her own hospital, and comparing notes with her. Gil had been busy all afternoon, but that was okay. She had a list of people to see, and this separation was just the result of needing to be in two different places, rather than being terrified about getting too close to Gil.

She was on her way to his office, to share an idea with Gil, when she saw him out in the garden, digging one of the flower beds. He'd changed into a pair of worn jeans, and Clemmie stopped for a moment at the window to watch him. Many washes had the advantage of softening denim and making it fit very well. When that was combined with physical activity and a great body, what was a girl to do, but stand and stare for a moment?

Just a moment, though. Clemmie walked out into the garden, trying to keep her mind off the great body, because she was going home, and she couldn't take Gil with her.

'You're just off?' He straightened when he saw her, driving the spade into the freshly dug earth.

'Yes. I've an idea I want to run past you first. I see you've found something else to do.'

Gil chuckled. 'This is recreation.'

'You're sure about that? Looks like work to me.' Hard physical work maybe. But Gil was smiling and relaxed.

'What's your idea, then?' Gil's undivided attention always made her feel good. As if her ideas were worth hearing.

'I'd like to make a memory book, for Jahira and Sarah—'

'Jahira *and* Sarah?' He picked up on her point immediately. Memory books and photographs were one way that families were encouraged to help patients in the unit, but they were usually made for just one person.

'Yes, both of them. I was talking to them today and Jahira remembered something that Sarah didn't. They laughed about it, but I could tell that Sarah was a bit puzzled.'

Gil nodded. 'Forgetting things isn't confined to patients with brain injuries. It can be a different process, though.'

'Exactly. The difference between forgetting where you put your car keys and forgetting you even have a car.' Clemmie used the analogy she'd heard when she was a teenager and the manager of her gran's care home had explained dementia to her. 'That puts a responsibility on the people around a patient with a brain injury. They're a repository for their memories, but all memory is subjective.'

'You mean that Sarah can tell Jahira the facts, but she might leave things out that were important to Jahira, and her feelings about those facts will necessarily be slightly different.' He stopped to think for a moment. 'And you're talking just about Sarah and Jahira, are you…?'

He was far too perceptive. But then, the whole point

of what Clemmie was saying was that memory was a two-way process sometimes.

'Not entirely.'

His face softened. 'I don't want to put pressure on you, Clemmie. Whatever you want to tell me about things that happened that I don't remember...' Gil shrugged. 'It's all a bonus.'

There were things that she definitely *didn't* want to tell Gil. Clemmie was feeling guilty about keeping things from him, but it was better he didn't know about their brief love affair. It would put too much strain on their working relationship, and on the friendship that she was beginning to value so much.

'It's not you, Gil. It's the situation that makes me feel pressured. Wanting to explain things to you and knowing that I can't because I was looking at things through my eyes and not yours. You can be a storehouse for facts, but memories are a very different thing. Sarah's struggling with the same thing—she can tell Jahira what happened on any particular day, but she can't tell her how she felt or see it through her eyes.'

Gil brushed his fingers across the back of her hand. The small gesture told Clemmie everything. About how he was struggling now, and how important this all was to him.

'So Jahira's memory book will be all about how she fits in. With Sarah, with her family...'

'Yes. The memories in it are theirs, and Jahira can add her own to them. Maybe it'll help her work things out a bit.'

Gil nodded. 'I think it's a great idea. A nice slant on something we do so often that we don't always think about how it might really work. Is there anything I can do to help?'

Clemmie laughed. 'You're not just talking about Jahira and Sarah, are you?'

His gaze melted into hers. 'No. I have a personal agenda, too.'

That sounded so much like one of Gil's smiling invitations up to his room at the conference hotel. Her memories changed everything, turning Gil's everyday charm into something he probably didn't mean it to be.

'It's been a good talk, Gil. Thank you. I'll suggest the idea to Jahira and see what she and Sarah think about it.'

'I don't need to tell you to go gently. You have a talent for that without my interference.' He turned suddenly, bending to pick up a bottle of water that was propped on the grass and taking a swig. 'If you've got a moment, I have something to show you.'

Always. These days she always had a moment for Gil, even if it meant missing her train. There would always be another train, and Clemmie's fear over holding on to her time with Gil was diminishing.

She followed him over to a patch of earth behind the greenhouses, and Clemmie saw four big plant cloches. Gil opened one of them, parting the leaves carefully to reveal a large red strawberry.

'Our first one. They're coming into fruit a little later than mine at home.' He grinned up at her.

'Wonderful!' Clemmie crouched down next to Gil to examine the plants. 'You'll have a lot more soon. There are plenty of little ones there.'

Gil nodded, reaching out and picking the strawberry. 'Hold out your hand.'

It looked very tempting. 'No… Gil, you should save it for someone else…'

'Too late. I've picked it now. When the others are ready I'll get everyone out to pick them and we'll share them out, but you can't do that with just one.' He gestured towards the building. 'And no one will see.'

They were hidden behind the greenhouses and this felt like a delicious secret. Clemmie held out her hand, and Gil dribbled some of the water from his bottle over the strawberry to clean it. Clemmie picked it up and took a bite.

'Mmm… That's…so good. Try it.' She offered the remaining half of the strawberry to him.

'My hands are dirty…' He grinned suddenly. 'And I'm rather enjoying the look on your face.'

'And you're not going to share?' Clemmie joked. 'Try it.'

She held the strawberry out, and Gil took a bite. A sudden, potent reminder of feeding each other strawberries, on a warm day. Only then, they'd been sprawled across Gil's bed.

'That's good. You finish it.' His gaze was on her mouth, and Clemmie shivered as she took the last bite. A memory that they could both keep, which echoed the memories only she had. It couldn't do any harm, out here…

She couldn't tear her gaze from his face, and as Gil slowly rose to his feet, she followed. They were standing close, but even that physical proximity was less potent than the look in his eyes.

'Clemmie…' He murmured her name, and suddenly she had no choice. Clemmie reached up, pulling his head down so she could plant a kiss on his lips.

One wasn't enough. Of course not. What could she have been thinking? Gil's hands circled her waist, not quite touching the fabric of her dress. She didn't care if he got a few smudges of dirt on her—she just wanted to be close to him. For their bodies to touch when they kissed again.

Somehow that happened, even though she wasn't aware of moving towards him. His kiss was just as spectacular as the last time, and still so different from anything she'd experienced. That was because it was Gil doing the kissing, and his gaze that she seemed to be falling into.

But this was wrong. She could be honest with him, to a point, if they were friends. She could keep that hard-won self-determination. But if they went any further, she'd have to admit the things she hadn't said, their relationship and the mistakes she'd made as a result of it. She'd have to be prepared to give herself to him completely, because that was all she knew how to do with Gil.

When she drew back, he let go of her immediately. He gave a nod, but his eyes were full of questions. Then it hit her.

This was his first time. He didn't remember kissing her before, and he didn't know how much she liked it. She reached up, brushing her fingers against his cheek.

'That was a lot better than strawberries.'

He grinned, a look of relief showing in his face. 'Strawberries? I've just forgotten strawberries?'

Clemmie dug her fingers in his ribs and he laughed. 'I'll have to reacquaint you with strawberries, Gil. No one should forget them.'

His gaze searched her face, and then he nodded. He understood. He knew that their history together outweighed anything that they could do now, even if he couldn't remember all the details.

'You're right, Clemmie. It wouldn't be smart to take this any further.'

'However nice it was.'

'Nice doesn't really cover it.' Gil heaved an exaggerated sigh. 'Don't you have a train to catch?'

Trains. The old excuse had come to their rescue this time, because if she stayed here much longer Clemmie was going to throw caution to the wind and kiss him again.

'Yes, I think I do. Have you finished here?' Maybe he'd walk her out. She still couldn't quite bring herself to leave him.

'No, I've a bit more to do. But I'm missing you already.' Gil knew what they had to do and was pushing her gently in the right direction.

'See you tomorrow, then.' Clemmie was missing him too, and missing everything else that had followed their very first kiss.

As she walked back towards the unit, she heard the sound of his spade cutting into the earth as he started digging again. Maybe this gardening thing wasn't so crazy after all. Clemmie could do with a little activity, to take her mind off the tingles of pleasure that were still coursing through her. Perhaps if she ran all the way to the station, she could catch her train.

Neither of them had mentioned their kiss yesterday, and Gil felt that was the best way to handle it. Let it be one, isolated incident that made no promises and set no precedents. But it had changed them both subtly.

It felt almost as if they were a couple, as they walked

out of the rehab unit together at lunchtime, going to the cafeteria to buy coffee and sandwiches and then on to the park, to meet Sam. Gil saw her sitting on a bench, moving the double buggy back and forth, and as they got closer, he could hear the sound of the twins crying.

'Hey. Where's Yanis? You didn't come down here on your own, did you?' Gil put the coffee down on the bench, along with the sandwiches and a bag of apples that he'd brought along with him.

'No. He's popped into Neurosurgery to do a couple of urgent things.' Sam sighed. 'I'm not even allowed in the building.'

'Quite right, too. You're on maternity leave.' Gil grinned. When he'd called Sam to ask about meeting up, Sam had declared that she would be delighted to pop into the rehab unit, and Gil had suggested the park as a compromise.

One of the twins had settled a bit, and the other was still crying. Gil bent, and, when pulling a face didn't work, he picked the tiny baby up, walking around in a circle and jiggling her in his arms. She miraculously stopped crying, and when he looked up, both Sam and Clemmie were staring at him.

'You're a baby whisperer, Gil!' Sam grinned broadly. 'Or is this just your natural charm?'

Clemmie was smiling too, and Gil avoided her gaze, concentrating on the baby in his arms. A kiss was one thing. He hadn't anticipated that being in close proximity to both Clemmie *and* the twins would make his heart melt so very quickly.

But whatever Clemmie was thinking or feeling, she was keeping it to herself. She sat down on the bench, taking two of the cardboard cups from the holder and passing one to Sam. The two women introduced themselves, without any need for Gil to intervene.

'Shall I take them for a walk? Um… Aurelie seems a bit happier now.' Gil felt a trace of reluctance in letting the tiny baby go as he bent to put her back into the buggy.

'Nice try, Gil. That's Charlotte.' Sam grinned. 'If you don't mind, walking always does seem to settle them. Don't be too long, or I might eat your sandwiches. I'm really hungry.'

'Help yourself.' Gil shot Sam and Clemmie a smile and started to push the buggy along the wide path that ran around the edge of the park.

'What do you think, then, ladies?' As he walked, he bent towards Charlotte and Aurelie, checking that they were both all right. 'Will Clemmie be okay on her own?'

Of course she would. Gil had the same confidence in Clemmie that he had in Sam, and when he glanced behind him, the two women were already deep in conversation. Coffee in the park would go perfectly well without his input, and he was much better employed in keeping the twins quiet.

Gil named a few of the trees and shrubs that he could see and threw in a couple of gardening tips for good measure. Charlotte—or was it Aurelie?—began to fret a little and he picked up his pace.

'Hey, none of that. I'd like you to think about something for me.' The little one quietened down and Gil kept talking. 'There's this person I know…'

He knew that the twins couldn't focus on him properly at this distance, but the sound of his voice seemed to be keeping their attention. It was soothing to Gil as well, finally being able to say the things that he hadn't shared with even his closest friends.

'She's beautiful and kind, and good at her job. Great sense of humour—you'll find that's important in a partner when the time comes.' He hoped that Aurelie and Charlotte were taking note. This was all useful information for them.

'We've got a past, though. That's not a good thing, in case you were wondering. And it's confusing for me because I don't remember it. That's a very long story, so I'll skip that part. My main worry is that I don't want to hurt her. I know I hurt her before, and I don't think she's told me everything, even now.'

Gil felt his eyes mist with tears, and he blinked ferociously. There was something about talking to a baby that set your emotions going. Two were an even more potent mix.

'But I just can't back away from her. I…um…' Aurelie and Charlotte didn't need to know the details of exactly how he felt about Clemmie.

'To be honest with you, I kissed her yesterday. I didn't mean to—it just happened—but it was the best kiss…' Gil fell silent, reliving those moments as he walked.

'I don't want to make the mistakes I made the first time around, though. Even if it means we'll only ever be friends, I think it's better to take what we have and be grateful for it.' He stared down at his two confidantes. 'What do you think?'

Charlotte and Aurelie seemed to agree. At least they didn't voice any objections. Gil smiled down at them both.

'Thanks, ladies. Great chat. I appreciate it.' He could see two pairs of eyes beginning to close and reckoned that he'd given the twins enough to think about for the time being.

'Gil!' He heard Yanis's voice behind him and turned. 'Where's Sam?'

'I left her with Clemmie, back on the bench where we found her.' Gil grinned. 'Sam's looking after the sandwiches, so if we hurry, there might be some left.'

Yanis laughed, peering into the buggy at his daughters. 'Nice job. Now they're asleep, shall we go see if we can rescue some lunch?'

Gil nodded, and the two men turned, walking back towards where Clemmie and Sam were sitting.

'Sam's been very keen to meet Clemmie. She seems nice...' Yanis floated the idea.

Gil didn't take the bait. Sam was one of his dearest friends, and he'd become close to Yanis as well, even though he'd only known him a short time. But he'd got his answer from the twins, who were very good listeners and less challenging to talk to than anyone he'd ever met. Even Anya could take a leaf from their book.

'She's a great doctor. Lots of good ideas. I think this working relationship is going to benefit us both.'

Yanis nodded, raising his arm to wave as he saw Sam catch sight of them. Clemmie looked up from the writing pad she had perched on her knees, and her smile seemed warmer than the sun.

It was nice. A summer's afternoon in the park, and friends to share it with. Even if this wasn't all that Gil wanted from his relationship with Clemmie, he was determined that it would be enough.

CHAPTER TEN

CASUAL. NOT TOO casual because she'd be working. Not too smart because it was Saturday, and she wasn't going to the hospital. Smart/casual. Or casual/smart. After half an hour of looking through her wardrobe, Clemmie wasn't entirely sure what the difference was.

This shouldn't be so difficult. She and Gil were going to be spending an afternoon giving the budget proposals a final look-through, uninterrupted by the many other calls on his time that made it much easier to do it at his house than at work. What she wore wasn't going to make the slightest difference to that. Clemmie reached for the dark red dress that was her current go-to piece for any occasion, and slipped into it before she could change her mind again.

Maybe they'd talk a bit, as well. Since Gil had promised lunch, it would be rude to sit there in silence, and Clemmie was beginning to value the time they'd spent getting to know each other again. And if not, the afternoon wouldn't be a complete washout because the budgets would be finished and ready to send off. Clemmie now understood exactly how they worked, and how to get the very best from the money available, and that was an achievement in itself.

'Go with the flow, Clemmie.'

She murmured the words to herself as she glanced into the mirror. This wasn't the battle of wills that she'd had to endure with her ex-husband, who'd had a habit of deciding what he wanted from each and every transaction and sticking to it come hell or high water. It was perfectly possible to spend an afternoon with Gil without arming herself with a thousand answers to questions he probably wouldn't ask.

She picked up her briefcase and car keys and snagged the bag of macadamia nuts that she'd bought to take with her from the kitchen. Hopefully he still liked them, and if he didn't, then she could always eat them herself. Because this afternoon, she *was* going to go with the flow.

It was just lunch. Simple enough. Someone cooked, you sat down and picked up a knife and fork, and you ate.

But Gil saw every day how the simplest things in life could suddenly become mountains to climb. How many times had he patiently picked up a dropped knife or fork and encouraged someone to try again?

'Not the same thing, Gil.' He moved his finger quickly before it suffered the same fate as the cucumber he was slicing. 'There's no reason you can't do this, so just get on with it.'

The doorbell put him out of his misery, by prompting a wash of excitement. The same feeling that engulfed him every time he saw Clemmie, and which came to his rescue and propelled him into action.

How did she do that? It was the same question that occurred to him every time, as well. Clemmie was standing on the doorstep looking like the combination of the girl next door, who he'd known all his life, and an intoxicating new paramour. Effortlessly beautiful. Although he imagined that probably *some* effort had gone into her appearance—her hair shone as if it had been brushed a hundred times, and her eyes looked even more luminous with the application of a little make-up.

'Are you going to let me in?' She grinned at him. 'If not, perhaps you'll bring a chair out and I can wait here in comfort.'

Gil stepped back from the door, still speechless with admiration. Clemmie either didn't notice or maybe she just liked the effect that she had on him. He very much liked it too, so that was one thing they could agree on.

She was a charming guest. Pushing a bag into his hands and looking around her with obvious curiosity. Clemmie peered through the open door of the sitting room, and then gave him a little smile, as if she took pleasure in finding out what all the rooms in his house looked like. When he showed her through to the kitchen, she saw the bowls that were standing ready on the counter.

'Hm. Peanut sauce and a chicken marinade. That's not so difficult to guess. We're having chicken satay?'

'Yep. It's the Malaysian version.'

'Of course. You learned to make it in Malaysia?'

He must have mentioned that he'd been to Malaysia, but Gil didn't remember. Clemmie did, though, and that didn't seem quite as much of a challenge as it had once been.

'No, I wasn't much interested in cooking when I went. I got the recipe from a book, but it tastes much the same.'

'I can't wait, then.' She smiled again, and this time Gil remembered to return the gesture. 'If it tastes as good as this marinade smells, I'll have to get the recipe from you.'

'You can help if you like.' Gil unhooked an apron that

he never used from the back of the door, and she nodded and took it. She had to fold it over at the waist so it would fit her, but she looked enchanting in it.

Clemmie grilled a mean satay, as well. The same recipe tasted a great deal better when she cooked it, or maybe it was just her company that made the difference. Gil pulled the awning down to shade the paved area at the back of the house, and they ate outside. Coffee, macadamia nuts and the first two pears from the tree, which had obligingly ripened this morning, were an easy dessert, and then they set to work.

It took all afternoon to check through the budgets and assemble the package, to be sent off on Monday. Finally they sat grinning at each other, the wrapped parcel sitting on the table between them.

'Done. This is the first year I've had them in early.'

'Thanks, Gil. I've really learned a lot from this.'

'Coffee? Or do you think something to drink is a bit more appropriate to celebrate?' The solar-powered lights that he'd planted amongst the shrubs were beginning to glimmer faintly now, in the early dusk, and Gil gathered up the scrap paper from the table, taking it into the kitchen to put into the recycling bin. When he turned around, Clemmie was standing right behind him.

'Do you have the ingredients for that cappuccino cocktail you used to make? Only you need to go easy on the alcohol. I'll be driving later.'

He'd made her cappuccino cocktails. And he'd shared his own, very special secret recipe with her. The thought hit Gil like a blow to the chest, because he knew exactly what that meant...

The echoes of his own shock registered in her eyes,

and Clemmie's hand flew to her mouth. 'I've said the wrong thing, haven't I? I'm sorry…'

'It's okay.' He smiled, trying to make a joke of it. 'I only used to make cappuccino cocktails for very special people.'

Clemmie reddened a little. 'Special as in…good doctors? Valued colleagues?'

She knew that wasn't what he meant. And finally Gil felt that it wouldn't be so bad to ask, even if it was in a relatively roundabout way.

'People I like. My brother and I read about them when we were kids and tried them with instant coffee and some wine we managed to sneak out of the kitchen.'

Clemmie winced. 'Ew! That sounds horrible.'

'It made us both sick. We spent a good portion of our teens perfecting the recipe and I managed to get it right for his twenty-first birthday. I don't remember sharing that recipe with anyone else. It was always our thing.'

'I'm honoured, then.' Suddenly her gaze met his. It seemed to draw him in, and before he could stop himself, Gil had taken a step closer.

'Was there anything more than just cappuccino cocktails, Clemmie?'

She thought for a moment. Clemmie must know the answer. She was just wondering whether she'd tell him or not. Then she stepped towards him.

'Yes, there was something else.'

The look in her eyes almost brought him to his knees. Clemmie laid her hand on his shoulder, as if testing him out, and he smiled. Then she stretched up, planting a kiss on the side of his mouth.

'There was this, too.'

Not just that. Fire seemed to be dancing between them,

following the path of her fingers as she caressed his cheek. Gil reached for her, and when he gingerly laid his hand on her back, he didn't have to pull her close. Her body just seemed to melt against his of its own accord.

'And this?'

She nodded.

'I can't think how I could have forgotten...' Right now it seemed that this moment would stay in his memory for ever.

'I...wasn't sure how to tell you.' She looked up at him, twisting the corners of her mouth down.

She should never do that. Gil didn't want to ever make her regret anything. He leaned down, to drop a kiss on the side of her mouth and smooth away the frown. She shifted in his arms, turning her lips towards his, kissing him.

This time, he couldn't bear to let her go. She was so sweet, and yet so passionate, stirring the echoes of what felt like a long-lost memory, but in truth was just a part of a dream. One of those dreams about the ideal woman that no one ever expected to find. Somehow he'd managed to find Clemmie twice...

And then she broke away from him. Had he done the wrong thing?

'How about those cappuccino cocktails? We could always get back to this later...' Her smile told him that kissing her had been exactly the right thing.

And now she was doing the right thing, too. It gave him a bit of time to process the sudden shift in their relationship, and how he felt about it. And something to do while he was processing...

Gil walked over to the kitchen dresser, opening the top cupboard and reaching for the drink bottles. 'Can you remember the proportions?'

'I think so. You make the coffee and we'll see if I get it right. I know that Kahlua is the main one.'

Gil nodded, flipping the switch for the coffee maker and fetching ice from the freezer to cool the mixture. Watching her examine the bottles and line them up in order of importance on the counter. Order, amongst all the chaos that was pounding in his heart.

'Don't tell me...' She smiled up at him, studying the bottles carefully and then rearranging them. Gil shook his head and she looked at the bottles again, swapping two of them around.

'Interesting.' He grinned down at her. She'd remembered that Kahlua was the principal ingredient, but got some of the others mixed up.

'That means it's not *quite* the same as your recipe.'

Gil shrugged. 'Maybe it'll be better.'

'Let's see, shall we?'

Gil reached for the cocktail shaker and handed it to her. Clemmie carefully measured out the spirits, and then poured the iced coffee onto the mix.

She poured the mixture into glasses, adding the ice-cold milk that he'd frothed. Then he led her back outside, to sit in the warm scent of the evening air.

'Here goes...' She clinked her glass against his and took a sip. 'Not bad.'

Gil tried his. 'Not bad at all. In fact, with a bit more Kahlua I think it's better than mine.'

Clemmie grinned. 'We'll have to try that another time.'

Another time... Gil smiled. She'd just widened everything out, so that everything didn't depend on this moment. This night. She'd allowed him the time to come to terms with a relationship with someone who he knew so little about, but who knew so much about him.

'Another time. Yeah...' Suddenly he didn't need more time. He could trust Clemmie to let him know whatever he needed to know. He leaned back in his seat, savouring the moment as it swirled around him in the gathering darkness.

But it was slipping away. Clemmie had finished her drink and they'd sat for a while enjoying the warm silence of the evening, but now she was sliding towards the edge of her seat. Using that body language that announced that she was about to go and leave him alone with his thoughts. The ones that only included her.

'It's been a good day, Gil. I hope we can do this again.'

Maybe he should wait. But having Clemmie here with him in his home felt so different from being with her at work. He couldn't quite fathom why...

Then it hit him. Everything they'd done and said at work had been centred around how they'd felt seven years ago. Here, surrounded by the everyday and without constant reminders of the fallout from brain injury, it was all about how they felt now.

When Clemmie got to her feet, he saw a fleeting moment of regret on her face. She felt it too, that freedom from the chains of the past. It was all he needed to know, and he rose, taking her into his arms.

What might have been a kiss goodnight turned into something much, much more. Something that burned into him, a beginning rather than an ending.

'I'd love it if...you stayed a little longer.' He tried not to put too many expectations into his words.

She smiled, her eyes dark in the failing light. 'On our first date?'

That was the heart of it. 'My first. I can live with that if you can.'

'Since it's not my first, I can make an exception.' She reached up, her fingers tracing his cheek. 'No expectations, eh?'

'I have little to base any expectations on.'

Clemmie kissed him again, and made him into a liar. Her kiss let him know exactly what to expect from this evening, and it was all good.

Clemmie had resisted this for so long. And yet now that the time had come, it was so easy to do. Maybe they could break that final boundary and be together. Not just ignore the secrets of the past, but come to terms with them…

She shivered suddenly in response to the thought, and Gil stilled. Waiting for her to say something, but she wasn't sure what to say. She wanted him so much, but Gil's honest gaze deserved her honesty in return.

'It's okay. Whatever you're thinking.' Gil's murmured words gave her strength. Maybe it *was* okay.

'I…' Clemmie took a deep breath, looking up into his eyes. 'There was someone else. After I met you…'

He nodded. 'You owed me nothing, Clemmie. You thought I'd deserted you.'

All the same, she should tell him now. Maybe leave out the parts that made it obvious she'd fallen into Harry's arms as a result of Gil's actions…

'You need to know that—' She fell silent as he laid his finger across her lips.

'Let me tell you what I need to know. Was there someone else when we were together?'

Clemmie smiled at the thought. 'Seriously, Gil? There was no time for anything or anyone else.'

'Sounds as if we had our priorities straight.' He gave her a wicked smile. 'Is there anyone else now?'

That was an easy question, as well. 'No.'

'It's the same for me. There was no one else then, and there isn't now. If you want to know more, I can tell you about the couple of brief flirtations in between, that never went anywhere.'

Clemmie shook her head. 'I don't need to know. I'm glad you weren't lonely.'

'I was lonely. When I found you, I realised why that was. I think that even though I didn't remember you, I always knew that there was something missing.'

That was more than enough information. Clemmie kissed him and he responded with a new hunger. This time, his hands didn't shake when he touched her. It was a lot for someone to deal with, but it seemed that Gil had come to terms with it all a little quicker than she'd imagined he would, and in exactly the way she wanted him to.

No expectations.

That was hard, because she couldn't help wanting this to be the same as it had been last time. But Gil was a changed man, in so many ways. Not so driven, and without that brash confidence that had allowed him to challenge her so deliciously.

And then he made *that* move. The one that she'd loved so much, the one that made her feel as if she were the one and only person in his world. Seen and heard, and capable of so much more than she'd thought. One arm coiled around her waist, pulling her tight against him. Gil was staring down at her, the fingers of his other hand caressing her face, his kisses following their path. Watching her closely, his lips curving into a smile when she sighed her approval. All hers...

And she knew exactly what he wanted. He'd never seemed to tire of exploring her body, how it fitted with his and every way that she reacted to his caress. When she pulled away from him, she saw self-doubt in his face, but when she took his hands in hers and guided him back through the open door and into the darkened sitting room, he smiled.

'Clemmie…?'

She pushed him down onto the sofa, silencing him with a finger across his lips. Two silhouettes, taking their time to renew what had once been everything.

As she began to unbutton her dress, he leaned to one side, reaching to switch on the lamp.

'You're far too beautiful to do this in the dark.'

It was how he made her feel. How his gaze made her feel, following each and every movement she made. Making her hands shake as she slipped the soft fabric from her shoulders. He gave her all the confidence she needed to walk slowly towards him, climbing onto his lap, her legs astride his.

'Clemmie… Please talk to me…'

'Don't you know what comes next?' She started to unbutton his shirt and he grinned.

'I have a good idea. I guess you already know I like to play a little first.'

'So do I.' She leaned forward, kissing his cheek. 'Am I going too fast for you?'

He shook his head. 'You have perfect timing. But I need you to talk to me. Tell me what you're feeling.'

What she was feeling had always been so important to him, and that was what had bound them together, in a way that Clemmie had never experienced with anyone else. He'd seemed to know instinctively, but of course it had been the result of watching and listening. Gil did that so well that it had seemed effortless.

'Take all the time you need to catch up. In fact, I insist that you do.' Her lips brushed his ear as she whispered, 'I want to see a little more of you.'

He was still there. The Gil that didn't know what else to do with a challenge other than meet it head-on. He leaned forward, so that she could pull his shirt off, and then back again, his fingers running lightly across her body. *Now* she could say it. In the heat of a warm night, she could tell him all of the things that she liked best, whispering them into his ear without needing to mince her words. And he followed through, doing everything that she asked of him.

'Did you do this before? Telling me exactly what you want?' He grinned, acceding to her request to unfasten the catch on her bra.

'No. You like it?'

'Very much. Particularly the finer details.' His hand covered her breast, the thumb brushing the nipple in a move all of his own. 'You?'

'You don't need to ask that, do you?' Clemmie had already shown him how much she liked this intimate conversation.

'I guess not.'

'Then do it again...'

Gil chuckled. 'Like this?'

She was beyond telling him now, but her sigh was enough of an answer. He lifted her against him, kissing her breasts until Clemmie groaned with the sweet agony of it all. 'Stop...please. You're going to make me come...'

'That would be a bad thing?' He let her sink back down onto his lap.

'It would be, if I didn't have you inside me.'

'I was hoping you might say that.' He kissed her, sliding forward in his seat and lifting her up in his arms. 'You want to go upstairs?'

'Yes.' All she wanted now, after this long and delicious foreplay, was to dispense with words. Have him take her in all the ways he'd taken her before.

Gil carried her upstairs. The bedroom was lit only by moonlight, slanting in through the windows and across her body when he laid her down on the bed. He swiftly closed the curtains, leaving the door open so that light from the hallway could illuminate the room.

Clemmie watched as he undressed. His body was still the same. Strong and immeasurably beautiful. And he still hesitated for a moment, one hand brushing his chest as if he was in some doubt about whether she liked what she saw. He'd done that the last time, taking nothing for granted.

'Come here, Gil.'

He took a moment to open one of the drawers in the dresser and take out a pack of condoms, and then he did as he was told. Batting her hands away when she tried to remove her briefs, so that he could do it himself. They were beyond words now, each knowing that all they wanted was to be finally together.

She cried out as he slid gently inside her. Then again, as he lifted one of her legs, pushing further. Clemmie closed her eyes, gritting her teeth, trying to make this last just a little longer.

He stilled suddenly, leaving her in an agony of frustrated desire. 'Open your eyes, Clemmie.'

When she did so, she could see that he too was very close to the edge. But even now, the most important thing to Gil was that they should keep the bond that had grown again so naturally between them, and that they should make love staring into each other's eyes.

'Now let go.'

Did she dare? After everything that had happened? There was really no choice in the matter, because every instinct was telling her that she wanted to feel what he'd do when she did.

'Take me with you, Gil. Wherever you want us to go.'

He nodded, rolling them both onto their sides. Lifting his weight from her leg, and then twisting his body, so that when he slid inside her again the angle was different. A little less friction, but much more depth, and his free hand was able to reach any part of her body.

Gil was calculated and precise. He made it last until he'd told her everything that was on his mind, how beautiful she was and how much he loved everything they were doing. Building her up so that when the orgasm came it was so strong that it might have shaken them apart, if he hadn't been holding on to her so tight.

And then his. She felt him stiffen and swell inside her, and then give himself to her with a helpless roar of feeling. It felt better than it had before, because now they knew each other in ways they hadn't when they'd first met. They were no longer just charmed lovers... They'd had to forgive each other and build this new relationship from the ruins of the old.

She snuggled into his arms, and he covered them with the light duvet that lay on the end of the bed. Holding on to him so that maybe she'd figure in his dreams.

'You okay?' Clemmie felt him kiss the top of her head.

'No. I'm a lot better than that.'

'Me too.' He hugged her and Clemmie lay quietly by

his side. His fingers brushed her shoulder, and he shifted a little closer. 'You're sure? You're very quiet…'

'Don't you want—?' Clemmie stopped herself. 'You don't want to sleep, do you?'

'That's not number one on my list of priorities. Why…?' He puffed out a breath. 'You're telling me that the last time we did this, I just rolled over and went to sleep afterwards, aren't you?'

'You were very tired. You said you'd been working some long shifts before you arrived at the conference.'

'Don't make excuses for me. You *are* telling me that I went to sleep.'

'I didn't mind. I liked watching you sleep.' Clemmie propped herself up on her elbow and saw the pained look on Gil's face.

'Don't. I can't believe that you didn't kick me out of bed for falling asleep on you.'

'We were in your hotel room, so it would have been difficult. Anyway, you're very cute when you're asleep.'

'Always good to know.' He rolled over, covering her body with his. Holding her so tenderly that it felt she was melting into him again. 'And maybe you were a bit more accepting of bad behaviour in others then.'

There were some things that Gil didn't need to be told; he just saw and understood them. But he was wrong about this.

'It didn't seem so surprising to me that people would ignore what I wanted.' She shook her head when he went to protest. 'You were the one who challenged that and made me understand what it was like to be seen. We've both changed, Gil.'

'I'm not so stressed out and tired, and you're comfortable with telling me what you want.'

Comfortable wasn't the word for it. Telling Gil what she'd wanted and having him respond to that had been exhilarating. 'Don't you know that already?'

He bent to kiss her. 'I loved it, too. So much that I'm going to demand you do it again. You can go to sleep, or… Strawberries maybe? A back massage?'

'Can I have both?'

He grinned, disentangling himself from her arms and pulling on a pair of jogging bottoms. 'That'll be my pleasure…'

Gil was trying so hard to make it all up to her. He didn't need to. All he really needed to do was to be the same man who saw her and heard her, and who she'd fallen in love with the first time around. They could leave all the hurt between them where it belonged, in a past that he didn't remember.

CHAPTER ELEVEN

CLEMMIE HAD STAYED until Sunday evening. It had been wonderful, something that Gil hadn't been able to hope could ever happen. But it had, and it was better than he could have ever imagined. They'd walked down to a small restaurant for lunch, sitting outside. Tables and chairs stretched out across the cobbled street, which was closed on Sundays to make a pedestrian walkway that buzzed with life. Then they'd gone home and made love again. Gil was beginning to wonder whether this was all he'd ever need out of life. Good food, the warmth of the sun, and Clemmie. The first two reminded him of Australia, and Clemmie reminded him of everything that felt right in the world.

It was no surprise that it couldn't last. After she'd gone home, to prepare for the week's work ahead of them, Gil had sat alone in the garden. In the quiet of the evening, doubts buzzed around him like mosquitoes.

There was so much she hadn't told him. Would she ever have admitted that they'd slept together if it hadn't been for the cappuccino cocktails? The drip-feed of information was like a leaking tap. You could lie awake all night waiting for the sound of the next splash of water.

He knew how hard this had been for Clemmie. And

he didn't blame her for keeping things back; she'd found herself in an impossible situation. The thing that worried him the most was that she'd kept the things back that she knew would hurt him. The things he'd done that made his head and his heart throb with guilt.

But he couldn't let her go now. When they made love, he knew that she was holding nothing back from him. In time, everything else would follow.

He went to bed early, and her scent on the pillow was enough to lull him into a deep, dreamless sleep. In the morning, he took his bike from the lean-to in the garden. It had been a couple of weeks since he'd gone for a long ride, and that always cleared his head. A turn around the cycle paths in Richmond Park was what he needed, and there was plenty of time before he needed to be at work.

'Been for a swim?' Gil's hair was still wet when Jahira appeared in the doorway of his office.

'A shower. I cycled to work this morning. What are you doing here, Jahira?' Patients weren't barred from any part of the unit, but they very seldom came to the part of the building that housed the offices.

'I want to ask you something.'

'Okay. Come in and take a seat.' Jahira was hanging on to the door handle to steady herself and Gil got up to offer his arm. She shot him a ferocious look.

'What's the point of me walking all the way here by myself, if you're going to go and spoil it?'

Gil chuckled. 'Sorry. You made it from your room to here without your walking frame?'

'Yep.' Jahira walked unsteadily across the room, sitting down in a visitor's chair with a bump.

Now probably wasn't the time to remind her that she

shouldn't overdo it and fall. Gil sat down in the other visitor's chair and gave her a smile. 'Nice job. I'm really impressed.'

Jahira grinned. 'Yeah. I'm a bit puffed now.'

'So how's your memory book going?' Clemmie had shown him various bits and pieces, sparkly stars and hearts, and a sheet of beautiful hand-printed paper that she'd gone out to buy one lunchtime, and Jahira had explained to him exactly what the empty album on her desk would contain.

'Good. Sarah's learning a few things about me. My mum brought in a load of photos from when I was a kid.'

Jahira was still just a kid; she was only seventeen. But she was learning to shape her own life again, and see where she fitted in with the people that she loved. It was a process that never failed to inspire Gil, because everyone did it differently.

'That sounds great. Will you show it to me when it's done?'

Jahira nodded.

'So what did you come to see me for?' Gil prompted her. 'Assuming it wasn't just to show off about how far you can walk, that is.'

'Oh. No, it wasn't. I've got a problem. It's Edward.'

'Okay. Tell me about it.' Gil wondered if the two of them had fallen out.

'He's got a girlfriend.' Jahira frowned, obviously reconsidering the word. Gil gave her a moment.

'A lady friend?'

'Yeah. She's a senior citizen. And Edward really fancies her. His wife died, you know.'

'Yes, I'm aware. How do you know all this, Jahira?' Gil almost didn't like to ask.

'Because he introduced me to her when she came. He had his best waistcoat on, and I'm sure he was wearing aftershave. I know he wants to take her out, but he can't. He's proud.'

The speech therapist was clearly making great strides with Jahira. For one moment Gil wished that the girl had decided to express herself on a different subject and then dismissed the thought. He'd seen Edward helping Jahira in the garden, talking to her when she became frustrated with her efforts to pick up the small seeds she'd spilled on the table. Jahira was trying to do something nice for her new friend, and this was exactly the kind of thing that he encouraged here. Everyone helping everyone else.

'Okay. You have something in mind?'

Jahira nodded. 'We could put a table in the garden and make them tea and cakes. Like a date.'

It wasn't such a bad idea, at that. The walled garden would be perfect, and Gil knew that although Edward made a point of never complaining, he felt the loss of his independence keenly. A treat for his lady friend might be just the thing he needed.

'It's a kind idea, Jahira, but we have to make sure that Edward really wants us to do something like this, so you're going to have to ask him. Take Clemmie with you.'

Jahira nodded. 'Yeah, Clemmie will know what to say. I can bake a cake if you like. My mum's got lots of recipes.'

'That sounds really nice. But first of all we'll ask Edward, shall we?'

'Okay. Thanks.'

'My pleasure. Would you like to go back to the lounge now? I'll ask Clemmie to come and see you as soon as she gets here.'

Jahira nodded, getting to her feet and taking Gil's arm. The effort of getting here had clearly taken some toll—she was leaning on him—and Gil made a mental note to mention to the physiotherapist that Jahira's enthusiasm sometimes outstripped her capabilities.

'You've got a bike, then. You'd better tell me that you wear a cycle helmet.'

Jahira's words came right out of the blue. Her own injury had been caused by colliding with a car while cycling to college, and her parents had told Gil that it had been the one morning that she hadn't worn a cycle helmet.

'Yes, I do. Thank you for reminding me.'

'Can I see it? Your bike.'

'You can't ride it, if that's what you're asking. Your balance isn't good enough yet.' And getting back onto a bike might be more difficult than Jahira imagined. Gil understood her impatience, he'd felt that same impatience himself, but it was important that she didn't try to do too much, too soon.

'I don't want to ride it.' Jahira pressed her lips together. 'I think I'd like to just look at it, though.'

'Okay, that's fine. Today's a bit booked up but I'll bring it in tomorrow, and you can look at it all you like.' Perhaps he would mention the idea to Jahira's mother first, just to make sure.

'Thanks. Edward says that when you mess up with something, you have to take a breath and try again.'

It was good advice, although Edward had probably been talking about spilled seeds at the time. Maybe Gil should heed it himself. Giving up on Clemmie because *he'd* messed up didn't seem fair. He had to face his own mistakes and shortcomings, and deal with them.

'Yeah, he's right. But sometimes, with the big things, you have to give yourself a bit of time.'

When he arrived back in his office, Clemmie was sitting in one of the visitors' chairs. He closed the door behind him, walking behind his desk and sitting down. He didn't dare get too close. Even the desk between them was fast becoming a temptation...

He needed to get a grip. Avoiding horizontal surfaces while in her presence wasn't going to be practical. Clemmie had that mischievous smile on her face that he adored so much and he couldn't help grinning back at her.

He held out as long as he could, staring into her eyes, and finally she broke. Her hand flew to her mouth as she started to giggle, and Gil began to laugh, too.

'So we did it, then.' The look on her face left Gil in no doubt about how she felt about that.

'Yeah, we did.' Gil could almost feel the touch of her lips on his, still. 'You look beautiful today.'

'So do you.' She lowered her gaze suddenly. 'I'm sorry I didn't tell you.'

'Hey.' He wanted so badly to reach out to her, but when Clemmie looked up at him, being caught in her gaze seemed a good second best. 'I know why you didn't tell me. You didn't want me to know how much I'd hurt you.'

'You didn't mean to, Gil.'

'No, I didn't. That doesn't make me feel any better about it, but that's for me to deal with.' Now that she was here, Gil didn't want to talk about how guilty he felt. He just wanted to see her smile again.

'We can put it behind us?'

He couldn't deny her anything. 'Yeah. The future's a nicer place than the past.'

'Thank you.' She smiled suddenly and Gil promptly forgot that anything else existed.

'There's a new tea shop in the town centre. Want to come and try it out with me at lunchtime?'

'A date?'

'More a working lunch. I thought we might leave the date until this evening.'

Clemmie's smile broadened. 'That sounds perfect, Gil. I can't wait.'

'Me neither.' They didn't need to rush things, this time. They had a second chance, and Gil wanted to make it work, however difficult it had all seemed last night. This morning it didn't feel so much of a mountain to climb.

'So what's on the agenda for today? While we're both looking forward to our date tonight?'

'Would you believe another date? I was talking to Jahira just now, and she's had an idea…'

Clemmie had been juggling several different projects in the last week, but she'd arranged everything. She'd decided that Edward should wait in the garden for his lady friend, Caroline, and so Maggie was put on alert to watch for her arrival. There had been activity in the kitchen, which Gil had largely been excluded from, and Jahira was bubbling with excitement. Clemmie had made sure that Edward was looking extra-smart today, and wheeled him out to the garden to sit under a large sunshade, at a table with fresh white linen and silver cutlery that she'd borrowed from somewhere and brought in.

'I don't know about this.' Gil had decided to keep Edward company while he waited, and it seemed that he had last-minute nerves.

'She'll love it.'

Edward surveyed the table in front of him. 'I don't have much to offer her.'

Edward wasn't much of a talker, usually buckling down and getting on with whatever task presented itself. He was clearly very nervous.

'I can relate to that.'

Edward glanced up at him. 'Jahira told me that you were in here, some time ago. With a brain injury like hers.'

'Yes, that's right.'

'Young fellow like you shouldn't have any difficulty with the ladies, though.' Edward raised an eyebrow.

'That's not the point. I looked at what I'd been before the injury, and I reckoned I'd never be the same again.' Gil wondered whether Clemmie would mind him saying a bit more, and decided that she'd be cross with him if he didn't.

'For a long time I thought that no woman would accept me the way I was. But I've met someone, and she's made it perfectly clear to me that she would have accepted me then, the same way she does now.'

Edward smiled. The same kind of lopsided smile that Gil had been able to offer, and he could see now that was enough. Edward was perceptive and kind, he could talk about all manner of things and places he'd seen in the course of his career, and he was a gentleman. He had a great deal to offer.

'Good show. That's one thing you can say about the ladies. We're none of us good enough for them, but they don't seem to mind about that.'

Gil chuckled. 'No, they don't.'

'Just as well, I suppose,' Edward mused, seeming a little happier about the prospect of his afternoon tea.

They didn't have too long to wait. Caroline had arrived promptly at the appointed time. Gil saw Maggie, who had deserted her post for once, at the back door of the clinic, pointing the way to the walled garden. Carrying a bag that was no doubt stuffed with things she'd brought for Edward, Caroline walked along the path towards them.

'Here goes nothing,' Edward muttered under his breath, and Gil got to his feet, leaving him alone to face what was probably one of the biggest challenges he'd meet here. It went against the grain, but Clemmie had been adamant that Edward should greet Caroline on his own.

Jahira was hidden behind a spreading rhododendron that stood on the outer side of the wall. She looked just as nervous as Edward.

'What if I made a mistake? What if she just wants to be his friend?'

'Then it's a nice tea on a sunny afternoon. What's not to like about that?'

Jahira shot him an annoyed look. 'You really don't understand, do you?'

Gil understood, better than Jahira could imagine. He still had mixed feelings about whether he'd ever been good enough for Clemmie, but now wasn't the time to share them.

'It's all set now. You'd better call Clemmie.'

Jahira nodded, pulling her phone from her pocket and fumbling with it. She could manage autodial now, but her nerves were making it difficult. Gil resisted the instinct to help her, knowing that doing things for herself was a lot more valuable to Jahira.

'What's happening?' A woman's voice sounded from

the other side of the wall, and Jahira stiffened. Gil stretched up, peeping over, and smiled.

Edward had made it to his feet when Caroline arrived, and Gil mentally congratulated the physio for working so hard with him to make that possible. Caroline was standing, her hands over her mouth, obviously thrilled. Edward made a gesture towards the chair that had been set opposite him and waited for Caroline to sit down before he lowered himself back into his seat.

'We're good. She's sitting down and she looks really pleased.' Gil was starting to feel excited now.

'What are they saying?'

'I can't hear. Come along—you're up now. And take your walker.'

Jahira pulled a face and grabbed the walker, the two menus that Clemmie had printed out in the basket that was fixed to the front of it. Clemmie had worked her magic with Jahira as well, helping her to plait her hair in a complicated, one-sided arrangement that made the shaved side of her head look as if it were a fashion statement, and choosing a bright top for her to wear.

As expected, Jahira abandoned the walker as soon as she got to the entrance of the garden and walked the last few yards on her own. She delivered the menus to Edward, who handed one to Caroline. Then Edward gestured to an empty chair and Jahira sat down.

Okay, so that wasn't part of the plan. But Caroline was studying her menu carefully and smiling, and Edward was talking now, looking far more relaxed. If it worked, it worked.

Clemmie appeared, walking out from the back of the building carrying a laden tray, and his heart lifted, the way it always did when he saw her. Reckoning that the little group in the garden would be all right for a few minutes on their own, he went to meet her, relieving the cook who was following of her tray.

'How's it going?'

'Okay so far. She looks pleased.'

'Oh, well, that's a good sign, eh?' Clemmie grinned up at him, her usual optimism breaking through and calming Gil's own fears.

They carried the trays into the garden. Clemmie had found a cake stand from somewhere, and arranged sandwiches and scones on it, along with two slices of the delicious-looking cake that Jahira and her mother had made together, in the rehab centre's kitchen. There were little tubs of cream and jam for the scones, and a good supply of napkins, in case Edward's shaking hand made any mess. On Gil's tray, two pretty china cups and a matching teapot, with a tea cosy.

'This is wonderful. Thank you so much!' Caroline exclaimed.

'Edward's our friend, so we helped him do it for you.' Jahira grinned.

Gil had been hoping that Jahira wouldn't say the wrong thing, but he'd underestimated her. It was exactly the right thing to say and Caroline beamed at Edward.

Clemmie finished unloading the trays and poured the tea. Edward added milk, using his good hand, and pushed one of the cups across the table to Caroline, who picked it up and took a sip, then nodded her approval to Edward.

'You have everything?' Clemmie took her phone out of her pocket and put it down on the table next to Edward. 'Maggie's on speed dial, and if you call her when you've finished, she'll get hold of me.'

'Thank you.' Edward gave Clemmie a look that made

all of this worthwhile, and she smiled back at him, grabbing Jahira's hand and coaxing her to her feet to leave the couple alone now.

'You think they'll be okay?' Clemmie asked as she and Gil walked away.

'With half the unit watching out of the windows, and Jahira standing guard outside? I can't see what could happen to them.'

Clemmie's elbow found his ribs. 'That's not what I mean. Where's your instinct for romance?'

Gil chuckled. 'If you don't know by now, I'll have to try a little harder.'

'You're fine, just as you are. I think Edward will be, too.'

CHAPTER TWELVE

CLEMMIE HAD STAYED LATE, to catch Jahira's mother when she came to visit that evening. The afternoon tea had been everything she'd hoped it would, and Edward had confided afterwards that he'd suggested that he and Caroline might see a little more of each other when he came home from rehab. To his surprise and relief, she'd replied in the affirmative, wanting to know why on earth it had taken him so long to ask.

Clemmie walked back to Gil's house. He'd be home already, after having grabbed up some paperwork that he'd said he needed some peace and quiet to finish. Clemmie hoped that he'd be done by now, and that the rest of the evening would be theirs to enjoy.

He was sitting in the garden, staring out at the apple trees. Clemmie sat down with him and he turned, smiling.

'Got all your pruning sorted out in your head?'

'That's not going to be until February. It gives them a chance to grow after you've cut the dead wood back.'

'So what's up, then?' Something was obviously bothering him. 'Edward's over the moon. When I left he was polishing off the rest of the cake with Jahira and her mum.'

'That's nice.'

There was something in his eyes. A longing that matched her own, along with regret.

'What's up, Gil?'

He heaved a sigh. 'Do you ever wonder? What might have happened if I hadn't had the brain bleed. If I'd called you.'

There was a whole weight of sadness and mistakes in that seven years. Clemmie nodded. 'Yes, I wonder.'

'I know that you didn't want to talk about that, Clemmie. But our relationship's changing. I love that it is, but it makes for different boundaries.'

He was right. Being with Gil was wonderful, but there was more to talk about. Clemmie would have to choose her words very carefully.

'It's difficult.'

He nodded. Maybe he'd decided that it was all too difficult. There were risks involved in telling him more, but the last week had taught Clemmie just how much she wanted the reward.

'I guess we both need a push.' She looked at him hopefully. Gil hadn't let her down yet, and she couldn't imagine a situation where he could.

'I guess we do. Something pushed me today.'

Suddenly he got to his feet, walking into the house. He reappeared moments later, holding a brown paper bag, folded over at the top.

'What's that?' Gil put the bag down on the table and she peered inside. He'd been to the handmade chocolate shop and bought her favourite truffles. 'Are they for me?'

Gil chuckled. 'You know they are. Not yet, though…'

Clemmie took her hand guiltily out of the bag. 'You're right. After we've talked…'

He shot her an unfathomable look, sitting down opposite her. 'Truth or Dare, Clemmie. You want to play?'

Clemmie raised her eyebrows. 'With chocolate?'

He nodded.

'Gil, have you actually ever played Truth or Dare before? You're not supposed to reward someone with chocolate if they decide not to tell the truth.'

'I've played it. Think about it this way. If I don't tell you the truth, then I'll have to eat one of them, which means that's one less for you. Which I'm not prepared to contemplate, because I love watching the look on your face when you eat truffles. If, on the other hand, you decide not to tell the truth, then you don't have too onerous a dare. That's working pretty well for me as a concept.'

He'd been listening, to all she'd said. He knew that she wasn't finding it easy to be the one who remembered when he didn't, and he was giving her a way out. She might take it if she needed it, but she wanted this chance to share more.

'So you're planning on telling the truth, without expecting me to do the same.' Clemmie pushed the bag away from her into the centre of the table. 'I think you underestimate the effect that chocolate has on me, Gil. It's far more likely to loosen my tongue than tequila shots.'

'Then perhaps this is a bad idea.'

He reached for the bag and Clemmie laid her trembling fingers on his. The one thing she knew for sure was that Gil wouldn't hurt her. It was only the secrets that could do that, and if they were ever going to move forward, perhaps some of those secrets needed to be told.

'It's not a bad idea at all. Can I go first?'

He nodded. 'Of course.'

Clemmie thought hard.

'What happened today? To push you?'

'I was talking to Edward and he said that he didn't have much to offer Caroline.' He started to answer without any hesitation. 'It made me think, because I felt that way after my TBI. I could have called you a lot earlier than I did, but I looked at the photo and you were so beautiful and full of life... I put it off, and by the time I was at a point where I felt that I did have something to offer, it was too late.'

Clemmie took a deep breath. It hurt, but knowing the reason why was helping her to understand. 'I would have taken you, Gil. Any way you were.'

He nodded. 'I know. I told Edward as much.'

'Good. That was one piece of good advice for him, at least.' Clemmie couldn't leave it there. 'Supplementary question?'

He nodded. 'Be my guest.'

'How do you feel about that?'

That was harder for him to answer, and Gil paused for a moment.

'Guilty. Full of regret.'

'You shouldn't. I understand—' Gil held his hand up to stop her.

'You asked how I felt and I told you. There's no blame here, just the truth.'

That was reassuring. Clemmie reckoned that Gil might have some awkward questions for her, and this 'no blame' policy would certainly work in her favour.

'Okay. Your turn.'

He thought for a moment. 'When we were first together. There was something you wanted to tell me.'

Cold fingers of panic squeezed Clemmie's heart. 'You said you didn't need to know.'

'I didn't. I don't now. It's none of my business. It seemed important to you at the time, and I wonder if it's still important now.'

Clemmie grabbed the bag of chocolates and Gil reached out, putting his hand over hers.

'That's probably an unfair question. Take a pass on the dare.'

Clemmie rolled her eyes. 'You really *don't* know how chocolate works, do you, Gil?' She unwrapped one of the truffles, putting it into her mouth. 'I want to tell you.'

He nodded, taking the bag from her, a quiet smile hovering around his lips. Okay, so he wanted to make sure it wasn't just the chocolate talking. Probably wise—she could have eaten a few more of these.

'I was married for a short while. It only lasted for eighteen months and...' She shot him a pleading look. It was past time that she told him, but that didn't make it any easier.

'It's been seven years. I'd be shocked to hear that you hadn't had a life.' Gil seemed to be taking the news well.

'Harry and I were at school together. He had a bit of a crush on me when we were in the sixth form, but I made it clear that all I was interested in was friendship. I thought he knew that, but...' Clemmie shrugged. Harry had renewed his interest in her at just about the time she'd realised that Gil wasn't going to phone. Maybe he'd sensed her sadness and vulnerability. But Gil must never know that.

He nodded. Waiting.

'It was a bit of a whirlwind thing. Harry was determined it was the right thing for us and I should have listened to my doubts.'

'Why didn't you?'

Clemmie shrugged. 'I needed an anchor, something stable. Harry was so attentive, so sure about everything, and I was grateful to him for that. I thought it was love. But all he was really seeing was someone who would reflect what he wanted. Harry could be very manipulative in getting what he wanted, and I found out that it had been a deliberate thing on his part. We separated and the divorce came through earlier this year.'

'I'm sorry that he made you unhappy. You deserve more, Clemmie.'

Clemmie reached out, putting her hand in his, and he wound his fingers around hers. So warm and reassuring. It was possible to forget that she hadn't told Gil the one secret that she knew would really hurt him. That she'd married Harry because of the way that Gil had broken her heart.

'Thanks for understanding.'

'I don't, not really. I don't understand how someone could try to control you, when you're perfectly capable of ordering your own life. But I'm hoping you made that very clear to him.'

Clemmie smiled. Gil's protectiveness wasn't the rigid, controlling kind that Harry had demonstrated. 'Yes, I did. When I finally came to my senses.'

He squeezed her hand, seeming to forget all about truths or dares. Warmth ignited in his eyes and it would be so easy to leave this conversation where it was and start another very different conversation. The intimate give and take of their lovemaking.

But she'd started and she wanted to finish. 'Harry made things very difficult after I left him—it was as if any contact was better than nothing, even if it was conflict. He haggled over everything that I hadn't been able to squeeze into my suitcase, even my clothes. He emptied out our joint bank account and I had nothing. I went to see my parents and they let me stay with them for a few months. But my mum kept asking me whether I was ready to go back home to Harry yet. She just couldn't see that it wasn't my home and that it never really had been.'

'She didn't see how you really felt. Didn't see *you*.' Gil unerringly picked up on the point of what Clemmie was trying to say.

'No. A few of my friends clubbed together and lent me the cash for a deposit on a bedsit. It wasn't much but it was mine. When I got the money to pay them back, they wouldn't take it. They said that they were glad to see me away from Harry, and that I was to put the money towards a mortgage.'

'I'm glad you had someone to support you. You have your own place now?'

'Yes. I don't have much furniture...' Clemmie grinned at him. 'That's why I haven't asked you over.'

'I was wondering. I'd like to come and visit you, if that's all right.'

'I might put you to work. There's a lot to do still.'

'That would be my pleasure. Supplementary question?'

Clemmie nodded.

'How do you feel now? About being seen and heard. It seems that your parents really let you down, and that must have been a crushing blow.'

'To be honest, they did more than I expected them to. But I've made choices, and I've built a new life. It's my choice to be with you now, Gil, and one of the reasons for that is that you do see and hear me.'

He leaned across the table, kissing her. 'Always,

Clemmie. Seeing you and hearing you is the best part of my day.'

'Can we leave it behind, Gil? Everything that's happened?' That was really the only question that Clemmie needed to ask.

'I wouldn't be here if I didn't think so.' He answered without hesitation.

She shifted from her seat, rounding the table and sitting back down on his lap. Gil wound his arms around her, holding her tenderly. Something had changed, and it had changed for the better. The secrets and the lost time were starting to be acknowledged, and Gil's understanding was weakening their hold.

'Are you done with this game?' He kissed her.

'I'm really glad we talked.' Clemmie kissed him back. 'And yes, I'm done with it for the moment.'

'Good.' He reached for the bag of truffles. 'Because I'd really like you to explain to me exactly how chocolate works for you...'

There had been something different in their lovemaking. It was no longer a way of forgetting all that had happened between them, but of celebrating their bond and strengthening it.

Gil had made a late-night snack, because they'd missed dinner completely. Clemmie sat cross-legged on one of the chairs on the patio, wearing only one of his shirts. She looked great in any outfit, but that was the one he liked the best. The stray smudge of chocolate on the collar was a great accessory.

'Can I ask you another question?'

'You make that sound as if I have the ability to say no to you.'

'It's always an option.'

Yeah. Dressed like that, and with the sweet remembrance of her caress still on his skin. Clemmie really did underestimate herself.

'Ask away.'

'What about your family? I'm not close to my mum and dad now, but we did at least have a chance to repair the relationship, even if it didn't work out. It's not so easy for you, with your family in Australia.'

'It's hard to sort things out when you're depending on phone calls. But it's better. I talk a bit more and so do my mum and dad. When Mum yelled at me for not telling her about the TBI sooner, it was a bit of a wake-up call.'

Clemmie smiled. 'That's nice. That she yelled.'

'Yeah, it was.' It had been the start of a change in their relationship, which had allowed some admission of frailty, even if Gil still tended to gloss over any difficulties he had in life.

'They're mellowing a bit as they get older. My dad retired last year, to everyone's surprise. He's substituted hobbies for work, and he pursues them pretty relentlessly, but there's something about sitting on a boat and dangling a fishing line into the ocean that defies too much stress.'

'Even if they're big fish?' Clemmie's eyes widened.

'They're big fish.' Gil held out his hands to indicate the size and her eyebrows flew up. 'There's quite a bit of competition about who can catch the biggest, but there's still that element of going and catching what you eat that keeps him grounded. A bit like growing what you eat, only strawberry plants don't usually put up so much of a struggle.'

'It sounds as if you have a better relationship with them now.'

Gil shrugged. 'I've never really had a *bad* relationship with them. Just a little dysfunctional maybe.'

Clemmie took a deep breath. Clearly she had something on her mind. 'Will you do me a favour?'

'Depends what it is…' Gil returned Clemmie's steady gaze. He really couldn't deny her anything. 'Strike that. The answer's yes.'

'Will you go and see them? Or at least call them and start a dialogue. Let them know if you're in a bit of a jam.'

Gil thought about the prospect. His parents weren't so bad; he actually really liked them. Talking with Clemmie had convinced him that he really didn't share enough.

'Any particular reason for that request? I've already said yes, but I'd like to hear your thinking.'

'My relationship with my parents has broken down irretrievably. Yours doesn't sound as if it has, and… You should hold them close, Gil. Don't leave it until it's too late.'

He reached out, brushing her cheek with his fingers. 'That's a very fine and generous thought, Clemmie. You're right.'

Gil wondered if maybe Clemmie could be convinced to come with him. He'd love to take her on a tour of Australia and have her meet his family. Renew a few ties himself while he was there. That was a question for later, though. The last week had tipped his world upside down, but it was still a little early to ask her to fly more than ten thousand miles to meet his parents.

But it was something to look forward to. He reached out, taking her hand and drawing it to his lips. Clemmie shifted from her seat, sitting on his lap.

'Are we good?' He kissed her and she snuggled into

his arms. Of course they were good, but he just wanted to hear her say it.

She looked up at him, her face shining in the darkness. 'Yes, we're good. Although it's getting a little chilly out here.'

'Come back to bed, then.'

CHAPTER THIRTEEN

GIL WAS FAST coming to the conclusion that there was nothing he wouldn't do for Clemmie. Their relationship had been a helter-skelter ride, where missed opportunities, anger and guilt had all done their best to break them apart. But somehow they'd stayed together. Growing and moving forward, leaving the past behind.

Gil felt that he could finally look to the future now. Clemmie remembered so much more than he did, and she'd been three steps ahead of him in this relationship, but she'd waited for him to catch up with her. Now he was ready to take her hand and run towards the future.

'Would you like to go for a bike ride tomorrow? Explore Richmond Park a bit.'

He asked the question as casually as he could. They didn't usually plan their weekends, taking everything as it came, but a little structure wasn't a bad thing.

'I'd have to perch on your handlebars.' She was packing her briefcase, ready to leave work for the evening, and she looked up, grinning at him.

'The bike shop I go to does hires.'

'I'm not going to go whizzing around Richmond Park, dressed in Lycra. I don't think my legs are up to that.'

'I don't know about that. You have wonderful calves.'

She raised her eyebrows and Gil smiled. 'But I was thinking more of a nice Saturday morning ride, to enjoy the scenery.'

'All right. As long as you don't go too fast.'

'I'll stay behind you all the way.'

Clemmie snorted with laughter. 'You will not. Half the pleasure is a nicely shaped rear in front of me to keep my sights on.'

'So sad. You make me feel as if you only want me for my body.' Gil opened his office door before she could reply and Clemmie poked her tongue out at him.

He locked the door behind them, wishing Maggie a good weekend as he walked through Reception. Clemmie went to get her things from her locker, and Gil waited for her outside. The fact that they often left the unit together hadn't excited any particular comment because their work was so closely connected and Gil's way home was in the same general direction as the station, but it was as well not to be too obvious.

'We could follow that path...' Gil pointed across the road to the cycle track that ran around the perimeter of the park. 'Then cut through the woods. I'll be keeping my nicely shaped rear within your line of sight at all times.'

'I'm looking forward to that.'

'If you like it, I'll buy you a bike for Christmas.' The conclusion that he'd been working towards sent a little tingle of pleasure down Gil's spine.

'For Christmas?' She looked up at him, her cheeks reddening slightly.

'Only you'd probably have to keep it at my place. Unless you have cycle lanes where you live.'

'No, there are none close by. And I live on a pretty

busy road, so I'm not sure about cycling there.' Clemmie linked her arm with his. 'Probably best to keep it here.'

Christmas seemed a long way away at the moment. But they'd just made a plan, which took it for granted that they'd still be together then. *And* they were walking past the main entrance of the hospital, arm in arm.

'Are we going too fast?' Clemmie removed her hand from the crook of his arm suddenly.

'I'm comfortable with this speed.'

'Me too. Only it's probably best not to make any overt expressions of affection in front of the hospital. Not until I leave next week.'

'So sweeping you off your feet and kissing you is out of the question, then?' Gil liked the way her cheeks became a little pinker when he teased her.

'Absolutely. None of that until we're officially not working together any more.'

'Agreed. Reluctantly, because I very much want to kiss you at the moment.' It felt as if they'd taken another important step, and Gil wanted to mark the moment somehow. The first time they'd talked about the future, knowing that the past had loosened its grip on them. When they got back to his place, he'd make up for lost kissing time.

Clemmie had fussed a little over what to wear, and Gil assured her that jeans and trainers were absolutely fine for the kind of bike ride they were going on, and that they'd be hardly working up a sweat. He walked down to the bike shop the next morning and she was waiting for him as he wheeled the hired bicycle up the front path.

'Ooh. It's a nice one. Not too racy.'

'It'll go at a good speed, and it has gears.' It was a

sturdy bike, without being too heavy, and if Clemmie liked it he'd get her one like this.

'I don't know how to use gears.'

'Don't worry about them for the moment. I'll show you how when we get to a hill.' He reached into the bag that hung from the handlebars. 'Here's the most important thing.'

Clemmie nodded. 'A helmet. And it matches the bike, as well. Mint green.'

'Yeah, don't be put off by the colour. It's a good helmet that will protect you if you fall off.' And she looked very cute in mint green, her dark hair giving a lift to the colour.

Clemmie tried the helmet on, and Gil checked that it fitted correctly, adjusting the strap carefully under her chin. That wasn't totally necessary from a safety point of view, she was perfectly capable of doing it herself, but Gil just liked doing things for Clemmie.

'We're going now? I'm ready.' Clemmie stepped astride the bike, trying out the brakes.

'Yep, if you like. I'll just go and fetch mine.'

Clemmie's fitness might come from constant activity rather than gym work, but she had stamina and strength. Gil already knew that. He'd tested every part of her body, measuring its balance and power against his. She rode ahead of him for a while, setting a very respectable pace.

They stopped for a while, when the path wound upwards into the woods, and he showed her how to use the gears. After a few hiccups, she got the hang of it, and they rode to the top of the hill and then turned to make their way back down.

'I really like this. It's not as much work as it looks.'

She rode beside him on the wide path, careful to leave plenty of space for pedestrians, and an overtaking lane for other cyclists. 'Oops!'

She wobbled, almost coming off the bike as three sports bikes shot past her down the hill. Gil instinctively stretched out his hand, but she regained her balance. But the other cyclists were going too fast, and as they hit a bump in the path further down, one of them swerved violently.

'Go...' Clemmie obviously wasn't confident about going any faster down the hill, but she urged Gil on. She could see the same as he had—the guy had been going at such speed that he'd practically flown off the bike, landing a good six feet away at the side of the path.

He got to the man before his companions had a chance to turn around and pedal back up the hill. But before he could stop him, the guy had got to his feet.

'Hey. Are you all right?' Gil would have preferred he'd stayed down a little longer, so that he could check him out before he started to move around.

'Yeah, I think so...' The man grinned, squaring his shoulders, and then doubled up with pain. 'Agh!'

'I'm a doctor. Sit down for a moment and let me take a look at you.'

'Uh... Yeah, thanks.'

Gil walked the man slowly over to a nearby bench and sat him down. His first instinct was to check on his head, but he could see that the guy's cycle helmet was undamaged and that was a good sign. All the same, he carefully unbuckled it, taking it off.

'Did you hit your head?'

'Don't think so. Came down on my shoulder. Bloody stupid... Going far too fast.'

Gil was inclined to agree with him, but that wasn't his first concern at the moment. He felt someone jostle him from behind, trying to move him out of the way, and then heard Clemmie's sharp rebuke.

'Give him some room, please. My friend and I are both doctors.'

'What kind of doctor?' There was a hint of cockiness in the male voice that replied.

'The kind you're always pleased to have around when someone falls off their bike.' The crispness in Clemmie's tone brooked no argument, and Gil smiled, imagining that her expression was just as fierce.

'Give it a rest, Brad.' His patient tried to move but his face creased in pain.

'You too. Stay still, please.' Clemmie sat down on the bench beside him. 'I'm Clemmie, by the way.'

'Nathan. I'd shake your hand but...'

'You'd have to move to do it. So we'll give that a miss, shall we?'

Clemmie had already fetched the first-aid kit from Gil's bike, and was unzipping the bag. She handed him the penlight and Gil checked that Nathan's pupils reacted correctly to the light. He could feel no bumps on Nathan's head, and he seemed to have no other symptoms of concussion.

'Looks like it's just his shoulder,' Clemmie murmured, gently moving Gil on to the next thing on his to-do list. He nodded, glad of her prompt. His own experience meant that he was always very careful about the possibility of anyone bumping their head, and Clemmie was watching over him, carefully guiding him.

They removed Nathan's cycling top, and even the most cursory examination would have been enough to reveal that he'd broken his collarbone, and probably one of the small bones in his wrist, as well. Clemmie unfolded two triangular bandages from the first-aid kit, helping Gil to immobilise Nathan's arm.

'Thanks. That feels much better now.' Nathan seemed about to try to stand, and Clemmie stopped him.

'We'll need you to come down to the hospital, for an X-ray. It looks as if you've broken your collarbone, and possibly your wrist.'

'Really? It doesn't feel too bad.' Nathan tried to sit up a little straighter and grunted in pain. 'You might be right...'

Now it was just a matter of getting him there. Calling for an ambulance seemed to be the only way, but the crew might have to walk to get to them, as it was unlikely that the ambulance could navigate the narrower parts of the track. Then Clemmie nudged Gil, pointing down towards the bottom of the hill. An off-road parks department vehicle had drawn up, and a couple of men were surveying a felled tree.

'That'll do, won't it?'

It would. Gil sent one of Nathan's riding companions down to talk to the men, and within ten minutes they were helping Nathan into the vehicle and their bikes were being loaded onto the back. The driver manoeuvred slowly and carefully down the hill, taking them round to the park entrance that stood opposite the hospital, and then driving them across to the entrance of A & E. There were a few raised eyebrows from the ambulance crews who were waiting there, but as soon as they saw Nathan, they set about helping him from the back seat and into a wheelchair.

'Thanks, guys.' Nathan gave them a smile as a nurse wheeled him away to be examined. 'Sorry to spoil your Saturday.'

'No problem. Take care...' Clemmie gave him a wave and turned away to retrieve their bikes, which had been propped up against the wall by the entrance.

Gil finally allowed himself a frustrated grimace. 'I take a girl out and what happens? Someone comes flying off their bike and we end up back at work.'

'Stop it.' Clemmie bumped her shoulder against his arm. 'What were you going to do, ride past and leave him there?'

'No, I suppose not.' Gil had wanted today to be perfect, though. The first day when their future seemed clear.

'Don't be so grumpy, then. Tell you what—why don't we walk over and I can show Jahira this bike?'

'She'll only want to try and ride it. One person falling off a bike is about as much as I can take in a day.'

'We'll just let her put the helmet on and sit on the saddle. You can hold the bike steady and she won't be going anywhere. You asked her mum whether it was okay to encourage Jahira to take an interest in cycling again, didn't you?'

'Yes, I did. Jahira's been asking her about getting a new bike, and her mum thinks it's a good idea as long as she keeps to cycle lanes in future. I'm sure she wouldn't object.'

'Well, then. We can take some photos for Jahira's memory book. There are plenty of pages to spare for the new memories she's making.' Clemmie reached for her cycle helmet, putting it onto her head. 'And I want to show off the cycle helmet, as well. I like the colour.'

Gil made a mental note that the bike he bought Clemmie—and the cycle helmet—would both be mint green. 'Okay, then. And then we'll go and get some lunch?'

'Sounds good to me.'

Suddenly the day *was* perfect. Because Clemmie was smiling.

Gil had been keeping things from her. On her last afternoon at Barney's they'd been working in his office and he'd received a call. He'd got to his feet, hurrying out of the room, and she'd followed him, wondering what was up. When he'd got to the patients' sitting room there had been a loud chorus of *'Surprise!'* and then party poppers, a cake and alcohol-free punch.

Everyone had traded kisses with her, apart from Gil. His would come later.

'I talked to my boss on the phone this morning.' Clemmie followed him into his house, putting her flowers down carefully in the hall. 'He's really interested in some of the things we've been doing in the last six weeks and wants me to write a full report. Compare and contrast the two units.'

Gil nodded. 'Sounds great. I'd be interested in seeing that. There'll be something I can learn from it, no doubt.'

'No doubt.' Clemmie liked the way that he always looked outwards, not locked into his own way of doing things. It was a professional and personal breath of fresh air.

He wrapped his arms around her shoulders, kissing her. 'I guess that means I won't be seeing so much of you next week...'

Clemmie turned her lips down in an expression of regret. 'Probably not. He's talking about a presentation at a meeting that's taking place the week after next, so I'll have to get it done next week. It'll probably mean a few late nights at work. I'll miss you—'

Gil put his finger across her lips. 'This is important. And just think—I'll be missing you more than I can say, so...' He whispered in her ear, telling her all the ways he might show her just how much he'd been missing her, when next weekend finally came around.

'That sounds wonderful.' This was more difficult than Clemmie had thought it would be. She trusted Gil and knew that history wasn't going to repeat itself. All the same, their fond goodbye at the end of the conference and everything that had happened subsequently were hard to banish from her thoughts.

'And just to make sure that you know where to find me.' He took her hand, leading her into the sitting room. An envelope was propped up on the mantelpiece and he handed it to her.

'What's this?' Clemmie opened the envelope and then started to laugh. There was a small card inside, with Gil's mobile number written on it. Along with his email address, his landline number and his direct line at work. Gil knew how she felt, and he was making this parting different from the last.

'Just to give you a few options.' He was smiling broadly.

'Thank you. I'll keep it safe.' Clemmie fetched her handbag from the hallway, taking out her purse and slipping the card into one of the pockets behind her credit cards. 'Would you like my numbers at home?'

'Yes, and your email address. I'll be calling you, and if you don't answer, I'll be turning up in person to find you.'

'With a glass slipper in your hand?'

'Yeah. Or a cycle helmet.' He kissed her and Clemmie flung her arms around his neck. This time, things were going to be different.

CHAPTER FOURTEEN

GIL HAD CALLED every evening, at nine o'clock on the dot. They'd talked about everything: the finer points of her presentation and what their days had brought. Gil had reported that the romance between Edward and Caroline was very definitely on, and that Jahira sent her love. The best part was right before they said goodbye, when he told her how much he missed her and that he'd call her again tomorrow. The warmth in his voice was always the same, always something that Clemmie could depend on.

She'd emailed the text of her presentation through to him every evening, and at lunchtime the following day there was always an email from Gil, answering questions and giving his own opinions on what she'd written. Clemmie arrived home at eight o'clock on Friday and decided she couldn't wait a whole hour to speak to him.

'What are you doing?'

Gil seemed a little out of breath when he answered. 'Digging.'

'Ah. Frustrating day?'

'It's been interesting. We had a new patient in and he's very angry. Very frustrated. He took a swing at Elaine at one point, but fortunately she managed to duck. Anya talked him down and I spent some time with his wife this afternoon, discussing how we can all help him. The situation's under control and he was much calmer when I left him just now.'

'That's good. Poor Elaine. I'm sure she doesn't need something like that.' The young nurse had become more confident in her role since Jeannie's fall in the greenhouse, and Clemmie hoped that this incident hadn't undone any of the work that Gil had done in reassuring her.

'I had a chat with her, and she knows it's nothing personal. She has all the makings of a very good nurse. How's your day been?'

Clemmie grinned. 'Productive. I've finished my presentation and my boss has given it the thumbs-up. Two thumbs, actually, and a *"Very well done, Clemmie."* Which was amazing because he's generally a man of few words.'

She heard Gil laugh. 'Of course he did. I think it's an exceptional piece of work.'

'Thank you. I couldn't have done it without you.' In so many ways. Gil hadn't just given her the experience of running a unit that she needed; he'd been there for Clemmie. Giving her the confidence to break new ground in her presentation, rather than simply report on her findings.

'You did it all by yourself. I just watched and marvelled. So you're free tomorrow, then?'

'Yes. Do you want me to come down to Richmond so that you're on hand if you need to pop into the unit to see your new patient? I have a furniture delivery coming first thing, but I'll be able to make it to you by lunchtime.'

'Or I could come to you. I've spoken with the doctor who'll be on duty tomorrow and he's perfectly capable of handling the situation. One of the things you learn when you're running your own unit: how to have confidence in your staff, and realise that the place isn't going to fall to pieces if you take some time off.'

'One of the things I'm going to learn? Or one of the things you learned?'

'All right. One of the things I learned. So how about it? I can come to you first thing tomorrow, or you can come down here if you prefer.'

Clemmie wanted Gil to come to her flat, but she supposed she should let him know what he might be in for. 'I could offer you a fabulous lunch and something glamorous to do in the afternoon, but you may find yourself putting some furniture together...'

'Where's your sense of adventure? Putting furniture together can be glamorous, too.'

'Well, I'm pretty excited. I've been sleeping on an old futon that someone gave me for the last six months, and now that my bedroom's painted and I've got some nice furniture, it'll be much more comfortable.'

'In that case, I insist on coming to you. You might need some help with the bed.'

Clemmie laughed. 'I definitely will. And by the way, you're to stop digging immediately, Gil. I don't want you working all of your frustration off on a patch of ground.'

He chuckled. 'There's only one cure for that kind of frustration, sweetheart, and digging isn't going to do it...'

The delivery van arrived at eight the following morning, and Gil's car drew up behind it while the men were stacking boxes in Clemmie's hall. He helped them in with the final few and gave them a cheery wave as they left. The door slammed behind him, and Clemmie found herself in his arms.

'I don't suppose you missed me, did you?' He grinned down at her.

'I missed you.' But now the past had been overwritten. That felt special.

'Mm. How much?' He crowded her back against the plastic-wrapped mattress that was propped up against the wall.

'Seriously.' She smiled up at him. 'You want to try it out already?'

'This is probably the last time it'll be at quite this angle...' He ran his hands from her shoulders to her wrists, and then pinioned her arms above her head.

Tempting. *Very* tempting. 'Far be it from me to add a note of practicality, but...what happens when things get a little bit too passionate and it falls on top of us?'

'I get to rescue you. And you get to be *very* grateful?' Gil gave her that playful grin that made Clemmie go weak at the knees.

She stood on her toes, planting a kiss onto his lips. As Gil moved closer, the pressure of his body against hers and the subtle give of the mattress against her back *were* enticing. All she needed to do was let Gil support her weight...

'You're right. It's not going to stay upright for much longer.' He stepped away from her.

'Tease! I was just starting to like the idea.'

His lips curved. Gil clearly was, too.

'I dare say we can prop it a bit more securely against the wall in the bedroom.' Clemmie opened the bedroom door, surveying the empty room.

'Sounds like a very sensible plan.' Gil kissed her. 'Are you sure I can wait that long?'

'Positive. Because you know I'll deliver...'

* * *

They'd unpacked the chest of drawers and Gil had helped her manoeuvre it into the bedroom, along with the boxes that contained the wardrobe. The bed had come next and had taken an hour to put together. Trying the mattress out, first vertically and then horizontally, had taken rather longer, but Clemmie had found it an enormously satisfying experience, and there was no doubt that Gil agreed with her.

It was so good having him here. Cooking together, and puzzling over the leaflet that gave instructions on how to put the wardrobe together. Clemmie loaded up the wardrobe and Gil took apart the steel-framed clothes racks that she'd been using, stacking them neatly with the flattened boxes in the hallway.

Waking up with him was even better. Feeling his warm body curled around hers, in a comfortable bed. Sunshine filtering through the window, and everything neat and tidy, her clothes folded in the chest of drawers and hanging in the wardrobe.

Gil made her breakfast in bed, and then insisted they finish the job. His car was bigger than hers, and the old futon and all the rubbish in the hallway could be crammed into the back, so that they could take it for disposal.

'Lunch?' He grinned at her as they drove out of the recycling centre. 'Or would you prefer me to cook while you stare at your new bedroom?'

'I'm taking you to lunch. Thank you so much for helping, Gil.'

'My pleasure. Thank you for making me a part of your milestone.'

It felt like a milestone. She'd finally got herself on

her feet, enough to furnish and decorate one room in her flat, at least. The others would follow. Everything else would follow.

Clemmie directed him to her favourite local pub, and they ordered their meal. She tipped her glass against his.

'I feel as if I'm finally getting my life back together again. I have my own flat and some furniture. And there's no more feeling as if I'm being held hostage while Harry tries to throw spanners in the works with the divorce.'

He took a sip of his drink. 'Two years must have seemed like a long time to wait, in those circumstances.'

'Five.' It had been a long time, but it was over now. 'A divorce only takes two years if both parties agree in writing. Harry refused to do that.'

'Five years? And you were married for eighteen months...' Clemmie heard the sudden tension in his tone and her heart sank. Stupid. She'd been basking in the pleasure of the weekend and let her guard down.

'Um...closer to a year.'

'You said it was eighteen months.'

Why did Gil have to remember everything she said? Or was it just all the things she didn't want him to remember?

'Yes. It was eighteen months, then.'

'You said that you needed an anchor when you married him. Do you mind telling me why?' He was obviously trying to keep this casual, but there was a hint of tension behind the questions.

'It was a lot of things, Gil. Can't we talk about something else?'

He nodded. 'Yeah. Sure.'

Saying it was easy. Gil was smiling and talkative again, but Clemmie could still see a cloud of doubt in his eyes. It was so easy to overlook Gil's vulnerability because he seemed so very strong.

And there was nothing wrong with his maths. Five years plus eighteen months was six and a half years. Leaving only six months for a broken heart and a rushed engagement.

He was quiet on the way back home, and as they walked back from his car, he put his arm around her shoulders, as if he wanted to protect her from harm. That he couldn't do, but after all they'd been to each other—all they *were* to each other—maybe they were strong enough for this. She let them into the flat, walking through into the sitting room.

'Okay. I'll tell you…'

Gil didn't want to know. All of his instincts were telling him that he should stop her now, and they could go on with their weekend. Go on with their lives. But Clemmie had kept this secret from him for a reason. It might well break them apart if she told him, but he'd never be able to touch her again if he knew that he'd done something that hurt her so much she couldn't speak about it. At least this way, they had a chance.

Gil sat down. He thought he knew what she was about to say, but he didn't dare believe it.

'One thing, Clemmie. If you're going to tell me, please don't leave anything out.'

She nodded, coming to sit beside him. Gil took her hand and gave it a squeeze, in the hope of communicating a reassurance that he didn't feel.

'I shouldn't have let you guess.'

That could mean one of two things. Either she shouldn't

have kept this secret, or she should have kept it better. Gil decided not to ask.

'What's done is done. Tell me now.'

Her mouth twisted. 'We had something special, you know that. It all happened so fast, but it seemed so right, from the very start. You heard me and you saw me. You told me that you loved me, and we exchanged numbers because we were going to...' A tear ran down her cheek.

Her words hit him like a hammer blow. 'You mean... we made plans.'

Clemmie nodded. 'Yes, we did. You said that you loved your work but you felt it consumed you sometimes, and that I'd made you see that there were other things in life. I thought that this would be a new start for both of us, and when you didn't answer my calls I...' Her voice dropped to a whisper. 'I thought you'd ghosted me, Gil. And that it was a cruel thing to have done.'

'I made promises and...then I broke them. You were right to think me cruel.'

Clemmie frowned. 'You're nothing of the sort. You were in hospital with a brain injury—how on earth could you be expected to answer your phone?'

Gil's head sank into his hands, in despair. She had to know...

'When I was recovering, I managed to get my phone charged and I deleted all the calls and messages that were on it. I couldn't accept what was going on in my life and I just withdrew. I didn't want to speak to anyone.'

Clemmie reddened suddenly, staring at him. Maybe she was putting two and two together and realising that he *was* responsible for all the hurt she'd felt.

'I don't blame you for that. It was a perfectly natural reaction to what had happened to you.'

'It was *me* that did it, not the TBI. You married Harry because I broke your heart, didn't you?'

She pressed her lips together. 'I needed someone who was present, and who wouldn't leave me. That was everything to do with where I was in my life back then, and nothing to do with you. I gave up on you too soon, because I was ready to believe that no one could care about me the way you seemed to.'

'Don't…' Gil felt tears prick at the sides of his eyes. 'Never believe it was your fault, because it wasn't.'

His TBI had been the turning point that had forced him to slow down and strike a better work-life balance, but deep down Gil had known that he needed to do that before then. What if Clemmie had sensed it, too? What if she'd given up on him because she'd known in her heart he would never change? All she was guilty of was a willingness to see the best in him.

But the worst was still there. He'd found a healthier balance, a better way to live his life, but he was still the same man. Still determined to succeed in whatever he did, which was really just another way of saying that he was driven.

He had no doubt that he'd told the truth when he'd said he loved Clemmie. He loved her now. Maybe that was the best reason of all to let her go.

'Can't you say something, Gil…?' Clemmie was looking at him imploringly. Despite everything, she still trusted him.

'I'm sorry.' How could he tell her that the only thing he could do to make things better was to leave, when it was the last thing in the world he wanted to do?

'I know this is hard and…' She shrugged. 'We both should have known that a completely new start wasn't going to be possible. And I'd understand it if you felt that you don't remember what happened between us because I'd put you under stress—'

'No. I won't hear you say that, Clemmie. You had no part in what happened to me. You make me happy now, and even if I can't remember it, I know you made me happy then.'

'Then *be* happy, Gil.' Frustration sounded in her voice.

He shook his head. 'That's not enough. If I can't know that I'll keep my promises, how can our relationship ever be a safe place for both of us?'

'It *is* our safe place. Don't take that away from me. I don't deserve it.' Her cheeks flushed a deeper red with anger, and suddenly Gil knew. This time wouldn't be the same as the last, because Clemmie knew that she deserved better and was strong enough to go out and take it.

'I'm sorry. I can't see a way forward and... I won't hurt you again.'

'What if I don't let you? What if I tell you that I'll stick with you and that we can get through this?' The way that Clemmie's eyes flashed, so defiantly, almost made Gil weaken.

'You'd have stuck with me when I had my TBI as well, wouldn't you?'

She didn't even have to think about it. 'Of course I would. What's wrong with that?'

Nothing. And everything. Gil had just realised how much Clemmie had forgiven him for, without even asking for an explanation. The woman in the picture hadn't deserved to share the bad days after his TBI, and Clemmie didn't deserve to risk her future with someone who had already hurt her so badly.

'You kept this from me, Clemmie. Because you knew it would change everything.'

She hesitated. In that moment, Gil knew he was right. 'I thought you'd be...that you'd feel responsible.'

'I *am* responsible. What I did then, the little things that added up to all that rejection and hurt, was less to do with my TBI and a lot more to do with the person I was. You've changed, but I'm still the same as I always have been. I can't promise to be the man that makes you happy and I won't settle for anything less.'

He'd said it now. There was no point in staying any longer, when he wasn't going to change his mind. Gil got to his feet, aware that Clemmie was staring at him. But when he walked away from her, she didn't stop him.

As he walked out into the sunlight, it seemed to sear into his brain, and the old sensation that he was about to lose his balance almost stopped him in his tracks. He had the strangest feeling that the world was unfamiliar, as if it had changed somehow when he wasn't looking.

Gil got into his car. This he could handle—he knew exactly how to deal with disorientation. Emotion and loss were less easily put aside, but if they allowed Clemmie to get on with her life and be happy, he'd take them.

He sat for a moment, breathing steadily and mentally checking that he was okay to drive. The world began to resolve itself into sharp focus again, but it was suddenly a harsher and colder place. Gil started the ignition and pulled away from the kerb.

As soon as she heard the front door close, Clemmie sprang to her feet, running to the window. Gil didn't look back. When he got into his car he sat for a moment, seemingly deep in thought, and one last thread of agonising hope held her motionless. Then it snapped as Gil started the engine and drove away.

This time she'd survive. Not because she loved Gil any less, but because she knew she had the strength to carry on. And because she had no regrets.

She'd taken the risk of loving him and she'd done it with her eyes wide open. Knowing what she did now, she would still have taken that risk, because her relationship with Gil had brought her closure. She'd loved him almost from the moment she'd met him, and now she knew that she hadn't made a mistake, in loving him then or in loving him now. Nothing could take that from her.

If Gil could only trust himself. If he could just believe in himself the way she believed in him. Clemmie knew that Gil loved her, and that he was only doing what he thought was right. That was the most heartbreaking part of it all.

She walked into the kitchen, opening the door of the fridge. There was a bottle of wine, and there was ice cream, too. But it was far too early in the day for either of those remedies, and she wasn't going to crumble the way she had before. This time it was going to be different.

CHAPTER FIFTEEN

'ARE YOU READY, Jahira?' Gil stopped in the open doorway of her room.

'No. Are you?'

Jahira could be a lot wiser than her years suggested at times. Gil laughed. 'No. I dare say I'll manage, though.'

'Me too.'

Gil had been intending to give Jahira a final barrage of encouragement before she left rehab today, but he reckoned that those few words pretty much summed it up. No one knew what the future would hold, but Jahira was ready for it, and that was all anyone could ask.

'You know where I am, don't you? Don't be a stranger.'

'I'll come back and check up on you.' Jahira grinned at him.

She'd caught Gil staring silently out at the garden yesterday and asked him what the matter was. Two weeks, and he still couldn't think about Clemmie without someone noticing the pain on his face. The only solution was not to think about her at all when anyone was around, but that was difficult when there was so much here to remind him of her.

'You do that. And don't forget, if you have any questions or difficulties...' Gil shrugged. 'It says all that in your discharge leaflet. Just put my number in your phone and use it, eh? Or I'll start to feel that you've forgotten me.'

Jahira gave a dry chuckle, picking up the phone that lay next to her chair. 'Can't have that, can we, Doctor? What's your number, then?'

Gil took his phone from his pocket and handed it to her. 'This is the number you can get me on twenty-four-seven. I want to hear about how you're doing when you go back to college.'

'That might be a long story…'

'I'll get myself a cup of tea.'

Jahira nodded, flipping his phone against hers. A beep announced that the two phones had linked up and exchanged numbers. It was efficient, but it didn't compare with the photograph that Gil still carried in his wallet.

'I forgot to show you this.' Jahira handed him an envelope, and he saw Clemmie's writing on it. Gil hadn't lost the feeling that Clemmie was close by, watching over him, and these small reminders of her always brought both pleasure and pain.

'What's this?'

'See for yourself.'

He flipped open the envelope, taking out the card that was inside. 'Puppies. Nice.'

'Cute. Puppies are cute.'

'All right. Cute puppies.' Gil grinned as he opened the card. He expected that Clemmie had thought they were cute, too.

Inside, a gift card for a chain of bookstores, and a message from Clemmie.

A little something to help you with your studies.
The world's out there, waiting for you to take it
by storm!

'Do you think Clemmie would mind if I called her?
To say thank you.' Jahira's words dragged Gil back from
the gaping hole of longing that was threatening to swallow him up.

'No, I think she'd love to hear from you. You can
give her the full story of exactly how you're planning
to take the world by storm. You have her number?' Gil
congratulated himself on managing to get the words out
without choking.

'Yeah. She gave it to me when she left.'

Gil decided on a change of subject. 'What time are
your parents coming to fetch you?'

'They phoned just now, so they'll be half an hour.'
Jahira rose from her seat, grabbing the walker that stood
beside it. 'I've gotta say goodbye to everyone.'

'I'm doing my morning walkabout. You're going my
way?' Jahira's bright independence was one thing. But
Gil knew that today was going to be an emotional one
for her, and she might like a little company.

Jahira grinned. 'Depends which way you're going,
doesn't it, Doc?'

Jahira was a little teary by the time her parents arrived,
but a hug from her mother and father made her smile
again. Then Sarah flung her arms around Jahira's neck
and the two girls started to talk excitedly, while Jahira's
mother packed the last of her things into her bag.

'I hear someone's going home...' A familiar voice

sounded behind him, and Gil turned to see Sam standing there, holding a bunch of flowers.

'Where did you hear that? You've got this place bugged?'

'Never you mind.' Sam tapped the side of her nose. 'I have my sources.'

Sam delivered the flowers into Jahira's lap, and the teenager smiled shyly, obviously only half remembering Sam's name. Her father stepped in, reminding Jahira that Sam was the surgeon who had operated on her, and shaking Sam's hand until her arm looked in danger of falling off.

'Haven't you forgotten something?' Gil smiled at her.

'No. Don't think so…' Sam looked around and then the penny dropped. 'Oh, you mean the twins. They're in Reception with Maggie. She's masterminding the cuddle rota. Yanis is keeping an eye out to make sure we don't lose one of them.'

'That's only going to get more difficult when they start walking.' Gil grinned.

'Don't, Gil. We're working on an event horizon of about five minutes at the moment. Anything beyond that, we'll take as it comes.'

And the next five minutes held a whole world of goodness for Sam. Her face was glowing with the kind of happiness that lived in each moment, always there and always sustaining her. Just thinking about it allowed Gil to breathe, as if some of it had rubbed off on him.

'I'm going to do the walk?' Jahira tugged at his sleeve.

Gil nodded. 'You'd better. You deserve it.'

'What's the walk?' Sarah asked.

'You'll see.' Jahira took her arm, ready to go.

General practice at the hospital was to discharge anyone

who had difficulty walking in a wheelchair. But Jahira was steady enough on her feet now and 'the walk' was more important. Her father picked up her bag and the flowers, leaving Sarah and her mother to walk on either side of her.

'I love this part...' Sam whispered, falling into step beside Gil, who was following Jahira, ready to step forward and steady her if she lost her balance.

So did he. He'd insisted on walking out of the rehab unit himself, seven years ago, and Gil knew just how it felt. And now there was a little more ceremony to it. Many of the staff and some of the patients had gathered in Reception, along with Edward and Caroline, who had come back to visit Jahira and stayed to see her off. When Jahira walked through, they all applauded.

Jahira's mother was so intent on saying goodbye and thanking everyone that she left Sarah to take Jahira's arm and lead her out of the main doors. Jahira took a deep breath as she stepped outside. Gil knew that feeling. It didn't matter that he'd spent most of his time in the garden when he was a patient here. That first breath of air that he'd filled his lungs with when he'd left the building with his discharge papers in his pocket had seemed so much fresher.

The two girls sat down on the bench outside the building, while Jahira's father went to fetch the car. Sarah was talking to Jahira, her arm around her shoulders, and Jahira was nodding and smiling.

'They're so adorable together.' Sam smiled. 'Teenage sweethearts...'

Gil chuckled. 'Yeah. I miss that feeling of having everything in front of me, sometimes.'

Sam's elbow found his ribs. 'Don't get soppy on me,

Gil. That "everything" that we had in front of us wasn't all plain sailing, for either of us.'

Very true. But the void he was looking at now wasn't all that appealing either.

'We both made it through, though.' Sam had, at least. He was still a work in progress. 'By the way, I'm going to be taking an extended leave soon. I'll be off from next week.'

'That's a bit sudden, isn't it? Are you going anywhere nice?'

He was keeping a promise. Clemmie was still here, still guiding him.

'I'm going back to Australia, to see my folks. I'll be away for six weeks.'

'Six weeks!' Sam's eyebrows shot up. 'You're sure you'll survive that?'

Gil shrugged. 'I'm going to give it a go. I won't be staying with them for the whole time. I thought I'd take the opportunity to just sink my roots into home soil for a while. Jack Llewellyn is going to be taking over the running of the unit while I'm away.' Jack had worked here as a doctor for three years now, and Gil was confident in his ability to keep everything running smoothly.

'I'm sure he'll do a good job. But tell him to call me if he wants to talk anything over.'

'Thanks. I will.' Gil was aware that Sam was staring at him thoughtfully. 'What?'

'It sounds like a great idea. But is everything all right? None of your family are ill, are they?'

'No, everyone's fine. It's just time I went, that's all.'

Gil leaned back in his seat on the veranda. His parents' house was situated in the hills around Brisbane, and at dusk the city was just a few pinpricks of light in the distance. The jacaranda trees were in flower, shedding carpets of iridescent purple blooms, and a huge mulberry tree in the back yard was in full fruit. Gil had spent the afternoon helping gather the mulberries, climbing up into the spreading branches and shaking them so that the ripe fruit fell onto a tarpaulin, spread across the ground.

His mother walked towards him, pulling on a thin cardigan and sitting down.

'Aren't you cold?'

Gil shook his head. 'Nah. If we were in London, I'd be doing laps around the veranda to keep warm at this time of year.'

His mother chuckled. 'Turned you into a tough guy, has it?'

Yes and no. Gil felt more vulnerable now than he'd ever done, as if there were an open wound around his heart that only Clemmie could heal.

'You should come for a visit. See for yourself.'

'The Tower of London in the snow?' Gil's Christmas card last year had obviously registered in his mother's mind. 'I'd like to see that.'

'You'd have to pick your time if you want snow. We get a lot less of it than the Christmas cards suggest. You're more likely to encounter cold winds and horizontal rain.'

'Sounds lovely.' His mother turned her mouth down.

'It's different. If you ever have six weeks to spare, I think you'd like exploring London.' The idea of his parents *ever* having six weeks to spare to do anything just for pleasure was a little alien to Gil. Although his mother didn't seem so tightly strung as he remembered her.

'You'd be surprised, Gil. I might just persuade your

father to take you up on that and we'll turn up on your doorstep, expecting you to show us around.'

'Nothing would give me greater pleasure.' Maybe Gil hadn't said that enough. He probably hadn't said it at all, reckoning that the idea would be instantly deemed impossible.

His mother stared out at the darkening horizon for a moment. 'You want to fix a date?'

'Yes. Be warned that if we do, then I'll hold you to it.'

'I guess I deserve that.' His mother's face suddenly seemed lined with regret. 'You know... I should have had more time for you and your sisters. When you were growing up.'

Gil shrugged. 'I never felt that. You were building your career. Doing things that mattered.'

'When did you stop saying what was on your mind, Gil? I'm quite aware of my own mistakes.'

'None of us is perfect. You always loved me and I love you back.'

His mother nodded, obviously pleased with the sentiment. 'I've realised a few awkward truths in the last few years, Gil. When the doctor told me that my liver wasn't in good shape and I had to stop drinking, it was a wake-up call...'

'What? You never said anything to me about your liver, Mum.'

'Stopping drinking did the trick.' Gil's mother waved his concern away. 'I'll show you the scans if you don't believe me. I dare say you'll understand what they mean a lot better than I do. And you're a fine one to talk. How long was it before you admitted to having been laid up with a traumatic brain injury?'

Gil stretched his fingers, staring at the two that obstinately refused to straighten as much as the others. 'I didn't want to worry you.'

His mother snorted her disdain. 'Stop it, Gil. You know that's an excuse as well as I do, don't you?'

'Yes, I do. And I'm going to make a change, Mum. Next time something happens I'll be calling you.'

'You'd better. I know how that all works, Gil. You were always the one that was most like me. Even when you were a toddler, I'd put something in your way and you'd just climb over it, however high it was. I encouraged you in that. In my eyes it made you strong...' His mother shrugged, staring out at the sunset.

'Stop beating yourself up, Mum. You gave me a great childhood and the determination I needed to face obstacles, and to change when I needed to. There's nothing wrong with that.'

'I'm glad you see it that way. And I'm glad you found a way to change sooner than I did.' His mother shot him an amused look. 'I still can't get my head around you in a garden. Having the patience to grow apple trees.'

'It helps that London has a bit more rain than you do here.' Gil shrugged. 'I'm not sure how much I've really changed, though. You said it yourself. I always had a driven streak.'

'Yes, you did. It's what you do with it that matters, though. I knew you'd changed pace, and that you'd made that work for you. I remembered that when I was told that I needed to lay off the booze if I was going to make old bones, because I knew I'd have to find another way to wind down and get a night's sleep.'

'And the yoga's working?'

His mother nodded. 'Much as the gardening is. I've come to love it.'

Gil sighed. He should have had this conversation a long time ago. 'I've been away too long, haven't I? I've missed all this, and I've missed you, too.'

'You're here now. I'm interested to know why exactly...' His mother leaned towards him, a querulous tone to her voice. 'Come on. I might have brought you up to deny your own weaknesses, but I'm officially changing my tune now. Let's see if you're the man I think you are...'

Gil laughed. His mother could never resist throwing down a challenge and he couldn't resist picking it up. Maybe she was right and it was what you did with that instinct that mattered.

'There was someone... Her name's Clemmie.'

'Nice name. She made you happy?'

More than he'd ever been. More than he ever would be again. 'Yes. Very happy.'

'I'm starting to like her a lot. Did you pull your socks up and make *her* happy?'

Gil chuckled. 'Yep. I pulled my socks up. It's complicated.'

His mother folded her hands in her lap. 'I'm retired, kiddo. I've got all the time in the world for complicated.'

Gil considered the prospect. He'd come all this way because he'd promised Clemmie he would, and she'd been right. If he really wanted to know what kind of man he was, this wasn't a bad place to start.

'I met Clemmie before I had my brain injury. I didn't mean to, but I hurt her very badly. She gave me a second chance, though...'

'That's good, isn't it?'

'Clemmie's a good person. She has a capacity for seeing the best in everyone.'

His mother nodded. 'You mean you think you're not good enough for her?'

Gil shrugged. That went without saying. 'I was proud, and I wanted to be the best in whatever I did. I wouldn't acknowledge my weaknesses to myself, let alone anyone else. That's what hurt her so much the first time, and I'm not sure I'm so very different now.'

His mother reached across, squeezing his hand. Gil wouldn't have dreamed of having this conversation with her a few months ago, but maybe this was why Clemmie had told him to come here if he ever reached a cross-roads in his life.

'You and me both. And yet look at us. Sitting here with a sunset, talking about it.'

Gil chuckled. 'It's not that easy, though, is it?'

'Forget easy. It's a matter of reassessing your goals and choosing a bit more carefully this time. Was it easy for you, coming here?'

No. It had been a leap of faith. Wanting his relationship with his parents to be different and trusting in Clemmie's judgement.

'Let's just say that this visit was well overdue.'

'Don't sugar-coat it, Gil—a *no* will do. But I'm grateful that you came. I'd be willing to bet that if you want to be with this girl, then you'll make that work, too. Nothing comes easy, but that's what we both do. We make things work. If she were here, I'd tell her that she can trust you to do that if you set your mind to it.'

Gil didn't reply, and his mother got to her feet, her fingers brushing across his shoulder as she walked behind him, in an expression of tenderness. 'I'm going to get some juice. You want a beer?'

Gil shook his head. 'Actually, I was going to see if I

could mix a virgin version of the cappuccino cocktail. One that doesn't just taste like a cold cup of cappuccino.'

His mother gave a dry laugh. 'Yeah, go for it, then. If you can manage that, then you'll manage anything...'

CHAPTER SIXTEEN

CLEMMIE HAD PROMISED herself that today would be the last day she'd have to clean paint spatter out of her hair before she went to bed. The kitchen ceiling was going to be painted by tonight, however many people called her. But now she'd climbed down off the ladder to answer a question from one of the junior doctors at work, which really could have waited until Monday, she might as well make herself a cup of tea.

It had been four weeks. She'd missed Gil every day and every night. She'd cried, and sometimes the weight in her heart seemed so heavy that she could hardly move. But she'd carried on. He'd shown her how to do that.

As she sipped her tea, her phone rang again. Clemmie looked at the caller ID and her sharp intake of breath sent the tea into her windpipe. She grabbed the phone, stabbing at the answer button, and then dropped it back onto the counter as she started to choke.

'Clemmie! Clemmie!' She could hear Gil's voice coming from the phone, but she was still fighting for breath and she couldn't reply. He was calling her name, sounding more and more alarmed, and then the doorbell rang.

Forget visitors, she had more important things to think about right now. Then she heard an urgent knocking on her front door and the sound of Gil's voice outside. He'd been right here, and must have found someone to buzz him into the lobby. Clemmie felt a wash of relief. Now all she had to do was get to the door...

Or not. From the sound of it, Gil had just put his shoulder to the door. Breaking it down didn't seem such a bad idea at the moment. Clemmie put her fist to her stomach, grasping it with the other hand, and bent over the countertop. One sharp shove and the liquid stuck in her windpipe suddenly dislodged.

The door gave. She could breathe now, but she was still wheezing, and Clemmie sank to the floor as Gil appeared in the kitchen doorway.

'Okay...' She held up her hand before he could lift her to her feet to perform more abdominal thrusts. Gil knelt down beside her, one hand rubbing her back and the other supporting her against his chest.

This was nice. He was tanned and smelled gorgeous. It would have been nicer if she hadn't been bright red in the face and wearing her painting clothes, but Clemmie could ignore that for the moment. She was safe in Gil's arms, and that was all that mattered.

'Are you okay?' His voice was laced with tenderness and concern.

'Yeah.' Her voice sounded a little weird as well, and Clemmie coughed to clear the rest of the blockage. 'What about my door?'

'The latch is broken, but it's still on its hinges. Shouldn't take too long for me to repair. Keep coughing...'

So he was staying long enough to repair the door. Right now, Clemmie couldn't care less what had brought Gil here. She just wanted him close. She coughed again, and then managed to take a deep breath without wheezing.

'That's better.' She tried to get to her feet but Gil was holding her tight. 'I'm okay now.'

He helped her up, supporting her through to the sitting room. Gil sat down on the sofa next to her, and when she leaned against his chest, he put his arm around her shoulders. That wasn't strictly necessary, but it felt good.

'What made you choke like that?'

'I…um… Do you remember when you dropped that pitcher of water and cut your hand?'

'Ah. Sorry to catch you unawares. Maybe I should have texted, rather than phoned.' Gil winced.

'No, I don't think that would have made any difference.' Clemmie was feeling better now, and she really should sit up straight. 'What are you doing here? I thought you were in Australia.'

'How did you know that?'

'I called Sam, about returning a book she'd lent me. She mentioned it.'

'I was there because… I promised you I'd go, Clemmie.'

'I shouldn't have made you promise. Since you're back so soon, it can't have been the right thing to do.' Clemmie grimaced at the thought of all that money wasted on plane tickets.

'It was the absolute right thing to do. It just didn't take as long as I thought it might. I had to talk to the people who've known me all my life to help me remember who I am. And what I can and can't do.'

He'd come to tell her that? Disappointment bloomed in Clemmie's chest and she pulled away from him. Suddenly the painting clothes *did* matter, because if she was only going to see him once more, she'd have preferred to look a little more presentable.

Then she saw the look in his eyes. Whatever he'd come for, it meant as much to Gil as it did to her.

'We should talk about this later. When you're feeling better.'

'I'm fine.' Clemmie sucked in a breath and puffed it back out again. 'See?'

'You're sure?'

This was killing her. Suddenly all she wanted was for him to say what he'd come to say and then go. He didn't even need to mend the door—that would be piling more pain onto a heart that was already hurt enough.

'I'm sure, Gil. Please will you just say whatever you're here to say.'

He nodded. 'I came back to ask you for another chance. I'm still the same man who hurt you. I always will be. I want to be the best at what I do, and I'll do whatever it takes to succeed. But my goals are different now, and I love you with all my heart. I won't leave you and I'll do whatever it takes to make you want to stay with me.'

Clemmie caught her breath. 'And once you've set your sights on something, you don't give up, do you?'

'No, I don't. You need to know that.'

It was *all* she needed to know.

'Yes, Gil.' She flung her arms around his neck, kissing him. 'We'll leave the past behind us—'

He laid his finger across her lips, smiling. 'The past is where all your strength comes from. All my determination. We're a little bit wiser than we were, though, and we know how to use what we have to make it work this time.'

'You saved my life today, Gil.'

He raised her fingers to his lips. 'I'm not sure about

that. Your front door is pretty solid, and by the time I got to you, you seemed to be managing...'

Clemmie shook her head. 'I *was* managing. And you still saved my life.'

Three months later

Gil had taken Clemmie to meet his family. After just a week, they'd felt like the involved and interested family that she'd never had, and she was already looking forward to his parents' visit to London.

They'd seen the ocean and the beach. The rainforest. And then there was the grand tour that Gil had promised. They'd driven through miles of red-brown countryside, seen kangaroos, and flown across the baked heart of Australia to Sydney and then Melbourne. When Clemmie had said she wanted to see penguins, he'd taken her to Phillip Island, and when she'd wanted seafood, they'd gone to an unassuming-looking beach restaurant that served the best seafood she'd ever tasted.

But they weren't the best sights. Watching him while he slept, or opening her eyes to find that he'd been watching her, was ever fascinating. His body, wet from the shower, or hard and smooth against hers, was an endless pleasure. Gazing into his eyes, and feeling the warmth spread through her.

'Two days to go.'

Clemmie flung herself down onto the bed in their hotel room. They'd been to one of the vineyards on the Mornington Peninsula this afternoon. In the south of Australia, the early summer weather was cooler than Brisbane, and the breeze smelled of the damp earth and the vines.

'Is there anything else you want to do?' Gil grinned at her. 'There's still plenty to see.'

'Maybe we take it easy for the next couple of days.' She propped herself up on her elbows. 'We've lots to do when we get back.'

Gil nodded. 'My new research project at the rehab centre. And of course there's the cooking...'

Clemmie chuckled. They'd decided that they wanted to live in Richmond, not just because Gil's place was bigger than hers, but because they both liked the area. It meant a slightly longer commute for Clemmie, but the fast train took her into the centre of London in under half an hour. And Gil had promised to have a meal on the table every evening when she arrived home.

'You don't have to cook every night.'

'Now that your promotion's official, you'll be busy at work for a while.' Gil pulled a face. 'Don't you like my cooking?'

'I love your cooking. I just don't want you to feel you have to be home every evening to make dinner. It can tie you down a bit after a while.'

He laughed, flopping down on the bed next to her. 'You can tie me down all you want. In fact, I might insist on it.'

'Right now?' She kissed him, rolling him over onto his back and pinning his arms above his head.

'Tempting... There's something I have to do first, though. I won't be a minute.' He lifted her off him, walking through to the seating area that adjoined the bedroom. Gil had insisted on a suite, as a special treat for the last few days of their holiday.

Could she be any happier? Clemmie very much doubted it. Commitment had allowed them to talk about all the things that had torn them apart, knowing they couldn't do so again. They'd taken their time and told each other everything. It had brought Clemmie a peace that she'd never had before, and she knew that Gil was happy, too. This holiday had been one sparkling day after another, because they loved each other and they were together. It was all she needed, and all she'd ever need.

'So what's the one last thing you need to do before we leave? Perhaps we should do that tomorrow?' she asked, when Gil returned.

'I think we should do it now.' He caught her hand, pulling her to her feet and opening the sliding doors that led out onto the wide balcony.

'Oh! What a beautiful sunset!' In the short time they'd been inside, the sky had become streaked with red, outlining the dark shapes of massive gum trees. 'And champagne…'

'Clemmie.' The note of urgency in Gil's voice made her turn, and when she did she saw that he was on one knee.

'Gil!' Her hand flew to her mouth.

'Give me your hand.'

She put both of her hands into his. She was trembling now, but so was he.

'Clemmie, it's been my good fortune to meet and fall in love with you twice. And I want to keep falling in love with you every day for the rest of my life. Will you be my wife?'

'Yes!' She pulled him to his feet, unable to wait any longer to hug him. 'When can we get married, Gil?'

He laughed, a carefree happy sound that said everything was right with his world. *Their* world.

'As soon as you like. Although I'd better give you the

ring first, just to tie up all the loose ends.' He reached into his pocket, taking out a ring and slipping it onto her finger.

Clemmie caught her breath. Two diamonds flanked an opal, which sparkled with all the colours of the sunset.

'It's beautiful, Gil. Thank you.' He had that goofy, can't-help-smiling grin on his face that she loved so well, and Clemmie flung her arms around his neck, kissing him.

As the sun went down, he popped the champagne cork and handed her a glass. 'I'd like to propose a toast. To all our new adventures.'

She tipped her glass against his. 'And new adventurers.' She knew that Gil wanted children as much as she did.

He grinned. 'I'm looking forward to that, as well.'

'As soon as you like, Gil…'

His kiss told her that they wouldn't have long to wait.

* * * * *

COMING SOON!

We really hope you enjoyed reading this book.
If you're looking for more romance, be sure to
head to the shops when new books are
available on

Thursday 28th October

To see which titles are coming soon, please visit
millsandboon.co.uk/nextmonth

MILLS & BOON

THE HEART OF ROMANCE

A ROMANCE FOR EVERY READER

MODERN

Prepare to be swept off your feet by sophisticated, sexy and seductive heroes, in some of the world's most glamourous and romantic locations, where power and passion collide.

HISTORICAL

Escape with historical heroes from time gone by. Whether your passion is for wicked Regency Rakes, muscled Vikings or rugged Highlanders, awaken the romance of the past.

MEDICAL

Set your pulse racing with dedicated, delectable doctors in the high-pressure world of medicine, where emotions run high and passion, comfort and love are the best medicine.

True Love

Celebrate true love with tender stories of heartfelt romance, from the rush of falling in love to the joy a new baby can bring, and a focus on the emotional heart of a relationship.

Desire

Indulge in secrets and scandal, intense drama and plenty of sizzling hot action with powerful and passionate heroes who have it all: wealth, status, good looks…everything but the right woman.

HEROES

Experience all the excitement of a gripping thriller, with an intense romance at its heart. Resourceful, true-to-life women and strong, fearless men face danger and desire - a killer combination!

To see which titles are coming soon, please visit

millsandboon.co.uk/nextmonth

MILLS & BOON

Coming next month

CHRISTMAS MIRACLE IN JAMAICA
Ann McIntosh

Chloe took a deep, audible breath and then said, "I'm pregnant."

The words made no sense to him. And yet they must have, because his heart stumbled and an icy pit opened up in his stomach.

"And before you ask, yes, the baby is yours. If it isn't, then we'll need to contact the Vatican about a miracle, because you're the only man I've been with since I left my husband two years ago."

Her words came at him as though from a distance. The frigid sensation had spread from his belly to form a band around his chest, causing the fleeting thought that perhaps he was having a myocardial infarction.

Then Chloe's face softened into an expression so beatific, all other thoughts flew from his head at the sight.

"It's actually a true miracle to me," she said, her voice low and so full of joy it melted the ice in his torso. "I was told I wasn't able to conceive because of endometriosis. So—" She paused, her chin tilting up to that pugnacious angle he'd come to know so well. "So what I wanted you to know is that I'm keeping this baby, and if you don't want to be involved in his or her life, I can assure you my child will lack for nothing."

He knew he should say something, but try as he might, nothing came out. And it felt as though he'd been turned to stone. All he could do was watch as Chloe gave him a small smile and stood up.

"I'll let you get on with your afternoon," she said, and then she was gone.

Pregnant? With my child?

Sam's brain couldn't seem to grasp the concept, and he finally staggered to his feet, not knowing where exactly he planned to go.

Endometriosis…

His heart stopped, and a wave of nausea had him swallowing against the thickness rising in his throat.

Chloe's pregnancy was high-risk.

His legs gave way again, and he plopped back into his chair, momentarily overcome by fear so strong it dulled the edges of his sight to darkness.

What would be worse, he wondered dully: losing a child you never knew existed until it was gone or a second one you suddenly realized you wanted almost too much?

Because, just then, Sam realized the baby growing in Chloe Bailey's womb meant more to him than he'd have ever expected.

That baby—his child—was as much a miracle for him as it was for its mother.

Continue reading
CHRISTMAS MIRACLE IN JAMAICA
Ann McIntosh

Available next month
www.millsandboon.co.uk